Although Lee Jarrett dreads facing it, it's looking more and more like his own grandfather is a double murderer who has never been caught. As beloved as he is to Lee, this is a transgression that, no matter the circumstances, his grandson cannot forgive.

Lee discovers a map showing the far wilderness where his grandfather once lived when the murders occurred, a drawing that he hopes, among other things, might hold answers to the old man's guilt or innocence.

Following said map, however, is a life-threatening gamble. Bud, a restaurant owner near those same mountains, had cautioned Lee once about venturing into that country, saying, "Wouldn't try it if I was you, young feller. Never forgive myself if I heard the Demon had you for supper one night."

Then too, there was the ominous warning at the bottom of the map itself: "When stone runs blood and dies the flood, there be your prize but the Demon lies."

BURNT TREE FORK

a novel

J. C. Bonnell

Riverfeet Press

Dedication

To Sheila, my Queen and the love of my life: For one brief moment in eternity, she walked upon this earth and made it a better and brighter place.

Riverfeet Press
Livingston, MT 59047
www.riverfeetpress.com

BURNT TREE FORK: *a novel*

J.C. Bonnell

Fiction

First e-book edition 2018

Edited by Andrea Peacock

ISBN-13: 978-1-7324968-4-2

LCCN: 2020909480

Second printing

This title is available at a special discount to booksellers and libraries. Send inquiries to: riverfeetpress@gmail.com

Cover art by Robert William Doyle

Typesetting & Interior Design/Layout by Daniel J. Rice

Mayfly illustrations by Timothy Goodwin

Eagle illustration by Paul Rice

Riverfeet Press is proud to be Made in Montana.

BURNT TREE FORK

a novel

J. C. Bonnell

PART ONE

CHAPTER ONE

Most of his young life, Lee Jarrett had been chasing that pretty white horse on a merry-go-round, the one that was just up ahead but always out of reach. His latest version was Eden Brook, a storied "River of Gold" far over the mountains in West Virginia, and loaded with beautiful trout that had never seen a hook, or so his new friend Bud claimed. This quest turned out differently, however—he finally caught up with that pretty white horse.

His journey began on the Burnt Tree Fork. That first day on the river had gone well until late afternoon at the Gardino's gate. On it hung a crude sign, "Go A Way or Git Shot." Grinning at them from a nearby fence post was the bleached skull of a bear, a bullet hole dead center of its forehead.

Joining Lee in his search, but reluctantly, was Tom Drew, his best friend. After studying the Gardino's sign, the two young men eyed one another, the same question running through both their heads: Was Bud's "River of Gold" worth it?

High mountains walled them in on all sides, their flanks choked with dense greenery. The heavy Appalachian air suddenly grew smothering.

At the back of the Gardino's land, a high, rocky cliff loomed. Pressing close to a rusty barbed wire fence, Lee motioned for his friend to follow toward the escarpment. Thick brush shrouded the fence, making it hard to see the other side. When the fence dead-ended against the cliff face, Lee swung his pack down.

Parting the brush, the two young friends peered across the barbed wire. Muted sunlight cast long shadows onto the field. Around 30 yards or so from the cliff face was a tired, one-story cabin. Between it and the cliff, a long field of new corn stretched to the fence on the far side. The front of the cabin faced the river, but the back watched them.

"Lift the wire," Lee whispered, pointing to the bottom strand. As he rolled under, he smelled a strong, pungent odor.

After Tom followed and stood up on the other side, he sniffed his shirt. "Crapola, what's that smell?" he asked, his voice hushed.

"Remember what Bud said about them guys pissing to mark their territory, you know, like wild animals?" Lee gave a nervous snicker.

Tom swung his pack onto his shoulders. As he did, it caught a fence barb and the sound twanged through the quiet evening like a string on a bass fiddle.

Holding their breaths, both men froze and checked the cabin.

In the dim light, Lee could make out a small human figure on the back porch in a stuffed chair. After staring for a moment, his eyes got used to the shadows. Sunken deep in the faded chair was a sad-looking, little old man. His head was shoved down between his shoulders, like it was tired and seeking refuge inside his chest. He was wearing a baseball cap with the letter "P." Sticking out from under his cap was hair, or what passed for hair. Straight and coarse, it jutted out at all angles. It reminded Lee of scarecrow straw, but gray. Three large hounds lay on the porch around his feet, their heads toward the two young men. Lee could not tell whether they were dozing or watching.

As they stood in the evening hush, Lee heard a baseball game being broadcast. His eyes found the small radio beside the man and something else more disturbing. Lying across the chair arms in front of him was a double-barreled shotgun, a big one.

Lee elbowed Tom, pointed and made a trigger motion.

Tom saw it too and his eyes rolled skyward.

The two young men remained motionless. Finally, Lee waved but the little seated figure didn't move. At that point, Lee was convinced he was dozing, although he did consider he might be dead.

Sensing an advantage, the young men began creeping past the cabin. Just then, Tom's net came loose, falling from his pack onto an old tree stump. The dull strum of metal on wood sliced through the evening quiet. They froze and their eyes snapped over to the man on the porch, now only 30 some feet away. The biggest dog stood up and growled. The seated figure stirred, mumbled something and the dog sat down again, only now watching the two men. The old man tilted his face up slowly and sniffed the air, like an animal scenting prey.

Tom whispered. "Your damn after shave."

The man turned the radio down, moved one hand near the shotgun triggers and grinned at them. The few teeth he had left were jumbled fence posts. No longer harmless, he now seemed like a grotesque gnome.

Pointing up the valley, Tom called, "Howdy, friend. OK if we go through?"

The man spat on the porch. One dog sniffed it and lapped it up, then its neck hairs straightened and it growled. With that, the whole pack rose and began pacing back and forth, all the while snarling, their eyes glued on the two young men.

Both took one step upriver in the direction Tom had pointed.

With that, the old man cocked both hammers, swung the big shotgun in their direction and began motioning them back down-river. As he gestured, he grunted something low. At the grunt, the dogs bounded off the porch but held at the bottom of the steps, snarling and clicking their teeth.

"Okay, what now, Jarrett? This jay-bird wants us to go back ... and he's got a gun."

Lee wiped his forehead. "Could be bluffing."

Tom studied the black, empty eyes of the two large barrels. "You do realize, don't you, that this guy could just be the tip of the iceberg?"

"Tip of the iceberg?"

"Yeah, maybe Bud didn't tell us the whole story."

His look questioned Tom further.

"There could be a lot of worse things waiting for us up ahead, a lot worse." Tom motioned back down river. "What do you say, Jarrett?"

Lee's eyes swung back and forth between Tom and the little man with the big gun.

Tom pressed him further. "Hell, we could be back at camp this evening downing a couple cold ones. What do you say? Let's get the hell out of here."

Lee's shoulders slumped. They should have listened to Bud, he thought, and gone through the Gardino's after dark. Tom was right. They hadn't signed up for this, getting shot. For a long moment, he studied the country up the Burnt Tree valley, all the while fingering his wading staff. "No dammit, no, no," he said finally, "we're gonna go on."

Hands on his hips, Tom sighed. "Okay, buddy, it's your ... our funeral. Just remember whose idea it was if you get an ass full of buckshot."

The two young men stood motionless for a long moment, beads of sweat running down their faces.

Finally, Lee's jaw line hardened. "We haven't done nothing wrong, T.D. He's got no right pointing a gun at us."

"But he is, Jarrett, he is."

Lee called to the man on the porch. "This isn't right, mister. We're not bothering you. We just wanna go through."

Still, the man kept the shotgun trained on them.

"That worked well, what else you got?"

3

The corners of Lee's mouth carved down.

Tom yelled at the old man. "C'mon mister, call off your dogs." He held his hands up and open. "We don't want no trouble."

Lee followed with, "Yeah, mister, we just wanna go fishing."

Tom shot his friend a wry look. "Fishing, are you crazy? How about just staying alive?"

Still no answer came from the man.

Tom spoke to his friend out the side of his mouth, his tone patronizing, "So, Jarrett, this wild-goose chase of yours, your precious 'Little River of Gold,' is it worth getting shot for?" Tom's upper lip curled. "If it is, then what do you say, let's get the hell out of here?"

Tom often needled the other man about his endless quest for the ideal, his rejection of any imperfection in his world. Once in a while, after similar but fruitless searches, Tom would begin calling Lee Goldilocks or Goldy, as in the 'Three Bears' fairy tale, for always wanting things just right. Often, on such occasions, when Lee would grow weary of the hazing, he would snap at the other man. Tom would then back-off for a while, although he always returned to it later, especially when Lee was most vulnerable.

Occasionally too, Tom would ride Lee about something else very personal to him, his fly rod, tying it to the other man's fixed beliefs about right and wrong. The rod was ivory with dark windings. "The perfect rod for you, Jarrett," he would always note, "black and white."

After eyeing the man on the porch with the gun and the valley upriver, Lee's teeth clenched. "Okay, T.D., let's do it, let's make a run for it."

Tom whispered, "It's a shame ol' Bud never covered this part when he was selling us on this trip, how not to get shot."

As they tightened the straps on their backpacks, the dark barrel ends, like two lifeless eyes, watched them

"We'll go on four, okay Jarrett?"

Tom began counting.

When he got to three, Lee held his hands up. "Hold up, I just remembered something Bud said." Swinging his pack to the ground, he rummaged through it until he found one of the bottles of Old Log Cabin whiskey Bud had sold them. Plastering on a cracker-friendly smile, he held it up, waved it back and forth toward the man and set it on the stump.

"Are you crazy?" Tom cried. "That's the last thing that'll charm this guy, moonshine. Hell, that's their business. They're up to their ears in it now."

For several long seconds, the little man ran his eyes back and forth between them and the bottle. At last, his mouth gaped open and he flashed his best gnome-grin. He grunted something at the dogs and they slunk

4

back on the porch. Uncocking the shotgun hammers, he turned the gun away from them, resting it across the chair arms again. Turning the radio up, he closed his eyes and sank down in the chair.

Tom motioned upriver. "C'mon, Jarrett, let's get the hell out of here before he changes his mind."

As Lee wheeled to follow, the radio came in clearer, "... and so that about wraps it up, folks," the announcer was saying. "The Bucks win it three to two in the ninth," and the voice faded again. That fit with the little man's hat initial, Lee thought.

Lee and Tom began running as hard as they could toward the fence marking the end of the Gardino property. Their breaths were coming hard and the heavy packs were throwing them off balance. Every time they looked up, the fence seemed farther away. At last, though, their outstretched hands found the barbed strands. Crawling under, they flopped down on their backs on the other side. After exchanging glances, they began laughing, rolling from side to side. Then, still on their backs, they recounted the whole Gardino episode, occasionally bantering with one another over some detail, each followed by more high-pitched laughter.

"I know what Bud meant now," Lee said. "You know, when he told us to take along some liquor."

"Only got one left though. Say, can you answer me this? If the Gardinos are swimming in this stuff, like Bud said, why the hell would he want our store-bought?"

Lee shrugged. "Bud did say the old man loved the sauce."

Holding up his canteen, Lee said, "God bless Bud," and he took a long swig of water.

Doing the same with his canteen, Tom added, "God bless Old Log Cabin."

Both men laughed up at the clear June sky.

"Hope there's no more Mr. Shotguns like this upriver," Lee said.

Tom gave a wry smile. "Are you forgetting old Crazy's ghost?"

"Aw dag."

CHAPTER TWO

Two evenings before, everything had been fine, no Gardino's, no shot-gun, no running for their lives. Tired and relaxed after a day's fishing, Lee and Tom had just finished their meals in a homey little restaurant huddled in the remote mountains of West Virginia.

As both men shoved their chairs back, the waiter nodded toward their plates. "How was them chops?"

Lee answered, "Not bad," but the other man with a crewcut gave two thumbs up.

"Where y'all from?" the waiter asked.

"Over 'round Eastbrook," Lee answered.

The waiter slapped his thigh. "Knew it, dammit, knew you was West Virginia boys right off. Could tell by the way you talked. I got a good ear." Wiping his right hand on his apron, he offered it to Tom. "Forgetting my manners. Name's Bud, Bud Smith."

"Drew, Tom Drew," he answered, shaking Bud's hand. Pointing to the other young man at the jukebox, he added, "The pretty one there with the blond hair, that's Lee Jarrett."

Lee never looked up from the jukebox. "Jealous."

"Nah, I like being ugly," Tom said, his eyes amused. "That way, nobody bothers me."

Lee walked over and shook the waiter's hand. The smell of bacon grease and cigarettes greeted him. The waiter's sleeves were rolled up and he had hairy arms. Lee motioned toward his friend. "Tom here, he's a big hero over our way, sports. Folks 'round Eastbrook call him T.D. Not for football though, for scoring with the girls, or so he claims."

"And what about you, Mr. Hot-Shot?" Tom asked. "As long as we're bragging, what about all them baseball records of yours?"

"Don't change the subject, T.D." Looking at Bud, Lee thumbed toward his friend. "Tom here claims he's a real Romeo with the girls. Can't prove it by me."

"That's Mr. Romeo to you, Jarrett." Turning, he spoke to Bud, after winking. "But as long as we're talking love lives, how are things with you and your ol' gal, Cathy?"

"Pru? I told you the deal there."

Bud had been following the playful needling between the friends, but the girls' two names seemed to confuse him. He looked from one young man to the other for help.

Tom noticed and a patronizing grin slid across his face. "Pru, that's Lee's nickname for Cathy. Her real name's Cathy Pruitt."

She was one of those pretty white horses Lee was always chasing on his carousel, only this one he was able to corral.

"Where are you fellows staying?" Bud asked.

"We're camped down by the Tree, Burnt Tree Fork," Tom explained. "Got in late last night."

"Don't get many strangers up this way," Bud said, glancing out the window at Tom's truck. "You've been up here before, haven't you?"

Tom nodded. "Yeah, we camp and fish the Tree every chance we get. Never stopped in your place before though. We usually fix something back at camp on the Coleman, but we got in late from fishing tonight, a little tired, didn't feel much like cooking."

"Thought I'd seen it before," Bud said, "the blue Chevy truck." He handed them the check. "How long are you here for?"

"Got a week off from work," Tom answered, jerking his thumb toward Lee. "But this guy's still sponging off his folks. He's got no deadlines."

"Where's work?" asked Bud.

"Welles' lumber mill over at Eastbrook," Tom answered. "Doesn't pay much, but for a one-horse town, what's to expect?"

"They gave you a whole week off, huh?" Bud asked. "That's pretty good in my book."

"Yeah, around the same time every year, early June. But the time off, I earned it."

Busying himself behind the counter, Bud asked, "Fishing any good?"

Lee answered. "Just a couple o' dinks."

"Nowadays," Bud said, "the Tree has too much people dirt. Too many camps, people, roads. Throw in a few mine tailings and beer cans and you get the picture. Don't get me wrong, they love this river, them city folks. Trouble is, they're loving it to death. Whatever they do ends up in the river and it doesn't do it any good. City folks don't seem to get that. Yes sir, too damn much people dirt."

Bud worried a stain on the counter with his dish rag. "Wasn't always that way. You shoulda seen this gal in her younger days. She was something. Pure as new snow back then and loaded with native brookies. They won't put up with bad water, you know. Has to be clean. Browns ain't so picky."

Lee's head bobbed like he knew that.

"Poor guys," Bud added, "them dinks you caught, fish truck probably dumped 'em in last week. What kind of flies did you use?"

"Little of everything," Lee answered. "Casto Special, woolly worm with a spinner, Royal Coach too."

"Got a couple o' flies in the back that'll work better for you on the Tree," Bud said. "I'll dig 'em out for you."

"C'mon, Jarrett, tell Bud the real reason we struck out today." Tom nodded toward his friend. "This buddy of mine always stops by St. Peter's, his church over at Eastbrook, before he goes fishing. Says a prayer to the fish gods. He claims the church has to be empty though when he stops in. If anyone else is there, it's no good. Go figure." He grabbed Lee around the neck and squeezed playfully. "Fish prayer of yours didn't work today, did it buddy?"

Lee pushed him away. "You're full of it, T.D. That's not why I stop by church, to pray for good fishing."

"Then what?" he asked, grinning.

Lee studied his friend momentarily. "You wouldn't understand."

Tom winked at Bud. "Have it your way, Jarrett, but whatever you did at St. Pete's didn't work." He chuckled. "Who knows, maybe you didn't stay on your knees long enough."

"Up yours."

The waiter went on about the fishing. "You fellers are here in prime time, early June, but no one's done any good lately. But like I said, it wasn't always that way." He gestured in a wide circle around the restaurant. "See for yourself, gents. All bagged in the old days in Burnt Tree country."

Both young men surveyed the dozens of trophies decorating the knotty pine walls. Stationed here and there between them were paintings, idealized sylvan landscapes and old photos of sports smiling proudly alongside scores of dead fish and animals. Behind the counter was a sign that read, "Jesus is love."

The waiter motioned back over his shoulder. "Restaurant's all mine now. Used to be Mom and Pop's. They opened the place in the '20s, named it after the mountains hereabouts. I kept it, the name, 'Spruce Mountain Restaurant.' But they're gone now, Mom and Pop."

Just then, a motorcycle rumbled up outside, its motor almost deafening. It revved twice with deep growls and cut off.

Bud peaked through the shutters. "Uh oh, trouble."

8

CHAPTER THREE

Two bleary-eyed young men, both wearing cheap sport coats and bad ties, threw the back door open. The smaller man had a weak chin and dark eyes, like buckshot pellets. He was wearing tennis shoes with white socks and a baseball cap that read, "Chew Mail Pouch." The bigger man was powerfully built through the shoulders and upper back and his arms were too long for his sport jacket. Lee was certain both were wearing their Sunday best. As the men weaved past Tom and Lee's table, the bigger one yelled, "The Swede's back and I'll have you know it." Turning back, he took his hat off and threw it toward a coat tree near the door. When it missed, he laughed hysterically. "Who said I couldn't hit the floor with my hat?"

"Johnson," Bud acknowledged the bigger man. "Ratliff," he said to the smaller, his tone stony for both.

Ratliff removed his jacket and hat. Over his close-set eyes, a dark widow's peak crawled down his forehead. From there, his hair was slicked straight back with some thick, greasy substance. It looked like motor oil, 20/50 grade.

"Let's get out of here, T.D.," Lee whispered. "Them two look like trouble." Picking up the check, he walked to the register.

Meanwhile, the little man with the buckshot eyes sat at the counter spinning around on his stool, eyeing the bigger one for some direction.

Taking off his jacket, Johnson called to Bud as he started down the hallway, "Gotta use your terlet."

"Out of order," Bud answered.

Johnson wheeled about unsteadily. "Aw, for Christ sake, Bud."

The only other customer in the restaurant was an old man. He was sitting at a table near the hallway drinking coffee and reading his newspaper.

Stopping at the old man's table, Johnson leaned on it stiff-armed, cutting off his reading light. The seated man never looked up.

On Johnson's upper right arm was the tattoo of an American flag in color, and just above that, a blue ink cross. Seemingly irked by the old man's indifference, Johnson shouted, "How's the coffee, Tombstone?"

The old man seemed startled. His nose was just a few inches from Johnson's when he looked up. Frowning, he leaned away, his eyes playing curiously over the other man's face. "Tsk, tsk," he uttered, shaking his head and returning to his newspaper.

Johnson glanced over at his little friend who was busy spinning a butter knife on the counter. Unlike the Swede's powerful biceps, Ratliff's upper arms were scrawny, hardly wide enough for a two-syllable tattoo.

"What's the matter, Tombstone," Johnson demanded, "you hard of hearing? I asked you a question, how's the coffee?" When the old man ignored him again, the Swede picked up his cup and drank his coffee down in one swallow. "Hmm, good," he said, wiping the back of his hand dramatically across his mouth.

The old man still never looked up from his newspaper.

"What's in the news, old feller?" Johnson demanded, ripping the newspaper from his hands. "Let's see," he said, doing a quick mock read.

Lee suddenly heard a voice growl at Johnson, "Leave him alone. He's not bothering you." He recognized the voice. It was his, and he wished he could take it back.

"Yeah, Johnson," Bud added from behind the counter, "you two behave yourselves or I'll call the cops."

Turning from the old man, Johnson tossed the newspaper aside and staggered behind the counter. "I just remembered," he said to Bud. "You called them on us last time, the cops." Wrapping one arm around the owner's neck, the Swede squeezed until Bud's face reddened. Relaxing his hold momentarily, he gave Bud a long, sloppy kiss on his forehead. "Aw Bud, don't 'cha love us anymore?" he asked, his tone mocking.

"Get off me," Bud demanded, trying to shove him away. The big man only tightened his arm lock more.

Winking at his friend, Johnson spun Bud so his back was to the counter.

That was Ratliff's cue. With Bud facing away, he began loosening the salt, pepper and sugar caps.

Still holding Bud fast, Johnson said, "Hey, Bud, I got me a new gal." He dangled a set of keys in the other man's face. "She's parked outside. Wanna meet her?"

Back at their table, Lee whispered low to Tom out the side of his mouth, "Can you imagine any girl wanting that big ox's hands crawling over her?"

Trying to hide his amusement, Tom stifled a belly laugh.

10

The Swede stopped wrestling with Bud, shoved him aside and tossed his keys to Ratliff. Eyes narrowing, he looked straight at Lee. "Didn't catch what you said there, Bub, about my new gal."

"Nothing," Tom answered for Lee. "He was just kidding around, didn't mean nothing." Tom laid a tip down. "Let's head out, Jarrett."

As they got up to leave, Johnson and his little friend swaggered over to their table. The big man's eyes hardened toward Lee. "Was you funning me, bub?"

For an instant, just one absurd instant, Lee thought about answering "Yeah," then running like hell for the nearest exit. But with Tom at his elbow, showing color was not an option, so he met Johnson's eyes boldly, despite the fear behind his own.

To Lee's relief, Tom cut in. "We don't want no trouble, mister." He held his open palms up toward the Swede. "We were just leaving."

Johnson thumbed toward the parking lot. "That your blue pickup?"

Before either could answer, Ratliff prodded the big man in the ribs. "Ask blondie there what he said when we was funnin' Ol' Tombstone."

The Swede turned toward Lee again. "Yeah, what was that crack you made?"

Lee's mouth suddenly filled with sawdust. He swallowed hard and answered, surprised at the bravado in his voice. "He wasn't bothering you none, the old guy."

Tom broke in. "The truck. That's mine, why?"

Before the Swede could answer, his hand discovered the coins Tom had left for a tip. He pivoted unsteadily toward his little friend. "I'd like some music, Rat. Wouldn't you like some music?"

The little man eyed Tom. "Sure would, Johnny."

With that, Johnson picked up Tom's coins, dropped two in the jukebox, blindly punched a tune and pocketed the rest.

Rat grinned for the first time. He had two oversized incisors.

As the music began playing, Tom fingered his wristwatch. Walking over to the jukebox, he jerked its plug from the wall, and the music trailed off in a string of sour notes.

The big man waved his middle finger in Tom's face. "Here's your change, buddy."

Eyes unafraid, even defiant, Tom answered Johnson's fierce gaze with his own. Never blinking or losing eye-lock, he slid his wristwatch off.

Before Tom could put the watch into his pocket though, Johnson grabbed for it. "Lemme see that," he demanded.

Tom tried pulling away, but the big man held on. Almost nose-to-nose, the two men wrestled for the watch, each searching for a submissive tell, but none coming from either man.

11

Bud picked up the phone and yelled from behind the counter, "Cut it out, Johnson, or I'll call the cops."

Glancing at the owner, the Swede hesitated, then let go. Turning abruptly, the big man headed toward the back door, his little friend scurrying behind.

Once the door slammed behind them, Bud walked over to the two young men. "Sorry about that. Them two is trouble when they're together and drinking."

Tom slipped his watch back on his wrist.

"You guys better stay inside till they're gone," Bud added, looking out the window. "They're probably headed to the square dance over at Thompson's. A regular Saturday night ritual. They get the girl fever, you know, all the hot ones they fancy they're gonna meet at the dance. They need the drink for courage though." He winked. "A real test of manhood for some fellas, asking a pretty young thing to dance. Strikes more fear in some guys' hearts than meeting up with Ol' Scratch himself. Anyway, they get all plastered, stop in here on the way and give me a hard time. Of course, I call the cops and they throw them in jail. Those two never learn though." He wiped his hands on an apron. "All the jail time does is get them sore at me." He paused. "Isn't doing my business any good neither, scaring off my customers."

Lee fished some change from his pocket and handed it to Bud. "Here, that big guy took your tip."

"You fellers don't owe me a thing, but thanks anyway." Bud glanced out the window past the crackling, red neon sign.

Johnson and Ratliff were talking beside Tom's truck, the bigger man's foot resting on a cement block.

"I'd better call the cops." There was growing concern in Bud's voice. "Them two are trouble. You guys stay inside."

Tom looked out the window and his lip curled. "Son of a bitch," he cried. Hat flying off as he jumped up, he ran toward the back door, throwing it open with a loud bang and sliding his wristwatch off as he ran down the steps. Lee and Bud hurried close behind.

There beside Tom's truck was Johnson, now standing on the cement block and urinating into Tom's gas tank.

Lee had seen Tom fight before. When his friend's lip curled and that silver watch came off, the one his deceased father had left him, someone got hurt, and most often, it wasn't Tom.

At the last second, the big Swede saw Tom's fist coming and tried rolling away from it. Even though it was only a glancing blow on his cheek near the mouth, it sent Johnson rolling in the cinders nearly the length of the truck. Stunned that anyone would dare strike him, the big man got to his feet, dazed but more sobered now. He threw his head back to get the hair out of his eyes and looked down at the blood he had just wiped from his mouth. His private parts still dangling, he snorted and charged at Tom.

"Get him, Johnny," the little man squeaked.

Knees flexed and bent at the waist, Tom danced gracefully out of the way of the other man's wild charge.

Stopping to tuck away his genitals, but not bothering to zip up, Johnson came at Tom again, only this time more in control, fists up and pumping.

Tom's shoulders were hunched, and his elbows down close to his body, and he was staring hard into the other man's eyes through his own rotating fists.

Hard breathing, both men circled one another for a few seconds in the half-light from the restaurant windows, each feeling the other out. As they did, an occasional car went by with its horn blaring, its occupants yelling something inaudible.

Bending to one side at the waist, Tom slammed a hard right into the other man's ribs and when Johnson grunted and dropped his left, Tom pivoted his upper body and came over the top with a right to the Swede's jaw that would have dropped a bull and it did.

The big man's knees buckled and he dropped straight down, then fell back and lay there beside an old barbed wire fence, its rusty strands loose and dangling. Tom danced over the big man, still holding his fighting pose.

"Enough, enough," whispered the fallen man, holding one hand up in submission.

When Tom put his fists down and turned away though, the Swede grabbed his legs from behind and tried wrapping the loose barbed wire around them.

Like a halfback dodging a linebacker, Tom easily danced away from Johnson's grasp and the barbed strands. Rocking back one step and gathering himself, Tom kicked the big man viciously under the chin with the toe of his shoe. Johnson's body crumpled, he dropped face down and it was over, this time for good.

Ratliff picked up a wooden stake lying nearby, but after eyeing his fallen hero and Tom for a few seconds, threw it down. Sitting beside Johnson in the gravel, Rat tried comforting the big man. "C'mon Johnny," he whispered in his ear, "let's head over to Thompson's, pick up some tail."

"Help me up?" the big Swede asked meekly, his speech slowed and bloody saliva stringing from his mouth.

Flexing his hand, Tom walked over to the window alongside the restaurant.

In the light, Lee could see his friend's right hand, although rock steady, was bleeding. Lee's own hands were shaking and he hid them in his pockets.

Tom held his bleeding knuckles out toward Lee. "Better head back to camp, soak these in the river."

Bud called from the steps at the side door, "You fellas c'mon back inside. Let's have a look at that hand."

"It'll be okay."

Bud walked over to Tom and looked at his knuckles. "Nah, c'mon. I got some ice."

When the motorcycle roared to life, Tom and Lee looked over. Johnson, his fly still open, climbed onto the back.

His vision distorted from the beating, the big man looked at the restaurant owner, trying to decide which image to address. Fishing through his pockets, he threw some change on the ground. "For ol' Tombstone," he mumbled, "a newspaper and coffee."

With that, Rat gunned the bike and they rumbled off into the night.

"Don't think they'll be stopping off here again any ways soon," Bud said to Tom, smiling. "About time someone took the starch out of them two. Feel like I owe you."

"Forget it," Tom said. "He was asking for it"

"I know their kinfolk, good people," Bud said. "Them boys ain't bad when they're sober. Big trouble though when they're together and liquored up."

Bud walked toward the side door and motioned for Lee and Tom to follow. "C'mon, we'll sit a spell and gas. I'm putting the place to bed anyway. Coffee's on me."

Hands still shaking, Lee twisted Tom's gas cap back on. "Bud's right, T.D. Better get some ice on that."

Standing in the doorway, the owner called, "I'll throw in dessert."

"Got any fudge?" Lee asked. "Peanut butter fudge?"

Bud smiled and shook his head no. "Got some pie though. Like I said, on me. The least I can do."

"What kind?" Tom asked.

"Cherry, homemade," Bud answered. "Best in Spruce County, whipped cream to boot."

Tom gave a pursed smile and nodded. Chuckling, he pushed Lee playfully. "Peanut butter fudge."

CHAPTER FOUR

After closing the restaurant, the owner brought pie and coffee to their table along with ice in a towel. Thumbing toward Tom, he spoke to Lee. "Your big fella sure knocked the snot out of that Swede. No one's going to kick sand in his face."

Lee followed his lead. "Yeah, a regular Charlie Atlas."

"How's the pie?" Bud asked.

Both men nodded their approval.

"A pitcher, huh?" Bud asked, studying Lee. "Played a little ball myself over at Greenfield High." He pointed to a dusty team picture on a shelf behind the counter with a yellowing baseball alongside. "A left fielder I was. Pretty good hitter too." He stood up and struck a batting pose. Then, over his left shoulder, asked, "You any good, Lee?"

"Won a couple," he answered.

"Don't go modest on us, Jarrett." Tom turned to Bud. "Best damn leftie in these parts. Surprised you haven't heard of him. All he did was set the high school record for shutouts this year, state and county both. Never lost a game either, no sir."

"Yeah?" Bud answered, seemingly impressed. "What year are you in?"

Making a fist, Lee showed Bud his class ring. "Just graduated, class of '50, St. Peter's in Eastbrook."

Thumbing toward his friend, Tom spoke to Bud. "This whole trip's on me, my present for him graduating." He pointed to the owner's yellowing baseball on the shelf. "Yes sir that little stitched ball earned him a full scholarship ... Hillsboro State. Does that answer your question, how good he is?"

"Wow, Hillsboro State. Free ride and all, huh?"

"Of course, I taught him everything he knows about baseball," Tom said, "but who gets the scholarship?" He nodded toward Lee. "Mr. Lucky. Where's the justice?"

"What're you gonna study there, Hillsboro?" Bud asked.

"Not sure, writing probably, stories and such," Lee answered. "Never written anything good yet though, nothing worth selling."

"Who're you kidding, Jarrett? You're going there for baseball and girls." Tom smirked. "Writing's for sissies anyway."

Bud frowned. Picking up a newspaper, he scanned the front page. "College might keep you out of this." He pointed to a headline on the front page about war in Korea. "You know, if this mess blows up."

Tom shoved Lee's shoulder. "He's always writing something in that journal of his. Takes it everywhere."

Lee's eyes were pulled to a landscape on a nearby wall. In it, a lone figure was fly fishing a small, orchid-blue mountain stream with lush greenery embracing him all around. "Can't explain it," he said. "I need to feel, make others feel."

Tom sneered.

"I like to do a bit of that myself, young fella, story write." Bud stopped and lit a cigarette. "Even took a write-away course in a magazine once. Helped some. My English is not so good, but you probably noticed. Keep trying though."

"Ever been published?" Lee asked.

Bud shook his head, but crossed his fingers. "Got a good one to write about someday though." He looked at Tom. "You a college boy too?"

Tom made a sour face. "Not in the cards, not for me." He stood up and walked toward the back door. "Gotta take a leak."

Bud motioned toward the john instead.

"Thought it was busted?" Tom asked.

"That was just for the biker boys. Every time they stop in here they plug up my john with paper towels. You know, deliberately, think it's funny. Do you have any idea what a plumber costs nowadays?" He motioned toward the john again. "No, go ahead with my blessing."

After he had gone, Lee moved his chair closer to Bud's and motioned toward the john. "A little sensitive about college."

"Yeah, thought I touched a nerve."

"We've been friends since around..." Lee scratched his head. "Around '47. He went to Eastbrook High, but my parents sent me to Catholic school, St. Peter's. Summers, I played American Legion baseball, so did Tom. That's where we met. We didn't have much in common at first, me and him. He was a junior and I was a freshman. He was an all-star catcher and I was just a skinny kid with baseball dreams and not much else. Something clicked between us though."

"Know what you mean," Bud said. "Sports'll do that, tie guys togeth-

16

er." He motioned toward the picture of his old team on the shelf. "Hell, we still keep in touch."

Lee continued. "Anyway, Tom took me under his wing and taught me to pitch. I wouldn't have any of those records if it wasn't for him, no scholarship either. After that, we hung out a lot, baseball, fishing, mostly summers. Long story short, we became best friends." Lee glanced toward the john. "Always will be too." His fingers played with the pepper shaker.

"Surprised he's baseball," Bud said. "With them beefy shoulders, I took him to be football, a fullback or lineman. You though, young feller, it don't surprise me none you're a pitcher. You have the perfect build. Once you get that tall frame of yours cranked up, lots of arm speed."

"I'm sure he coulda done that too, played football," Lee agreed, "but had no time for that after losing his father. From what I heard, things were running smooth as glass for their family until he up and died suddenly. Tom was around 14 or so at the time. Mr. Drew had a bar but not much else, no insurance, savings, nothing. No sir, didn't leave them much, except for a ton of bills. Tom did have an older brother, but he was a priest and you know what they make. Top it off, their mother got sick too." He tapped the side of his head.

The other customer, the old man, stirred at his table.

Bud called to him. "Make yourself to home, Jim. You know where the coffee is." He turned back to Lee. "Anyway, you were saying his mother wasn't right upstairs."

Lee went on. "Family didn't have much and so Tom had to help out. That meant giving up sports and any social life. He got part-time work, evenings and weekends during the school year. Had more time in the summers though. Only reason we got together.

"After high school, he had his pick of scholarships. Turned them all down though. Had to find full-time work. No good paying jobs 'round Eastbrook, so he had to grab what he could. That's why the mill."

"So he drew the short straw, huh," Bud said, shaking his head. "Boy, the road is full of pot holes for some folks."

"He's still got one dream left though," Lee went on. "He wants to be a pilot someday, U.S. Air Force, hoping Uncle Sam'll pay him to fly." Just then, Tom returned from the bathroom. "Anyway," Lee finished, "his brother, David, used to catch me once in a while when Tom wasn't around. Pretty fair athlete himself. Did I mention he was a priest?"

"What about my David?" Tom called as he walked toward their table.

"Just telling Bud how much you guys, you and David, helped me with baseball." As Lee forked the last piece of pie to his mouth, it fell onto his white t-shirt. "Damn," he said. Dipping his napkin in a water glass, he began dabbing at the stain, only making it worse.

Bud walked behind the counter and poured himself some coffee. He stopped and studied the picture of a grizzled, fierce-looking mountain man on the wall near the cash register. "Like I was saying, I got me a good story to write about someday. Least ways, I think it's good. Could make me a fistful of dollars too."

He walked back to their table and set the coffee pot down. "It's all about how this little ol' river got its name, the Burnt Tree. Has everything you'd want in a juicy story—love triangle, gold, murder, even a demon. Leastways, that's what some folks call him, Crazy Dan. A true story too, well, mostly. Folks don't know which is which anymore." He stopped and called to the old man who was half dozing now. "How's the new pup working out, Jim?"

Hearing his name, the old man roused, threw up his hand but never answered.

"Jim got a new pup. His old dog up and died. Jim there, he's the best banjo player in these parts. I swear, a feller's feet ain't his own once he starts in to picking. Now where was I? Oh yeah, the river. I was about to tell you fellas how it got its name, Burnt Tree." He glanced at Lee. "I don't want you messing with it though, my story, writing it up yourself. You gotta promise."

Snorting cynically, Tom nodded and Lee held up his right hand.

CHAPTER FIVE

Bud scooted his chair closer. "Family named Jagger, same last name as that bald, Hollywood actor guy. They were early settlers to the region hereabouts. Had two sons, one named Dan, the other I don't know. This here story's about Dan. Don't know what became of the younger brother. Anyway, the story goes that around the early 1890s, Dan, a giant of a fellow, built a homestead smack-dab in the middle of nowhere. It was wa-ay up on the headwaters of Burnt Tree Fork alongside the river, just east of a valley and brook called Amanda's. Amanda was her name you see, Dan's wife, and everyone reckoned he named both after her. Still marked on the maps that-a-way too."

"When did you say this all happened," Lee asked, "late 1800s?"

"I know where you're headed, young feller," Bud said. "If it happened way back then, how come I know about it?" He thought a moment. "To be honest, it's a hodgepodge story, what I'm telling you. Part was in the papers at the time. You can still read about it at the library over at Wilkens. Some is legend, the rest is just hand-me-down retellings." He studied Lee momentarily. "Not to cut you short, young feller, but if you don't mind, hold off on your questions. My head ain't what it used to be. Nowadays, I get sidetracked if someone just farts."

"Sorry," Lee said, stifling a smile when Tom squeezed his knee under the table.

Bud picked up again with his story. "As I was saying, that family, the Jaggers had a place way up the Tree. Alongside their home were two giant oaks, one on each corner. They was the biggest trees for miles 'round, hear tell. A big, beautiful cabin they had too, finished pine walls and oak floors, all hand sawed and sanded. Leading up to the front door were three huge granite steps. They musta' weighed a half-ton apiece. It would have taken a monstrous strong fellow to wrestle them in place." He stopped. "Of course, he could have used horses.

Anyhow, chiseled into the side of the bottom step was the year they were married, 1896.

"Somewhere along the way, Dan decided a jaguar would be their family crest. It don't take much of a stretch to see why. Your big cat, the jaguar, isn't but a couple letters over from the family name, Jagger. Hear tell, Dan's temper matched that creature's too, wild and fierce when riled. Old timers who claimed they saw their cabin back then said it had a big brass knocker on the front door, the head of a big angry cat, a jaguar with fearsome eyes, flattened ears and barred fangs.

"Anyway, he and his young bride homesteaded there for a spell. They had a perfect little life for a couple years, just the two of 'em. Of course, it weren't easy making a living back then, them being on the edge of nowhere, but they pulled together. Dan hunted, fished, trapped and she put up the stuff they grew and kept their little home warm and cozy ... yesiree, they had it all."

He stopped and looked back at the kitchen. "Gotta turn that grill off. Don't need no fires. Did I mention Dan and her was newlyweds?"

Lee nodded.

"No neighbors in that neck of the woods either, that is except for a feller in the next holler over. He was a strange sort they said. Some kind of nature man. Always using plants, herbs and such to try and cure things. Folks claimed he could make strange things happen too. You know, wizardy stuff. Now that does sound a bit farfetched, don't it?

"Dan was young back then, and even though he and this other feller were about the same age, folks thereabouts called the other man Papa, Papa Joe. Probably because he had long hair and a beard down to here." He gestured to his belt. "Looked older than he was, you see.

"Like Dan, Papa was a horse-sized fellow too. Always sported a black, wide brimmed hat, or so folks claimed. Come to think of it, from old pictures I've seen, most fellows in those days had long hair, beards and hats like that. Dan too, I reckon. It was the custom back then, you see." He pointed to Tom's head. "The hats were sorta like your buddy's there, only wider brimmed."

Tom took his off and tossed it on a nearby chair.

"Now where was I? Oh Yeah, Papa Joe. Another thing about him. He had this mean- looking, half-moon scar on his left cheek. Always bothered folks back then how he come by it, but most were too scared to ask, and so, they had to settle on their own imaginings—It seemed that Joe had a knife fight once down in Argentina with a jealous Norwegian sea captain over a beautiful Spanish dancer. Joe killed the other man, self defense, but got cut bad himself." Bud made a cutting motion at his own cheek. "Everyone was happy with the outcome though ... save for the sea captain, that is. It just so happened, Joe liked his women well versed in how to please a man down below, which she just happened to have a doctorate in, and then too, she liked her lovers' faces carved up some. Made 'em look more macho, I guess, at least in her eyes. Anyway, that's the tale the locals settled on, a bit far-fetched, but romantic too.

"Then too, a less fanciful telling made the rounds. This one claimed Dan gave it to him, the scar that is, a sort of reminder who was boss up there on the Tree. You see, they were neighbors, but never buddies.

"Speaking of Papa Joe, there was an interesting backstory to that fellow. Lost his wife to the fever years before, or so folks claimed. They said he was a big city doctor once, but when he couldn't save his own wife with Johns Hopkin's medicine, it destroyed him. He began looking for other ways of doctoring, the black arts and such. Who knows? Some claimed he had a son back East, too.

"Seems as though most men carried big knives back in them days. Joe's was a big, mean-looking, curvy thing. Carried it on his right hip because he was left-handed, see." Reaching across his body, Bud demonstrated how Joe might have drawn it out, doing so in one long, dramatic motion.

"On his own hip, Dan toted a big blade, too, but on the other side. A wicked looking hunk of iron it was too, razor sharp like Joe's, only straight, not curved. Guess a fellow back in them days never knew what sort of critters he might come across in the mountains, both four and two-legged. Folks claimed Dan even had a name for his, his knife that is." He scratched his head. "Can't for the life of me recollect what it was?" He tapped the side of his head. "Little guy upstairs ain't what he used to be. "I can tell you this much, neither one of them fellows was the kind you'd want to run into on a dark night in the woods."

Tom pointed to his knuckles. "Mind if I get more ice?"

The owner motioned him toward the kitchen. After he left, Bud tamped his cigarette out in an ashtray, but the butt was still smoldering when Tom came back. "Anyway," he resumed his tale, "things must have gone haywire in paradise around 1898 or so because two old ginseng hunters stumbled onto their smoldering cabin. It was burned to the ground except for them three stone steps, then leading only to a pile of ashes."

Lee worried the last of his pie crumbs.

Bud gestured to Lee's plate.

Lee waved him off.

"Well, gents," Bud picked up again, "inside their burned-down cabin on the charred bed springs was Dan's wife and Papa Joe, both shot in the head and toasted well done. They buried her, least ways what was left, next to the burned down cabin. Planted him nearby, too.

21

"They knew it was Amanda 'cause she was the only female woman 'round those parts back then. As for Papa Joe, they knew it was him because they found that big, curved knife of his alongside his well-done carcass. Its handle was gone, but the blade was still hot, like it had been forged in hell.

"Then, as if things weren't strange enough already, a few days later her body just up and disappeared. Yes Sir, someone came along and dug her up, what was left, and carted her off. Of course, it had to have been Dan who done it. He couldn't stand the thought of her sleeping up there beside that other fella, Joe. They figured he must have laid her to rest in some secret place, hoping to sleep beside her someday, but no one knows where. I can tell you this much, it had to have been a beautiful place where there were heaps of daisies all around. Did I mention she was partial to them?

"Top it off, Dan just up and disappeared himself. To this day, no one's seen hide or hair. Folks said he was the kind of fellow you could drop off most anywhere in the wild though, mountains, swamps, it made no difference. He'd make himself a shelter and live off the land as long as he had to. Most any kind of weather too. All he needed was a rifle, axe and good knife.

"Another odd thing too," Bud added. "Those big oak trees I mentioned, the two beside their cabin alongside the Burnt Tree. When the ginsengers found things, they said one tree was still smoldering, charred to a stump, but the other was okay. Of course, the leaves on its cabin side were singed, but otherwise, there it stood, tall and proud as ever.

"So, you ask yourself, why'd that one tree live and not the other? Well sir, after they chewed on it for a spell back then, the best they could figure was that a big wind must have done the deed: blown them flames away from the standing one."

Bud stopped and looked from Lee to Tom. "Well, that's about it, gents, how this ol' river got its name, Burnt Tree. You see, don't you? It was because of that burned stump. Before that, it had some Indian name, the river that is ... but I don't recollect what it was."

"What did they think happened at the cabin?" Lee asked.

Bud leaned on the broom handle. "Truth be known, folks didn't know, not even to this day, not for sure. But the best they could piece together went like this: It was a love triangle gone bad ... as they always do. I saw his wife's photo in an old newspaper once. Pretty as a picture, she was. Anyway, the story went that Dan caught them in bed together, Joe and her, couldn't forgive either one, especially her. Murdered them both in a jealous rage.

"But why the love triangle? Why not murder-suicide or lovers' suicides, Joe and Dan's wife?"

Bud fingered the salt shaker. "What clinched that for most folks, the three-way lovers' version, was written in the dirt outside the cabin. From the tracks, it looked like Dan and Joe had a terrible fight, and Papa cut him before getting stuck himself. Then, they figured Dan musta dragged Joe's carcass back inside and for lover's spite, tossed him on the bed alongside his wife before setting the fire.

"Also, they found bloody boot prints leading into the forest, Dan's they figured. Trackers said he was favoring his right leg. They followed his bloody trail for quite a piece before losing it in a swamp. Did I mention Joe was left-handed?"

Lee nodded.

"You see where I'm headed, don't you?" Bud asked. "It stands to reason. If Dan's wound was on his right leg, it had to have been Papa who done the cutting, him being left-handed."

The red neon sign in the window crackled.

He thought a moment. "There may have been other reasons folks settled on the love triangle too, beside the signs in the dirt. That version, perhaps, made the most sense to folks, what they might do themselves or want to do if their sweethearts cheated on them. Then too, you can imagine how back in those days, or today for that matter, finding them two in bed together, like they did, would set everyone's sex fancies at full gallop." Bud chuckled to himself. "Hell, most likely folks settled on the love triangle 'cause it made the juiciest telling."

Bud worried a stain on the table with his waist towel. "Now that I'm thinking about it, there was another version that also set gossipy minds to racing. In that one, there was treasure. That tale went this-a-way. Dan struck it rich somewhere up on the Burnt Tree, but never told Joe. Stands to reason though, he would have told sweet Amanda. But they figured somehow Papa Joe wormed it out of her. Maybe some under-the-covers talk, if you get my drift. Anyway in that telling, Dan killed her 'cause of both, the cheating and blabbing about the gold."

At the mention of "gold," Lee's eyes lit up.

"Now you see don't you, why folks gave him that name, Crazy Dan, Crazy Dan Jagger? It was because he killed the thing he loved, murdered her in a jealous rage, 'cause she wasn't perfect enough to suit him, like the rest of his world up there, or like he dreamed it was." Bud stood up and swallowed the last of his coffee. "Damn, that's a good batch, even if I do say so. Think I'll whip up another. What about you fellers?"

Lee nodded yes, but Tom covered his cup with a hand.

Whether by chance or design, Bud left them with a tease. "There's more about that gold too. Be right back."

After Bud walked away, Lee asked, "Good story, huh?"

"You mean a nice try for a big tip," answered Tom, chuckling.

"What do you mean, T.D.? He's just telling us a good story."

"C'mon, use your head. He doesn't get that much business up here. He's gotta milk who he can."

"That's a crappy attitude. You gotta trust folks more."

"Crazy Dan, love triangles, murder, sounds like touristy B.S. if you ask me."

Bud returned and sat down.

"Say, Jarrett, didn't your grandpop live around here once ... about the same time as ol' Dan too? Hell, they could have been friends in them days, Crazy Dan and your grandpop." He winked at Bud. "For that matter, Ol' Crazy might have been your grandpop."

"Not funny, T.D."

"Where'd I leave you guys?" Bud asked.

"Something about gold," Lee answered.

Bud quickly found his story-rhythm again. "I'll get to that shortly, but back to Dan. Like I said, after they lost his trail, he just up and disappeared and no one ever saw hide or hair of him again, not to this day. Of course over the years, some folks would say they spied him once in a while. They would swear they glimpsed him just as he disappeared around a bend in the river, or into the forest just beyond their headlights when they were driving along some dark country road. Said they recognized him by his long hair, beard and wide-brimmed hat. Mind you though, I don't put much stock in them ghosty tales." He made a drinking motion.

"Stranger yet," he added, stroking his chin, "My Pop always claimed that in June for years after, they'd find fresh daisies on the old stone steps to their cabin. Left there by Dan, folks reckoned. Of course, if that even happened, how could they know who left 'em? On the other hand, June was her birth month and daisies was her favorite flower."

Tom kicked Lee under the table and he elbowed back.

Hand to the side of his mouth, Bud lowered his voice. "Then years later, a tale made the rounds about Dan's gold. I don't know where it came from or how it got started, but according to that version, Dan found a foot-wide seam of quartz somewhere up the valley with veins of gold lacing all through it. Them two go together, you know, quartz and gold.

"Before long, folks hereabouts were digging up half the county looking for it. That's what happens when folks let their imaginations stampede. Of course, if Dan did strike it rich somewhere, it'd still be up there, the gold." Bud leaned his broom against the wall, walked behind the counter and began rummaging through a drawer. "There you are," he spoke to something inside it. He tossed a small charred stone to Lee. "Jim

McCloud, dead and gone now, always claimed he fished that little guy out of the ashes of Dan's cabin."

Lee turned the stone over and over, his interest growing. Underneath the charring were amber crystals with what looked like gold tinseling through it.

"But who knows," Bud said, "Jim could have been pulling my leg. Hell, no gold has ever been found 'round these parts. Wrong kinda rock, or so the experts claim." He glanced at the stone Lee was inspecting. "Then again, I've always heard gold's where you find it."

Wide-eyed, Lee looked over at his friend. "Did I ever tell you Grand-dad left me some stones he found in the mountains?"

Tom held Bud's stone up and grinned. "See, I told you they could be the same guy, your grandfather and Crazy Dan. Say, what's his first name, your grandfather's?"

"Dallas, why?"

Tom thought a moment and grinned. "Hell, they even got the same initials, Dan Jagger and Dallas Jarrett."

Lee gave him a middle finger.

Walking toward the counter, Bud called back, "Excuse me a second. Gotta get that ham bone out of the freezer. Bean soup, tomorrow, almost forgot."

"What a load o' cra-pola," Tom said, after Bud left.

"What are you saying, he's lying?"

"You're kidding, aren't you? Don't you see he's playing us? Now he's trying to get us to chase Ol' Crazy's gold?" He sneered at the stone on the table.

"C'mon, why would he do that?"

Tom looked at him in disbelief. "For money, Jarrett, ours. Jeez, wake up?" He thought a moment. "Okay, let's say we fall for that gold mine story of his and what the hell, we decide to look for it. Just where do you think we're going to get our provisions? It's not like there are a dozen stores just down the road. There's nothing up here, nothing. We'll have to get them from dear ol' Bud, that's where. Money out of our pockets, into his. Get it? Ten to one, he's got a map with an 'X' too, that he's willing to sell us."

"You're full of it, T.D. He knows we like the Tree, like hearing about it. You told him so yourself. Besides, he wants to know if it's a good story to write about someday, that's all."

"Don't get me wrong," answered Tom. "I'm not blaming him for wanting to make money. He's just looking out for Bud, what everyone does. I just don't like him digging through our pockets for it."

Sitting down at their table again, Bud chuckled. "I'm not one to push scary stories and such, mind you, but nowadays, anytime a hunter or fisherman comes up missing around these parts, they say the Demon, meaning Crazy Dan, had him for supper." He winked and added, "If you get my drift." He cocked his head and listened like he heard something in the night, then took a long drink of coffee, his eyes big over the cup's rim. "B.S., I say to that spooky stuff." He motioned around in a wide circle. "With all that wilderness out there, dollars to donuts, them fellers just got lost. Easy to do 'round here."

After fishing through his pockets, Bud laid a small compass on the table. "Me, I always take this little guy along when I'm tromping around out there, just in case. Always points me toward home. Of course, a big knife's good company too." He played with the compass. "Got an extra in back in case you're interested." He gave a patronizing smile. "But you fellers have no use for one, seeing as you're just here for the fishing. A compass is for fellers who are looking for adventure, ready to tackle the big green mystery out that door. But I understand, you guys are playing it safe, looking for more house-broke adventures, like fishing. Can't say I blame you neither."

Tom bumped Lee's chair hard. "Excuse me," he mocked.

"But back to those lost fellows. You gotta learn quick up in them mountains, else you go under. Nature weeds out the slow ones. I reckon that's why they call it survival of the fastest."

A patronizing glance flitted across Tom's face.

"But like I was saying, over the years, some do swear they've seen it, the Demon, usually after dark. Still out there guarding the mountains and his gold, they figure. Spotted sometimes by folks who don't tell fibs neither, leastways not regular. Personally, I think it's a load of crap."

The owner blew at some dust balls under a nearby table and they ghosted across the floor. "Don't know how I missed them fellows," he said. "I'll get 'em later."

"But who knows, maybe Dan is still up there somewhere, and he did have them lost souls for supper, like they say. After all those years though, he'd have to be awful long in the tooth and wild-looking ... a bit crazy too."

The red neon sign in his window buzzed and crackled. When Bud walked over to turn it off, Tom whispered, "He's not fooling me with that chicken-dare stuff either."

"What's your problem now?"

"Hinting we're scared if we don't bite and set out after the gold. I'm telling you, Lee, he's playing us with all these stories."

"Dag, don't be so cynical." Lee grinned. "Sounds like that demon business is spooking you."

Bud returned to their table. "So, my story, what do you think?"

"That's a keeper," Lee answered. "Wish I could use it, but I promised." This time, when Tom kicked Lee's leg under the table, he kicked back.

Bud smiled. "I thought so, thought it was a good one. Always nice to hear it from someone else." He pointed to the fading cherry stain on Lee's t-shirt. "Looking better."

"OK if I get some water, soak it some more?" Lee asked the owner, gesturing toward the kitchen.

As Lee walked away, Tom called, "Give it up, Jarrett. The fish won't mind it."

After he was gone, Bud asked, "Your buddy, he likes daring the gods, don't he?"

Tom questioned him with his open hand.

"Wanting what they got."

His look questioned Bud further.

"Perfection."

Tom's mouth did a wry smile.

Lee came back and sat down, still worrying the stain.

Bud made a fly casting motion. "You fellas gonna try your luck tomorrow, the Tree?"

Both nodded.

"Well, maybe it'll pick up soon," Bud said. "She'll never be like she was in the old days." Walking behind the counter, he took a framed picture from the wall and brought it to their table.

It was a yellowed photo of two smiling men holding a long stringer of trout between them. There was a river in back of them. An inscription at the bottom read, "Burnt Tree, 1922."

Bud's face softened. "Man on the right's my Pop."

Reaching for the photo, Tom brought it closer. "Nice stringer."

"Wow," Lee added.

Bud lit a cigarette. "The wife is always after me to quit. Told her I did, but I always sneak a couple after she's gone to bed. Probably oughta listen to her though." The cigarette ash under his nose grew longer. "Ashtray," he said, "back in a second." As he walked away, he called back, "Yeah, fishing on the Tree was great back then. Only place like it nowadays might be Eden Brook."

Lee's eyes jumped over at Tom, alive with new interest.

"Go on, Bud," Lee said. "Eden Valley."

The owner glanced over at a verdant landscape painting on the wall. "Well, when we first came over the pass at daybreak, but still high up, it caught my breath. So beautiful, it made my insides shiver. It was a wide valley, not like those little hollers down your way. You could hardly see from one end to the other.

"The whole valley floor was green with splashes of gold flowers everywhere. I'm no Arthur Burbank, but I'm pretty sure they were daisies."

Tom hid a smile behind his hand.

"West, at the valley head were two big mountains. The one in sunlight was taller, the other in darkness, but both tops were poking through clouds. They were so high and far off that their forests looked like charcoal-green moss. They seemed unreachable.

"Holding the valley captive to the north and south were mountains back of mountains, the far off ones with that blue Appalachian haze. Some had their tops chewed ragged by a jillion years of wind and rain, yet still shaking their stony fists up at the heavens."

Tom gave a low hiss.

"I read in a National Geographic that them mountains was once giants, so big that the Himalayas was like their little brothers. Pleases me to think they remember that time.

"Anyway, busting out of those mountains at the head to the west, wild and untamed, was Eden Brook. It wove down Eden Valley, pressing close to the mountains to the north. I swear, those shimmering riffles looked like brushed gold under that new sun."

Tom cleared his throat.

"The whole stream was around..." He stopped and stroked his chin. "Maybe 10 miles or so long if you pulled on both ends and took out the bends. The brook itself was about as wide as your two-lane road, counting the shoulders."

Bud walked over and wiped a nearby painting with his sleeve, leaving it slightly askew. It was similar to the scene he had just described.

Tom looked at Bud askance, suspicious that Bud had made up the Eden Brook tale and borrowed his description from the painting.

"Where was I?" Bud asked when he came back.

"You had just come over the mountains into Eden Valley," Lee answered.

"Right," he said. "Anyway, we rode on downstream to where Eden Brook left the valley and emptied into the main river, the Burnt Tree. You know, just to see it. Glad we did too. Two giant slabs of limestone were guarding the entrance to Eden Valley, with Eden Brook gushing out between. Carpeting both banks, down to where it spilled into the Tree, was a path of gold."

"A path of gold?" Lee asked.

Intent on his telling, Bud waded through the question. "Speaking of those limestone slabs at the Eden Valley entrance, they looked like the gates to some magical kingdom, the kind you see in a child's fairytale book, old and all tapestried with vines and green velvety moss.

"Pop said the Seneca Tribe used to call that entrance to Eden Valley their 'Spirit Gates.' Claimed the valley was sacred to them, that their Great Spirit lived there. Afterward, we hiked a mile or so on up the Burnt Tree itself, you know, just to get a gander at it too."

"What was it like?" Lee asked.

"More good country, but not your Eden Valley, lots of boulders and whitewater that way. We turned back when we saw storm clouds riding our way along the spine of the mountain."

Bud downed the last of his coffee. "Either of you boys care for a little nip of Old Log Cabin whiskey? You know, brighten your evening?"

Both men waved him off.

"Don't do it often, understand, but think I'll give myself a snort. Hope you fellers don't mind."

As Bud rummaged through the counter cabinets, Tom elbowed his friend. "I'm telling you this bird's after our money. We didn't go for the gold mine story, so he's trying something else. It's you he's working on though."

Lee returned a blank look.

"Aw c'mon, Jarrett. He read you like a book, you and that 'pretty world' nonsense of yours. You know, how everything's gotta be perfect, from your nose hairs to ... whatever. Eden Brook's just the latest. He's counting on you biting and me going along. And another thing, did you get a gander at that wall painting he dusted? It looked just like what he was describing, Eden Valley ... doesn't that make you question what he's feeding us?"

Walking over, Lee examined the painting closer and straightened it.

Tom snickered. "I liked it better crooked."

Stepping back to inspect it, Lee shook his head. "Aw, he wouldn't make up a story like that."

"Are you kidding?" Tom asked. "We know he lies to his wife, the smoking." When he saw the owner coming back, he shushed Lee with a hand.

Bud poured two fingers of whiskey into his cup. "Both you fellas of drinking age, ain't you?" He held the half-empty bottle toward them.

Both waved him off again and he screwed the cap back on.

"You said you and your father checked out the Burnt Tree," Lee said. "What did you do after that?"

Bud thought a moment. "As well as I recollect, it was late afternoon, so we rode back up Eden Valley and camped alongside Eden Brook."

"Eden Valley," Lee asked, "what was it like?"

Tom's fingers drummed on the table.

Thinking a moment, Bud picked up with his story. "Well, that first evening we hobbled our horses in a wide meadow on the south side of the river. Lots of belly-high sweet grass for the horses, and plenty of flowers for our tired old eyes.

"Never another human sign all the time we was there, but we saw plenty of big cat and bear sign. No old fire rings, cigarette butts or boot tracks like you'd find back on the Tree. No sir, no people dirt up there.

"Up the valley on a cliff face though, Pop did see some Indian drawings. He said they looked old, that whoever made 'em was sleeping under the grass by then ... most likely.

"When we made camp that evening, the sun was just setting between them two big mountains at the head of the valley. Damnedest sight.

"Pop started a cooking fire and sent me to fetch water in Mom's white enamel bucket. Doubt he told her he'd packed it along. Her best one, you see. I done like Pop said, dipped water from a cold spring that bubbled up from the mountain's heart, then spilled down into Eden Brook.

"Anyway, when I came back, Pop was about to dip himself a cold drink from my bucket when he let out an, 'O-o-oee!' I held up a firebrand. There, circling the white bottom was a fingerling brookie, its back amber-olive. 'By cracky, Boy,' Pop yelled, 'we're gonna have milk and honey tomorrow, boy, milk and honey.' Never seen him so tickled."

A door opened behind them and they all turned.

Behind the counter, a pretty teenager was pouring a glass of milk. "Hi, Daddy," she called.

Bud waved back. "Daughter," he said. "Just finished high school. Helps us run the place. Kind of lonely for her sometimes, though. Not much happens up here, off the beaten path."

Tom asked, "How is business?"

Bud wig-wagged his hand. "We get by. Picks up some in hunting, fishing season. Money ain't everything. Wife and I like it up here."

"We're getting sidetracked," Lee said.

"You're right, young feller. Where was I?" he asked himself. "Oh, yeah, you were asking about Eden Brook. Anyway, Pop went upstream with his fly rod, and I went down with my old bait-casting outfit and worms. I can tell you this much, both of us was plenty excited.

"Eden Brook kept its promise too. I caught more brookies than Carter's got liver pills. Nary a hook mark on any of 'em. Most was 8 to 12 inches, some 14, but all fat and sassy. Beautiful too, like that wild home they was living in.

"Some of their gill covers flashed like gold under wet glass. I don't

Brook of yours, that's pie in the sky stuff." He glanced down at the calluses on his hands. "Besides, I only got a week off."

"I've been thinking about that too," Lee said. "Today's the fourth and you don't have to be back to work till a week from this coming Monday, June 13th."

Tom nodded.

"Tomorrow's Sunday. Let's say we take tomorrow to get everything ready. That still leaves us seven whole days, assuming we drive back to Eastbrook late Sunday night. That way, we'll have three days to look for Eden Brook and three, maybe two to hike back. And let's just say we do get lucky and find it, that'll give us one whole day to fish water most guys just dream about." He tried gauging the other man's reaction. When he could not, he added, "C'mon, T.D., what do you say?"

"In your dreams, buddy, not mine."

"Yeah, but isn't this my trip, your graduation gift for me? Leastways, that's what you said, or was that a load of B.S.?"

Tom's finger ran mindlessly around a knot swirl in the wooden table-top. "Yeah, but let's be reasonable."

Both young men looked up when the back door opened.

"Help me out here, Bud," Tom said, "talk some sense into this guy."

Bud frowned.

Tom motioned toward his friend. "This goofball wants to look for your—"

Lee cut him short. "Got a question, Bud. How would you feel if we looked for it, your Eden Brook?"

"Eden Brook?" Bud repeated, surprise in his voice, seemingly. He turned toward Lee. "Ever read 'Big Two Hearted River'"

Lee shook his head no.

"Story about a young feller who was chasing an ideal. In this case, an ideal fishing trip by himself. He was a lot like you, except he was just back from a war and trying to deal with some bad things that happened there." He looked at Lee knowingly. "Check it out sometime. I think you'll recognize some stuff."

Lee frowned.

Bud thumbed toward Tom. "Your friend here's right, young Jarrett. You'd just be chasing your tail looking for that stream." He glanced at the head of a bear on a nearby wall, its teeth bared. "No sir, you don't wanna mess with that country. I'd feel mighty bad if something happened to either one of you fellers and you was never heard from again, and all on account of my ramblings." His voice lowered. "Hell, you could run into The Demon, ol' Dan Jagger himself, up there some dark night and him just licking his chops and grinning your way, like a Chessie Cat. What then?" He slapped his knee and chuckled. "Seriously, I wouldn't risk it if I was you, son."

"But you did it," Lee said. "You made the trip."

Bud dismissed Lee's words with the back of his hand. "Wouldn't do it again though, ever. No offense, but it's too far, too wild, dangerous for you guys. Best listen to your friend here, young Jarrett. Forget about Eden Brook and just go fishing.

"But why couldn't we do like you did," asked Lee, "get some horses, go over the mountains? You could draw us a map so we wouldn't get lost."

"No one stables horses 'round here anymore," answered Bud. "Not since the war."

"Dag," Lee said.

"It wouldn't do you fellas no good anyhow, even if there were horses. I don't recollect the way over them mountains. I wasn't paying much attention to the trail when we done it back then, you see. Left that to Pop.

"You see, I was just a kid at the time, a dumb, snot-nosed kid, with lots of other things on my mind. Coulda been almost anything, anything exceptin' work." He rolled his cigarette back and forth between his fingers. "More'n likely, it was some pretty young thing I was trailing at the time, if you get my sense."

"But why couldn't we hike up the Burnt Tree, find it that way?" Lee asked. "End up the same place, wouldn't we?"

"Up the Tree?" Bud asked. "My God, counting all the river twists and turns, a feller might go a hundred miles that-a-way and never run in to another soul."

"But if we did, how far would it be," Lee asked, "you know, till we come to Eden Valley?"

Stroking his chin, Bud looked at the ceiling. "Uhh, I'd say 30, 35 miles of wild, hard country, maybe more. Sure you guys are up for that? Won't be no picnic. You never know what you might run onto either," he said, grinning, "or who."

"Piece of cake," Lee answered. "We're young, in good shape and done plenty of hiking. All we'd have to do is 10 or 12 miles a day." He spoke to Tom. "Just like I figured, it'll take us three days to find it two, maybe three back and whatever's left over is gravy." He mustered his most plaintive voice. "So, Bud, is it okay if we look for it, your Eden Brook?"

The owner's fingers drummed on the table. "Um-m ... guess so," he said, reluctance in his voice. "Your funeral, but like I said, keep it under your hats."

Lee smiled broadly. "Wild horses couldn't drag it out." He slapped Tom's shoulder playfully. "Right T.D.?"

One corner of Tom's mouth fell down.

"C'mon, T.D., it's not like you, ducking a challenge."

Tom stared off into a dark corner of the restaurant.

"Sure ain't for sissies," cautioned Bud.

Speaking out loud but to himself, Lee began planning more of the trip. "'Let's see now, we'll need time to get ready, pack our gear, break camp and what else? That'll probably take us most of tomorrow, Sunday." He turned to Bud, his excitement growing. "Of course, we'll need some provisions. You open Sundays?"

Bud tightened the lid on a sugar dispenser. "No, but hell, I'll open up for you boys."

Tom smirked, knowingly.

"And could we get one of those compasses you showed us?" Lee asked. "We'll need it now. How was it you put it?" He paused, trying to remember. "'... To tackle the big green mystery out that door.'"

Bud smiled wryly. "You fellows know not to get metal near it, don't you, the compass? Won't read right if you do."

"Sure," Lee said, his eyes sliding over to Tom. "And Bud, could you give us a hand with directions?"

From behind the counter, the owner got a pad and pencil and began drawing a rough map, trying to explain things as he drew. Tom half-listened, but Lee followed every detail.

"I've only been a dozen miles or so up the Tree myself, understand," Bud said. "There's a trail alongside the river that far. The rest you'll have to figure out on your own. I do recollect Pop saying it was easy to get lost after that, so a feller had best not wander too far off the river." A smile played around his eyes. "No sir, I wouldn't wanna hear the Demon et you for dinner."

Bud frowned. "And, oh yeah, forgot to mention. About where the trail ends alongside the river is a family named Gardino. Italian I think. None too friendly, but you gotta cross their land to get up-river. Shot at me once, years ago, when I was fishing up that way. They got a pack of big hounds too, mean as all get out. Best stay clear if you can."

"Crapola, what's their problem?" Tom asked.

"Think they own the whole damn river, both banks. They got themselves a still up there somewhere, you know, for making moonshine. For what it's worth, they do make the best shine 'round these parts. You can tell by the bubbles, you know. When you shake it, if they're small and go away quick, you got a good batch."

The two young men nodded like they knew that.

"I've been known to take a swig of it myself a time or two," he added, wiping his lips like he could still taste it. "Damn good stuff. The mother died a few years back. She used to keep them in line some. Just the old man and his two sons now. You gotta watch out for them boys, especially. They're mean. Most weekends, the old man sends them over to Wilkens with a batch of shine. Sometimes though, they get all liquored up and stay there. Best hope this is one of those weekends.

"Not that the old man's a peach. He's the one who shot at me that time. He can't chase after folks like he used to though, bad hips and knees." A wry smile played around one side of Bud's mouth. "He lets them hounds do it for him. That old codger's a real rummy though. Don't matter to him whether it's his own or store bought."

Tom shook his head. "That's all we need this trip, some crazy moon-shiners. Any way around?"

"Take too long," Bud answered. He pointed to a squiggly line on his drawing. "Now this here's the Tree." He turned the map around for the two young men, placed a star alongside the river and tapped on it. "And this is where the Gardino's live, see. The valley kind of bottlenecks there. There's a swamp on the west bank and high cliffs on the other. Their cabin is in between.

"Some folks claim they mark their property with urine, you know, like wild animals. Best give 'em a wide berth, go through after dark. He looked at Tom. "Keep your eyes peeled for the old gent. He sits on the back porch sometimes with a pack of dogs, nursing a big, old double barrel."

"We don't want no trouble," Tom said, "especially that kind."

"And, oh yeah," Bud added. "Wouldn't hurt to take along some store-bought whiskey, just in case. A feller never knows when some Old Log Cabin might come in handy. Both of you is of drinking age, ain't you?" he asked, his eyes mocking the question. "I know I asked before, but just checking. John Law says I gotta."

"Bet you just happened to have some to sell us too." Tom said.

Lee shot his friend a sharp look.

"Don't matter to me where you get it, son, from me or someone else, but if I was you, I'd take some along."

"So, T.D., you up for it, searching for Eden Brook?"

"No sir, not me," he answered, waving his hands back and forth. "Be a cold day in hell."

CHAPTER EIGHT

After passing the Gardino's that first day, they no longer had a clear trail to follow so they stayed mostly to the river, hiking along the bank or wading when it was shallow. Although it did keep them from getting lost, the river seemed endless, snaking on and on forever up the valley.

On the early evening of the second day, Tom stopped under a tree alongside the river and wiped his forehead. "I've had it," he said.

Lee collapsed in the shade beside him. Turning up one shoe, he pried a piece of gravel from its tread.

Tom eased his shoes off and dangled his feet in the water. "Got a raw place starting," he said, pointing. "My marching foot."

Lee questioned him with a look.

Tom slapped his left leg. "This is the one they give the commands on, you know, when you're marching. Bet you didn't know that, Jarrett, that they marched in the Air Force."

Lee pointed to his friend's foot. "Those Eden Brook waters will fix that up just fine." He winged the gravel from his shoe out into the river.

Tom watched as the moving waters swept the rings away. "We both know this is a waste of time, don't we? Like I said, we could be downing a couple cold ones back at camp right now, instead of this." He pointed to his foot.

"Aw, lighten up. Think of it like baseball practice in the old days. Remember, those summers, hotter'n hell and muggy, both of us sweating blood to get in shape. Remember?"

"That was different. There was a payoff, we got to play ball."

"Well?" asked Lee, motioning to the sylvan wilderness surrounding them. "This isn't a bad payoff for starters."

"You know what I'm saying. We'll never find that Eden Brook of yours. No payoff, except maybe for blisters."

Lee eyed him skeptically. "Are you still sore about buying those provisions from Bud?"

"And that's another thing. What saps, spending good money on a wild-goose chase like this."

"You can't know that, not for sure," Lee said. "And what if you're wrong and we do find it?" He thought a long moment. "Let me put it to you again, only this time borrowing from Bud. Once, just once in your life, wouldn't you like to fish a stream whose pure waters bubbled up from the heart of a mountain, or hold a living brookie with gold plated gills in your hands ... or know that your boot tracks are the first there, at least in the last twenty years?"

Tom studied the water swirling around his feet. "Nah, this is the river I got, the one that's here and I can see, feel." He splashed his feet in the water. "But tomorrow's day three. I'll give you till then, like promised."

As night fell, they made a fire in a small clearing and ate their sandwiches beside it. Dog tired, they crawled into their sleeping bags and Tom was soon breathing heavily.

Before going to sleep, Lee made some notes in his journal, most centering around the Burnt Tree. He included their story filled evening with Bud at the Spruce Mountain Restaurant, and Tom's needling him about his grandfather and Crazy Dan being the same man. The Jagger tale captured his imagination also and he made some entries about it, ending with, "Dan Jagger's world is still up there somewhere on the Burnt Tree, only now sleeping under a half century shroud of leaves and dirt, with only a moaning night-wind for company."

Later that night, Lee had a dream, a bad one. He dreamt about something that had happened a few weeks earlier one evening. His parents had gone to a movie, and he and Pru were in the house alone. They were making out on the couch in the den and after one long, passionate kiss, she said, "Sounds like rain."

He knew what that meant, any mention of rain on her part when they were making out. It was a red flag, mutually agreed upon, whether rain was threatening or not, that things were going too far and it was time to slow down.

Pru seldom wore makeup. She didn't need to, nature had done the job for her: eyes traced in dark brown lashes, cheeks faintly rouged and pouty lips shaded in heart of rose.

Every time he went too far and she stopped him, he was disappointed in himself. He would always tell her he was sorry, go to confession, do the penance and promise the priest never to do it again ... but he always did.

She did hate getting her hair wet, though, and so when rain actually did begin drumming on the roof that evening, they went to his parents' bedroom to find her a headscarf before she went home.

The chenille cover on his parents' bed had not one wrinkle. Uncluttered night tables, each with its own matching lamp, sat on either side of the bed. Hanging over the bed on the wall was a large paint-by-numbers seascape that his mother had done years earlier. In it, the ocean looked stormy and angry. She had done a good job at keeping the colors inside the lines.

Perfectly balanced on either side of his mother's chest of drawers, as though measured in micrometers, were his parents' wedding picture and a family portrait.

Looking for a scarf, Pru searched the top drawer, careful not to disturb anything. She found a rosary and held it up. The beads were clear crystal and faceted. They caught the overhead light, and gave off a pink, silver, blue iridescence. The rosary's cross was silvered, like the one Pru wore on a chain around her neck, alongside the heart locket her father had given her.

Opening the next drawer, she found a headscarf. Under it was a document. "Hmm, marriage certificate," she noted, "your parents." About to close the drawer, her eyes caught the number 32 on the paper and she hesitated. Curious, she picked the document up and skimmed a few sentences. "Says here your parents, Stewart and Evelyn, were married in January, '32."

"So?"

"You were born in June, that same year."

He looked at her blankly before it soaked in. "Lemme see that," he said, jerking the paper from her hands. Sitting on the bed, he read and reread it. "My God, you're right," he said, "she was pregnant before they got married." Shoulders sagging, he let the paper drop to the floor and stared vacantly at the painting over the bed.

She sat down beside him. "Sorry, honey, if I hadn't been so nosey..."

He looked at her, surprised. "Not your fault," he said, staring at his parents' wedding picture.

She followed his eyes. "I know you think what they did was wrong, honey," she said, stroking his neck, "but maybe some good came of it too."

His eyes snapped around toward her.

"It gave them someone to love," she explained, pointing toward him and smiling. "Me too."

He scowled. "What are you saying, what she did was okay? We both know better. Why are you trying to whitewash that?" He glanced at her heart locket. "That sounds like your old man talking, that nonsense about right and wrong shifting."

She placed her hand high on her chest. "Sorry," she said, "I know you don't like hearing it, but it is what he believed ... so do I, but you know that."

He studied his parents' wedding picture again. "And her always on her soapbox. This is right, this is wrong, Lee," he said, his tone mocking. "Do the right thing, Lee. Do like you been taught, Lee. And all the while, her preaching one thing and doing another. How two-faced."

Despite Pru's further efforts to console and reason with him, he remained adamant that his parents' sex before marriage and hypocrisy afterward, more particularly his mother's, were terribly wrong and unforgivable.

CHAPTER NINE

In the lengthening shadows of the following day, Tom slumped down on the grassy bank of the Burnt Tree.

Lee sat down beside him, leaning his hiking staff against a tree.

At the higher elevation, the forests were mostly spruce and pine, not like the hickory his grandfather had used to make Lee's staff. That wood was found lower down around Eastbrook. Lee was pleased the old man had made it for him, especially out of hickory. True, the evergreens around them were more majestic and they smelled sweeter after you cut them. Even so, the hickories were harder, sturdier, more like his grandfather.

After curing the sapling, the old man had stripped the bark and rubbed warm linseed oil into it. Then, he had fire-hardened the tip and drilled a hole in the handle for a lanyard. His grandfather had one like it, except the old man's was bigger and heavily scarred.

When he first handed the staff to his grandson, he said, "Here, this might ease your trail some ... or another fellers'. Pay no mind to her gnarly crooks. She ain't perfect, but she's the one you got."

"OK, Jarrett, as promised, there's your day three. And still no Eden. What do you say, let's hit the sack early, get a good night's sleep before headin' back tomorrow."

Lee slumped over against his pack.

That evening in the fading light, they lay on their sleeping bags, finishing the last of their peanut butter and jelly sandwiches.

"Can't believe there's no sign," Lee said. "Thought for sure we'd run into it today, at least the stone gates. You know, like Bud pictured."

"Give it up."

"How far you think we've come?"

Tom nursed a blister. "Hard to say. Thirty miles, probably more."

Lee pointed to Tom's foot.

"It'll be okay, mostly downhill going back."

Lee took a longing gaze upriver.

Tom followed his friend's eyes. "Don't even think about it, Jarrett."

"Wha-at?" Lee asked, a faint smile playing around his mouth.

"You know what."

"Shame, just one more day and I know we'll find it."

"Hold it right there, buster. In case you've forgotten, I gotta job to think about. Look, add it up, it took three days to get this far. We'll need three back and one day to break camp and drive home. That's four total. I can't afford it, another day."

Before Lee nodded off that night, he jotted a few lines again in his journal. He wrote mostly about the beauty of the country they had traveled through that day, the challenges they had overcome and a line or two about Tom's griping. He made another entry about that day too. It was something he had held back from Tom, something that had been compelling him to sneak anxious looks back downriver ever since it happened.

Earlier that day, he had fallen behind. Tom had just disappeared around a river bend up ahead and Lee had stopped to take a breather. He was looking at the branches of the spruce trees across the river, noting how their new tips looked like mint-green bottle brushes, when he caught a movement far downstream. It was just a glimpse as he was turning his head, but he thought he saw a large figure moving alongside the river next to the trees. It was just an impression, but the figure looked to be wearing a big, wide-brimmed hat. When he studied the river harder in that direction, however, it was empty. Uncertain of what he had seen and trying to avoid Tom's ridicule, he kept it to himself.

That night Lee dreamed again, and as on the previous night, this dream also centered on an actual event. It had some bad in it, but some good too. The bad was about Pru and him breaking up, the other was meeting Mary Lou Harris.

As he approached Pru's house in the early evening, he saw that she was not waiting for him on the porch as usual. It was then he saw the young girl next door, the one whose family had moved there recently. Sitting on her front steps, she waved when she saw him, but he did not wave back. Turning impulsively from Pru's house, he strolled toward her, uncertain why. As he drew closer, he could see she had a peanut butter jar in her hand.

"Hi," he called over her gate, "I'm Lee Jarrett."

She looked to be around 16 and just beginning to stick out in all of the right girl-places. She was wearing tight, cut off denim shorts. Her legs, tanned light-maple, carried her toward him. She was long-waisted and taller than he first thought. Her rich, brunette hair was pulled to the back of her head in a mussed pony-tail. Up close, her face had good skin and features. Although she did not have classic beauty, she had arresting walnut-brown eyes like Pru's and a Chiclet-white smile.

Opening the gate, she motioned him in, started to walk away, but turned back. "I know who you are," she said, "you're Cathy's guy." She pointed to herself with a peanut buttered index finger. "I'm Mary Lou, Mary Lou Harris."

"Mary Lou, huh? Lou, Lou," he said, weighing the name and nodding with approval. "I like it, Lou ... Louie."

"Louie?"

"Yeah, a name I've always liked. Favorite movie character too."

Her face puzzled.

He shrugged. "It's not important."

"Not sure how I feel about it, the name."

"Maybe it'll grow on you." He smiled to himself. "Just be glad I'm not into cartoons. You know, movie characters: Bugs, Daffy."

Her mouth puckered, holding back a smile. Scraping the last dollop from her jar, she licked it off sideways between her lips, all the while her big chestnut-brown eyes catching and holding his. Afterward she wiped her hands on her shorts and held one out toward him.

Her hand was soft and warm when he shook it. He pointed to the Pruitt house. "Pru, I mean Cathy, she said your family was new to East-brook. Where you from?"

"Other side of Wilkens, Burnt Tree country," she answered. "Just me and mother. Daddy's gone now, years ago."

"I've fished the Burnt Tree," he said. "Just stopped over to say hello, that's all." He paused, uncertain whether or not to say why he really came over. Deciding to chance it, he began, "None of my business, understand, but I've seen a lot of boys hanging around here. Eastbrook's a small town and people talk. A girl can get a bad rep sometimes, even if nothing's happened."

Her eyebrows lowered. "What are you trying to tell me, Lee Jarrett?"

For a long moment, he stood there awkwardly. It was those damn eyes he told himself. "Uhh, forget it. Like I said, none of my business."

She smiled, seemingly amused at his discomfort.

He sniffed the air. "Wood smoke?"

Giggling, she pointed to her hair. "That's me," she said. "Too warm for a fire last night, but mother fixed one anyway. We usually had a wood-fire going at our old place. She misses that smell sometimes, wood smoke. Claims it makes her feel less homesick in Eastbrook. Guess I sat too close to it last night."

"Good smell," he said.

She smiled

He glanced at her denim shorts. "Aren't you cold?"

She tittered. "I like wearing them."

A female voice called her name through a screen door.

Turning, she wiggled her index finger goodbye.

"See you, Louie," he called.

Her eyes said she was amused, but her face read mock displeasure. As she walked away toward the house, her pony tail jogged subtly back and forth, and so too her backside, a budding rear with fine promise.

She glanced back at him over her shoulder, then down at her behind and back up at him, her eyes playful. He was surprised she had checked to see if he was looking and embarrassed he had been. "Little minx," he thought to himself.

There was something else about her too. As they talked, some part of her was always moving, gracefully so, an eyebrow, a shoulder, a hand, like she had a finely tuned engine, a Rolls Royce engine, purring somewhere deep inside. He had seen other girls do that when they were nervous or being flirtatious. With her though, it seemed to come natural; whatever her reason, he found it sexy as hell.

When he walked back to the Pruitt house, Pru was sitting on their front porch swing.

"Hi, honey," he said, sitting beside her.

She frowned and motioned toward the young girl's house.

"Went over to say hi," he explained. "Just her and her mother. She's just a kid. No man around to help out, keep her straight."

Pru motioned toward the Harris' house, her eyes amused. "She's stuffing socks in her bra now, told me so."

He smiled wryly.

"Can we talk?" she asked, her voice serious.

"Uh oh, I know that tone."

Blanche, Pru's mother, opened the door and gave him her usual cold stare.

"Hi Mrs. Pruitt," he said. "Feels like an early spring, doesn't it?"

Blanche gave him a stony nod. "Cathy, I'm starving."

"I'll fix something shortly, Mother. Give me a minute."

Mrs. Pruitt glided stiffly back inside, like a metal decoy in a carnival shooting gallery.

"Can't she do that," Lee asked, "fix her own food?"

"Claims she likes it better when I do it, the taste." Pru shrugged.

He shook his head.

"Can't help it," she said, putting her hand to her forehead. "She needs help and there's no one else. You know that. I don't mind though."

"What was it you wanted to talk about?" he asked.

Tears welled in her eyes. "Aw corn. You know how mother feels about you," she began. "She thinks you're a nice young man and all, but that it will never work out between us because—"

He finished her sentence, "because I'm Catholic, right?"

"Sorry, honey," she said, "but you know how she is. Still blaming Daddy's leaving on that, their different religions."

"But Pru, why do we have to keep paying for what your father did? I'll never run out on you. That's being a coward."

She stiffened. "You're right, Daddy caused a lot of pain, but like I've told you before, perhaps some good came of it also, his leaving."

His eyes rolled up. "Would you run that by me again?"

"Wherever he is, I believe he's a happier man," she said, "now that he's free of all the bickering and fighting they used to do. At least it pleases me to think so."

He scowled. "That sounds like your father talking again, his crazy notion that good and bad comes from everything, and that you've swallowed whole. If you ask me, your father was looking for some way to get himself off the hook. You know, for running out on you two."

Her eyes moistening, she placed her hand high on her chest. "You didn't know him, Lee. He wasn't like that." She thought a moment. "Perhaps I was to blame for some of what happened, the fighting especially."

He tilted his head in a question.

"We always had a special bond, Daddy and me." She paused, weighing her words carefully. "I've never told anyone this, Lee, but mother was resentful of that, at least I think she was, and that led to some of their quarreling. Who knows? Maybe if I had given her more attention, like I gave him, things might have been better between them."

He looked through their porch window alongside the swing. Mrs. Pruitt's favorite figurine, the one she titled the Joker-Clown, was resting on the coffee table inside. Although the ceramic's details were finely painted, Lee did not like its cold hardness when he handled it. "But you can't blame yourself for what they did," Lee said, "for what she did." The porcelain statue was facing the front window, the way Mrs. Pruitt always liked it positioned. "Why are you bringing this stuff up now?"

Pru caressed his cheek with the back of her hand. "You know how much I love you, Lee Jarrett, but mother wants us to stop seeing one another, only for a while though, six months or so. Claims it'll help us see things more clearly. She said then, if we felt the same way about one another, she wouldn't stand in our way."

He looked out at the approaching twilight.

"I know what's in the back of her head," Pru went on. "She's hoping I'll meet someone else, someone with the same religion, and it'll be all over between us. She's wrong though, honey. I'll never change how I feel about you, ever."

"Okay, I get what she wants, but what about you? What do you want?"

She pushed the swing with her foot and they began swaying back and forth. "I just thought that if we gave Mother her way one last time and proved her wrong, that she'd stop trying to break us up."

"But you didn't answer me. What do you want?"

She touched her chest again.

He studied her for a long moment.

"For me, honey, please?"

He melted. "Dag, so how long are we talking?"

"This is April. Let's say from now till September, late September, around the time you're starting college."

"Any phone calls?"

"Maybe one just now and then," she said, looking at her hand. "Mother said I should give your ring back too ... as a sign. You know, that we'll stick to it, staying apart."

Lee's eyes rolled up. "But that's yours, it'll always be yours, no one else's."

"Hey, buster, in six months I want it back, hear?"

"But that's your, our engagement ring."

"Still is," she said, beginning to twist it off her finger. As she did though, it slid off unexpectedly and she dropped it. Falling on the top cement step, it made a dull ding, and then bounced down the next two steps before landing in the grass.

She scrambled after it, easily finding it, and after a brief inspection in the fading light, confirmed it was okay. "Sorry," she said. Taking his hand, she placed the ring in his palm, folded his fingers over it and kissed them. "Sorry about the sizing tape."

He glanced at his watch. "I gotta scoot. Dad asked me to help him this evening."

For several seconds, they stood clinging to one another. Lee could hear a voice shouting on a radio somewhere. The only word he could make out was "Jesus."

Pru motioned her head toward the voice. "Religious station. I don't know what she gets out of it. Guilt, I'm guessing. But the only one that comes in clear at night."

When he turned to leave, she held onto his hand and followed him to the edge of the porch.

As they kissed, she began shivering.

"Cold?" he asked folding her into his arms and rocking her gently until she quieted.

After walking down the front steps, he turned back.

She held her open hand out toward him and he did the same. "Love you, always have, always will," she said.

"I'll think of you often," he called, managing a lame smile and pointing to his hair. "Especially when it rains."

Eyes moistening, she whispered back, "Hope it rains a lot." Long after he disappeared, she sat on the top step, staring after him into the night.

As he walked into the early darkness, he felt her sizing tape on the ring. "He would leave it on for when she took it back." His thumb also found something else, a new scratch from when it fell on the cement step.

Lee's parents always liked Pru. When he told them about the breakup, they were disappointed until they learned it was just for a few months or so. He glossed over the real reason for the separation though, never telling them it was because he was Catholic.

He told them instead, that Mrs. Pruitt felt they were getting too serious and were too young to be doing that, and therefore, they should have a cooling off period and maybe see other people. Then, after that, if they still felt the same about one another, she would withdraw any objection.

When Lee woke up from his dream in the middle of the night, frogs were peeping in a small marsh across the Burnt Tree. His grandfather once told him everything had to be just right for them to mate: time of year, temperature, moon phase and so on. Lee closed his eyes and listened. Their voices were joyful and filled with promise.

Later that night, he had a wet dream, not about Pru but about the young girl next door, Mary Lou Harris. He thought it strange that he dreamt of her. That morning, he lingered in his sleeping bag, concerned that Tom might tease him if he noticed the spotting on his shorts.

Lee's notebook was on the ground beside him. The cover was wet and he wiped it off with the tail of his shirt.

"We got heavy dew last night," Tom said. "Clear skies, you shoulda known better and covered it up." He hit Lee with a rolled up sock ball. "Get up, sleepyhead."

Lee threw it back. "What for?" he asked, rolling over and facing away.

"Are you still sore about losing Eden Brook?"

He rolled back toward Tom. "Last night, I thought about what you said before, you know, about needing four days to get back. Just for argument's sake, let's say we search one more day, but take three days to get back to Eastbrook, not four."

"Forget it, Jarrett."

"Hear me out. That means we have to make up for losing that one day, right? Well, for starters, let's cut out the fishing we said we'd do. That'll save us almost one whole day itself. The trip back should take less time too because we'll know the way and it'll be downhill, mostly. You said so yourself. Of course, we could travel after dark but I don't think we'll need to. Anyway, all that should get us back in camp Sunday so we can pack, drive home and get in late that same night. That way," he finished, his tone mocking, "you'll be back Monday morning so you can punch your happy little time-clock."

"It ain't gonna happen, Jarrett, another day."

"But T.D., is this my trip or not?"

"Aw, jeez, not that again."

"If you do like I'm asking, give it one more day, I won't bring it up again, ever, promise."

"Your word?"

Lee held up his right hand.

Tom studied him pensively. Picking up Lee's staff, Tom hurled it toward him. Spinning end for end, it landed on a large, flat boulder between them, and balancing there, spun a few turns before falling off to one side. For a moment afterward, Tom drummed his fingers on his pack. "Got a better idea, Jarrett. Tell you what let's do. You still trust in that God of yours, don't you?" Not waiting for Lee to answer, he went on. "Let Him decide about Eden Brook."

Lee arched an eyebrow.

"Let's spin it, your staff, on that flat rock. If the tip end stops toward you, we'll give it one more day. If at me, then we head back right now, if in between, we'll do it again. You put so much stock in that God of yours, let Him decide. That fair or not?"

"Thought you didn't believe in that religious stuff."

"I don't, but anything to shut you up."

For a long moment, Lee considered Tom's proposal, and although suspicious, agreed to the terms.

"I'll spin it," Tom said, "okay?" Holding it by the middle, he centered it on a large rock. When he asked, "Ready?" and Lee nodded yes, he gave it a hefty turn, using both hands. It spun evenly for several seconds, then slowed and began to wobble. On its last slow turn, the tip swung toward Tom and stopped.

Lee made a sour face.

Teetering there, it fell off the boulder to one side, handle end down, its momentum standing it straight up, and then, almost as if something willed it, the tip end fell over pointing toward Lee.

Lee slapped his knee. "Hot diggity."

"Now hold on," Tom said, jumping up. "You know I meant when it stopped spinning on the rock. Not afterward, not when it fell off."

"Don't change the rules, buddy. You gave your word, said where it pointed when it stopped. You gave your word."

Tom gave the other man a long disgusted stare. "Aw crapola," he yelled up at sky. "I'm warning you, Jarrett, I better not lose my job over this."

"C'mon T.D.," he said, patting him on the back, "we'll find it today, I'm sure of it."

Picking up the staff and handing it to Lee, he said, "Blunder on ... Moses."

CHAPTER TEN

Face dirty and streaked with sweat, Tom collapsed on the ground in the late afternoon sun. "That's it, Jarrett, I've had it. There's day four, like you asked."

Taking off his pack, Lee dropped down beside him. After removing his hat, he took a long drink from his canteen and poured some over his head. He fingered the chain around his neck with the compass. "I've been thinking about our getting lost the other day. It could have been a false reading on our compass. We might have held it too close to metal when we checked it. Could have been anything: your net, my canteen, whatever. Bud warned us about that, remember?"

From where they sat, the river snaked on and on alongside the spine of the Spruce Mountains. Lee could see far up the valley, and there was still no sign of Eden. If it truly was there, and he was beginning to have doubts himself, his prize was swallowed up by the vast, smothering greenness. "Dammit," he said, looking up river at the distant mountains, their tops hidden in clouds. "I know it's just up ahead a piece. C'mon, T.D., we still got some daylight."

Tom shook his head. "Not on your life, Jarrett. Gesturing to the ground, he added, "Right here's where I'm camping tonight." He glanced at the river and rubbed the dark stubble on his face. "Maybe clean up a bit too."

"Dag, T.D. Don't quit on me now. We're close, I can almost taste it."

"Remember our deal, buddy ... hey, I got a better idea. Let's do some fishing, what we came for, or is the Tree not good enough anymore?"

"Up yours ... twice."

Tom began rummaging through his pack. "C'mon, let's give it a shot." Shading his eyes, he looked at the late sun. "Besides, the cool water will feel good."

Lee slammed the staff down on the ground. "Quitter," he yelled, but with no sincerity in his tone.

"That frigging Bud," Tom said, continuing to rummage through his pack. "Thirty miles my ass. Bet we've covered 40 already." He motioned up the valley to Lee. "Go on chasing smoke if you want, I'm goin' fishing."

Despite the higher elevation, the day had been blistering hot and muggy. Just below them was a green shaded pool at the base of a towering cliff.

Sweat stinging his eyes, Lee began digging in his pack for his fishing gear.

"Wanna go up or down?" Tom asked, pointing both ways at the river. Lee motioned upriver. "Borrow your net?" he asked.

It was a cheap net, the kind you could buy at any hardware: green plastic handle, aluminum rim and black cotton mesh-bag.

Tom hesitated. "Guess so," he said, tossing it over. "It did almost get us shot."

Lee stuck his fingers through a tear in the net and held it up for Tom to see. "What the hell?"

"Do you want it or not, Goldie, the net?" He tossed him an apple. "That's the last o'them."

"What's for supper?" Lee asked.

"What do you say we skip sandwiches and have some real grub for a change," Tom said. "Let's open that Spam we've been saving and fry up the last of the potatoes." Feeling around in his pack, he pulled out two cans of beer, Barbarossa, Lee's favorite, and held them up.

"Where'd those come from?" Lee asked.

"Here," Tom said, setting them on a rock, "find a cold spring upriver and toss them in. We'll have 'em with supper." Momentarily, he studied the sky to the west. "Doesn't look like rain, but better cover your stuff anyway."

They often drank beer on their trips, downing enough just to feel good. Lee knew his parents wouldn't like him drinking so he only told his grandfather about it. He and Tom liked to drink it with a little tomato juice mixed in. It seemed to smooth the bite. Red Eye they called it at the local bars.

As Tom started down river, he called back, "It may be too late, but if you run across any ramps, pick 'em and we'll throw them in with the potatoes."

Lee hiked up-river a mile or so before stopping. On the way, he sank their beers in the main river where an ice-cold spring spilled in, anchoring them down with a big rock.

On the high river-bank, he slipped the two sections of his rod togeth-

Tom was there ahead of him, naked from the waist up and wringing out his shirt. He called to Lee, "Get a fire going. I'll try to find some dry wood."

After Lee rolled some rocks together, he tore the labels off several cans and, using Tom's knife, cut some curled slivers off a dry stick. He punctured a sap bubble on a nearby pine tree, smeared the sticky resin on the shavings and lit the small pile of tinder. Crisscrossing Tom's dry kindling over the flame, he soon had a good fire going.

Tom began stripping off the rest of his clothes and shoes. "Better get your stuff off too. Don't want Mrs. Jarrett's little boy catching a chill."

Naked, except for their hats, they placed their clothes on rocks near the fire and did the same with their shoes, gapping the tops open with sticks.

"Dag, I'm hungry," Lee said. "Your turn to cook."

While their cold-handled skillet heated near the fire, they cut up potatoes and onions, cubed the Spam and sliced the last of their bread. Lee huddled close to the fire and warmed his hands as Tom fixed their meal.

Later, when he handed Lee a full plate, he added, grinning, "There, maybe that will hold you ... for five minutes or so."

Heaped together in the middle of his plate was a steaming mound of food, and on the side was a thick slice of his mother's homemade bread. Lee held his fork skyward in approval.

Just as Lee was slathering some blackberry jam over his bread, the other man yelled, "Hey, our beer?"

"Aw shit," Lee answered, "forgot 'em in the storm."

"Where'd you put 'em?"

"In the river where a cold spring dumped in. Put a big rock on them too."

"Tsk, tsk, should have done like I said, sunk them in a spring."

Lee glanced at the river, now creamed coffee. "How'd I know it was gonna flood? Sorry."

After their meal, Lee scoured their plates in a side stream, using the tips of some spruce branches. Cedar boughs were softer on your hands, but he couldn't find a tree nearby. When he came back to their camp, he called to his friend, "Damn, my feet are cold. Gotta get me some waders. Dad's are too big."

Tom dug a bottle out of his back pack. When he held it up, firelight danced through its amber liquid. "Glad we listened to Bud."

After taking a long swig, Tom recapped the bottle and tossed it to his friend. "Here, this'll warm your dingle berries."

Lee never liked drinking straight whiskey but was ashamed to admit it to his friend. He tipped the bottle up and took a long, show-off pull. It tasted like triple Listerine on a strep throat but he didn't let on. Just as he was about to bring the bottle down, Tom gestured toward the back of Lee's hand. On it was a stripe of fresh blackberry jam. Theatrically, Lee licked at the daub, bobbing his head up and down with each tongue stroke and smacking his lips afterward.

Tom shook his head and grinned.

As the evening light faded, the two sat there in the fire's warm glow, passing the bottle back and forth until it was nearly gone.

Suddenly, Tom jumped to his feet. "Hey, Jarrett, our party's dying." With that, he picked up Lee's wading staff and stepped gingerly in his bare feet to the outer edges of their campfire's light. "Alright, mister, let's see that famous Jarrett arm. C'mon, show me what you got." Locating a flat rock, he took a batter's stance over it, pounded home plate once and began waving the staff and wagging his behind. "Just remember, buddy, I taught you everything you know."

Lee gathered a few pebbles lying nearby and backed up until the distance satisfied him. Winding up dramatically, he threw a half-speed pitch toward his friend's makeshift base.

Tom sent it and the next two pitches far out into the night. "C'mon hotshot, don't slow- pitch me with that junk. Where's the good stuff?"

With that, Lee reared back and whizzed two swinging strikes past him.

"Okay, buddy, you asked for it," Tom said, pounding home plate. "I'm sending this one back to Eastbrook." His last swing ripped the night air with a powerful whoosh, but he missed again. "Lucky pitch." As he walked around the campfire, Tom cracked the other man's shin playfully with the staff. "Good arm, rookie."

Lee shrugged.

Tom sat down and studied his friend across the fire. "Why can't you be satisfied with just plain good, like the rest of us? Why does everything have to be gold-plated, from the part in your hair to the bows in your shoelaces? Hell, even when things are perfect, you ain't happy ... not for long. Why are you like that?"

"C'mon, don't go psychiatric on me. We've been over all this before. Sure, I like my ducks in a row? Who doesn't?"

"But it seems like you want 'em all lined up ... just for you."

Lee scowled.

"Me being that way I understand, but you?" A smirk played across his face. "Thought you people were all about watching out for the other guy ... you fish eaters."

Lee caught the scent of needling ... moreover insincerity. "You're full of it, T.D. You know that?" he said, dismissing Tom's notion. But it struck a cord.

"Gotta see a man about a horse." Tom said. Tripping on a root, he melted into the darkness. A few minutes later, he came back, weaving unsteadily and humming a tune off key.

Lee recognized it. "What movie's that from?"

Tom gave him a long whiskey-stare.

"That song, what movie?"

Swaying, Tom giggled. "Don't know. You're the big *Casablanca* fan though, right?"

Lee nodded.

"That movie, why's it so special?"

Lee thought a moment. "Good story for one thing." He clapped for Tom to toss him the bottle. "That and the main characters, decent people, mostly." He stopped and thought. "But conflicted over the right thing to do."

Mockingly, Tom stuck his finger down his throat. "And that's another thing, your Bogie, talk about a dumb sap, sacrificing his own happiness for a stranger. No sir, not me, buddy. You wouldn't catch me givin' up something like that, what's-her-name, for nobody."

"Ilsa," Lee answered, "her name was Ilsa." With that, he walked to the edge of the firelight.

Tom called after him, "Don't let Ol' Crazy get you,"

"Funny man, funny man." As he relieved himself, Lee knew he could never be strong enough to do what Rick did, give up Pru. "*Casablanca*," he said when he came back to the fire, "Pru's favorite song's from that movie, *As Time Goes By*." His face softened when he mentioned her name.

"So you and her are broke up, huh?" Tom asked.

"I told you the deal there already. You really are drunk T.D."

"C'mon, play it again, Sam." He snickered at his own synthesis.

Lee sneered. "We're not split up, just not dating right now. Only for a while though, six months or so. Her mother's idea, sort of a trial separation to prove we're serious. But we still talk on the phone ... once and a while."

Tipping the bottle up, Tom nearly drained it. "So what's so special about her, your Pru?" he asked, his tongue growing thicker.

Lee eyed him skeptically.

"C'mon, tell me, what's the killer recipe for Jarrett's perfect girl? What's she got that other girls ain't?"

"Aw, dry up."

"Would sa-ay your 'Casablanca' darling, Ilsa, be good enough? Would she pass the Goldie test?"

"You're drunk, T.D. and enough with the Goldie crap."

"Whatever you say. C'mon, would she pass?"

"Yeah, yeah, sure," Lee answered, "whatever."

"No Jarrett, seriously, what's a girl gotta do to make your list?" He started to hand him the bottle, but then drew it back, and turning sideways, held it close to his chest. "No, you gotta give me your perfect girl checklist first," he said, his tone almost coy.

"Hey, your watch," Lee said, pointing to the other man's wrist.

"It's back at camp in the wood bag," Tom said, his tone patronizing, "like always. Same place I told you to leave your good stuff. After you drop it in though, shake it to the bottom. Last place a thief is gonna look."

"Afraid you might have lost it, the watch. I know what it means to you."

"Don't change the subject." Tom held the bottle out toward him again, and then pulled it back when the other man reached for it. "C'mon, what is it, your secret sauce for Miss Right?"

Lee's eyes rolled up, "Okay, I'll play your game." He thought a moment. "Well, for starters, she's gotta be kind and unselfish, but not a wet noodle ... strong-willed but not controlling."

"An-nd?" Tom asked, sticking the bottle out toward him and pulling it back.

Lee's eyes turned serious. "She's gotta be honorable too, keeps her word, no matter what."

Tom held his hands up in surrender. "What B.S. You don't want a girl, you want a saint. I give up," he said, handing Lee the whiskey. "You're hopeless."

Lee emptied the bottle. It was going down smoother now.

"Tell me," Tom asked, "you ever known a girl like that, a real one? Not a made-up movie girl."

For a long moment, Lee considered the question.

"That's what I thought," Tom said. "Ain't no such gal, never was. She's just a dream, your perfect gal." He smirked. "It's like Bogie in that other movie where he was a detective looking for a bird statue, a gold one." He scratched his head. "Can't remember the title. Anyway, it's like Bogie said at the end, '... the stuff dreams are made of,' only he was talking about the bird statue because it turned out to be lead. Point is they're both dream stuff, Bogie's bird and your fantasy girl."

"You're all wet, T.D. She's like that, my Pru is."

"Speaking of her," Tom said, "remember you telling me once you and her made vows that you'd be faithful, always. Swore it on a rosary, I think you said."

"Yeah, what about it?"

"That's Sunday School crap. No one does that, keeps their word, no matter what."

"We do, Pru and me."

Tom studied his friend. "About that—"

"What are you saying now, you don't believe in giving your word, keeping it?

Tom hesitated, considering the question. "Sure. I believe in promises, make 'em all the time, but sometimes the cost is too high and I end up breaking them. That's what most do, Jarrett, grow up."

"What about your brother? Is that what he does?"

"Father David?" Steepling his hands over his nose and mouth, he worried the question for a long moment. "You gotta think twice about that. Not the same as promises to people. As you know, I'm not a big fan, but David gave his word upstairs. You don't mess with that ... besides, he promised our Dad too. That's the other thing you don't mess with either, your word to the dead."

Lee shook his head skeptically. "Not everyone thinks like you, me first and the hell with others."

Tom thought a short moment. "Take that movie of yours, *Casablanca*, and your precious Ilsa. Some dish, but what do you think she and Bogie were doing in his room that last night? After they were done kissing, they made out. Of course, they never showed that stuff on screen back then, but you're supposed to assume it." He pumped his fist toward the floor.

Lee scowled.

Tom went on. "And all the time, she'd given her word to Victor what's his name. Like I said before, the cost was too high to keep her vows, giving up Bogie, the man she loved."

"She wouldn't have done that, T.D. She was married. Sure, Bogie and her were in love and they kissed, but that's as far as it went. She wouldn't have done that, break her marriage vows. If she did, how could either man ever trust her again?"

Tom steadied himself against a tree.

"You're drunk, T.D."

"Maybe so, maybe so," Tom said, slurring his words. "But you gotta wake up, my friend." He made three attempts to snap his fingers, failing each try. "That church of yours has your head all screwed up. Got you believing it's bad, watching out for Lee."

Lee shook his head and gave a patronizing smile.

"Laugh all you want, buddy. I used to think your way too, but I wised up. Ain't your way in nature either. It's dog eat dog there. Your books agree too, your science books. Survival, me first that's the number one rule of life. Check it out."

Lee snapped the twig he was holding and tossed it in the fire.

Eyes narrowing, Tom studied his friend. "Take, for instance, those promises you and her made. She may just want to play the field now, see other guys, and feels bad about going back on her word to you. Maybe that's what this trial separation is all about. She figures it may not hurt as much in six months, the kiss-off. Hell, it's not like she doesn't care about you at all."

Lee's eyes narrowed. "You trying to say something?"

Tilting his head and pressing his lips together, Tom studied his friend for a long moment. "All right, all right, have it your way, Jarrett," he said finally. "Anyway, lighten up."

"Trust me, she just wouldn't do that, toss me aside like you're saying, not Pru."

The fire burned lower but the coals were still hot orange. Rolling over and gathering some kindling, Tom threw it—along with Lee's hiking stick—into the fire.

Jumping up, Lee kicked the staff out of the flames. "Are you crazy?" he yelled.

"What's the big deal? It's just a crooked old stick. I could find you a better one with my eyes closed."

"I like this one," Lee answered.

"C'mon, Jarrett, toss it back in the fire, let it burn." Pausing, Tom smirked. "On the other hand, maybe you'd best hang onto it. Sort of a reminder, a souvenir about what you learned on this wild goose chase."

He looked at Tom side-eyed.

"Next time, maybe you'll think twice. You know, when you get another one of those rainbow-chasing notions, like Eden Brook, up your behind. Save us both a lot of time and trouble."

Lee threw a piece of kindling at him.

Warding it off, he tossed it into the flames. Seemingly mesmerized by its sparks, Tom watched as they danced wildly up the smoke column. His head dropped to his chest and he dozed.

As he did, Lee stared into the fire's hot embers. It disappointed him, not finding Eden Brook, but it irked him even more, Tom being right: It had been just another wild goose chase.

Tom jerked awake. "Hey, our party's dying again, Jarrett," he said, standing. He then began dancing unsteadily on his heels around their fire. Totally naked, except for the wide-brimmed hat pushed back on his head, he started swinging his shoulders first one way, then the other. Elbows and knees flailing wildly, he began tapping his hand over his mouth and howling up into the night sky.

The flickering light played over Tom's thickly muscled frame, but his distorted shadow on the surrounding trees looked like some hellish creature from a nightmare.

Lee glanced down at his own body, strong and athletic, but slight compared to his friend's. Noticing Tom's growing member when he stopped dancing, Lee trapped a smile. "Better go soak that in the river," he said, gesturing.

Tom glanced down and gave an amused smile. "Just thinking about Abby, Abby Wilson."

Lee looked at him blankly.

"Guys at the pool room say she's the hottest piece in Eastbrook." He motioned for Lee to join in the dancing.

Together, the two whirled in the flickering light, round and round the campfire, their feet oblivious to insults from the sharp stones or sticks on the forest floor. The tree-tops and stars overhead spun in rhythm with their wheeling until at last, glimpsing one another naked across the fire, their hangy-down parts jumping wildly and out of sync with their dancing, they collapsed on opposite sides of the campfire and pounded the ground, laughing and howling until their sides ached.

"Gonna bring this up in confession?" Tom asked.

"Just your part," Lee answered.

"Boy, if your mom could see her little boy now," Tom said, "pickled and dancin' naked."

Bending over, his rear toward Tom, he patted his cheeks with both hands.

Tom laughed a high-pitched laugh, but then stopped abruptly. He stared hard across the fire at his friend, like he was trying to get him in focus through the smoke and sparks. "That's it, isn't it, the why?"

Lee's face straightened.

"The answer to why nothing's ever good enough for you."

His eyes questioned Tom.

"Your mom, nothing's ever good enough for her either. I've seen it. Dammit, that is it, her little boy's trying to please his mother."

"You're full of shit, T.D."

"Don't feel bad, it's what most guys do. Me too, I guess," he chuckled. "Same reason we're always cleaning off the sides of toilet bowls with our streams at home, trying keep things spotless like they like it, our mothers. With you though, Jarrett, it's a religion, trying to do that, make life spotless."

"So now you're a God-damned philosopher." He waved his hand dismissively. "You're drunk, T.D, that's Old Log Cabin talking."

"Maybe, maybe so, but tell me honestly, how would she feel about all this, the drinking, the dancing?"

"She'd be okay with it, she knows I drink some," Lee lied, his eyes wavering. "I've told her."

The other man looked at him sideways.

"She's not like that, not like you're saying. She knows I'm no saint," he hesitated. "She ain't either."

"Who're you trying to kid? I know your mother, buddy."

Lee twisted his mouth to one side. Picking up his journal, he thumbed through it, stopping at a page. "By the way, how's your brother?"

"David? He's okay," he smiled to himself. "He wasn't no saint in the old days either. Back then, he'd have joined in the drinking, the dancing too. Why'd you ask?"

"Something I never got, T.D. Your family, why the different religions?"

"Think about it. Dad, Catholic. Mom, Baptist. He wanted us both raised Catholic and Mom went along. Not crazy about it though. Don't get me wrong, she was proud of David, but after Dad died, she made me go to her church. Guess she wanted at least one son raised Baptist, believing like she did. Didn't take with me though. I wised up." He pointed to his head. "Did I mention she's losing it?"

Lee nodded. "Sorry."

Tom slapped his thigh, and flicked off an insect. "Lucky I brought something along for these little nasties." Rolling over, he dug two cigars from his backpack, two Rum-Soaked Crooks, lit one and tossed the other to Lee.

After lighting his with an ember, Lee took a long pull and blew the smoke over his body.

Tom did the same. "Forgot to ask, how's your grandfather?"

Lee smiled. "Seventies going on 17. But I can talk to him better than Dad."

"Why'd you bring my brother up? Something about him in there?" he asked, pointing to Lee's journal.

"Aw, you know how people talk in Eastbrook. It's nothing, really."

"Yeah, what's the nothing?"

"My mother, she heard he was messing around with some young gal in the parish. I told her she was all wet. He wouldn't do that, not Father David. I thought the rumor might hurt his chances. You know, for being the head guy in a parish someday."

"That's B.S. about him messing around, pure B.S. Who told her that?"

"She didn't say," Lee answered, leaning his journal against the log beside him.

"If you find out, let me know, okay?" Tom said, jabbing his finger at Lee. Reaching across his body, he slid his hunting knife from its sheath. Taking it by the blade, he drew it back over his shoulder and hurled it sharply end over end. With a hollow thunk, it pinned Lee's journal to the log beside him, quivering there afterward.

"Jeez, what the hell did you do that for? What if you'd missed?" Picking up the empty whiskey bottle, he threw it at the other man.

Tom deflected it, and it shattered on a rock.

Working the knife back and forth, Lee pulled it from the log. "Why'd you do that?"

The knife-handle was elk-horn, rough textured, mottled brown and ivory. Tom always kept it razor sharp. It was his father's and the most prized possession he owned, next to the wristwatch. Lee held it up and firelight danced on its polished shank.

"I know you've been eyeing that baby for a long time, Jarrett. Who knows, maybe it'll be yours someday. Not till they throw the dirt in on me though."

Lee examined the half-inch long slit in his journal, and then began paging through it.

"Don't worry Shakespeare; your precious journal ain't ruined. If it is, I'll buy you a new one. Besides, there may be worse cuts than that down the line."

Lee's head snapped up from his journal. "How's that?"

Tom looked away. "Gotta take a leak."

"Wait a minute, what's that mean?"

"Just running my mouth, that's all. Forget it."

"You can't say something like that, T.D, and just clam up. I thought we were friends. You got something to say, say it."

For a long moment, Tom gave the other man a studied look. "Okay, you asked. It's about her, your ol' gal."

"You trying to be funny now? What about her?"

"Don't get sore at me."

Eyes fixed on Tom, he leaned forward.

"Okay, okay. Just remember, you asked for this, buddy. Anyway, I was cutting through the park one night, a week or so ago. You know, the park over by Cathy's house, Sawyer's, and I saw her. She was with Kenny Harte." He stopped. "Sure you wanna hear this?"

"Go on, go on, you saw her and Kenny Harte, and..."

"Anyway, they were on top a picnic bench, her dress up and him on top. Going at it pretty good too." He threw a stick in the fire. "Christ, I gotta draw you a picture?"

Lee scowled. "You're lying. You're a God-damn liar. She wouldn't do that, not Pru."

Tom held his hands up in mock defense. "Hold on, partner. Just telling you what I saw. Don't be sore at me."

Lee studied him hard across the fire-light. "Is this another one of your sick jokes?"

"No, Lee, I swear. Just telling you what I saw."

"Straight?"

He held up his right hand. "Swear, Lee, my father's grave."

"He could have been forcing her."

"Didn't look that way."

Lee's teeth clenched together and his jaw slid sideways, "Son of a bitch," he cried up at the night sky, "son of a bitch."

"Sorry, buddy. Just thought you ought to know. I almost let it slip at the restaurant."

Lee's head slumped to his chest and he asked without looking up. "You're positive?"

"Yeah," he answered softly. "Hell, maybe it's for the best. Like I said, those mixed marriages don't work. Saw it in my own family."

Like in a trance, Lee sat motionless, staring blankly into the fire.

"I know how you're feeling, buddy. There are some things a guy just can't get past." He spat into the fire and wiped his mouth with the back of his hand. "I know I couldn't." He stood up and stretched. "We better hit the hay. Things will look different in the morning, Lee."

When he heard his name, he looked up at Tom but through him.

As Tom passed him, he squeezed Lee's shoulder. "Cheer up, buddy. You'll find another gal, a better one. When she comes crawling back though, Cathy, you can tell her to kiss off. Serve her right, after what she did."

Thunder growled in the distance and it started to rain again. The drizzle began playing a happy tune on their tin cook-ware.

Down by the river, a granddaddy bullfrog was booming, calling all interested gals to his party.

Later, when Lee crawled into his own bag, sleep would not rescue him from his pain. It did give him plenty of time to think though.

To begin with, he had never liked Kenny Harte. He always thought the guy was sweet on Pru. Besides that, he was a cock hound, and worst of all, a bragging one, and obvious about it too, always licking his upper lip when he was on the trail of anything with a monthly. He was a good pool player though, but you had to keep an eye on him. When you weren't looking, he'd move the balls to gain an advantage. If nothing else though, he was predictable. Like clockwork he'd show up at Pru's church every Sunday. Outside on the steps after services, he'd leer and fawn over every girl there, including Pru, all the while licking his upper lip.

CHAPTER ELEVEN

On their return back down the Burnt Tree, neither man spoke much, but the river's mystique threw a scare into Lee. There was a sense that something, some foreboding presence, was following them. He never acknowledged it to Tom, but he found himself at dusk, glancing back up the misty river into the shadowy forest. If the same presence crept into a dark corner of Tom's mind, he never let on.

Other than that, the return trip was uneventful. They even passed through the Gardino's property without incident, but after dark. And although they kept mostly to the bank because the river was still rain-swollen, they made good time. Perhaps because the return trip was familiar, or as Lee reasoned, mostly downhill, they took only three days to get back, arriving at their truck Sunday afternoon.

As they were hurriedly packing, Tom threw the ice chest on top of Lee's fly rod, breaking the tip. "Damn, sorry, buddy," he sympathized. "I'll get it fixed."

Face pained, Lee pensively whipped the broken tip back and forth, finally resting the rod beside his wading staff along the back of the bench seat in the truck's cab.

Hanging on Tom's mirror was a key chain with a miniature ruler. Lee had given it to him once as a joke after the other man had been boasting about the size of his genitalia.

As Tom drove, he flipped his visor down to shield his eyes against the afternoon sun. There on the back was a small pocket where Tom said he always kept condoms. Pinned on the visor beside it, was a silvered religious medal.

Lee bent forward to get a closer look at the image.

"St. Christopher," Tom explained. "My brother's idea ... thinks I drive too fast."

"Thought you didn't believe in that voodoo stuff?"

"I don't, but it keeps my brother happy. If you ask me, he's just being foxy, trying to make me feel guilty."

"Guilty?"

"Yeah, reminding me I'm the bad brother, not good like he is."

An hour or so later, Tom grew sleepy and Lee drove.

The radio had been playing Tom's favorite music, country. After they changed drivers and Tom drifted off, Lee searched the dial for some pop tunes. Failing this, he turned back to Tom's station, just as they were playing Hank Williams,' *Lovesick Blues*. He left it on for that number, but then turned it off.

His knuckles grew white on the steering wheel. "Just wait, damn you, just wait," he cried at the radio. Tom stirred but did not awaken.

Once, when they came over a rise in the highway, two vultures were picking at a dead fox in the middle of the road. The birds flew into a tree when the truck neared. Slowing, he stopped at a pull out.

There were no skid marks near the fox. It did not appear the car that hit the animal had slowed or even tried missing it. Other cars had run over it too.

Its body was stiffening and flies were buzzing around. Lee dragged the fox to the side of the road with a stick, and knelt beside it. Too busy dodging passing cars, the vultures hadn't had time to tear its soft underbelly open yet. A breeze danced across the animal's burnt-orange tail, teasing its fur alive once more with its old devilry. Lee rested the stick on its chest for a long moment.

As he walked back toward the truck, he saw Tom's face in the passenger mirror.

When he climbed in, Tom was resting on his side with his back to the driver.

"I saw you sneaking a look back there, T.D."

"What the hell was that?"

Lee spoke to his back. "You wouldn't understand."

When Tom didn't bite, Lee went on. "How'd you like to be Dunlopped a few dozen times? I dragged him over to the side so he wouldn't have to eat no more of them."

"Still trying to recolor the world, aren't you, make it look all pretty and nice?"

Lee hissed at his back. As he pulled onto the highway though, he peered in his side mirror. No longer bothered by passing cars, the vultures were tearing open the fox's white underbelly. He shook his head. "After you're gone, wouldn't you like to be remembered as more than just road-kill?"

Tom didn't answer.

As Lee watched the highway, a suspicion began eating at him that Tom was pleased Pru had betrayed him. He didn't know why he felt that, he just knew it was gnawing at his insides.

He glanced at his wading staff on the seat back. There was that too, he thought. In a way, Tom had also cost him Eden Brook. From the start, he had never believed in it, not like Lee had.

Lee's thoughts began to darken even more as he followed the black ribbon of macadam into the young evening. From time to time, he glanced at the back of his dozing passenger, each time with a sense of growing resentment.

They pulled into the Jarrett driveway around eight in the evening. As they unloaded Lee's gear in the back yard, neither man spoke much.

Before driving off, Tom waved to Lee's father who was burning trash. From his truck window, he said to Lee, jabbing a finger at him, "I'll call you, but remember what we talked about. You know, about who comes first."

After Tom left, Lee's father turned to his son. "How was fishing?"

"So-so."

His father poked at the burning fire. "But you knew that going up there. Something else?"

Lee plucked an empty Oleo carton out of the trash can nearby and tossed it into the fire. When the fat inside crackled, the young man's eyes slid toward their picnic table.

"We lost a chance for some real good fishing."

His father looked up from the fire.

"A restaurant owner up there, Bud Smith was his name, he told us a story about a great trout stream way over the mountains, headwaters of the Burnt Tree. He said it was marked Amanda's Brook on maps."

"Never heard of it. Maybe your grandfather, Ol' 40 Grit has. He was raised 'round that country."

Lee then told his father the rest of the story, including the part about Bud's father renaming it Eden Brook. "That restaurant guy, Bud Smith, said he fished it himself when he was a youngster in the 30's. Claimed it was loaded with brookies, most never seen a hook. We searched but never found it."

"Get lost?"

"T.D.'s fault. We were this close," Lee said, holding his thumb and index finger up with a tiny bit of daylight between. "But he got nervous about getting back for his job."

"Can't blame him for that, son." He poked at the fire.

"Bud told us another tale, too," Lee said, giving a nervous chuckle. "A yarn about some crazy old guy who lived near the same stream we were looking for, Eden Brook. He said he lived there in the late 1800s. His name was Jagger, Dan Jagger.

"Anyway, the owner claimed this guy had a perfect life until one day out of the blue, he just up and killed his wife and a friend. Bud said it was a lovers' quarrel, maybe over gold. Afterward, he burned their bodies and vanished. Never heard from again. Interesting though, Bud claimed the ol' guy named that valley after his wife, Amanda, same one he killed."

"Sounds a bit fishy, that tale."

"T.D. tried riding me about it afterward. Claimed that crazy old guy, Dan, coulda been my own grandfather. You know, 'cause of both living there around the same time. He wasn't serious though, T.D., just riding me. It didn't bother me none."

"Speaking of Ol' 40, he's been asking about you. Anxious to hear how your trip went. Wondering when you were coming back. He's around here someplace."

"I'll catch him later." He picked up the compass Bud had sold them. "About Eden Brook. Tom never had his heart in it, searching for the brook, not like I did. He just went through the motions to keep me happy. He claimed it wasn't even real, that we were just chasing our own tails. But that guy, Bud, he swore it was up there somewhere." Lee paused and shrugged his shoulders. "Then again, like Tom said, Bud coulda been playing us just to get our money. You know, so we'd buy stuff from him if we went looking for it."

"Don't toss that dream away, son, Eden Brook. You may need it again someday." His father turned and poked the fire with his stick. "How about tending this for a spell? I gotta help your mother."

Lee pointed to his camping gear. "Okay if I store this stuff first?"

His father motioned him away.

When Lee's mother heard the screen door open and shut, she looked up from her apple peeling and smiled.

Picking up a table knife, he pointed to a fresh pie cooling near the window.

"Sit down," she said, wiping her hands on her apron. "I'll make you a sandwich. Meatloaf all right?"

He waved it off.

"You okay?"

"A bit tired, that's all, the trip."

She glanced at the seat of his pants. "You losing weight?"

He cut a piece of pie, poured himself a glass of milk and sat down at their kitchen table.

When she felt his forehead with the back of her hand, the silver cross around her neck caught the overhead light.

71

Rolling his eyes and pulling away, he sing-songed, "I'm ok-ay, Mom, I'm ok-ay."

"Why don't you wear your Miraculous Medal anymore, the one I gave you?" she asked, "Saw it in your drawer the other day."

"Why were you in my room?"

"Just dusting, It was open, the drawer."

"I told you, Mom, I'll take care of that, the dusting."

"Wish you'd wear it though, Lee, the medal. Father David blessed it for you special. I saw it was tarnished. Is that why you're not wearing it?"

"I just don't wanna wear it right now, Mom, that's all."

"By the way, Pru called while you were gone."

His eyes shot over to his mother. "Pru ... why is she calling here?" he asked, his voice irritated. "What did she want?"

"Lee-e, why are you being so hateful? I thought you liked her."

He glanced at the apple pie with the missing piece.

She followed his gaze. "No more, mister. The rest is for supper."

On his way through the dining room, he bumped against a chair, jarring the table. Hesitating, he checked to make certain he had not disturbed her arrangement—the six chairs were still stationed directly across from one another, her lace doily was laid out exactly in the center of the table, and two blue candles were plumbed straight and spaced evenly on either end with the white and blue flowered centerpiece in the middle.

After storing his gear in the closet in his room, he sat down on the bed. A small wooden cross was on the wall over his head. Reaching up, he took it down and placed it in the drawer of his nightstand.

On a shelf on the far wall was a stuffed doll that Pru had made for him. It was a uniformed baseball player, and it sat smiling down at him from its perch.

He gazed softly at the framed picture of Pru on his nightstand, the one taken on the Burnt Tree. Penned at the bottom in her lovely script were the words, "Love you, always." He lay down on the bed on his back and held her picture up. "But are you my Madonna or my Magdalene?" he asked the face, mildly surprised at his own clever metaphor.

It was true, he thought to himself, Pru and he had come close to doing it numerous times, but what Tom claimed didn't sound like something she would do. And yet, Tom was certain it was her. But then, maybe he was mistaken, that or stretching things. Father David said as much once himself, that sometimes his brother could be full of it when it came to tales about girls.

But when was it he last saw that lip-licking Kenny Harte? It was a few weeks earlier in May, he decided, on a Sunday morning and a few weeks after their separation, Pru and his. After Sunday mass, Lee had strolled over to her church, just a short distance from his own, hoping to see her.

Services had just let out and Tracey Smith, a friendly acquaintance of Pru's, was standing near the bottom of the church steps. Her back was to him and momentarily he mistook her for Pru. They did look like sisters. Everyone said so. Once she turned sideways though, he saw it was Tracey.

Pru was standing near the church doors with Kenny. The two were talking and laughing. It was then he remembered him touching her, slipping his hand part way around her waist and whispering something in her ear. She had smiled, but worst of all, not pulled away.

That guy was only after one thing and transparently so. Why couldn't she see that?

Then too, that last night with Pru at her house could have been a kiss-off, like Tom said, her effort to let him down easy. His eyes hardened. "Damn you, damn you to Hell," he cried at her framed picture, hurling it against the wall where it shattered.

His mother called from the bottom of the stairs.

"It's okay, Mom. Just a water glass. I'll clean it up."

In the drawer of his nightstand were more pictures, some just of Pru, and others of them together. Alongside the pictures was the tarnished medal his mother had given him and Father David had blessed. He began tearing up all of the photos, stuffing the pieces in his pockets. Shaking the glass shards from the frame, he folded her picture and jammed it into his pocket also.

He looked out his window, and his father was motioning for him to come down.

As Lee walked toward him, his father said, "I was about to give up on you." Pointing to the bin with his fire-stick, he added, "Tend to that till it burns down good." He motioned toward their house. "I'm gotta help your mother."

Their fire bin was a round, wire mesh crib. When Lee fed it the pieces of Pru's pictures and jabbed at its flanks, angry flames leaped into the night sky.

One edge of Pru's photo, the one where she wrote "Love you always," was sticking out through the wire mesh on the side. He started to pull it out, but just as he reached for it, flames shot out and licked the back of his hand. He jerked away and grunted, then looked at his hand in the firelight. It wasn't red, but it stung sharply and he could smell the singed hairs.

A cool breeze whipped up, twirling a few embers skyward. Out of the darkness, his grandfather's beagle loped toward him, ears flopping like socks on a shaken clothesline. Lee looked around for the old man. When he did not find him, he stuck his face down next to the dog's muzzle, hoping for a lick. "Miss me, Dan?" he asked. The dog wagged his tail once but that was it.

From when he was a pup, Dan had been devoted to his grandfather. As for others though, including Lee, while never unfriendly, he was, at the same time, aloof, like a cat.

At the edge of the fire's glow, a large human form materialized. Dan padded over and sat on his haunches beside the figure.

"Hey, Granddad," Lee called.

The old man, his father's father, was living with them in a spare bedroom downstairs for the past seven years since his own wife, Lee's grandmother, had died.

"What are you up to, boy?" He was wearing what he called his dut hat, and holding his favorite blue, enameled cup.

Granddad had two hats to his name, both felt, wide-brimmed fedoras with low crowns. The gray one he originally called his church hat. He always kept it crisp and clean and wore it to people-places where he was less comfortable, like church, the grocery store or the barber downtown. His other hat, a brown one, he originally named his dirt hat and he wore it when he was working, fishing or afield, places where he felt more at home. It was misshapen, dirty and stained. "Broken-in just right," he would always brag. Needless to say, it was the hat he preferred.

Never one to take himself too seriously, however, his grandfather made light of his own labeling over time, altering the spellings of the fedoras to make their vowel-sounds match to his liking. Thus, church hat morphed into "chuch hat" and dirt hat into "dut hat."

Since the summer before, the dut hat had been Pru's favorite also. Granddad had loaned it to her in case it rained when Pru and Lee fished the Tree together. When she first put it on, it fell down to her eyebrows. She liked it anyway because it was grandfather's.

Lee pointed at the old man's cup. "Coffee?"

A warm fire-glow playing over his face, the old man gave a wink. "What else? Just the way I like it. Strong enough to melt your mustache and black as bear shit in a huckleberry patch." That's the way he always described it to his grandson, but rarely in front of Lee's mother. She was always asking the old man not to do that, use bad language around Lee. She always claimed he knew better, was educated. He never paid her much mind though.

Lee recounted the trip's highlights for his grandfather, including Bud's story about Crazy Dan Jagger, Eden Brook and their search for it. "We'd have found it too, Granddad, but we ran out of time. Tom had to be back and we got lost, more'n once too. Took some wrong forks."

Eyes amused, the old man said, "Eden, huh? Hell's fire, why didn't you start with something easy, like say, Shangri-La?"

"And the staff you made me, it got scorched." Lee snapped his fingers. "Dag, I left it in Tom's truck."

"How'd that happen?"

"Aw, we knocked in our campfire one night when we were fooling around."

His grandfather cocked an eyebrow. "Still okay for hiking?"

Lee nodded.

"Then I wouldn't fret." Stepping over to the fire-bin, his grandfather studied the charred edges of the photos sticking out the sides of the wire cage. "Setting fire to some bridges?"

The burn on Lee's hand was beginning to sting more and he blew on it.

"Fire bite you?"

When Lee turned his hand toward the flames to inspect the injury, his gold class ring caught the firelight.

"Ain't seen that for a spell either, your class ring," his grandfather said. "Last time, Pru was sporting it." His eyes tried capturing his grandson's. "Everything hunky dory between you two?"

The old man had the darkest pupils Lee had ever seen, black as obsidian. Sometimes they could be reassuring, other times unsettling, but always arresting.

"I, uhh, she broke a promise, Granddad, a big one," he answered.

"A leaf in the river, huh?"

"How's that?"

"Floating this way and that with her word?"

His shoulders sagged and he nodded once.

Limping slightly, his grandfather walked over to Lee and gave him a hard, squint-eyed assay. "That don't sound like Pru. She's a good gal."

Lee stoked the flickering fire bin, and shrugged at the towering face.

The old man pointed to a pine tree in their yard. "Try dabbing some sap on that burn. It'll ease the sting some." He took the poker from Lee. "You're probably tired from the trip. You go on up. I'll tend this." He waved his grandson away.

"I'll be heading off to college this fall," Lee called back. "We're still gonna do some hunting, aren't we?"

Grandfather smiled. Bright sparks from the fire bin wheeled over his head, but quickly winked out in the night sky.

Over the years, since he was 12, Lee and his grandfather had hunted and fished together. His father went with them once in a while, but he never loved it, not like they did.

yeah, left some money for you," he said, glancing at the top of Tom's bureau. "Not much, I'm afraid."

"Every bit helps."

"How's she been, Ma?" Father David asked though the half open door.

"Worse, I think. Mrs. Kincaid agrees."

"That's the way it is with that disease, or so I hear."

"Yeah, I know," Tom said, "Ma can't help it, but she's driving me crazy. I need to get away from her some."

When Father David pushed the door open, steam rolled out ahead of him. He had a white towel around his middle and his face was lathered with shaving cream. "But that's why we hired Mrs. Kincaid, to stay with her, get you some relief. And what about the trip you and Lee just took, didn't that help recharge your batteries?"

Tom chuckled. "You don't get it. There's a truckload of other stuff I have to do. When I get home from work, I'm dog-tired. Don't have the patience to deal with her, not like I should."

Father David paused a moment. "I know it's not fair, all this coming down on you, but it's the same answer we're always left with. Wish I could help out more, but I can't. I got a full-time job helping run the parish. That leaves just you, buddy, sorry. Besides, who'll take better care than you?"

"The other day, I found her shoes in the ice box, yelled at her like she was a child, even made her cry." Tom bowed his head and covered his eyes with one hand. "Jeez, can you believe it, made my own mother cry?"

Father David put his hand on his brother's shoulder. "Sorry, pal, I'll try helping out more."

"And oh, yeah," Tom said. "Mrs. Kincaid. We may lose her. She said her own husband's getting worse. She may have to stay home and take care of him. We may have to find another day time lady."

Father David ducked back inside the bathroom, leaving the door ajar. "Shame, she's good with Ma. Real kind, patient."

"By the way, thanks for helping out with Ma last week, our Burnt Tree trip."

"Lucky we found those ladies. Most caretakers don't like night-duty, only want day, like Mrs. Kincaid ... meant to ask, your trip, how'd it go?"

Tom didn't answer.

His brother asked again, only this time louder.

"Okay, I guess."

Sticking his head out the partly opened door, Father David studied his brother briefly. "Something happen?"

"Aw, we wasted most of the trip chasing smoke, searching for a hot trout stream that wasn't there. Lee's idea. That fits doesn't it, for him?"

"Doesn't sound like you had a very good time. I thought it was a crackerjack idea, you getting away for a while."

"The last night was pretty good, part of it anyway," Tom said. He then told his brother how the two had gotten soaked, stripped to dry off and afterward, drank some liquor and danced naked in the dark around their campfire. "I told Lee, in the old days, you'd have liked that part, maybe not the rest, but that part, the drinking and dancing naked."

A smile flickered through Father David's eyes. "Nuts," he answered.

"Just remembering the old days, brother."

"And that's what they are, brother, old days." The priest's face turned serious. "How'd it go, the rest?"

"So, so."

Father David studied his brother again, this time for a longer moment. "I'm going to finish cleaning up," he said, starting to close the door. "Catch you later."

Tom stuck his foot in the door. "Uhh, there was something else."

The priest waited.

"The trip, something happened between us, Jarrett and me." Another silence followed. "Pru, you remember her, don't you? Lee's girl, Cathy Pruitt?"

"Sure, sure I remember her. Those two have been sweet on one another since forever. What about her?"

Tom explained how he had told Lee about seeing Kenny Harte and her having sex one night in the park.

"My God, what were you thinking?"

"Aw, we were drinking and..."

"Jeez, how'd he take it?"

"What do you think?"

Father David blew air out of his puffed-out cheeks.

"Maybe I shouldn't have told him, but they were busted up anyway," said Tom. "Besides, it wouldn't have worked out, the different religions. You saw it in our own home."

"Maybe so, but you still shouldn't have. That was between them, Lee and her. How could you do that, your best friend?"

Tom turned away.

The priest checked his watch. "Mind if we talk later? I'm running late. Eating supper at the rectory with Father Moore. He likes his dinner on time. Lately, I've been in his dog house. Thinks I'm too liberal. I got off on the wrong foot with him to start. He didn't like me being assigned here in the first place because it was my hometown. It got worse when I let the kids call me Father D., you know, for David. He didn't like that either. But other stuff too."

"There was something else," Tom said. "Mind if we talk while you're showering?" Stepping inside and closing the door behind him, he put the toilet seat down and settled himself. "This won't take long. You won't be late."

"Better not."

"What's the something else?"

"Somebody's been spreading rumors about you around Eastbrook, about you fooling around with some woman in the parish. I know it's ridiculous, gossip like that, just thought I'd tip you off, what some folks are saying."

There was no response from behind the shower curtain.

"David?"

"What else?"

"Nothing, just like I said, that you were messing around with some woman, that's all."

Father David was silent behind the shower curtain again, only this time longer. "Let's just say I have a big decision to make ... and soon."

"What does that mean?" Tom asked ..."My God, you are, you are fooling around, aren't you? You are, aren't you? What the hell are you thinking?"

His brother slid the shower curtain open. "You're lecturing me now? That's rich. Let's just say I need to make my mind up about something, something to do with her. Let's just leave it at that for now, all right?"

"Make your mind up?" Tom cried. "Make your mind up? Jeez, about what? What is there to decide? You're a priest, end of story."

"You wouldn't understand. It's between me and Him," he said, motioning toward the ceiling. Sticking his hand out of the shower curtain, he pointed to a dark towel.

In a daze, Tom handed it to him, washing his own hands before leaving.

CHAPTER THIRTEEN

A couple of days later, Tom pulled up in front of the Jarrett house. When Lee heard Tom's motor, he gathered his baseball glove, journal and college papers. "Down in a minute," he yelled out his bedroom window. On his way out the back door, he called to his mother who was clearing the dinner table, "Might be little late, Mom, ballgame at Fremont."

Lee's father, who was sweeping the back porch, called after him as his son bounded down the steps, "Fill out them papers, bub."

"Got 'em," Lee yelled back, waving them over his head. As he climbed in the truck and threw his things on the seat, his father called again, "No later than midnight, hear?"

Speaking to Tom, he motioned back toward his father's voice. "Still thinks I'm a kid."

"You're lucky to have one, a father."

"Where's my staff?"

Tom snapped his fingers. "Forgot, I'll drop it off later." He pointed to Lee's papers and tipped his chin up in a question.

"Aw, more forms, college."

"Thought you were through with that."

"Boy, do you have a lot to learn. Seems like that's all I've done lately, jump through their paper hoops, most asking for the same information. They don't have to be in till July, a week or so yet, but Dad's on my case to get 'em done. Bet I've filled out two dozen of these already." He chuckled. "Nah, more like four or five. Just feels like two dozen."

For a half hour or so, Lee tended to the forms until Tom turned off the road to Freemont. "Where we headed, T.D.?"

Tom pointed out the front window toward the darkening sky. "Looks like our ballgame's gonna be rained out. Let's swing over to Martin's instead. You know, do something different."

Lee made a sour face.

"What's wrong?" Tom asked, slowing the truck and pulling to the side.

"Just not in the mood tonight, Martin's."

"Aw, c'mon, Jarrett. Let's grab a beer, talk to some girls. Just for tonight, that's all, c'mon."

"I don't know."

"It'll do you some good. Get your mind off her, your old gal. Just what the doctor ordered. Don't worry, I'll get you home in time so your mother can tuck you in."

Lee hesitated, and then shrugged. There was a baseball on the truck's dash and he picked it up. It felt smooth and crisp in his hand, pristine except for one dark scuff.

They parked outside Martin's. "Let's sit a spell," Tom said, "may be a bit early." He glanced at a scab on the back of Lee's hand. "How'd you do that?" he asked, pointing.

"Aw, I was burning some trash, pictures and stuff."

Just then, a car door slammed and Tom looked out the truck's front window. "Jeez, there's Dixie Ann Morgan and she's by herself."

"So it's Dixie Ann Morgan and she's by herself." Lee mocked.

"Don't you get it, dammit? That's real hot stuff, or so I hear. She's alone too. There's usually two, three guys buzzing around but she's alone. We got her to ourselves. Don't know for how long though, so we better act fast." He slapped Lee on the leg. "How'd you like to crawl in the sack with that tonight?"

"My God," Lee said, "settle down."

Dixie Ann walked across the parking lot toward the front door of Martin's Tavern, stopping just outside to adjust her bra. She wore a white dress with a red print and a thick, black belt wound tightly around her waist. Her flawless white skin and wavy brown hair were beautiful, but her lipstick color wasn't right for her face and her cheeks were over-rouged. She carried her body royally, chin high, shoulders back, like she knew she held some regal power, which she did ... over her male subjects.

Opening the truck door, Tom motioned for the other man to follow.

"You go on," Lee said, pointing to the college forms. "I wanna finish these first."

"Okay," he answered, walking away, "but I'm telling you, we gotta grab that before someone else does."

When Lee opened Martin's front door later, a cloud of blue cigarette smoke streamed out into the young night. Stepping inside, he felt the throb of country music pulse through the floor and into his body. From somewhere in the blue cloud, he could hear the high-pitched laughter of girls. He followed the laughter through the haze.

Once his eyes adjusted to the dim lighting, he spotted Mary Ann leaning against a nearby wall. Tom had his knee between her legs and was kissing her hard.

After she walked away, Tom came over to Lee and pointed to the ladies' room. "Got her all hot and bothered," he said. He sidled closer to his friend and began speaking low, all the while watching the rest room door. "All we have to do now is dance with her a little, buy her two, three beers, you know, get her feeling good, and we're home free. I'm telling you, Jarrett, that's a sure thing if we play our cards right."

"You enjoy," Lee said, pointing toward the bar. "I'm gonna grab a beer."

"Aw holy crapola." Tom said. "I just remembered. We can't do her in the truck. The back's full of furniture. David's helping some lady move."

He needn't have concerned himself about a place to bed her. After eight beers and two hours of dancing in the hot hall, Tom finally persuaded her to come with them. Once she hit the muggy night air outside, however, she threw up all over her dress.

Sensing his plans for a fantasy evening of wild sex fading, Tom punched the air and swore up at the night sky. "Damn, double damn."

Lee went back inside and asked the bar tender to call a cab. Once back in the truck, Lee said, "Maybe we should stick here till her taxi comes."

Tom looked at him askance. "Are you kidding?"

As they drove away, she was sitting on the curb in a daze, her legs gapped open, her soiled dress bowed down between her knees and a string of saliva trailing off her chin.

Not quite the love-Goddess Tom had in mind, Lee thought.

"Let's head over to Kelly's," Tom said, "I need a drink."

"Consolation prize?" Lee asked.

Tom was not amused.

CHAPTER FOURTEEN

The Wilsons lived in a small, wooden-frame house with unpainted gray shingles, most of which had begun to crack and curl. Close out their back door were train tracks.

On their mantle inside was a ceramic Madonna, a yellowing wedding picture and an old clock. Behind the mantle, the wallpaper was faded and sooty.

The clock struck four. Weary from years of marking time for the Wilson's ups and mostly downs, the clock seemed to be struggling now to find the strength to carry on for the rest of the family's story.

Her back to her mother and eyes closed, Abby Wilson sat on a worn raglan throw-rug just off their kitchen. As Mrs. Wilson combed her daughter's long, brown hair, she hummed.

Outside, a chicken landed on the unpainted window sill, tried balancing itself, but then fell off.

"What's that song, you're humming, Momma?"

"*Lavender Blue.*"

"Teach me so I can sing it?"

"I will."

"Sing some country, Momma. I like country."

"I know you do, dear."

Abby began petting the white, slumbering cat beside her. When she did, it stretched and began purring. "Don't you think Pocaho's pretty, Momma?"

"Prettiest cat 'round here."

"Aw, you're just teasing. Pocaho's the only cat 'round here." She tilted her face up. "Think I'm pretty, Momma?"

"Very pretty."

"Why don't the girls at school like me?" She looked at her mother squarely. "Is it 'cause I'm dumb?"

Her mother looked away momentarily. "You're not dumb, Abby. Don't listen to those girls. They're just jealous." She thought a moment. "You see, God gave all of us good points and weaknesses. Those girls at school have both too. But you've got things they don't have."

"Like what, Momma?"

"There's pretty outside and pretty inside, Abby. Pretty outside's looking nice, pretty inside is treating others right. God gave you both, dear. You're pretty outside and in."

"They call me 'Little Digger Girl' at school, the other girls do. Why do they call me that, Momma? Is it 'cause Pa works in a cemetery? What's wrong with that?"

"Nothing, dear, not a thing. That's good, honorable work, being a caretaker at a cemetery. She measured her words carefully. "Some folks have funny notions about what's good and bad. Sometimes, they look down on others 'cause of what they do for a living. That's wrong, Abby, doing that."

Her daughter's eyes were drawn to the chair at the dining room table where her brother used to sit. "Is that why Joey left home, Momma, 'cause of where Pa works?"

"I don't know why your brother left home."

Abby held her wrist up in her mother's face. Around it was a woven, yellow and white gimp band. "Like my bracelet, Momma?"

"It's lovely, dear."

"Made it myself. Bea showed me how."

Her mother smiled and nodded.

"Think he'll be back some day, Momma, Joey?"

"Hope so, girl, I hope so."

As her mother stroked her hair, the comb caught on her daughter's necklace. "Sorry," she said, leaning forward to untangle it.

Abby touched the pendant on her chain. Turning, she hugged her mother's leg. "It's the best gift you ever gave me, Momma. Thank you, thank you."

She played with her daughter's locks. "Your hair surely is nice, girl."

"The boys at school think I'm pretty, I can tell. There's this one boy. Danny Dell's his name. He drives a red Thunderbird. I like him a lot. Bea thinks he likes me, too."

"How is Bea? Haven't seen her in a spell. You two have been friends since grade school."

"I'm meeting her this evening at the teen center on Main."

"Back by 10, girl. Remember, school tomorrow."

"But the school year's almost done, Momma."

"Soon, but not yet, girl." Mrs. Wilson stroked her daughter's hair with her hand. "Someday you'll meet a nice boy, Abby, one who loves you. That's very important, you know, that he loves you and you love him. Do you understand?"

"I know, Momma, I know. You done told me that before."

"Anyway, you'll get married someday and..." Not far off, a train whistle wailed. Her mother's eyes rolled toward the sound. The ground began to shake and the little house trembled. A few moments later, a steam locomotive rumbled past just outside their back door.

The cat jumped to its feet.

Abby reached down and stroked it. "It's okay Pocaho. Go back to sleep. Tell me again, Momma, why you named her Pocahontas."

"Later, dear. Like I was saying before though, someday you'll meet a nice boy and Pa and me, we'll have a fine house, but not near no tracks. You and your family will come for picnics on Sundays, and Pa will make ice cream and the kids will play croquet in our big yard."

"When we do, would you fix fried chicken, Momma? I like fried chicken."

Mrs. Wilson smiled a tight-lipped smile.

"He spoke to me today after school."

"Who did, dear?"

"Danny Dell, ain't you been listening?"

"Don't say ain't, Abby. What did he want, this Danny?"

Her daughter shrugged.

Just then, their front door opened and Wilma, her sister, stepped in. Two years older than Abby, she was pretty, but her face was sad, so too her posture. She kissed her mother on top the head and tapped Abby's head lightly.

Abby swiped at her sister's hand but missed.

After getting a drink from the kitchen sink, her sister disappeared into the bedroom that she and Abby shared.

After she closed the door, Abby asked, "Why is Wilma sad, Momma?"

"She and her Sammy broke up. She'll be all right, though. Just give her some time."

"I'm gonna get me a job at the Five and Ten, Momma, like Wilma did when she was 18. Buy some nice clothes, a car maybe. What can I buy for you, Momma?"

"We'll see, Abby."

Just then, there were footsteps on the front porch, deliberate and plodding. Stopping just outside their door, the footsteps were followed by two loud clumps on the floor entry.

Mrs. Wilson's face brightened. "It's Pa."

Unsmiling, her husband came through the door in his stocking feet. There was a dark aura about him. His charcoal clothes were ringed with sweat, and he had a dark beard, like coal dust had been ground into his face. He hung his gray hat on a peg, walked over to his wife, put his hand on her shoulder and kissed her on top the head.

Mrs. Wilson put her hand on his. "Tired, Pa?"

He didn't answer. After setting his lunch pail on the counter, he plodded toward the back door. "Gotta wash up," he mumbled.

"Pa's tired," Abby said.

Out back, the pump handle creaked as her father stroked it.

Turning, Abby looked up at her mother. "Don't Pa like me no more? He used to play with me, called me his Tuddybug."

She stroked her daughter's cheek. "Of course, your father still loves you, Abby. He loves all of us, but he works awful hard. It's just that he's tired sometimes when he comes home. It's not always easy, serving your family. Takes more backbone than some men's got."

"What's that mean, Momma, serving your family?"

"Always being there for them, putting their needs and happiness ahead of your own. Like that new fence he got us to keep the chickens from getting run over in the road. That's love, Abby, serving your family. That's being a real man."

When the clock on the mantle struck five, her mother walked to the kitchen.

"Can I help with supper, Momma, can I set the table, can I?"

The hint of a smile on her lips, her mother nodded yes.

Afterward, Abby went to her room, Pocaho trailing along. Her sister was lying on one twin bed.

"Sorry about you and Sammy," Abby said.

Her sister fought back tears.

Abby could hear her mother humming in the kitchen. After glancing in her direction, she closed the door.

"What is it?" Wilma asked.

Abby shushed her with a hand. "I wanna ask you something."

"Yeah?"

"Promise not to tell?" she asked, her question just above a whisper.

Wilma nodded yes.

"I got a date tonight, around eight, with that fella I told you about, Danny Dell. He said he'd take me for a ride in his red Thunderbird. Didn't tell Momma though." She giggled. "His Thunderbird, he calls it his 'Love Machine,'" she added, touching her pendant.

"Abby, Momma wouldn't like you—"

"Now you promised, Wilma."

"What was it you wanted to ask?"

"Can I borrow your loafers, the ones with the new pennies?"

Wilma thought for a long moment.

"Please?" begged Abby.

Her sister grudgingly nodded. "But don't get 'em dirty."

"Thank you, thank you, thank you," Abby gushed, kissing her sister's hand repeatedly until she pulled away. Although they were slightly too big after she slipped them on, Abby still fawned over the shoes.

"They'll fit okay," her sister said. "Just put Band-Aids on your heels." Glancing at her closet, she added, "And you can borrow that yellow skirt of mine you like too, the pleated one with the white flowered print. Just for tonight."

After Abby pulled her sister's skirt out of the closet, she caressed the garment. "You're such a good sister," she said, starting toward her.

Still on the bed, Wilma held her hands up. "No more kissing, please."

"Thank you, thank you," Abby said, blowing her an air kiss as she walked toward the bathroom. "I gotta shower now. Don't wanna get it smelly, your skirt."

Wilma pointed to the loafers. "Take good care of those, and don't do anything dumb, hear? If you do, Momma will skin me."

When Abby returned from the shower, her sister was still on the bed with one arm over her eyes and breathing deeply. Abby dressed quietly, placing a Band-Aid on each heel as her sister suggested. Checking the mirror on their dresser before leaving, she had to stand on tiptoes to see the skirt and shoes. She giggled at what she saw.

As she opened the front door later to leave, she called, "I'm leaving, Momma, bye."

Her mother stuck her head out the kitchen door. "Remember, girl, back by 10." Then she added sternly, "And mind what you been taught."

Abby touched her pendant.

Before closing the door behind her, she heard her father ask, "Where's she going, Momma?"

"Over town," Mrs. Wilson answered. "She'll be all right. She's meeting Bea."

As Abby stood at the bus stop outside her house, she felt something brush against her legs and looked down. "Pocaho, you get on home," she ordered.

The cat retreated a few feet toward their house, but lingered in the shadows.

She ran toward it, stamping her feet. "Go on home now."

This time Pocaho scurried to the bottom of their front steps, stopping there.

"Go on up, Pocaho, go on, get home. You don't wanna get runned over."

In true cat fashion though, Pocaho sat down, staring back at Abby and refusing to budge. Even later, when Abby took her seat on the bus and looked out the window, the cat was still lingering at the bottom of their steps.

Abby stood outside the teen center for half hour or so, but no Danny. Just as she was about to give up though, she heard it, the unmistakable rumble of a souped-up engine. As the sound came closer, she brightened. Suddenly, there he was, Danny Dell, coming toward her in his red Thunderbird, the engine throttled back. Seated beside him was one of the girls who called Abby names at school. As the "Love Machine" slowly rolled past, both looked at Abby and laughed. Then, with engine revving and wheels screaming, Danny sped away into the night.

Abby's shoulders fell and she shuffled toward the bus stop down the street.

CHAPTER FIFTEEN

Nursing their cokes, the two friends sat in Tom's truck outside Kelly's Restaurant in Eastbrook.

Tom pointed toward a young girl who was approaching them on the sidewalk. "My God, is that who I think it is?" he asked.

As she came closer, Lee could see she had long, rich brunette hair, good legs and a nice figure.

"Holy crapola, it is, it's Abby Wilson," Tom whispered. "Hold me down, Jarrett. Remember, I told you about her up on the Tree. Guys at the pool room say she's hotter than summer asphalt. How'd you like a little taste of that?"

"So she's Abby friggin' Wilson," Lee mocked. "My God, I may have to hose you down."

"Don't you get what I'm saying, Jarrett? That's prime tail, boy. Scoot over and make room." He stuffed Lee's college papers inside his journal and tossed it onto the floor. "Roll down your window, quick," he ordered.

"Careful with my shit," Lee barked.

"To hell with that, Jarrett. I got a boner I could hit in the majors with." He leaned across Lee and smiled at the young girl. "Hi Abby, where you headed?"

She walked over and stood by the truck on Lee's side. "Bus stop," she answered, pointing. "I'm going home." Up close, she was even prettier. She had kind, dark brown eyes, clear skin and full, red lips, Pru lips. Around her neck was a delicate silver chain, but the pendant was down in her white blouse between the 'V' of her breasts. Her pleated skirt was a yellow flowered print.

"What time is it?" she asked.

"Around eight," Tom answered.

She was wearing loafers and each had a bright copper penny in its insert.

"Like your shoes," Tom said, fawning.

She brightened. "My bus don't come for an hour though. Gimme a lift home?"

"Sure, hop in," Tom said. After she slid in between the two young men, he leered at her and stuck out his hand. "Hi, I'm Tom Smith." He nodded toward Lee. "That's Lee Jones."

"How'd you know my name?" she asked.

"Uhh, do you know Suzie Bennett?" Tom asked.

She shook her head yes.

"She told me."

Lee looked at him side-eyed.

Her hair had a clean fragrance. She tittered once. "My sister's shoes is too big. I got Band-Aids on the heels to make 'em fit." Giggling, she looked down at her shoes.

When Lee glanced down at her gimp bracelet, she noticed and held it up in his face. "Made it myself, like it?"

He nodded.

Tom flapped his shirt collar. "Sure is hot tonight, don't you think?"

Abby fanned herself too.

"I hear Sawyer's Park is the coolest place in town, 'cause of the trees and all," Tom said. "Want to check it out, cool off, talk a while? You know, before we run you home?"

"Aw Jeez," Lee said. "What the hell are you doing, T.D.?"

He glanced at his friend knowingly.

At Tom's question, Abby hesitated, but then shrugged indifferently. "I gotta be home by 10."

"Drop me off at Fourth," Lee said.

"What's your hurry, Jarrett?" he asked. "I heard your dad. You don't have to be back till midnight." When they came to the street where Lee wanted to get out, rather than stopping, Tom hit the gas and barreled on toward Sawyer's Park.

"Aw dag," Lee said under his breath.

"Do you know Danny Dell?" Abby asked Lee.

He shook his head no.

"He drives a Thunderbird." She played with the chain around her neck. "Boys at school think I'm pretty," she said, pausing. "You think I'm pretty?" she asked Lee, tilting her face sweetly up toward his.

He shook his head yes. She was too, borderline beautiful.

"Girls at school laugh at me. Call me names. My friend Bea says that's 'cause they're jealous. Boys like me though. I can tell. But them girls, they ain't gonna laugh for long. I'll be 18 soon. Momma says I can quit school then and get me a job downtown at the Five and Ten."

Her body language was like a child's. Although mildly exaggerated, it seemed honest, always confirming what she was truly thinking, feeling. Lee found it refreshing after the dissembling ways of some of the other girls in Eastbrook.

"Her eyes slid over to Lee. "Do you think I'm a good girl?"

"This ain't right," Lee said, leaning forward and speaking across her to the other man. "And you know it."

"I do," Abby answered her own question, "I think I'm a good girl."

Lee squirmed in his seat.

"My daddy, he works in a cemetery," she said, her tone serious. "You scared of that place?" she asked Lee.

He didn't answer.

"I am," she said, hugging herself. "All them dead people rotting away down there in the dark. It's spooky. Momma says they're waiting for something, some sign. They'll be up top again someday when they get the right sign." Her eyes grew bigger and she shuddered. "I don't wanna be around when they do."

"Never thought about dead people that way," Lee answered, eyeballing Tom.

"You're funny," she said to Lee.

Just as they turned into Sawyer's Park a rabbit darted across the road.

"Hope Pocaho's okay," she said.

"Who?" Lee asked.

Her face saddened. "My cat, Pocaho. She followed me to the bus stop at home. Hope she found her way back okay."

Tom looked over at Lee and snickered. "I wouldn't worry about it, Abby."

"Just hope she's okay, that's all," she said, her voice trailing off. They passed Sawyer's Oak sitting alongside the road in the park. Famous locally, it was a massive tree with limbs almost like the arms of some giant creature. They came to a deeply rutted, muddy section. When Tom gunned the engine, the truck fish-tailed back and forth on the narrow one-lane road. As it did, Tom twirled the steering wheel back and forth.

Abby giggled and stomped with delight like a happy child.

They pulled into a secluded area and just before Tom shut the engine off, Lee could see a picnic bench at the far edge of their headlights.

Abby turned to Lee, her hand over her heart. "My Mama says it's okay. You know, to have sex, as long as you love one another, the boy and you."

Tom reassured her, "Yeah, we love you, Abby, we both do." He flipped the visor down and removed a condom from its pocket. He got out and helped her slide out on the driver's side. As Lee watched, Tom pressed her up against the fender with his body. He began kissing her hard, all the while massaging her pelvic area with one knee. When she squirmed and began moaning, he took her by the hand and led her away into the darkness.

"Bye," she called back sweetly to Lee.

Tom led her to a picnic bench 100 feet or so in front of the truck. "After you get your clothes off," he said, pointing to the bench, "get up on there." While she did as he directed, he undressed, afterward kneeling and doing something with one of her loafers. Just as he started to climb up on her table, however, he gave a low cry, "Ouch, dammit."

"You okay?" she asked, her concern sounding genuine.

He touched his knee and flinched. "A damn splinter," he answered.

"Yeah, me too," she said, pointing to her elbow.

He felt it and it was wet. "Jeez, you're bleeding. Why didn't you say something?"

"Aw, it'll be all right."

He ran his fingers lightly over the table top across the grain. "My God, there are splinters everywhere."

He studied her momentarily. "Be right back," he said, walking away toward the truck.

When Tom suddenly appeared out of the dark at the truck window, Lee jumped. "Dag," he said, "you scared the hell out of me ... what's up?"

Tom pulled a blanket from behind the seat. "She's on one of the tables, but the whole damn thing's loaded with splinters," he said, rubbing his knee. "Got one myself when I climbed up."

"So the blankets for you, huh?" Lee asked, his tone sarcastic. "That's my ol' Tom, always thinking of the other guy."

Tom gave him the finger as he walked away.

Back at the bench, he carefully spread the blanket under her.

"Thank you," she said sweetly. "How's the splinter?"

He shrugged.

"Here, I'll make it all better," she said, her voice ringing honest. She kissed her fingers and gently touched the wound on his knee.

He hesitated, seemingly stunned. "Aw, Jeez," he said, blowing air out his puffed cheeks..."why the hell did you do that?" For a several seconds, he stared at her and then out into the darkness, all the while chewing on his lower lip.

"What's wrong?" she asked.

"Nothing," he answered, getting down off the table and starting back toward the truck. "He'll be along shortly, Lee."

As Lee sat in the truck with the windows down, all he could hear were muffled voices in the direction of the picnic table.

Suddenly out of the darkness, Tom was there again at the truck window on the driver's side. His pants were draped over one shoulder, and he was wearing only undershorts and a t-shirt.

Switching on the cab light, Tom held his hand out. In his palm was a new copper penny.

Lee frowned.

"It's hers, Abby's. Pried it out of one of her loafers when she wasn't looking." He snickered.

"What the hell is wrong with you, T.D.? Why would you do that?"

"Aw, lighten up. I'm just funning her. Don't get your shorts in a wad. I'm gonna give it back—by the way, hope you were paying attention before."

The other man's look questioned him.

"Didn't you see what I was doing with my knee? That and breathing in her ear. Drives 'em crazy. Try it sometime."

Lee sneered.

Tom slid under the steering wheel. "Okay, I had a little taste. Pretty sweet too, I gotta say." He licked his lips theatrically. "Your turn."

Lee motioned away.

Tom glowered at him. "You gotta be kidding. Your first and you're turning it down? My God man, look." He turned the headlights on. She was laying there, naked, one hand shielding her eyes from the headlight glare. "I told her you'd be along in a jiffy. She's waiting for you, go on."

Lee glanced out the front window and scowled. "What the hell are you thinking, T.D.?" He reached over and turned off the headlights, Tom laughing as he did. "That girl's not right upstairs. You know what I mean. This is wrong."

For a long moment, Tom studied the other man. "This ain't about Abby, is it? It's about Pru. You're still trying to keep your promise to her, aren't you? In case you've not been paying attention my friend, she's already broken hers. Seems to me, you've got a little payback coming."

For a long moment, Lee wrestled with the other man's words until Tom tossed something on the seat beside him. It was a condom wrapped in gold foil with one edge torn.

Haltingly, Lee moved in the shadows toward the bench and Abby, the other man chicken-clucking behind him.

Somewhere in the dark ahead, he heard her whisper his name sweetly. Stumbling forward and groping blindly, he bumped into the rough edge of her table and caught a splinter.

His jaw tightened. My God, this could be the same table where Kenny and Pru did it.

Suddenly, he sensed the near warmth of her body. He reached out for her, tentatively at first. By chance, his hand found her abdomen, near her pubic area. "Sorry," he said.

"That's all right," she answered.

Under his fingers, he felt a long, thin, slightly raised blemish. "What's that?"

"'Pendix scar from when I was little," she answered. "Hurt for a whole week 'fore it busted. Daddy was mad at me for not saying something. Said I acted like I had no sense." She snickered.

The trees cast a dark veil over the table and he could see her only vaguely. She was on her back on a blanket, completely naked. Her knees were raised slightly and her thighs open. Most arrestingly though, he could see she was looking up at him, unashamed, innocent.

Just then, Tom turned the truck's headlights on and off once.

"You son of a bitch," Lee yelled. In that flash of lights, Lee saw for the first time the pendant resting on the pale skin between her breasts and he hesitated. It was a silver cross.

She caught his hesitation. "Don't you wanna love me?"

Just then, the moon slipped out from behind a cloud and he glimpsed her clearly for the first time. He had never seen a girl completely naked before: her body, alabaster in the pale moonlight, was more beautiful than anything he ever fantasized.

Darkness cloaked the indecision in his eyes.

CHAPTER SIXTEEN

Pants over his shoulder, Lee walked back to the truck.

Grinning, Tom doffed his hat. "So you finally gave it up, you son of a gun. Congratulations." When Lee opened the door on the passenger side to climb in, the other man tossed him a baseball. "Here," he said, smiling broadly, "a baptismal gift, me to you."

Sliding in, Lee tossed the ball on the seat and turned the radio down. "Hey, why'd you do that?" Tom asked, pointing to the radio.

"I couldn't hear you," Lee answered. Motioning back toward Abby, he said, "We should be getting her home. Okay if I check for ball scores?" Playing with the dial, Lee found a faint sports station.

"I hope you can get my music station again, Jarrett. Had a hell of a time finding it."

Shushing him, Lee cocked an ear down close to the speaker.

"Dammit, I need some music," Tom said, getting out of the truck and disappearing toward the picnic bench and Abby.

A few minutes later, he came back carrying the blanket, and standing next to the truck, he snapped on the truck headlights.

Standing barefooted on the picnic bench in the truck's lights, dressed only in her panties and bra, was Abby.

"She's gonna do us a little show," Tom said, walking toward the bench and motioning for Lee to follow.

"C'mon T.D.," Lee said. "We should be getting her home."

"What songs do you like?" Tom asked her.

"Country mostly. Cindy William's my favorite." She stuck her chin out proudly. "Momma says I sound just like her."

Tom began to clap. "Okay, let's hear one, Abby, sing one of Cindy's."

Her first song was done off-key, and the second, although better, was out of sync with her swaying and dancing. Still though, she sang honestly.

Lee began clapping and humming to help her find the rhythm. Once she winced, but soldiered on with the singing.

A splinter, Lee thought.

When she finished, Tom clapped and whistled wildly.

Too wildly, thought Lee.

At Tom's approval, however, Abby beamed childlike, even curtseying. "You Are My Sunshine," Tom called to her. "Know that one, Abby?" Lee nudged the other man and tapped on his watch. "It's·close to 10. We gotta be getting her home."

Abby's confidence growing, she began belting out his request.

All the while, Tom was dramatically waving his arms like he was conducting some grand orchestra, often glancing over his shoulder to gauge Lee's reaction.

When she was almost done, Lee clapped quietly. "Nice, Abby, thanks, we better be going though." Lee walked over and switched the truck-lights off.

"No, no. Just one more, one last song," Tom pleaded, switching the lights back on. This one's for Lee, Abby. It's his favorite. "Do you know *As Time Goes By?*"

Lee's eyes snapped over at the other man.

She shook her head no.

Tom hummed the first chorus for her.

"Oh yeah, I've heard Momma singing that along with the radio." With Tom's prompting, she tried it, sometimes singing behind him, sometimes along with him, and other times just humming when neither could remember the lyrics.

When she finished, Lee said, "C'mon Tom, you're embarrassing her now, yourself too."

"Just one more chorus, Abby. For Lee, do it for Lee, it's his favorite. Then we'll go, swear."

She nodded sweetly, and when Tom gave her a cue, she began again.

Lee scowled at the other man, but when he turned toward Abby, he showed a good face.

The second chorus of the song was her best. Her swaying became more in rhythm with her singing and she remembered most of the words. As before too, she sang unashamedly, but this time her voice rang even more true and pure in the lonely night.

The spell of her singing prompted both Tom and Lee to grow silent and sobered momentarily, each man sliding into his own valley of shame prompted by the disparity between his own character and Abby's: her innocence a counter to Lee's guilt and the young girl's honesty a contrast to Tom's deceit.

"It's starting to sprinkle," Lee said near the finish of her song, "Got any Band-Aids?"

"Band-Aids? What the hell?" he asked, pointing to the cab. "Glove box." Lee rummaged through the compartment until he found one. He then walked over to the bench. "We're going home now, Abby." Grabbing her by one arm, he put her over his shoulder and carried her back to the truck, setting her down behind it. He handed her the Band-Aid. "For your foot, the splinter," he said. "I'll get your clothes."

When Lee started back toward the picnic table, Tom stopped him with a hand. "Tsk, I'll get 'em, Jarrett," he said, shaking his head. "Jeez, before it's over, you're gonna make me a candy-ass too."

Lee shrugged.

While Abby dressed behind the truck, the two men stood out front. "Gimme that penny of hers," Lee whispered. "I'm gonna give it back to her."

After searching his pockets, Tom shrugged. "Musta'dropped it somewhere."

"Aw jeez, T.D. ... gimme some light." After he switched it on, Lee searched through his pocket change until he found a penny, a tarnished one. Walking to the back of the truck, he called Abby's name softly and she answered. "I found a penny on the ground," he lied. "Must have come out of your shoe. Throw me your loafer and I'll put it back in." She did and he replaced it.

When Lee got back in the cab though, Tom hissed at him and shook his head. "Always spoiling the fun."

Once all three were seated in the truck, Tom fiddled with the radio, trying to find his music station again.

"Find Cindy Williams," Abby urged, "play her, play her."

Lee looked out the window at a star that had found its way through the overcast.

Tom followed his friend's gaze. "I read someplace that most of them burned out a million years ago, they're all gone, even though we're still seeing them." He looked over at Lee and grinned. "Sort of like them promises you and Cathy made."

Lee shot back an angry look. "You go to hell."

Reaching over, Abby put her hand over Lee's and squeezed it. "Don't feel bad," she whispered, "it's all right. I still love you."

Trying to fathom her remark, Tom frowned at Lee for a few seconds, finally shrugging when he couldn't.

"What am I sitting on?" she asked.

When Tom flipped the cab light on, Lee pulled his hand from hers.

Reaching under herself, she pulled out the scuffed baseball.

Tom chuckled, took it from her and threw it on the dash.

As they drove, the ball rolled back and forth, alternately showing the blemish then the clean side.

Lee grabbed it and jammed it down in the pocket of his jacket. When he glanced over, her pendant flashed under a passing streetlight. All the way to her house, his knee smarted from where he caught a splinter on the bench.

While they were driving, she found his hand again in the darkness and pressed something into his palm.

Lee did not look, for fear Tom would notice.

"What time is it?" she asked suddenly, urgency in her voice.

Lee read his wrist watch in the dash light. "Almost 11."

"Momma's gonna skin me alive."

Leaving his headlights on in the dark, drizzly night, Tom pulled over on the left side of the road in front of Abby's small, one-story frame house. Out front, a two-lane highway crowded up close to their front wooden steps. The only room lit was the one inside their front door.

"Gotta run," she said when they stopped. "Love you both."

Not until Tom got out did Lee look down at what she had pressed into his hand. It was her gimp bracelet. Lee helped her slide out on the passenger side. Holding onto her hand, he said, "And Abby, you are a good girl. Don't let anyone tell you different."

As Lee climbed back inside, Tom's face puzzled at his friend's remark.

Lee slid over to the driver's side, resting his head against the partially opened truck door with his left elbow out the open window.

"How's about one last kiss, Abby?" Tom asked.

"No, my parents," she said, looking up at the house. "Aww," she cooed, "there's Pocaho in the window. She seems upset."

As she turned to walk to the steps, Lee called to her softly, "And Abby ... remember what I said."

Smiling sweetly, she looked back at him as if saying goodbye.

Suddenly, a flash of light streaked by the driver's window, followed by a dark blur and a dead-sounding thud, and Tom and Abby disappeared. One second they were there and the next they were gone.

At the same instant, Lee felt a sickening blow to his head and a sharp stabbing pain in his left shoulder that shot across his back clear to the other side. Everything went blank then, followed by several disjointed, blurry scenes and just bits of those.

CHAPTER SEVENTEEN

When Lee opened his eyes in the hospital room, his mother was sitting in a chair beside the bed. Her head was bowed and her fingers were worrying a string of rosary beads.

He had a sickening throb in the back of his eyes, like when you swallow an icy drink and the pain radiates from the back of your throat up through your head. He tried rolling over onto his left side, but could not.

He recalled having a dream, a bad one.

Laying her rosary on the chair arm, she patted his hand. "I'm here, Lee, and everything's all right. Stay off your left side though, dear."

He looked over at his left shoulder. It was in a sling and seemed lower than he remembered. When he tried scratching his head, he felt bandages.

"Take it easy," she said, pulling his hand down.

"What happened, Mom?"

She hesitated. "The doctor said you might be a little fuzzy at first. It's June, dear, 1950."

He chuckled cynically. "My God, Mom, I'm not that out of it. I know what month, year it is."

"Sorry, dear, rest now."

When she started to sit down, Lee grabbed her arm, his face questioning hers.

She paused for a moment, but then asked, "Last night, do you remember any of it, Lee, the accident?" She hesitated. "You were hit by a car, you and Tom. It sideswiped his truck on the driver's side."

He remembered pieces of what she was saying and realized his dream was real.

"Doctor Gladstone, he just left," she explained further. "He took some x-rays. You're all fine, except for here." She placed her hand on her left shoulder. "It's broken." Then, pointing to her forehead, she added.

"And a few stitches up here. The doctor, he doesn't think they'll leave a scar though." She wiped one eye.

He had been half-listening up to then, but in the middle of her words, the evening came back in focus. All of it, including Abby, the picnic bench, the dark blur in the darkness outside her house, the sickening thud. He remembered all that followed too—flashing lights, sirens, the ambulance ride, and finally the hospital with the doctors poking and probing and testing and finally, the policeman's questions afterward.

Lee glanced at the wall clock. It read six.

Following his eyes, she explained further. "It's morning Lee, early morning. The doctor said you kept dozing off right in the middle of his exam. Said not to worry though, your head tests were normal."

"Tom?" he asked. "How's Tom?"

"Hold on," she said, walking toward the door. "I'll get your father."

Lee didn't like the look she gave him. "Something wrong with Tom?" he asked. Sitting up and swinging his feet over the side, he searched for his shoes.

She walked over and swung his legs back on the bed. "Now, Lee, don't upset yourself. She pulled the sheets back over his legs. "Stay in bed till the doctor comes back, please."

Despite her pleadings, he sat up and swung his feet over the side again. "What room's he in?"

Palms down in a settling motion, she said, "Okay, okay, have it your way. About him, Tom, it's too early to say. His foot, it was badly injured. Doctors are still working on him, I think."

"My God," Lee said. "Which one, which foot?"

"Left, I think," she answered. "Why?"

"Aw shit," he whispered, "Air Force." Lying back on the pillow, he closed his eyes. A few seconds later though, they snapped open and he sat up in bed. "Did they get the bastard?"

"Lee, your language."

"The guy that did it, they catch him?"

"The other driver?" she asked. "Some young fella from down near Lost Run. Your father talked to the police. They said he'd been drinking. That's what comes from drinking and driving."

Lee studied her. "You ready for sainthood?"

She sat back in her chair. "Lee, what a mean thing to say. I just meant—"

"Forget it."

She eyed him skeptically. "Not a scratch on him though, the other driver. Like they say, drunks and babies."

He lay back and closed his eyes again. Bastard, he thought.

"By the way," she asked, "what were you guys doing out that way? I thought you were going to a ball game over at Fremont."

"We were just giving someone a lift home, Mom." The dull light from his bed lamp caught the silver cross dangling from his mother's rosary. "A friend of T.D.'s, named Abby." Pausing, he asked, "How's she doing?"

There was a gentle knock at the door and his father stuck his head in. "Evelyn," he called to his wife, motioning her outside.

After she left, Lee could hear their agitated voices in the hall.

Momentarily, his parents reentered the room. "How you feeling, pal?" his father asked, trying to sound casual.

Lee touched his left shoulder and made a face.

"Could have been worse, a lot worse," his father said. "All of you could have been killed."

Catching the nuance in his father's words, Lee frowned and sat up. "All of us?" he asked. "All of us?"

His father fingered the brim of his hat. "That little gal you guys were with last night, what was her name, Abby? Her chest was crushed, couldn't save her." He hesitated. "She died."

"Oh, my God," cried Lee. "My God. Oh, my God," he repeated, swaying back and forth, his head in his hands.

"No pulse when they brought her in. They worked on her for almost an hour but couldn't get her back." He paused, and then added, "Freak accident. The other driver, young man named Downey, claimed he didn't know the road. Said he couldn't see the white lines because it was dark and rainy. Anyway, he drove to the right of Tom's headlights, like he was supposed to. He said Tom was parked on the wrong side of the road."

Lee dug at the bandages on his head.

"Sorry about your little friend though, buddy," he said, his voice low and breaking slightly. "We just thank God you're okay."

His mother covered her eyes with a handkerchief and her shoulders began shaking subtly.

"You know what I mean," his father went on, his voice just above a whisper, "your injuries, that they're not more serious." He gently squeezed his son's good shoulder.

"But T.D., will he be okay, Dad?"

"Doc Gladstone said he'd drop in later to check on you again," his father said, trying to escape his son's eyes. "Might even let you go home today. He wanted to take one last look, make sure you're okay before he released you. You know docs." His father pointed to a nearby closet. "Your clothes are in there, if he gives you the go ahead." He smiled. "Ol' 40 Grit's outside in the hall. He's busting to see you."

Years back, his father had nicknamed Lee's grandfather after that coarse grade of sandpaper, 40 Grit. It matched the old man's character perfectly.

After his father left, the old man stuck his head through the partly opened door. He was balding on top with hair like steel-wool at his temples. "You all right, boy?" his grandfather asked, a smile broadening his curved down mustache.

"Hey Granddad.

"Sorry about your little friend, that girl," the old man said. He stared blankly out the window. "It hardly ever seems right, a young person dying. A fellow always knows that kind of thing can happen, hears about it all the time, but it's seldom anyone he knows. It's always some stranger the next county over, or just some fellow in the newspaper. A body's never ready when it happens to one of his own, someone he knows, cares about." He studied his own reflection in the window momentarily, like he didn't recognize it. "Life is loss, son."

Lee sensed he was talking about something that happened in his own life.

"Hear anything about Tom, Granddad?"

As his fingers worried the brim of his chuch hat, the old man studied his grandson hard for a few seconds. "Just that his foot was hurt bad," he answered. "But I saw your little friend downstairs before they carted her off, the Wilson girl. Pretty young thing. Strange what a fellow notices at a time like that. She had Band-Aids on both heels and one on her big toe. Don't know where her socks were. Her loafers were on the gurney. They looked brand-spanking new. Strange though, she had a fresh copper penny in one shoe and a tarnished one in the other. Folks generally try to match 'em."

Lee started to say something, then stopped and covered his eyes with his forearm.

The old man studied him. "I know the Wilson girl's dad, Tom. Shame, damn shame. But how's your wing?"

Lee shook his head.

"So things ain't perfect. For now though, let's work with that." He pointed to his own forehead. "Your goose egg?"

"We just wanted to give her a lift home, Granddad, that's all." He avoided the old man's gaze. "We were just trying to do something nice."

"Hell's fire, where'd you get that notion, in them pretty picture shows over town?" The old man's eyebrows lowered. "That good's bound to come from good?"

"But that's not all, Granddad. What happened, the car hitting her and all, it was my fault, in a way. She'd started toward her front steps, and I called to her to say something nice. Anyway, when she turned, that's when it happened, the car hit her. If I hadn't—"

Granddad put his hand up. "Hold it right there, Lee Jarrett. The last time I checked, you're just like the rest of us, a cast member in this here opera. Not the director, least ways, not yet you ain't."

The young man's cheeks puffed and he blew out a whoosh of air.

Just then, the door opened and Doctor Gladstone, his eyes warm and fatherly, stepped inside. Nodding toward Lee, he spoke to his grandfather. "I think our boy can go home today, Dallas."

"Be heading out myself now," Granddad said. Just before closing the door, he added, tapping his chest, "And trust me, son, you'll find it in here, whatever you need."

When Lee got out of bed later to get his clothes, he was lightheaded. With just one good arm, it was hard to dress, especially when he tried buttoning his shirt and pulling his pants up. When he finished dressing and threw his jacket over his shoulders, he felt something in the pocket. It was T.D.'s baseball, the one he had given him as a prize for his first time. He turned it over and over. Still there on one side was the dark scuff mark. He tried gripping the ball with his pitching hand, but had no strength. When he slipped it back into his jacket, he felt something else. It was the gimp bracelet Abby had pressed into his hand the night before. He smiled at it weakly.

CHAPTER EIGHTEEN

Somewhere far off, Tom heard a name being called over and over, "Dr. Kline, please call radiology, Dr. Kline..." His eyes snapped open. He couldn't think; it was like his mind was swimming through sticky tar. A ceiling fan was whirling slowly overhead. "Where am I?" he asked the fan. When he got no answer, he looked around. His mother was seated in a chair beside the bed to his right. Her head was down in one hand and she was sniffling. Beyond her was a sterile-looking wall clock that read two, a large window with closed shutters, sunlight silhouetting its edges, and a closet, its door partially opened. Just inside the closet, the pale light from his bed-lamp caught the white canvas toe of a sneaker, his own he realized.

Hearing her son's question, Mrs. Drew looked away, and removing a tissue from her worn and faded pocketbook, she dabbed her eyes. When she turned back to him though and smiled bravely, the whites of her eyes were red.

"Mom, why are you crying?" Tom asked. "What's wrong?"

"Nothing, dear, nothing at all." Her voice was patronizing. "Just a car accident. You've been a little confused since they brought you in last night. Everything's all right though. I'll get your father," she said, easing out the door. Shortly, she stuck her head back inside. "Silly me," she said sweetly. "I meant your brother."

"How are you hitting them, young fellow?" an upbeat voice asked from a nearby bed. Propped up on one elbow and facing him, was a little man with a short gray beard. His eyes jumped with life. Near the foot of his bed was a wheelchair.

Tom's eyes dragged away from the other man when he heard footsteps at the door. It was his brother, David.

"Hey, how's it going, pal?" the priest asked, squeezing his shoulder gently.

Tom caught his brother's tone: too casual. "What's wrong?"

Father David took his hand away and frowned.

"Something's wrong," Tom said. "For starters, you're too damn bubbly."

Before Father David could answer, a short nurse with auburn hair and an ample body came through the door and stopped at the foot of Tom's bed. For a few seconds, she studied his chart. Two gold-colored, sea shell ear rings framed her pretty face. Above that, her nurse's cap was fluorescent white, its creases knife-sharp. "I see you're awake," she said, smiling. "I'm Nurse Judy." Glancing back at his chart, she asked, "Do you prefer Tom or Thomas?"

He returned a crooked smile. "Tom."

After taking his temperature and blood pressure, she asked, "How are you feeling, Tom?"

He nodded weakly.

She fluffed up his pillow. "Any pain?"

Tom shook his head.

She rested her hand on his shoulder. "If you do, let me know. Just hit that red button," she said, pointing. "I can give you something for it." She turned toward the other patient. "How are you doing, Coach?"

He gave her a thumb up. "Did you think about what I asked you, Judy?"

She looked at him blankly before pumping his blood pressure cuff.

"You know, about us running off together," he said.

"What would your wife say?" she asked, her voice playful.

"Hell, she can come along and watch," he answered, his eyes sparking with mischief.

Folding her arms, she tried striking a stern pose, but lost it and giggled.

"Got any scores for me?" the coach asked.

She shook her head as she read his temperature.

"Yankees, Orioles?"

She shook her head again.

"Damn," he said, snapping his fingers. "Did you tell your boy about that pitch, the one I showed you, how to grip the seams?"

She nodded. "He said to say thanks, he'd work on it. Now, let's have a look," she said, rolling his sheets down. Both of his legs were missing just below the knees.

Tom stared, stunned yet fascinated.

She sniffed the bandages and examined his legs above them. "Color's looking good, Coach. You'll be going home soon." Pulling his sheets back up, she said, "Promise me though, you'll take better care of that diabetes ... and behave yourself too," she added, playfully slapping his hand.

"I'll do it, for you," he said, pausing. "One or the other."

Nurse Judy walked to the door and looked back at Tom. "I'll be back shortly to check yours."

Tom frowned after her, frightened by a possible inference of her words. Clutching the top of his sheets, he hesitated, afraid of what he might see if he looked under, or more importantly, what he might not see. At last though, he raised the sheets, slowly at first. Once he could see both legs were still there, he lifted them all the way. His right foot was there like always, but at the end of his left was a large, white clump of gauze and bandages. His eyes snapped over to his brother.

Before speaking, Father David took a deep breath. "Sorry, pal." Shaking his head and placing his hand on Tom's shoulder, the priest spoke the words his brother was terrified he might hear. "They tried but couldn't save it, your foot."

Tom stared up at his brother, his eyes filling with disbelief. "They cut my foot off?" he yelled. "They cut my foot off?" he screamed the question a second time, a sob in his voice. "Oh, my God, they did, they cut my foot off."

Father David gently rubbed his brother's shoulder.

Arching his body back, Tom began rocking back and forth, all the while whimpering, "Mother of God, mother of God, holy mother of God..."

His mother squirmed and began weeping softly.

Father David's hand on his brother's shoulder, he bent down and whispered close in his ear, "It's okay, buddy, let it out, let it out."

At the priest's words, Tom stopped rocking, shrugged his brother's hand away and rested his forearm over his eyes.

The priest spoke low. "We're here for you, Ma and me. Your buddy too, Lee. He asked if he could see you, but I told him to wait. You know, till you get feeling better." When Father David got no response, he continued. "Lee was a bit luckier. Only broke his shoulder and got a few stitches on his forehead." He paused. "But that little girl they brought in with you. Abby, I think was her name. Not so lucky."

Tom uncovered his eyes and looked up at his brother.

"The doctors worked on her for a long time last night, but couldn't save her. Shame, pretty little girl."

Tom half-raised off his pillow and grabbed his brother by his jacket. "She's dead?" he cried, "Abby's dead?"

When the priest looked away, Tom released his grip and fell back on the bed. He closed his eyes again, whispering to himself over and over, "My God. Oh my God, she's dead."

"Wasn't your fault," Father David said. "They got the guy who did it.

He'd been drinking some. So don't go blaming yourself. This is hard to see right now, T.D., but all things serve His purpose."

Tom looked at his brother and laughed sarcastically. "You don't really believe that churchy B.S., do you?" He gestured toward the ceiling. "You know, about someone being up there who gives a shit about us."

Father David bristled. "You don't mean that, mister. That's your pain talking, not—"

"Shut the hell up,' Tom shouted. "You don't know a damn thing about it, not a damn thing." He turned his face toward the wall, away from his brother.

His mother placed her hand on Tom's back, "Please don't get upset, dear. It'll be all right. We'll take care of you, your father and I." Looking up at the priest, she asked sweetly, "Won't we?"

Father David scolded her with a look but she missed it. Taking her by the arm, he shepherded her toward the door and she followed passively. Once in the hall, he got a coffee and a picture magazine and seated her on a bench. He gently rested his hand on her shoulder. "Tom will be fine, Ma. I just want to talk to him a minute. Be back in a jiffy. You read your magazine, don't worry about a thing."

She patted his hand.

When Father David came back in the room, the patient in the other bed beckoned to him. Speaking low to the priest and extending his hand, he said, "Coach Sandy." Father David introduced himself and they shook hands. Motioning with his head toward Tom, the coach half-whispered behind his hand. "I know this is a rough patch for him and you folks and I'm sorry to butt-in, but I was wondering." He hesitated.

Father David tilted his head benignly, waiting for the coach to go on.

The coach pointed to a radio on his night stand. "When the big score-keeper put me down here, He gave me three loves: family, friends and baseball." He worried an end of his bed sheet. "Would it bother the young feller too much if I listened to a game?"

Father David gave a tight-lipped nod and motioned to keep it low.

The coach smiled, his eyes squeezing together.

Taking out a string of rosary beads, the priest seated himself beside the bed.

Tom hid his eyes under both forearms and pretended to sleep. Later, when he heard footsteps leaving, Tom peeked out from under his arms to make certain his brother was gone. In the eerie light from his bed lamp, he looked toward the closet. Through its half open door, he could see the one tennis shoe again.

As Tom lay there listening to the strains of the national anthem playing softly on the coach's radio, he felt his eyelashes moisten. Blotting them with his sleeve, he glanced over quickly to make certain the coach was not watching.

A few days later, a policeman came by wanting to talk to Tom. He was still in bad shape, so Father David talked to him instead. The officer explained that Tom was being ticketed and fined $200.00 for contributing to the accident—he was parked on the wrong side of the road with his lights on, confusing the other driver. He added though, that Tom could fight the charge if he wished.

The priest assured the officer that, considering his brother's low emotional state due to the recent tragic events, he would not be contesting the charge. Later, Father David paid his fine.

CHAPTER NINETEEN

The day after Lee was released from the hospital, he went to Sawyer's Park, uncertain why, and found the table he thought they had used the night of the accident. He ran his fingers over the table's rough, dove-wing gray boards. The signature of countless seasons was inscribed heavily in its grains. About to leave, he noticed something shiny under the table. It was a new penny. He dropped it in his palm and studied it for a long moment. Squeezing it gently, he looked up. "Oh, my God," he said up to the empty, cloudless blue sky.

A short while later in the Jarrett's back yard, Lee's mother wiped the clothes line and threw the white rag on the picnic bench beside Lee. It had dark streaks on it from the line, and he tossed it to the other end of the table.

"I hope Tom's not getting any of those phantom itches," she said.

"Phantom itches?" Lee asked, tossing his baseball in the air and catching it with his good arm.

"It happens sometimes when you lose a limb. You think you can still feel it even though it's gone. Hope Tom's not getting any of those."

"Yeah, bad enough losing his foot. Now he's got to keep scratching it?"

"Is it this evening you're going to see him?"

Lee nodded yes.

"Not fair," she said, "that poor boy lying in the hospital for a whole week and no visitors."

"Mom, I've called every day, told you that," he answered. "They said no company, no phone calls even, doctor's orders." He paused. "Besides, his mother's there, Father David too."

"Still not right," she insisted. "He needs someone he can let his hair down with, a friend, not family." She looked at him.

He got up to leave.

"Help me with the sheets?"

He held up one end with his right arm while his mother pinned the corners. On the last sheet, he dropped one billowing end, and trying to catch it, wrenched his bad shoulder. Gritting his teeth, he looked up until the pain backed off. The blue sky was still cloudless and empty.

"Sorry, dear, I can do the rest," she said, studying him afterward. "About the accident, Lee, that girl. That's not a very nice neighborhood where you were. A lot of trash lives down that way. I hope you weren't doing anything bad, nothing you'd be ashamed of, like having S."

"Aw, jeez," he said, "you mean sex."

She often did that, used just the first letters of words she considered bad, ones she thought were not proper for a lady to utter. In her mind it was okay to know the bad ones and think them, but saying them out loud was a different matter. Referring to the bad ones like that somehow sanitized them, at least in her mind.

As she wiped the clothesline, her cross pendant caught the noonday sun.

"You ever do that, Mom, break your word to God? You know, that way, sex?"

Her eyes jumped over to him. "Certainly not," she replied. "Lee Jarrett, why on earth would you ask such a question?"

"Granddad around?"

Eying him with suspicion, she shook her head slowly. "Something on your mind?"

He didn't answer her, but pointed to the house. "I'll be up in my room. If he shows, tell him I want to see him."

"By the way, a letter came from college. It's on your night stand."

Later, as he was lying on his bed gripping and re-gripping a baseball, there was a gentle knock on his door. His father stepped inside. "How's the arm, slugger?"

He waffled his hand.

The door eased open behind him and the dog ambled in.

"Hey, Dan," Lee greeted him.

The dog, after giving Lee a glance and cocking his head left, circled the room and padded out.

"Granddad around?" his son asked.

"He figured you needed some alone time. Mother said you wanted to talk to him about something." He clapped his hands for Lee to throw him the baseball. "Can I fill in for Ol' 40?"

Lee didn't answer, but chewed on his lower lip as they tossed the ball back and forth for a few seconds,

When they stopped, his father glanced at his night stand, "Mail, huh?"

He stopped chewing on his lip. "Yeah, college ... about that, Dad. I've been thinking. Maybe I should sit out a year. You know, college, till my arm's a hundred per cent."

"That reminds me," his father said, rolling over his son's notion. "I talked to Coach Bailey. He said your scholarship's safe, that there'd be plenty of time for you to mend before baseball next spring."

"It's not just that, Dad. Everything's all mixed up right now." His son looked down at the arm sling. "But what if it doesn't come around, my arm?"

"C'mon, Lee, the doc said it'd be okay. Besides," he added, "your mother's heart's set on you and college." He tossed the baseball on the bed. "She said you were gonna stop by the hospital this evening and see your buddy, Tom."

"Yeah, if he can have visitors."

"That's the right thing to do, Lee." He walked to the open door.

"But what'll I say, Dad? What do you say to someone who's just lost his foot?"

"This ain't about you."

His son looked away.

"Think what you'd want said if it was you, then you'll know what to say to him. Can tell you this much, a little kindness is never out of fashion. Let him do the talking. Even if he clams up, he'll be telling you something."

Before leaving, his father shut the door and leaned against it. "And another thing, bub, that little girl that got killed, her family, the Wilsons. You should have gone to her funeral. Your mother and I sent flowers, went to the burial and made excuses for you. Told her folks you weren't feeling well. They understood, but you should stop by their place sometime. You owe them that much." He paused. "Tom's different, he had an out for not going."

His son made a pained face. "Same deal there again, Dad. What do you say to a family who has lost their daughter?"

"Hell Lee, sorry is about all you can offer, all anyone can. Of course, it doesn't help much. Words can't cure what's ailing them, but that's all we got to give sometimes. You gotta mean it though. Folks can pick up on that."

The baseball fell from Lee's hand, hit the floor with a dull thud and rolled under his bed.

"Maybe we can help them with some money, but later," his father said. "Did your mother mention Cathy called? Third time this week. She asked about you, how you were doing. Call her."

Lee's teeth clenched together. Good luck with me doing that, he thought. "Close the door, Dad, would you, when you leave?"

There was a cheap mirror on Lee's bedroom wall; the kind distributors give to bars to advertise their beer. On its left side in black letters, it read Black Label. After one of the local taverns had tossed it in their trash, Lee fished it out and brought it home. His mother was always pressing him to get rid of it.

In its reflection, he peeled the bandage off his forehead. The right side was unblemished, but the other was branded with an inch of stitches. He glanced at the beer logo.

Looking in the mirror, he could see his night-stand where her picture used to be. His teeth clenched and his jaw slid sideways.

He jumped when his father called from the top of the stairs, "Say hi to Tom for me."

Lee gently knocked on the door of his friend's hospital room. When he peeked inside, Tom was sleeping, and his mother was resting in a chair alongside his bed. She smiled when she saw him, put a finger to her lips and motioned him back outside.

Once in the hall, she hugged him and thanked him for coming. She explained that Tom could go home tomorrow afternoon, but that he was tired, and it was best if he did not have visitors. She agreed though when Lee asked, "Can I drive him home tomorrow?"

As he left, she called down the hall, her hand over his heart, "The doctor said he'll be just like new again. They're going to make him a new foot."

Lee frowned.

When he arrived at the hospital the next day, however, he was told Father David had taken Tom home that morning. Later that day when he called the house, he got no answer. Lee tried calling a half dozen times more the rest of June, but each time, when he talked to Mrs. Drew, she said Tom would call him back, but he never did.

At this point, a question began creeping into Lee's head. Was Tom avoiding him, and if so why? More determined than ever to see his friend, Lee called his house and told Mrs. Drew he was coming over.

When Lee approached the Drew house, Father David's old sedan was out front. Mrs. Drew met him on the porch, explaining that no one was home, that Father David had taken Tom to the doctor in his brother's truck. He saw a curtain move at the porch window though, and as he left, he saw Tom's truck around back.

That clenched it for Lee about his friend: Something was definitely wrong. Tom was avoiding him.

The arraignment for the driver who hit Abby was set for mid-July. Neither Tom nor Lee had to be there. Lee reasoned, however, that Tom might attend anyway, whether due to social pressure, guilt over Abby's death or simply Father David's prodding, he wasn't certain. And so, on the chance that he might, Lee felt he needed to be there to confront his friend.

When Lee arrived at the courthouse, Tom was already there, seated up front alongside Father David and his mother.

Lee was shocked at his friend's appearance. Tom had a dark, scraggly beard, long, stringy hair and a haggard look. Besides that, he had lost weight and no longer seemed powerful and confident, not like Lee remembered.

There were not many people in the courtroom. Abby's parents were there, at least he assumed that's who they were. Seated alongside them also was a pretty young girl. Abby's sister, Lee assumed again. All were continually crying, Mrs. Wilson more than her husband and the girl, despite their best efforts to console her. Lee promised himself he would say something to them later.

The arraignment was brief. The defendant's name was called, Lawrence Downey, and a young man, his clothes dark and thread-worn, walked up and stood alone before the black-robed judge. He did not appear to have any legal representation.

Judge Maury Fein was bald but had a low, handsome forehead. He had a solemn demeanor when he charged the defendant with reckless driving, also informing him of the possible penalties should he be found guilty. Evidently he felt the young man was not a flight risk because he did not assign any bail.

As the state's criminal charges were read, the defendant continually wiped his nose to one side with the back of his forefinger. He kept his chin down on his chest and spoke low, and Lee could hardly hear him when he pleaded guilty.

All throughout the proceedings, Lee tried getting Tom's attention, intending to motion for his friend to meet him outside. When he finally caught Tom's eyes though, they were only sunken dark pits that drilled angrily back into Lee's.

The judge set his sentencing date for mid August and it was over.

In the hall outside afterward, Lee waited for Tom. At length, Abby's mother, father and sister came out. The sister had her head on her mother's shoulder. Mrs. Wilson was continually wiping her eyes and her husband had his arm around her. Lee turned away, but not before noticing that Mr. Wilson was wearing a suit, but his shoes were muddy. When Abby's father passed, Lee could smell mothballs.

Eventually, when Tom did not come out, Lee went back inside, but Tom and his party were gone. Evidently, he concluded, they had left by a side door. Hurrying out front to catch him before he drove away, Lee heard someone call his name. He followed the voice to an old truck. There, the face of one of his former baseball coaches was smiling out its window. Lee shook his hand. "Hi coach, what brings you here?"

"A permit," he answered. "Adding a room to the house." He pointed to Lee's shoulder. "Read about it in the paper, your accident. How are you doing?"

Lee nodded. "Thanks for asking."

"I know the other driver," the coach said, "Larry Downey. Good basketball player. Good character too, wouldn't lie. I could see it happening like he said though: dark night, bad weather and blinded by headlights. No one to blame, just an accident."

Lee's mouth twisted to one side. "I gotta be going, coach. Good seeing you."

"Keep in touch," the coach called as he pulled away.

Although Lee was not required to attend the judge's sentencing in mid August, he still wanted to be there, anxious to hear the decision. A couple of days before the judge's ruling, however, Lee came down with the flu. At his son's request, Mr. Jarrett took off work, attended the sentencing and gave Lee the highlights afterward—the state fined the defendant, $500 and suspended his driver's license for one year; the judge also gave him a stern lecture about drinking and driving.

"And that was it?" Lee asked

His father thought a moment and shrugged.

Lee shook his head. My God, Lee thought, he got off easy.

About to leave, his father turned back. "Oh yeah, outside, I ran into a policeman I knew who was at the accident scene. He said the defendant tested below the legal limit for alcohol. Also, he noted the young man could face a civil suit later ... you know, if the Wilsons wanted to."

After his father left, Lee slammed the door to his room and sat down at his desk. He picked up an envelope from his nightstand. It had a Hillsboro State logo. He tossed it in his drawer unopened.

That night he had a wet dream, a disturbing one. He was in Sawyer's Park on the picnic bench again with someone, Abby, he assumed, although he could never make out her face in the dark. It was just him and her though, no Tom. Just like that other black evening though, she was killed the same way when he dropped her off at her house. This time though, before the car hit her, just as she turned to look back toward Lee, like she had done that other fateful evening, it was Pru, not Abby.

When he awakened, he was angry at first he had dreamt about Pru, but on the other hand, he was glad. "Glad," he told himself, "that it was only a dream and she was not hurt, not in real life. He wanted to do that himself, hurt her like she had hurt him."

Lee needed to talk to someone about the accident and Pru...Tom also. But it had to be someone he knew, trusted, and who had counseling experience. Not his parents though, never them. He needed someone he could tell anything to and not be judged.

The next morning when Lee dialed the phone, the voice on the other end answered, "Father David."

CHAPTER TWENTY

Lee walked up to the rectory just as the priest was placing a box in the trunk of his black sedan. "Hey, kid, good morning," Father David said, "glad you called." He was sleepy-eyed. After closing the trunk, he pointed to it. "Supplies for St. Timothy's. I get out there once a month for Sunday Mass. This is my July visit. Hope you haven't forgotten how to be an altar boy." He reached out to shake Lee's hand. "How's the shoulder?" Before Lee could answer, he added, "Sorry I had to make it so early. Busy week, only time I had. You said on the phone you needed to talk. Thought we'd do it as I drive, if that's okay."

The front passenger seatback was laying down flat, its back resting on the edge of the rear seat. Following Lee's eyes, the priest explained. "Broken. Hope you're okay riding in back." He folded his neatly pressed jacket down on the front seat beside him with his communion case over top.

Climbing in the rear on the driver's side, Lee kicked the crumpled paper and trash on the floor aside. One piece had come partially uncrumpled. It was the picture of a beautiful model in a bathing suit.

When Father David returned, he touched a medal over his visor before starting the car. Turning to Lee, he said, "A little St. Christopher never hurts."

Despite the rumors about Father David that he had mentioned to Tom, Lee still considered him the ideal priest, someone with high ideals who could give good spiritual counsel and yet was down to earth. Indeed, the young man's high regard for the priest, prompted him to ask, "Can you answer me something, Father? Why do priests wear black?" He gestured toward the suit on the passenger seat. "You know, with all that black stands for, bad mostly, it makes more sense to wear white ... for goodness. What's with the black?"

Father David smiled. "Well, for one thing," he started to explain, but stopped. Rolling his window halfway down, he beeped his horn and waved to a man walking along the sidewalk. The other man threw his hand up. "Sam Connelly," the priest said, "… doesn't pay to snub the big donors." He paused. "That's a bit cynical, isn't it?" Turning in his seat toward Lee, he asked, "What's up? What was it you called about?"

"I need some advice from someone I know, can trust."

"Welcome to my office," he said, motioning around the car.

"The car accident and that girl who was killed," Lee began, "it's been eating me up—"

The priest talked over him. "The other driver that night, I heard the judge went easy."

"Yeah, considering what he did, he coulda gotten time if the charge was stiffer."

"There was a lot for the judge to consider."

Lee frowned in the car mirror.

"Downey, that was the young man's name. I made some inquiries. Folks said he had good character, never in trouble, nothing serious. Regular churchgoers too, his family, Catholic. Not much money though. The father couldn't work, mine injury, and the son's pumping gas, their main income. Oh yeah, he lost his mother recently too, cancer, and was taking it pretty hard. They said no drunk-driving record, but may have been drinking that night ... 'cause of losing his mother, probably." He paused. "But I'm sure the judge considered all this. A lot more too."

Lee made a dismissive gesture with his hand and drummed his fingers on the priest's seat back.

"Sorry," Father David said, noting his impatience.

"Your brother, did he fill you in on what happened that night, you know, with Abby and the rest?"

"Yeah, tragic," Father David answered, "but walk me through it anyway, your version."

Resting his forehead on his arms on the back of the driver's seat, Lee told the priest his side of that evening with Tom and Abby, ending with, "But I didn't do it with her, Father, I swear." His eyes were unwavering. "Still eating me up, though: A side of me wanted to."

Father David offered no response, but as he drove, he chewed on his lower lip, lingering doubt over Lee's denial about the sex written across his face. Looking over at his coat on the seat beside him, he tried sweeping some dust off with his hand. "Back to your question before, why priests wear black. Maybe it's a reminder that we're flawed too. Priests are just ordinary men underneath all the fancy robes, trying to help others, but searching for answers like everyone else." He stuck a finger down inside his collar and pulled it away from his neck.

Lee mindlessly worried the trash on the floor with the toe of his shoe. "Another thing, Father. You remember Pru, don't you, my old girl?"

"Yeah, a bully young lady."

"Well, me and her, we made promises." Lee then reviewed their history, including the vows of mutual fidelity, the religious differences, the temporary breakup, her suspected infidelity and his evening with Abby to try and get even. He concluded with, "But I still care for her very much, Father. What should I do?"

"Shame, she always seemed like such a nice girl, Pru," he answered, his tone suddenly officious. "But the church feels that, by and large, mixed marriages don't work." He reached for a knob on the dash beside an ash-tray that was filled with cigarette butts. "Care for a little music? Only gets one station, country."

"But Father, love, doesn't that count for something?"

The priest's dark eyes wavered in the mirror. "Takes more than that to make it work, a marriage." He fiddled with the radio a few seconds, but then gave up. "God, your faith, family comes first." He tapped on the steering wheel. "I know it's hard, Lee." He reached back, found Lee's hand and squeezed it. "But maybe it's best if you moved on, both of you."

Barbed wire hemmed the road in on both sides. A few Herefords were trailing along in the field to their right, one behind the other.

Afterward, neither man spoke for several miles.

Finally, Father David broke the silence. "I call driving to these remote parishes my 'Holy-Rolling Circuit.'" Smiling in the mirror, he made a circular motion with his forefinger. "Get it, 'holy roller, holy-rolling?'"

Lee's eyes said he was elsewhere.

"Something else?"

"Yea, your brother," Lee said. "Ever since the accident, he's been ducking me. I've dropped by the house, but all I ever get are excuses. We haven't talked in over two months. Is there something wrong?"

"It's not you. He's been avoiding everyone, me too. Stays in his room most of the time, there or hobbles to the back porch on his one crutch. Just sits there for hours sometimes, staring off into space."

The priest shook his head slowly. "Sad, my brother. Lost all hope, I'm afraid."

"Doesn't sound like him, not the Tom I know. He can be a bit cynical at times and hard-headed, but was never one for throwing in the towel."

"He wasn't always that way, Lee. Before Dad died, Tom was different. Back then, he had it pretty easy, not much responsibility. He did have plenty of idealism though and faith in God."

CHAPTER TWENTY-ONE

Father David was growing increasingly worried about his brother's downhill slide. Following the death of Abby and loss of his foot in June of '50, Tom had remained secluded in the Drew house far into the summer, his depression deepening.

That was why the priest was pleased to see his brother sitting on their back porch that afternoon. "Soaking up a few rays, huh?"

Tom was sitting barefooted in a chair, his chin on his chest. His blue-striped bathrobe was inside out. Leaning against the banister was his crutch. On the floor beside him was one leather work shoe, its laces missing. His hair was long, disheveled and his short beard scraggly. In his hands was a model balsa-wood airplane. He was spinning its propeller, seemingly mesmerized by the whirling blade.

Father David studied his brother momentarily, and then disappeared inside. Shortly, he opened the screen door and stuck his head out. "Has Ma eaten?"

Tom nodded but went on spinning the propeller.

David pressed him further, "Says she's hungry, hasn't eaten."

"She making good sense otherwise?"

The priest waffled his hand.

"Thanks for your trust, brother ... of course, I fed her," Tom answered, his voice raised and irritated. "I'm not that far gone, not yet."

Father David studied his brother pensively. "Sorry ... you're right."

Calming, Tom snickered. "But you're not gonna believe what she did. Get this. She asked if she could fix supper last night, and so I thought, 'What the hell, let her try.' Later, when I heard her messing around in the kitchen, I went in to check and sure enough, she was fixing supper. In a pot on the stove, she was heating three unopened cans of vegetables." He chuckled. "Unopened cans, mind you."

Father David's fingers curled into a tight fist. "What the hell is wrong with you? In case you've forgotten, that lady in there is our mother. She was wiping your butt before you knew your name." He paused. "You keeping up with her meds?"

Tom began crying. He hung his head down like a guilty child. As he did, his bathrobe gapped open. Under it, he was naked. Halfheartedly, he tried covering up. "Christ, I can't even take care of me," he whined, "let alone Ma."

"My God, man," Father David said, "you gotta climb out of this hole. You've been like this for months. I can't handle this alone. Mom needs your help ... so do I."

Tom gave him an inquiring look.

"Forget it," he said, waving his hand dismissively.

Tom looked at the stump of his leg, then at his brother. "You got problems? You got problems? Hell, I got nothing, nothing," he cried, crumpling the little airplane and hurling it into the yard. "Christ, man, where have you been? My life's over."

"Hell Tom, if it's flying, you can still do that."

"Sure, a one-legged Lindberg, that's me." He gave a cynical laugh. "No thanks."

"I'm serious. You can still get a license ... fly private planes."

"Still don't get it, do you? Never did. That's not the real air force," Tom said. "The U.S. Air Force, that's the real one." He looked down at his leg again. "You ever lost a foot? Get back to me when you do and we'll talk."

"You're right," the priest said, putting his hand on his brother's shoulder. "By the way, Cathy Pruitt, Lee's old girl, I saw her downtown the other day. She asked about you."

Tom's eyes narrowed. "What'd she want?"

"Just asked how you were doing, that's all. Hell, maybe she likes you."

"Who are you kidding? Who'd want a cripple?"

Father David's face softened.

"And save that bleeding heart look for your flock," Tom said. "Go save someone else and leave me the hell alone."

The priest waded through his brother's vitriol. "Saw Lee the other day, too."

"And forget about any end runs with him, getting someone else to do your pity work. No Cathy, no Jarrett, got it?"

"What ever happened between Lee and you?"

Tom's eyes fell to his one shoe, and then wandered across the fence to the cemetery. "His day's coming."

The priest's eyebrows lowered.

"Let's just say he's to blame for the mess that night," he said, patting his bad leg, "the whole damn thing."

Just then, a delivery man came around the side of the house with groceries. "Back in a jiffy with the money," the priest said to him.

The delivery man waited until the priest was out of sight before approaching Tom. Taking a bottle of liquor from inside his shirt, he exchanged it for a twenty. "Same order next Friday?" he asked.

Father David did what he could to help his brother climb out of his well of gloom. Once he had a local, one-armed service-veteran come over to their house and try bucking him up, and on numerous occasions, he had advertisements for flying lessons sent to their house. Tom remained resistant to all efforts, however, falling in his well even deeper.

Trying to be upbeat, the priest asked, "Hey pal, is it next week you get your new foot?"

"Maybe, maybe not."

"C'mon, the doc said you could start driving again, once you do."

"What for? So I can go downtown, pick out a street corner and sell pencils?"

"That's baloney. Your old job's waiting for you any time you're ready. Your boss said so."

"Grow up," Tom replied. "What's he gonna do? Fire a one-legged cripple? Bad for business. I'm a pity hire, and everyone knows it."

Nevertheless, Father David showed up at the doctor's office with his brother in tow, two deep furrows in the tile floor from where Tom's heels were dragging. The doctor, however, seemed pleased with the new prosthetic foot, especially the fit.

Tom hated everything about it though, from how it looked to how smelled. "Like nothing human," he described it to the doctor when he first sniffed it.

Most of all though, he hated the noise it made when he tried walking. He said it sounded like a hangman's rope rubbing on a limb, or like it sounded in the movies. The doctor assured him, however, it was new leather and the sound would go away once it was broken in.

Finally, showing his total disdain for the device, Tom left it in the doctor's office when he hobbled out on his one crutch. Apologizing to the doctor, Father David retrieved it and followed his brother to the car.

Father David drove him, or rather dragged him, to his first therapy session at Clarkston, a larger town 25 miles north of Eastbrook. After Tom filled out some forms, his eyes wandered out the office window to a large therapy room. There, one woman, using a bar above her head, was struggling to lift herself up from a wheelchair. She only had one arm.

Another patient, her eyes tearing and face pained, was inching along on prosthetic legs between two parallel bars. Tom looked away.

At the next appointment, as Tom stood waiting for the therapist, he heard a shrill whistle. Looking around, he spied a short, bald man waving to him. The man was leaning against a set of parallel bars with a referee's whistle in his mouth. Its lanyard was attached to a female attendant's neck. It was the coach, his hospital roommate.

Tom hobbled over to him on his crutch, just as the young smiling technician was playfully slapping the coach's hand. "C'mon, Amber," the coach said, "no harm, no foul. Just trying to get my old roomie's attention." He motioned with his head toward her. "This is my new gal. Amber meet Tom."

She had tawny hair and a ready smile.

Tom managed a token smile.

"How's it hanging?" the coach asked.

Amber looked away.

Tom turned his thumb down.

"Got a good one for you, young feller," the coach said.

Tom cocked his head, feigning interest.

"This feller picked himself up a good-looking hooker, you see, and took her up to his hotel room. Then, with his back to her, he started to undress in front of the mirror. Behind him, she starts doing the same: taking off her wig and falsies, removing her teeth and one glass eye and unscrewing her wooden leg.

"All the while, this feller is watching her in the mirror, dumbstruck at the change. You know, the Black Swan story, only ass backward. When she saw him looking at her aghast in the mirror, she straightened, and with her head high, asked proud-like, 'What's wrong? 'You see, she refused to devalue herself and tried to make him see that her missing parts were his problem, not hers."

Slapping his thigh, the coach laughed until he began choking and got red in the face. "Well, sir," the coach went on after he straightened, "this feller up and answers, disgusted but resigned to his declining prospects, 'All right, you know what I want, throw it over here.'"

Amber's cheeks reddened.

"You see, don't you," the coach said, "she had parts of herself missing, but the most important piece, the one she was fighting to hold onto, you couldn't see: her dignity." He motioned to himself. "I'm sort of like her, the hooker. I got chunks missing too." He glanced down at his leg stubs. "But the most important part for me, the one I'm fighting to hold onto, doesn't show either: It's finding courage within myself, the courage to go on, to keep fighting."

With a sweep of his hand, he motioned at the other patients around the room. "All them ... the same boat." He studied the young man for a reaction.

Tom offered only a weak smile.

"I'll give you a for instance," the coach went on. "Every once in a while, one of these folks starts feeling sorry for himself, gets his courage amputated, wants to throw in the towel. But then, he looks around the room and sees someone worse off who's not giving up and commences to working harder himself."

Tom looked away.

The coach patted his prosthetic legs. "Yes sir, one of these days," he spoke toward Tom but his words were aimed at the tech. "I'm gonna get me fitted with two Louisville sluggers instead of these. Then, me and Amber here are gonna go dancing some night when my missus goes to prayer meeting." He leaned close to Amber and whispered. "Run that past your old man, okay?"

She gave a coy smile and blushed again.

CHAPTER TWENTY-TWO

Although Tom eventually was able to replace his crutch with a cane, he was still unhappy with his new foot. Among other things, the hangman's-rope noise he detested before, was replaced by a new sound, a subtle squeaking. This new sound, he found even more distasteful than the old one. Uncertain why, but likely due to the dissatisfaction with his new foot, Tom held onto the crutch, alternating between the cane and it for support.

He began driving again and resumed his old job at the mill in the cutting shop. From the start, however, things did not go well, compounded by the use of his cane. He was having trouble keeping up with the shop demands: supplying lumber, disposing of scrap materials and moving the finished products to the next work space.

Unable to perform his old duties as he once did, he became easily frustrated, and this, in turn, led to several heated exchanges with his boss and co-workers.

For quite some time, Father David had been aware of his brother's drinking problem. In the beginning, he felt certain that if Tom could get over losing his foot, the drinking would stop, but neither one happened.

The priest's efforts to convince him to stop fell on deaf ears, so he talked to the man who delivered their groceries, threatening to have him fired if he brought any more liquor to Tom. That source dried up, but it did not end his brother's drinking.

Undeterred by his brother's efforts to intervene, Tom began driving or taking a cab to bars and liquor stores, having friends and winos purchase a bottle for him. It was on one such trip that he picked up some news about his brother that he suspected but did not wish to hear.

Tom rolled the back window of his taxi down and called to a wino standing in front of the liquor store. When the man came over to the window, Tom asked, "What's your name?"

"Stoney," he answered.

"Get me a bottle?"

"Hey, ain't you Tom Drew?" Stoney asked. "Damn boy, you was some ball player."

"Never mind that," Tom said, waving some bills. "Get one for yourself too."

"Saw you hit back-to-back homers once over at Wilkens," Stony said, weaving unsteadily. "That ump of theirs gave you a little home-cooking, called the first one foul. Foul, my ass, a foot inside the pole. But didn't bother you none. Next pitch, you did the same thing again, only this time put it over the center field fence. That one he couldn't call foul."

"Yeah, yeah," Tom said impatiently. "You want a bottle or not?"

The wino stood up straight, hiking up his pants with his forearms. "Hey, no need to get sore," he slurred, taking the money. He returned momentarily, and stuck his head through the window. "Heard about that," he said, pointing down to Tom's foot. "Damn shame."

"Just give me the bottle." Tom said.

"By the way, how's your brother, Father—"

"Just give me the friggin' bottle."

"You may be brothers, you two," Stoney went on, "but different, different as night and day. He's religious, you're not. He don't drink and ... you were one hell of a ball player, and well, he's..." He waved his hand dismissively and handed Tom the brown bag with his bottle.

As Tom twisted the cap off, the wino continued, his tongue growing thicker. "Shame though about that mess he's gotten himself into, your brother. You know, getting mixed up with that Heinz girl at church. Pretty young thing. Could happen to anybody. Shame, him being a priest and all."

Motioning the driver on, Tom yelled at him, "You're a damn liar."

Stoney's knuckles grew white on the cab's open window. "Hey, you got no right to—"

The wino was still leaning against the cab when it began moving. Even though the cabbie eased away slowly, it spun Stoney full around. He fell awkwardly, dropping his brown bag onto the sidewalk. Looking back, Tom could see the bag was wet; he tipped his own bottle straight up.

When Father David came downstairs a few mornings later, Tom was examining the hometown paper.

"What's new?"

"Just checking the help wanted ads. Looking for some part time help for Ma, like you ordered, sir." He gave a mock salute.

"Never mind," Father David said, "Forgot to mention. I found someone."

"Thanks for the heads up," Tom answered, his tone sarcastic.

"Have to run now. I'm saying mass this morning. By the way, she's dropping by later, Ma's help. Name's Joyce, Joyce Heinz. Be nice."

"Heinz, Joyce Heinz, that name's familiar," Tom said, tweaking his brother. "Say, isn't that your little playmate at church?"

Father David's mouth puckered. He pointed to his brother's open bathrobe. "Wouldn't hurt if you put some clothes on, shaved too."

An hour or so after his brother left, Tom heard a knock at their front door. When he opened it, there stood a tall, young woman with a good build, high cheekbones and an arresting smile. "Joyce, Joyce Heinz," she said, holding her hand out. "You must be Tom." Keeping both hands in his pockets, he turned and walked back in the house, leaving her standing at the open doorway.

Later that same day after work, Tom had just opened his truck door when he heard a voice behind him.

It was Jim Powell, the man who filled in for Tom during his absence. "Heard you got shipped back to delivery." he said, patting him on the shoulder.

"His mill, Mr. Welles, his rules."

"The ol' man called me in today," Jim said, "Gave me your old job in the cutting room. Hope there's no hard feelings. You know, the pay cut."

Not answering, Tom slid under the steering wheel.

"Just temporary though, I'm sure," Jim said.

Tom glanced down at the other man's feet.

Late that same evening after work, instead of going home as usual, Tom drove to Sawyer's Park. Why he went there, he wasn't quite certain. He parked just down the dirt road from the giant Sawyer's Oak. Both the park and the oak were named after one of the first families to settle the Eastbrook region. It was drizzling rain and twilight was fading. The skeleton of the leafless tree was stenciled in black. Pulling a fresh bottle of liquor from under his seat, he tossed the cap out the window and took several long pulls.

He pounded the dash with the butt of his fist, and when he did, the cigarette lighter jumped out and fell onto the floor. Picking it up, he pushed the lighter back in, activating it. When it popped out, he studied its glowing end for several seconds, seemingly fascinated by its orange coils.

Sometime later, after downing the last of the liquor, he started up his truck. The dark, massive trunk of Sawyer's Oak was in his headlights. In the dark night, its leafless boughs looked like some giant ogre reaching out for him.

He braced himself and gripped the steering wheel. Gunning the engine, he slammed the truck head on into the tree.

Later when he awoke, it was pitch black and he was sober. He was okay though, except for a bump on his forehead and a few minor bruises. His front bumper and grill were dented though. Later, he lied to his brother about the damage, blaming it on an accident he had on a rain-slick road. Although Father David did not press his brother on the matter, he didn't believe him.

A few days later, after entering the Drew home and kissing his mother on top the head, Father David motioned for his brother to follow him to the dining room. Once there, the priest asked, "Everything seems better, don't you think, Ma, the house?" He pointed to his brother. "Come to think of it, so do you."

Tom returned a sour look.

"So what do you think about Joyce?"

Tom giggled. "Nice tailgate."

Father David's eyes snapped over toward his brother. "What the hell is wrong with you? The job, smart aleck, the job she's doing."

"So-so, I guess."

"She said you didn't like her," the priest said, glancing toward the stairs. "Look, we need someone full time for Ma. I'm going to clear out that extra room upstairs so Joyce can move in, help take care of Ma."

"She's moving in here with us, huh, just like that?"

"She needs a place and it'll cut our costs. Only way we can afford full-time help."

"Who are you trying to fool? We both know where this is headed: You moving in also and you two playing house. She may be in a room upstairs, but you've got something else in mind ... something downstairs." He nodded toward priest's groin.

Father David's jaw line hardened. "After some of the stuff you're pulled, where do you get off lecturing me?"

"And how do you think Father Moore will feel about this cozy, little setup you have in mind, you and her? My God, are you trying to get tossed out of the church, is that it? And say, isn't there something in your Bible about not serving two masters? Which is it going to be?"

Father David was slow in answering: "I don't know."

"My God, man, you don't know? You don't know? You're a priest, end of story. Are you forgetting your vows?" he asked, thumbing up. "We both know I'm going to hell, but you? Then there's Dad. Are you going to break your promise to him too? You know, about being a priest?"

"It's not enough the town, my church are making me and Joyce feel like lepers. You too, huh?"

"Now you know how it feels, brother," Tom said, holding his hand out as if to shake the priest's. "Welcome to my world."

The priest slapped it away, "Are you crazy?"

Later upstairs, Father David found the key to their extra room in the dim hall light. He hesitated momentarily when he saw the bottle opener from his father's old bar next to it on the key ring. After unlocking the door, he began moving the stacked furniture. Once when he stopped, he could see the cross on the steeple at St. Peter's out the lone window. It was higher than anything else in Eastbrook. With his handkerchief, he dusted off the seat of a rocker in the corner and sat down. He rocked gently back and forth for several minutes. Finally, he locked the room back up and without saying anything to his brother, drove back to the rectory.

CHAPTER TWENTY-THREE

Despite Father David's warning not to visit his brother without his go-ahead, Lee watched as Father David and Mrs. Drew drove away from their house. When they passed, he slid down in the seat of his father's car.

In a maple tree overhead, an August locust was pulsing its raspy chant.

As he walked up the yard to the Drew house, he passed some of the priest's white collars drying on a clothesline. When he rounded the back corner of their house, he did not recognize Tom at first. It was not the face he remembered. Nursing a drink, Tom was sitting alone in a chair at the far end of the porch. He was staring over the fence at the cemetery next to their house. Beside him on the floor, was a half empty bottle of whiskey and one leather work shoe. Curiously, Lee thought at the time, the shoelace seemed too long. Also, like at the trial, Tom's beard and hair were long and unkempt. Leaning against the banister nearby were both a cane and a crutch. His good foot was bare and on the floor, but the leg of his amputated foot was resting on the seat of an armless chair in front of him.

Lee was stunned. For the first time, the truth of his friend's loss hit him. There was a smooth flap of skin pulled over the stump of his leg just below his calf. It looked like the end of a large pink, hairy grub. Lee looked skyward, half turning to leave, but then, setting his jaw, he turned back. "Hey, T.D.," he called, trying to sound casual.

Tom's head spun toward the voice. "Well, look who it is," he sneered, "Mr. Perfect himself."

Lee felt his jaw slide to one slide. As he walked toward the porch, his eyes caught the handle of his hiking staff sticking out of a trashcan. Pulling it out and walking over to the bottom of the porch steps, he held it up toward his friend. "Dag, what the hell?"

The other man eyed him suspiciously. "What do you want?"

"Hell of a question to ask your best friend. I called a dozen times. Why are you dodging me?"

Tom sat motionless, staring at Lee with those dark pits.

"Thought I'd drop by and see how you're doing. See if I could help." Lee's eyes were drawn again to the other man's leg.

Tom took his leg down from the chair. "Don't need your help, or any of your damned pity." He poured himself three fingers of whiskey and set the glass on his chair arm.

Lee patted his own left shoulder. "Don't know whether they told you or not, but I got hurt too, the car accident. Baseball may be over for me, college too."

Smirking, Tom downed his drink. As he started to get up though, he knocked his empty glass off the chair arm, and it shattered on the floor. "Ahh, shit."

"That's okay," Lee said from the bottom of the porch steps. "Where's your broom?"

Tom's angry eyes jumped over at him and he stood up.

"Jeez, just trying to help, T.D. Why are you sore at me?"

The other man didn't answer.

Still at the bottom of the steps, Lee glanced at his staff. "Hey, remember that time on the Tree we got hammered and danced naked after that rainstorm." He chuckled. "Them were good old times."

Tom's dark mood didn't lighten. "You've got a lot of nerve, Jarrett, coming over here." As he started to swing on his crutches toward Lee, his bare foot landed on some broken glass. "Son of a bitch," he yelled. Sitting back down, he began nursing the slivers from his foot, occasionally glowering at Lee. Pulling on his unlaced shoe, he hobbled to the top of the porch steps, glass shards crunching under his treads. Holding Lee with a fierce gaze, he touched his watch.

Lee's eyes wavered. "I feel bad about that girl, Abby. You know, what we did, missing her funeral."

"What do you want from me, a get-out-of-jail card? In case you haven't noticed, dear friend," he said sarcastically, "my life's over."

"You're not the only one, T.D. I lost a lot too," he said, patting his shoulder.

"But this whole mess," he yelled, stabbing his finger at Lee, "my foot, the dead girl, that's all on you."

Lee was stunned. "So, that's why you're pissed? You're blaming me for that night? Hold on, buddy. You had a part too. Doing her was your idea in the first place, remember?"

"You still don't get it, do you?" Tom asked, his words beginning to slur. "It was to help you, that whole damn evening was for you ... to get your mind off her, your old girl."

Lee's knuckles whitened on the staff.

"And oh yeah, about her, your old girl" Tom said. "Seems I made a mistake there."

The other man's lips tightened across his teeth.

"Turns out it was Tracey Smith with Kenny Harte that night in the park, not Cathy." A smirk spread across his face.

Lee scowled. "Then why'd you say it was her, Pru?"

"So I was wrong. What's the big deal?"

Lee felt the back of his neck and ears grow hot.

Tom explained further, but his voice had a cavalier edge. "I did think it was her at first. They look alike, her and Tracey. Everyone says so. Anyway, a few weeks after the accident, I heard Kenny bragging about doing Tracey around that same time and on a bench in Sawyer's Park."

"I still don't get it. Why didn't you tell me when you found out? I thought we were friends."

"What's the difference? It was dead between you two anyway, just needed burying."

Lee jabbed an angry finger at him. "Fact is, you knew the truth, but left me thinking it was Pru." He studied the other man skeptically. "Question is, are you lying now, trying to set me up once more, telling me it wasn't her, hoping it'll tear me up inside again, 'cause I broke my vow for nothing?"

"Believe what the hell you want."

Lee banged his staff down hard. "Dammit, I don't believe you. It was Pru that night, wasn't it? It was her you saw in the park. Say it, say it."

"Lee, Lee pumpkin eater," Tom sing-songed, "had a girl and couldn't—"

"That is it, isn't it? You're lying again to get even..." He nodded toward the other man's bad foot.

"Say it, say it," Tom said, his voice dripping with anger. "For being a cripple, right?" His eyes lazered down at the other man and something seemed to snap inside him. "Screw you, Jarrett," he cried, spittle showering Lee's face. He kicked at Lee's head with his good leg. The other man easily ducked out of the way and Tom's shoe flew off and into the yard.

Lee's eyes flashed. "You son of a bitch."

A sickening pallor washed over Tom's face. He curled his lip and slid his watch off. Uttering an animal like growl and swinging on his crutch, he pole-vaulted off the porch down onto Lee.

In the blur of that instant, just before his body crashed full force down on Lee, Tom's blue striped robe flew open and Lee saw he was totally naked. The blow slammed Lee to the ground on his back, knocking the wind out of him and pinning him there with both arms over his head. He felt like a bulldozer had landed on him, an angry, living machine that had hammered some vital life force from his body.

The leather shoe Tom had kicked at Lee was lying near the two men. Grabbing it, Tom began pushing its glass studded treads down into Lee's face.

Lee tried pushing back with his good arm, but the glass sliced his palm and blood began dripping into his eyes. Nor could he ward off the jagged shards as they came closer to his face, although he was straining with every muscle and sinew to do so. He was helpless, pinned there by the crushing weight of the stronger man. When the sharp crystals first sliced his nose and brushed his eyelashes, he snapped his face to the side, Tom's pressure pinning the back of Lee's right hand to his cheek. There, beside him on the ground was his wading staff.

Tom's crazed eyes, only inches from Lee's, seemed not to notice.

Mustering all his strength, Lee inched his bad arm over until he felt the staff, then slid it closer. Surprised by the movement, Tom looked over and for an instant, his pressure relaxed. When it did, Lee grabbed the staff with both hands and began pushing it up into the other man's throat.

Although the shoe pressure lessened, the other man's breath still blew hot in Lee's face. Suddenly, Tom changed tactics. Grabbing the shoe's leather lace with both hands, he snapped it down tightly over Lee's throat.

Lee's blood smeared staff was sticky, and although bowing severely, did not break.

Both men lay there sweating and breathing heavily, one pushing up with all his strength, the other down, each man trying to choke the other.

At last, after several seconds of straining, Lee's bad shoulder began to weaken, and the rawhide grew tighter against his throat. His eyes widened, and straining to draw each breath, he could hear raspy breathing, his own he realized. Suddenly, his air was cut off completely and he began thrashing wildly from side to side.

About to lose consciousness, he heard a woman scream, and suddenly, Tom's smothering weight rolled off of him. Gasping for air, he looked up into Father David's face.

"Stay out of this," Tom yelled at the priest, as he tried regaining leverage with his good leg.

Picking up his brother's crutch, Father David stepped between the two men. "That's enough," he shouted at Tom. "Cover yourself up," he added, pointing to his brother's private parts and his mother nearby. Helping him up, he tried steering Tom toward the house.

Lee sat on the ground, trying to regain his senses.

On the porch, Tom, barefooted but oblivious to the broken glass, broke free from his brother once and started back toward Lee. Father David corralled him again and wrestled him toward the front door. Just before the priest could herd him through it though, Tom managed to bellow, "I'm gonna kill you, Jarrett. Keep looking over your shoulder. Someday, I'm gonna be there."

"Next time, I'll be ready," Lee yelled back. Standing up, he brushed himself off and tested his left shoulder.

A few minutes later, Father David returned, carrying his brother's crutch. Lee could still hear the other man raging inside the house. Father David laid his hand softly on his mother's shoulder, and thumbed for Lee to go.

When Lee was half way back to the car, Father David caught up. "Ma forgot her shopping list. That's why we came back early. Lucky for you."

Pointing to Lee's cut face, he said, "Better tend to those, you might need stitches."

"But I don't get it. Why's he blaming me?"

"Sorry, Lee," he said. "He feels like he's got the Indian Sign on him, the whole world's against him. Not thinking straight."

When Lee looked in the car's mirror, his face was blood streaked. Spitting on a rag, he tried wiping it off. The damage wasn't as bad as he first imagined. There were some small cuts on his cheek and a deep one on his nose.

His right hand was a different matter. His palm was oozing bright red blood from three deep gashes. He wrapped the rag around his hand.

His neck was smarting too. In the mirror he could see a red welt around his throat, raw and beginning to swell.

He tried wiping the blood from the handle of his staff, but it only smeared bright rust. Glancing at the Drew house as he drove away, his knuckles whitened on the steering wheel. What a snake, he thought.

CHAPTER TWENTY-FOUR

Granddad stepped out of his old Ford pickup onto the rutted dirt road. "Thanks for tagging along, boy."

"Thanks for asking," Lee answered, his mouth a straight-line smile.

"Everything hunky dory?"

His grandson didn't answer.

Granddad looked at the dog lying on a blanket in the bed of the truck. "Dan's thanking you too." He pointed to the dog's tail drumming on the floor of the truck bed. "That guy's never happier than when he's hunting. Season will be here before you know it, and Dan needs the work. It'll feel good not toting a shotgun. Hot, muggy for September."

The dog jumped to his feet, stretched, cocked his head to the right, the way he did only for granddad, and searched the old man's face.

Lee looked up at the tall mountain across the wide field from the dirt road. The field was choked with wheat-colored sage and briars. There was a small, willow-lined stream wandering through the middle of the field. "What's this place called?"

"Belongs to a family named May," his grandfather answered. "Kinfolk of yours way back. Homesteaded here around the late 1800s. Folks said every spring when they plowed, they'd dig up old muskets and such from the Civil War." He pointed to the mountain towering over them. "That big boy there is May's Mountain."

The young man looked up at it. "Heard you talk about it, but never been here."

"You wasn't ready, neither was I."

A red bird called from a thicket, and his grandfather studied the gray clouds to the west.

Lee followed where the old man was looking. "What do you think?"

"Could rain, but it's the only day we got." He called Dan's name, slapped his leg and pointed to the field nearby. The dog padded along after him, the metal buckle on his dog collar sounding like a dull sleigh bell. As his grandfather climbed the rail fence bordering the field, he caught Lee's eyes and motioned for him to follow.

The young man caught up just as they were about to cross a brook. Its cold water was almost up to their groins. They waded around two oak logs submerged midstream, their trunks parallel to the flow.

"Dad said you used to be a good swimmer."

"Like a fish, boy, when I was your age."

"Them ribbons in your room for that?"

"Won most trying to impress the girls," he answered, chuckling and shaking his head. "They can sure tie a knot in a fellow's tail sometimes."

On the far bank, there were mink tracks in the sand. Bending over, the old man pointed to them. "That guy's missing a toe. More'n likely lost it in a fight over some gal. Won't stop him from fighting again though, or loving."

He pointed to the stream they just crossed. "Folks call that little fellow May's Creek.

"Of course, it ain't your Eden Brook, but still lots of secrets in its sweet music. Can teach you a lot about life." He bent over and cocked an ear toward the waters. "Hear it?"

His grandson gave him a skeptical look.

"But you gotta listen with more than your ears."

Dan started up the hill until his grandfather whistled him back and pointed toward another part of the field.

The dog, nose to the ground, began working back and forth.

Behind him, the two men began working the field, about 30 feet or so apart, kicking and beating the brush as they went.

"Keep your eyes peeled for copperheads," his grandfather cautioned. "Doubt it, but a fellow never knows. Might be a couple not holed up yet."

Lee glanced at the scars on his palm. Snakes again, he thought, great.

"I saw your face a ways back. Shaving with a lawnmower now?"

He glanced at the old man wryly. "Aw, Tom and me got in a fight, a bad one. He worked me over pretty good, like a sidewalk fell on me. Might have hurt me worse if it hadn't been for your staff. It's all smeared with blood now, mine."

"Still okay for rambling, ain't it ... hell's fire, son, that's the good stuff," he said, pointing to his own face, "them battle scars. They call it character nowadays." Gesturing to Lee's face, he asked, "Your parents, what'd you tell them?"

"Fell off my bike."

"Trying to duck one of your Dad's sermons?"

Lee's eyes were amused.

A rabbit suddenly darted out between them. Granddad whistled for the dog, pointed to the ground, and then trailed his hand along in the direction the rabbit had gone.

Dan studied Lee's grandfather, but would not come to where he was pointing. Instead, he began making a wide circle around the same area, his nose inspecting the ground.

Granddad shook his head. "Damn dog's like a cat, mind of his own. He knows we jumped one where I'm pointing, but he's got to find it himself. It's gotta be his idea."

Finally, the beagle struck the scent, straightened it out and began baying hot on the trail.

They both listened, smiling at the dog's voice, hoarse at times.

The old man smiled. "Sounds like he's been smoking again."

As Dan's music faded, Lee mindlessly traced circles in the dirt with his shoe.

Noticing, his grandfather asked, "Something gnawing on you?"

"Like I told you, Pru did something awful bad, something I can't get past. She'll be sorry though."

The old man pointed at his grandson's head. "Sounds like you've got some bad critters tromping around topside."

"Bad critters?"

"Yeah, some 'get even' ones. Bad idea, listening to them. They're all about 'me first.'"

"But if something's wrong, Granddad, it's wrong."

"Careful of your discards, son, throwing kings and queens away for aces."

"What's that mean?"

"Don't be tossing good folks in your deadwood for perfect ones."

The old man was always trying to do that: get his grandson to be content with the appaloosa he was riding on a carousel, rather than lusting after the pretty white horse just up ahead.

For a short moment, Lee considered his grandfather's words. "You're sounding just like her now, Pru."

The old man eyed him.

"Her father ran off years ago, but before he left, he filled her head with a lot of crazy notions. Anyway, he was a different kind of fellow, kind of Bahamian."

"Bohemian," the old man corrected.

"Anyway, I don't think he believed in God or any of that, an agno-agnos, something like that."

"Never mind, I got it."

The ends of Lee's mouth carved down.

"Don't be too hard on your mother, boy. Look at her side. I'm certain she had dreams once herself—college maybe, a career and a family when she was ready. I imagine she made vows too, promises upstairs," he said, nodding skyward. "But then, she fell in love, you was inside her and she lost her chance for all that, except the family part. Probably left her with a lot of regrets too, maybe guilt." He paused. "She doesn't want you making the same mistakes."

The old man took his dut hat off and looked at it, like he was seeing it for the first time. "So this is Pru's favorite, huh?"

Lee nodded.

He rubbed his fingers gently back and forth over its felt. "I'll leave it to her in my will."

A cricket began chirping under their log. The old man turned his ear toward it and listened. "They tell you when it's getting late in the day," he said. He put his hand on his lower back, arched his body and winced. "I'll be headin' there now," he said, pointing up the mountain. Motioning for Lee to follow, he started climbing. "Fetch Dan," he called back over his shoulder.

CHAPTER TWENTY-FIVE

Grabbing the dog by the collar, Lee began climbing steadily in the direction his grandfather had gestured. Over the better part of an hour, climbing all the while, he called the old man's name repeatedly, but got no response. At last, breathless, he broke through the trees into a clearing near the top. There, a wide valley opened up to the south. Hills fell away on each side, and in the far distance were the faint tops of the taller buildings in Eastbrook.

Off to his right, in a small meadow below him, was his grandfather. He appeared to be searching for something in the tall grass. Finally, he stopped and began stomping the weeds down in a small circle. He then knelt and began wrestling with a heavy stone, square on one end and round on the other. Finally he was able to tip it up on end. Pulling a handful of weeds, and using it like a broom, he began brushing the stone clean.

When Lee got closer, he recognized it was a grave marker. Walking up beside his grandfather, he looked down at the inscription chiseled in the face—A. J., June 1877 - August 1898. "Who's buried there?"

The old man studied him for a long moment. "High time you learned some family history. Your parents ain't gonna tell you."

"My wife, my first wife," the old man explained. "Not the one you knew, not your grandmother."

"Never knew that, Granddad. I thought grandma was the only wife you ever had. Any kids?"

His grandfather shook his head no.

"What was her name?"

The old man was silent for so long, Lee was certain he had not heard the question. "Uhh, Anne," he answered finally. "I called her Annie." He got down on his knees again and began clearing her gravesite, gently pulling weeds, removing stones and leveling the ground in front of the tombstone.

Lee joined in and Dan, certain it was all a game, began digging too. Grandfather stopped him though with a word and stern look. The dog, possibly hurt by the rejection but more likely bored, bounded off in search of some better adventure.

Lee and Granddad sat down in the tall grass next to her grave.

The wind suddenly gusted around their backs and down the valley. Granddad stared for a long moment after it and then glanced back at the tombstone. "My folks lived way out in the sticks," he began. "Things seemed all wrong for them in the village and just right way out where they were. They always seemed happy, never sick much, old too when they died.

"Of course, it makes some folks nervous, others being different, not following the herd. Makes them feel better if they can call you names, like odd, funny or strange.

"Annie and me just wanted to have a life like my folks did. Simple, peaceful, by ourselves, just living in one another's company. And we had it too, for a spell."

Lee glanced at the tombstone again. "How long were you married?"

A church bell pealed faintly in the distance.

"It's ringing too fast for a funeral," Granddad said. "More than likely a wedding." He studied his grandson. "Her and me, we were never hitched, official like you're asking. Never felt the need to. Of course, folks down in the village thought we were living in sin. But we loved one another and didn't see it that way. We were married all the same, boy, just not like you're asking.

"Anyway, we done that, built our house way out on the edge of nowhere."

"Where was this, Granddad, on the Burnt Tree? Was that where this happened?"

The old man studied his grandson. "Let's just say it was a far-off piece, boy, and leave it at that.

"Well, like I was saying, we was happy as pigs in slop for around three years, I reckon, just living way out there by our lonesome." His lip curled slightly. "That is, except for one strange fellow the next hollow over."

Lee didn't question him this time.

"That bird lived just a few miles from us in a one room, log cabin with a sod roof. He believed in herbs, spells and such. Hardly ever shaved or cut his hair. He was a big fellow, a woolly looking cuss, even for them parts. Living way out there that way, he had no one, so we tried being neighborly. Least ways, as much as he'd let us. Like I said though, he was an odd sort, even by back woods ways. He had a tender spot for animals though, birds too. He would leave scraps out and tend to them if they were ailing. He lived mostly on what he raised, we gave him or he killed.

"What was his name, Granddad?"

"John, that's what I called him. He did have a last name, and folks thereabout often called him by it." He stroked his chin. "I can't recollect what it was though. Only name I ever used was John. Wife called him Johnny.

"Claimed he was a doctor once in some big city back East. He said that before he came to the mountains, he had big dreams about serving God and curing the world, but then his own wife up and got sick and he couldn't even save her. They had one youngster, a boy, I think. Left him back east with her kinfolk.

"That John sure doted on my Annie though. Said she reminded him of his dead wife. He even brought her flowers every so often. Couldn't blame him much though. Pretty as a day in spring, Annie was. She had big brown eyes and was gentle as a fawn. He liked for her to read po-etry to him. Keats, I think. We had a book of his poems. It was bound with a brass, snap lock. She kept it on a shelf in our bedroom alongside some other books. Her reading seemed to calm him, gentle him some. I'd see him sneak peeks at her ever so often, kind of moony-eyed, when he thought I wasn't looking. We always figured he was harmless though." Pursing his lips, he shook his head. "Hell, how's a fellow to know what's in another's heart?"

The old man tilted his head up and sniffed the air. "Wood smoke, honey to this old snout. A bit early, but some folks are probably making apple butter." Looking at Lee, he asked, "Where was I?"

"You and Annie were living by yourselves out in the middle of no-where, except for this weird guy named John."

"Well, for three years," his grandfather said, picking up with his story again, "we had it all, her and me. Crazy in love and everything we needed just out our door."

"What was she like," Lee asked, "your Annie?"

The old man chuckled. "She had an impish funny bone. I remember once, she churned some butter. Ants got to it, but she ate it anyway. Got me to doing the same. We'd spread it on our bread, wolf it down with some wild cherry jam and giggle like fools.

"Other times, in the evening she'd dress up in my oversized coat, with knee high boots and a wide-brimmed hat that came down around her ears. Then she'd light a lantern, go out the back, walk around and bang on our big, brass door-knocker, like doomsday had come. Of course, I'd play along and act surprised when I opened the door. Then, half the next day, we'd giggle like fools every time we spied one another."

His grandfather took an apple from his vest and drew out his hunting knife.

He always called the big knife Stella. It was long and thick bladed with elk horn handles and a silver butt cap with the letter "J." The blade ended with a mean-looking, turned-up point. Its cutting edge was slightly curved in, worn that way, Lee assumed, from half a century of cutting and honing. Why he called it Stella, Lee never knew and was reluctant to ask. The name seemed right though, exciting, mysterious and yet dangerous, the way some women could be, at least in the movies.

Lee was always fascinated with the blade, both its frightening appearance and the dexterity with which his grandfather used it, like an extension of his hand.

The old man cut the apple in two and tossed his grandson half.

Lee bit into his. The corners of his mouth bent down and he spit it out. "Yuk," he said, hacking to clear his throat of its taste.

Seeing his reaction, the old man bit into his, then coughed it out too. He pitched the rest down the hill and motioned for Lee to do the same.

Granddad looked back at the grave. "Then she up and died." he said abruptly.

"What do you think happens when we die, Granddad?"

The old man studied him. "Remember them downed trees back on May's Brook, the ones in the water and how their trunks were all pointing downriver? I read once that's where everything's home was once, the sea, every living thing, trees too. Guess that's where they're pointing now, them trees, back toward home, same place we're all headed someday.

"I know it ain't the answer you're looking for, but it's the best I got right now. Least ways, till I get more news from the other side."

"How'd it happen, Granddad? How'd she die?"

"She went off smiling one sunny day in late August riding our old plow-horse, Savior Boy." he answered. "Off to gather a couple pails of blackberries from the next valley over, Sweet Springs, like she'd done dozens of times before.

"Lots of shade in that country. Big berries like that, shade, you know. We had a name for them, those big, fat, long ones. Called 'em sheep tits.

"She took along a bite to eat and some fresh water, but ran short and drank from a spring over that way. Told her never to do that, but it was a hot day and she was thirsty. I guess the water was bad 'cause a few days later, she came down with the fever.

"I decided to go for help over the mountains, and asked him, that fellow John, to keep an eye on her till I got back." His black eyes hardened like wet pebbles. "No sir, never should have trusted him."

"Anyway, riding hard day and night, it took me the better part of two days to make it to the nearest village. Lost the trail twice in the dark, that didn't help none. But the doc in town couldn't come back with me, fever epidemic there too. He gave me some medicine to take back."

The old man put his hand on his lower back and made a face.

"Arthritis?" Lee asked.

"Time I got back home, it was too late. I found our cabin burned to the ground with them two inside, both dead, shot in the head."

"Where'd all this happen, Granddad, around here?"

"Ain't important to the tale, boy."

"The reason I asked, your story sounds a lot like that restaurant guy's on Spruce Mountain. Remember me telling you about that once? That wild tale about Crazy Dan and how the Burnt Tree got its name."

"That was a nonsense tale, boy. This one's real."

"When they found them, what room were they in, Annie and the other fellow?"

"Bedroom, of course. Stood to reason. She was in bed sick and he was supposed to be watching her." He thought a moment. "My own damn fault.

"Pieced things together as best I could. Out of her head with fever, she must have gotten hold of my pistol somehow. I had it hid on a shelf in the bedroom behind some books. I found the scorched snap-lock of the Keats's book alongside the bedsprings. No sign of my pistol though. Buried in the ashes, most likely.

"Perhaps he was reading poetry to her, but had to leave for a short spell, maybe to relieve himself or get a drink. Hell, who knows, he could've just dozed off. Anyway, after he left or fell asleep, she must have snuck out of bed, found my gun, shot him dead, accidentally knocked over the lamp and turned the gun on herself."

"Where, where in the bedroom did you find them?"

He stopped and shot his grandson an annoyed look. "Where you headed with these bedroom question?"

Lee answered, trying to avoid his stare. "I was just wondering, that's all, wondering if things could have happened differently. You know, since you weren't there."

Granddad's dark eyes melted into hot tar.

Feigning interest in the burrs on his pants, Lee began picking at them.

From the right hip, the old man drew his big knife. Close in Lee's face, he poked the young man's chest hard with his finger and snarled. "It happened the way I said, boy. I was there and you wasn't. I seen it with my own two eyes. Besides, it was the only thing that made sense, what I told you." Granddad's spittle landed on his cheek.

Feeling his throat tighten, the young man leaned back and wiped his face. It was the first time he had ever seen his grandfather's eyes like that: fierce, like those of a big cat, an big, angry cat.

The drumming wings of a grouse nearby broke the tension. They beat slowly at first, then faster and faster. Lee had heard it before. To him, it always sounded like a basketball had been dropped from up high onto a wooden floor and left bouncing there.

The old man's face softened, and holding his breath, he listened to the drumming. "Frost on the pumpkins soon. That ol' boy's advertising for a pretty feathered gal to keep him warm this winter.

"Now hold still," he said to Lee. Using his big knife, he gently scraped the burrs off his grandson's jeans. Both were silent as he did so.

His grandfather stared up the ridge to where sunlight was dappling on the forest floor. "To wind things up, when I got back, it was all gone, gone forever, my darling and along with her, our sweet life together. She was the one true thing every fellow looks for in life, but most seldom find."

A strong breeze whipped around their backs and down the valley. Granddad stared after it, like his memories were blowing away along with it. "But I did," he added. "I found that one true thing." He spit on the ground. "No sir, my own damn fault for trusting him."

"Because he didn't keep an eye on her, that fellow, John?" Lee asked. "Is that why?"

The old man's eyes narrowed and for a long moment he studied his grandson skeptically. Indeed, it was for so long that Lee feared another angry outburst might be forthcoming. At last, however, he ended Lee's suspense. "What else?" he asked.

Eager to drop the subject now, Lee answered, "Just wondering, that's all,"

"Anyway, long story short," his grandfather continued, "I carted her up here later and buried her so she'd be close and I could visit." He stole a furtive glance at his grandson.

"Wow," Lee said, "that's some story, Granddad."

"Later, I got hitched to your grandmother, the one you knew. Lost her too in '43, but you was around for that. Of course, if Annie hadn't died, you'd never have come along," He slapped the young man playfully on his shoulder. "Not often I get someone captive up here who's gotta listen to my nonsense. Did I mention she couldn't have children, Annie?"

Lee shook his head.

Granddad crawled on his hands and knees to the edge of the clearing around the gravestone. There, among the weeds, a few hardy, yellow and white wild flowers were blooming. He pulled several, crawled back to her grave and laid them near the head. "She always liked them best, daisies." Dan began pawing at the old man's boots.

"Go on, ol' boy," his grandfather said, motioning him away. "Better hunt while you can. Winter's just over them mountains."

Rolling over, he used a sapling to help himself up.

CHAPTER TWENTY-SIX

As they turned to go, his grandson looked back at the dates on the gravestone. "She died young too," he said, "around my age." Continuing to stare at the stone but no longer seeing it, he thought for a long moment. "What's wrong with me, Granddad?"

The old man frowned.

"Girls, that's what it is. All I can think of anymore is girls. Every few minutes, girls, girls. That's what was on my mind too that night of the car accident." He pressed his hands to both sides of his head. "Can't get 'em out of here."

"And Pru?"

Lee thought. "Yeah, I think about her that way sometimes too, but I used to feel ashamed when I did."

"And now?"

He didn't answer. "Real girls, make believe girls, it doesn't matter. I find myself checking them out in magazines, underwear sections of catalogues, even cartoon girls in comic books." He turned away. "Don't laugh, but is it true what those ads claim in the back of magazines, you know, about being able to hypnotize 'em?"

With the last question, the old man trapped a smile.

"Some folks say that's dirty," Lee said, "having those thoughts."

The old man's eyes danced. "Aye God, boy, you take the cake." He chuckled through his words. "Hell's fire, we're all a bit crazy when it comes to them pretties." He put his hand on his grandson's shoulder. "Every young feller does that, paints pictures in his head about girls. When I was your age, I was hound-dogging everything in a skirt. Hell, just thinking about them used to make my tongue hang out a foot. Tell you this much. They can't rock us fellers for having 'em thoughts. If they could, we'd all have a bushel of knots on our noggins."

"But is it wrong, Granddad? You know, thinking about girls that way, doing things with them, to them?"

"Say, did I ever tell you about me and the Widow Taylor?"

Not the answer Lee wanted, he shrugged indifferently.

"Bear with me, son." The old man scratched his right temple. "It happened in church, right here in Eastbrook. Now don't get the wrong notion. I was never one for following the holy herd, but this one Sunday I was there, sitting back of the Widow Taylor. A fine looking woman she was, too. A little mileage on her tires, but she still had her figure. Anyway, when she was kneeling, I could see her skirt was trapped in her tailgate. I even remember the dress she was wearing, like it was yesterday. A flowered print, yellow and white.

"Lordie, she had a perfect fanny too. It poked out just right, like a fine West Virginny hill, good to look at but hard to climb. Well hell, what am I telling you this for? Every feller, from diapers to dirt, knows what I mean. Let's just say her behind was worthy of several hallelujahs and leave it at that.

"All through the service, all I could think of was reaching down and gently coaxing that skirt out for her. For me too, I guess. I tried pushing the idea away, but no matter how hard I tried, it kept dogging me. Whether the reverend was droning away up there on the altar or they were passing the exhortation basket around, that's all I could think of, freeing that pretty flowered print so it could brush any part of her hind quarters it had a mind to. I couldn't get it out of my head. I thought about it all through the hymn singing too.

"Do you remember me telling you once, Lee, about those little conscience-critters, the ones that are always ready to spoil a body's fun?"

Not waiting for an answer, he tapped his right shoulder. "Well sir, one of those pint-sized squirts was over here egging me to pull that skirt out, that it would be a good thing to do. That little fellow's reasoning went something like this: besides saving the widow embarrassment, should others notice the hostage skirt and commence to laughing at her, it could give me certain delights south of the border. He cautioned me, however, for maximum pleasure, not to yank the skirt out like some field hand bailing hay, but to nurse it out a midge at a time so it made certain parts of her tingle. Me too, if you get my drift.

"Now over here," he said, gesturing to his other shoulder, "was another Jiminy Cricket-sized feller. He was whispering in my ear not to mess with that skirt. He argued that while the other guy's points sounded good, dark notions sometimes come wearing their Sunday best. He offered that pulling on the skirt, rather than saving the widow embarrassment, might instead, startle her, goose her into a shout-out of the Lord's name, its tone never to be mistaken for religious fervor by the faithful ... nor forgiven. Then too, he noted how pulling on the skirt could dump me in a hornet's nest of trouble, casting me as a parish pariah with the church holies and prompting the minister to banish me to the front row where I would never again be tempted by skirts or back sides.

"Anyway, those voices got my head spinning so bad, first one ear, then the other, that I couldn't breathe. Finally. I had to bust through those church doors out into daylight and jerk my collar open. I thought to myself at the time, fresh air, that'll shake that notion out of my head.

"Once outside, I almost wore the church runner out tromping back and forth, tugging on that skirt still on my mind.

"Well sir, after gnawing on it for a spell, like Dan would an old soup bone, I made up my mind, and with that, I marched back down the aisle and took my place again, only now with a higher purpose in mind, or so I told myself. That day, however, the universe was having none of my noble nonsense. Wouldn't you know it, just as I was about to reach down and do my duty, services ended sudden-like and everyone began filing out, including the widow."

Lee put his hand over his mouth and stifled a laugh.

"As for the right or wrong of freeing that skirt from its fine living quarters: whatever I decided, some folks were gonna pucker and smile... same with the right or wrong of your gal-fantasies." He put his hand on his grandson's shoulder. "That don't do you much good, though, does it?" He thought a long moment. "Of course, it might help if you plumbed the why of them girl-dreams, see which shoulder critters are capturing your ears, the me or the her ones."

Lee's brow furrowed with a question.

Before he could ask it, his grandfather stopped him with a raised hand. "To hike down a different trail for a second, let's say I was a little quicker on the draw and had made it back inside before church let out, just in the nick of time to coax it out of its fine living quarters, that skirt.

He elbowed his grandson. "Some gals like that, you know," he said, his eyes snapping with mischief, "having their behind's fiddled with. Well, water over the dam, boy, but like I said, I wonder sometimes where things might have headed if I had teased that skirt out and the widow was one of them gals that did, you know, liked it. Gives me shivers just thinking about it." He made a mock shudder.

Lee slapped his leg and laughed out loud.

His grandfather looked at the dark-shading sky. "Time to skedaddle."

After crossing back over the ridge, they hiked down near where they started. Calling to Dan, the old man pointed across the brook. "Over there, dog." For a change, Dan headed in the direction he gestured.

A half dozen deer flushed from a nearby thicket. Their white tail flags bouncing, they loped down the hill and crossed the brook, stopping in the stream to look back.

The young man looked up as a small plane droned across the dark clouds. "Tom claimed it never would have worked between us anyway, me and Pru, different faiths. Her mother said the same thing, Father David too. He said the church frowns on it."

"What do you think?" his grandfather asked, fanning himself with his hat.

The young man shrugged. "Maybe they were right. I should have listened to them." He headed down the hill toward the brook. His grandfather called and motioned for Lee to follow him across.

Midstream, the old man stopped. After rinsing his hat out, he dipped water from the brook and drank from his hat. Water ran down the sickled ends of his granite gray mustache. He motioned for his grandson to do the same.

The young man inspected the water swirling around his legs and made a face. His wading had kicked up sediments.

"Have at it, boy, a little dirt won't hurt you none. Besides, ain't nothing but your own stirrings."

Lee bent down, dipped his hat and drank. "Tastes good, cold."

"Know why we dipped up here? Remember them deer that crossed below? Sometimes other critters can muddy your waters, both those at your feet and the ones in your head."

Once on the far bank, his grandfather bent over and retied his bootlaces, raising each pants leg as he did. On his right leg, starting just below his knee, then curving down and around toward his calf, was a white angry scar.

"How'd that happen?"

He followed his grandson's eyes. "Don't recollect. Knife might have slipped once when I was skinning a varmint."

Fearful the old man's eyes might fire-up like before, Lee didn't press him further. "Can we talk more on the drive home?"

"Hold your britches, Lee. Ain't that what we been doing?" There was mild irritation in his voice. "I got it, son, you're looking for answers. Well, I been chewing on that a spell."

Lee's tilted his head, wanting more.

"I know it don't sound that way, seeing as how I been running on so, but I been asking myself whether or not all my hot air is helping or not. Rather than being told not to touch a hot stove, a body can learn better sometimes if he touches it."

"Then, there's the other big question, why am I doing it, for you or me? Maybe your Dad's right. Maybe I'm just a preachy ol' windbag stumbling around in the dark, still looking for answers like the rest, droning on like I learned something big about life, but underneath it all, I'm just a scared ol' codger needing an audience to make him feel important.

"I gotta make sure I'm helping you for the right reasons, son." He motioned the dog across the brook. "Anyway, that's what I been wrestling with."

Lee skipped a flat rock downstream. It dimpled the waters three pools down.

"That wing of yours ought to be hunky dory come spring baseball."

"Not sure about college right now, Granddad. I need time to get my head straight."

"About what?"

Shrugging, Lee slid his hands deep in his pockets.

"This ain't about college, is it? It's about her, Pru."

Lee looked away, afraid his tight-lipped grimace would confirm the truth of grandfather's words.

The effort did not work. "Hell, son, no big mystery there. Go find yourself another Miss Right. There's your cure."

His grandson hung his head.

A hint of devilry played back of his grandfather's eyes. "I hear there's lots of them pretties over at Hillsboro. Who knows, maybe your Miss Right's one of them."

Lee returned only a straight-line smile, but he held onto the old man's words.

As they drove down the rutted country road toward home, both men rocked back and forth to the truck's crude rhumba.

The truck fishtailed in the muddy ruts several times. Once, when they came to a very bad section, his grandfather gunned the motor and cranked the steering wheel with its spinner. Without looking over at his grandson, he said, "Now tell me, boy. Don't this beat all of your carnival rides?"

"You said back there we'd talk more."

"Don't you beat all." The old man pointed to Lee's head. "All this time, you've been carrying that up there without spilling a drop. Hell, Lee, they may not be that hard to come by, the answers you're looking for. Maybe all a feller needs to play a good role in this here opera is the Golden Rule, the Eleventh Commandment, my favorite."

He downshifted.

"And who knows, might even earn him a bouquet or two at curtain call.

PART TWO

CHAPTER TWENTY-SEVEN

In the fall semester of '50, Lee registered at Hillsboro State, intending to major in Journalism. From the outset though, he was bored with school. Few of the freshmen courses held his attention, and he was ineligible to enroll in the more appealing offerings, either because they were upper-level or out of his field.

Early on, he tried following his grandfather's advice, dating some pretty young faces. He found no real chemistry, however, with any of them either.

Lee was temporarily by himself in the dorm room he was assigned. It was early in the school year, and he had made no close friends as yet, so he often worked out by himself at the gym, stretching his shoulder and lifting weights. Occasionally, he would throw a baseball if an assistant coach was there to catch him, but at moderate pitching speeds. He was not optimistic about his shoulder. It was not strong like it needed to be for pitching in a real game.

And so from the beginning of his freshman year, Lee felt like college was going to be a bust.

In November, he called home and tried convincing his parents that college was a waste of time and money and that he should quit. His father offered a strong rebuttal, but Lee was unconvinced until his mother got on the phone. All she did was shed a few tears, but with them, his will crumbled, at least for the time being.

Just before hanging up, she added, "And oh yeah, your grandfather said to say hello, too. His back's been bothering him. Won't complain though, but I see him favoring it."

In early November, Lee's fortunes changed for the better. He was assigned a sophomore roommate; a young man named Ray Osgood, also a baseball player.

The coach liked keeping his team in the same section of the dorm and team members in the same rooms together, often pairing an upper classman with a freshman, hoping the older player would keep the rookie in line. At least, that was his theory.

Ray was from Pittsburgh and was named after his father. The two young men hit if off right from the start. Like Lee, Ray had a baseball scholarship and the year before was Hillsboro's starting second baseman. Also, like Lee, Ray was Catholic.

The two friends worked out together, Ray catching him when he pitched, outside in good weather and in the gym when it was bad. Although Lee's arm was improving, it was still not right, not strong like it once was. During those fall months, however, baseball was the only thing that kept Lee from packing up and bolting for Eastbrook. That and Ray's girlfriend, Tammy Sturling.

A sophomore herself and from Pittsburgh, she was Catholic also and mind numbing gorgeous.

Naturally, Ray was crazy about her. He kept her picture on the nightstand beside his bed. Even had a white scarf of hers tied on his bedpost.

Lee was smitten with her too, although he tried his best to conceal it.

Ray was out most evenings with her. Although Lee enjoyed using this quiet time to write in his journal, Ray, noting his roommate was alone, insisted he come along on some of their dates. Consequently, Lee spent a lot of time his freshman year with his two new friends.

Just before Lee went home that first Christmas at college, his roommate unexpectedly gave him a gift. It was Ray's own baseball glove, a fielder's mitt, soft and broken in with a good pocket. Lee had admired it since the two started working out together.

"How'd you know I liked it?" Lee asked.

"Are you kidding? You've been making love to it ever since we met."

After that, Lee kept the glove on his bedpost. "Sorry, I got nothing for you," he apologized.

Ray shook his hand. "Merry Christmas, Lee."

At home, Lee tried convincing his parents again that college was not for him, but this time less convincingly. That effort ended with the same results as before. No sale.

The holidays, for the most part were uneventful for Lee, except for two pieces of gossip about Father David. Those tid bits, he picked up from his mother. Although she had whispered them behind her hand to his father at the dinner table, Lee knew they were intended for his ears also. She often did that kind of triangulation, got dirt to a third party by pretending to tell it discretely to a second. Lee went along with her charade, acting like he wasn't listening but hearing it all.

His mother claimed she had gotten both morsels from Gertrude Furste, a fellow church member at St. Peter's and the town gossip, although his mother was known to do a bit of tongue-wagging herself. Gert said she felt honor bound to pass on the information to his mother. After all, she noted, Father David was the Jarrett's friend, family priest and confessor. She said also that she had witnessed the first incident personally. It seemed that one evening near the baptismal font, she had seen Father David and a pretty young woman holding hands and looking moony-eyed at one another.

Then, a few weeks later, another crumb of gossip fell into Gert's lap. This second scrap was second-handed, however, and Gert's source had to remain anonymous, or so she claimed. After all, she told Lee's mother, she did have scruples. Anyway, she had heard from this unnamed source that a janitor at St. Peter's, while cleaning up after services, had seen the priest and a young woman kissing and fondling one another in the choir loft.

When he returned to school after New Year's, there was a sign tacked on his door: Lee, Happy '51, Tammy and Ray.

Two things would happen the following semester, however, that would recast their budding friendships that year and beyond.

The first took place one evening when the two roommates were having a few beers at a local tavern, the Mill Race. Ray asked Lee how he incurred his shoulder injury. Lee, his tongue loosened by their second pitcher of draft, told him not only about the accident but also about the entire evening with Abby, including the sex and her tragic death afterward. He even gave Ray details about the picnic bench and her abdominal scar. Afterward, somewhat ashamed and defensive, Lee explained to Ray that he knew it was wrong and had only done it because his girl had betrayed him. At the time, Ray said he understood and even sympathized, saying, "Hell, Lee, you're only human."

The other event that later altered their friendship occurred one winter evening. The two young men had just exited a local movie theatre, and Lee had said to Ray that it was a shame Tammy had to study that evening because she would have enjoyed the movie. It was then that Sophie Raynes, whom they both knew from art class, walked up.

Sophie was easy, or so Lee had heard. Cute, blonde and short waisted, there was a sense she was all bust and butt.

After nodding to Lee, she asked Ray, coquettishly, "Give me a lift back to the dorm?"

"Sure, why not?" he answered, his eyes rolling over toward Lee.

They all piled in the front seat of Ray's Ford coupe, Sophia in the middle. On the way, she glanced at the blanket draped over the seat back. "What's that for?"

"Picnics," Ray answered. "We like to picnic, Tammy and me."

As Lee got out of the car at the men's dorm, Ray said, "I gotta swing by the library after I drop her off. Finish some research."

It was after midnight when Ray returned, however, just as Lee was heating a can of soup on a hotplate. Ray's clothes were a mess. He explained to Lee that his car had a flat on the way home from the library."

Eyes amused, Lee asked, "So how'd it go with Miss Raynes?"

"Holy shit," he cried, like he just remembered. "That girl was all over me, Lee. Did you know she was like that?"

Lee's mouth puckered in amusement. "What happened?"

Eyes big and gesturing wildly, Ray said, "I pulled up at the dorm to let her out, turned to say goodnight, and she stuck her hand out like she wanted to shake mine. Instead though, she put my hand on one of her boobs and tried kissing me. Of course I pulled away."

"Of co-ourse," Lee mocked.

"Then she asked, 'What's wrong?'"

"'Are you crazy?' I answered. 'I'm going steady.'"

"'I got a rubber,' she said, rummaging through her hand bag, 'if that's the problem.'"

"'You got the wrong idea, Sophie,' I told her, getting out on my side, walking around and opening her door."

"'Then what's the blanket for?' she asked, climbing out of the car."

"Dumbfounded, I answered, 'Like I said, picnics.'"

"'Some boys,' she yelled, slamming the car door."

He looked at Lee directly. "Did you know she was like that, Jarrett?"

"I heard stories." Lee turned away from his friend, still trying to hide his amusement.

Ray pulled a towel and bar of soap from his locker. "Jeez, I need a long shower after that."

Lee was eating his soup when Ray returned from the shower. "Been thinking," he said, "your story about Sophie and the library sounds fishy."

Ray frowned.

"Are you sure you didn't get a little taste of that before you dropped her off?"

Ray smirked and hit him with his wet towel. Climbing into bed, he rolled away from his friend's light and was soon breathing heavily.

Lee stayed up until the small hours that night, trying to write in the jittery glare of his neon desk lamp. While paging through his journal, he ran across some entries about Dan Jagger and his grandfather. Somewhere deep inside, despite his denials to Tom, the other man's needling about the two men being the same was still bugging him.

True, their stories were similar; a blind man couldn't miss that. But that's as far as it went. In the 19 years of knowing him, his grandfather had never lied, as far as Lee knew. If the old man said his wife and neighbor were the innocent and tragic victims of the fever and circumstances, then that's the way it happened.

His grandson did concede, however, that since the two men once lived in the same region on the Burnt Tree and around the same time, they may have known one another. Lee made a mental note to ask his grandfather about that later.

By the time baseball season was over the following spring, Lee's arm was still not right and he had not won or finished a single game. Besides lacking his old arm strength and control, he was now having pain in his shoulder when he threw hard, worse with his curve ball. Coach Bailey, while patient and encouraging, suggested he have a specialist look at it. Ray tried bucking up Lee's spirits throughout, often calling his friend Mr. K, or just K., the common designation for strikeouts.

At the season's end, his parents drove Lee to Pittsburgh to see a specialist, Dr. Underwood.

When he examined Lee, his hands were cold. Later in the consult afterward, the doctor, using a lot of medical jargon, explained that Lee's break had been especially bad, that his collarbone had been shattered near his rotator cuff, accompanied by ligament and tendon damage in that area. It seemed that all this had prevented things from healing properly. "Without surgery, your shoulder will be fine for normal, everyday activities," Dr. Underwood assured him. "But for throwing a baseball, that's different. God didn't make shoulders for that in the first place," he said, "not even healthy ones."

Bottom line, the specialist said, he needed surgery. "Yes," Dr. Underwood assured him, "if you have the surgery and do plenty of therapy afterwards, you can probably pitch again." The doctor ended with a note of caution, however, pointing out that surgical results were never 100 per cent, and that Lee's throwing arm probably would never be like it was before the accident.

After the consult, Lee sat in the doctor's waiting room with his parents, trying to decide about the surgery. The doctor's prognosis, "Surgery never 100 per cent, his arm probably never like it was again," kept replaying in his head like a broken record.

Finally, Lee decided. He would postpone the surgery. He needed more time to think.

Returning to school, Lee told Ray about the specialist's findings, and then walked over to Coach Bailey's office.

"Have a seat, Lee," the coach said, pointing to a chair. "The doc phoned. Let's talk."

The young man's throat tightened.

The coach explained that he and his staff, after evaluating Lee's situation, felt they had to limit his scholarship the following season. On a positive note though, the coach said that if Lee was able to bounce back after surgery and have a good season the following year, he could have his scholarship fully reinstated.

After that, the coach was naturally sympathetic, but Lee was in a fog until the coach thrust out his hand saying, "Lee, have a good summer, and good luck with the surgery."

Back at the dorm, he sat on his bed with his head in his hands. Finally, his eyes slid to his baseball mitt on the bedpost. He threw it in the trash and kicked the can. Lying back and resting his arm over his eyes, he fell asleep.

When he awakened later, his baseball glove was on the bed and his roommate was sitting in the chair across from him. "Heard what happened, your scholarship," Ray said. "Sorry, pal. What now?"

"Don't know. I have to catch a ride home, talk to my parents. May not be back. A scholarship was the only way my folks could swing college."

"C'mon, buck up, K., things will work out. Hey, what about your clothes and stuff?" he asked.

"Aw shit. I forgot," Lee said. "My mind's not right. Guess I will be back. When do we have to be out for the summer?"

"Next Monday. Dorm fee's paid up till then."

"How long are you going to stick around?" Lee asked.

"Depends on my summer job, when it starts."

"Say goodbye to Tammy for me?"

"We're driving back together, Tammy and me, back to Pittsburgh. In case I'm not here when you get back, give me a call."

When Lee returned to Eastbrook and told his parents what the coach had said, they were understandably upset. Lee's uncertainty about his baseball future was tempered by his assumption that college was no longer in the picture, no longer something he had to endure. To his dismay, however, his parents, after an overnight's consult, announced that he could still attend Hillsboro. It seemed that, with some adjustments in their budget, they could manage it, pay for college themselves, regardless of the scholarship. Lee made a strong case against their sacrifice, but they were adamant and unified as before and he gave in.

Up in his room that evening, where he was her captive audience, his mother informed him she had news about an old friend, Father David. Feigning disinterest, Lee tossed a baseball in the air. His seeming apathy didn't deter her from continuing.

"They said that one night," she began, "when Father Moore was locking up, he heard noises. Investigating, he caught Father David and some young woman making out in one of the church pews. They had a big 'to-do' about it right there on the spot, him and the young priest, and Father Moore ended up putting him on probation. Notified the bishop too, I heard."

After his mother left, he dove into his journal. His fingers went again to the entries about Dan Jagger and his grandfather. Paging through those sections, he was finding, to his annoyance, more matches between the two men. For one thing, both wives had the same favorite flowers, daisies. Also, both narratives had similar story lines and characters.

CHAPTER TWENTY-EIGHT

Borrowing his father's car, Lee returned to college to clear his things out for the summer school arrivals. As he drove across campus, he saw Ray and Tammy sitting on a bench outside the library, their foreheads together.

Pulling up to them, Lee got out of the car and glanced at his watch. "Thought you two would be gone by now."

Ray rubbed Tammy's back. "She wants to go to summer school," he said. "Classes start next week, same as my summer job. I'll stick around till Sunday though. So what's new on the home front?"

As Lee tried explaining about his parents and college, he noticed they were only half-listening. "Okay, what's up with you two?"

Tammy held up her left hand and wiggled her fingers. A diamond ring sparkled back at him. She kissed her fiancee's cheek.

"You're kidding," Lee said with mock joy.

"Next spring, '52," Ray said. His eyes embraced hers.

"You son of a gun," Lee said, slapping him on the shoulder. "And you never even mentioned it."

"Afraid she might say no. Just asked her last night."

"Congratulations," Lee said, grabbing his roommate's hand.

When he hugged Tammy, she had a just-after-shower scent. It was Camay soap. He recognized the scent because it was the soap his mother used. Its pure, ivory hue and clean scent seemed somehow appropriate for Tammy though.

It was the first time Lee had held her that close; something primal clicked inside him. Whatever it was made him forget why he was hugging her. He just stood there awkwardly with Tammy's aura washing over him until Ray broke the silence.

"My brother has to be best man though," Ray explained. "Sorry, Mr.

K. When him and me were kids, we promised one another he'd be mine and I'd be his."

Lee's eyes pretended to follow what he was saying.

Ray squeezed her hand. "We're having dinner out tomorrow night, Tammy's favorite restaurant, Valley View." He nodded toward her. "Special celebration, her birthday, and our engagement, you gotta come."

"Nah, think I'll pick up my stuff and head back." Lee looked at Tammy. "Your birthday, huh? Sorry, I didn't know."

When she smiled, their eyes locked. Hers were deep blue, like in a picture of Oregon's Crater Lake he saw once on a calendar. He dove in, sinking deeper and deeper, drowning, but willingly so.

"What do you say," Ray urged, "stay over and have dinner with us? We'll sleep in our old room one last time."

He thought for a long moment.

"C'mon, Mr. K. Make it a foursome?" Ray coaxed harder. "It'll just be you and me, Tammy and her best friend, Lola, Lola Rush."

Lee frowned. "You trying that again?"

Ray slid one arm around Tammy's shoulders. "Matchmaking? Nah, we'd just like you to join us, wouldn't we, honey?"

She smiled at Lee.

"Hey, here's a little sweetener, Jarrett. How about we get the keys to the gym tomorrow morning and shoot some hoops, maybe get a pickup game going, or a little one on one, just you and me? Then we'll have dinner and hang out afterward. What do you say?"

"The evening, it's on you, right?"

Ray nodded.

"Sure about getting the gym keys?"

Ray nodded again. "Then you'll come, great," he said, patting him on the back.

Later that night in the dorm room, Lee sat by himself at the desk. His roommate was gone, out for the evening with Tammy. Lee had gathered his belongings and piled them beside his bed on the floor, intending to take them to the car when it was cooler.

The room was dark, except for his jittery table lamp. The light from it puddled on his open journal, only a knife slit marring the blank pages. Like Ray, Lee's muse also had stepped out for the evening. There were no familiar dorm sounds to keep him company either, most of the other students having gone home for summer vacation.

He worried his class ring with his thumb. From far back in the trees outside his open window, he heard a lone whippoorwill's call. It was a lonesome cry.

He lifted Ray's baseball glove off his bedpost, and then glanced at his roommate's bed. Both ends of Tammy's white scarf were fluttering toward him in a gentle night breeze. He tossed Ray's glove onto the floor with his other belongings.

The next day, after a pickup game in the gym, the two friends returned to their dorm room.

Lee went to the showers, but Ray lingered briefly, skimming a summer school catalog. About to sit on his bed, Ray saw a note was pinned to his pillow. It said call home.

When Lee came back from the shower, Ray was gathering some clothes and folding them in his suitcase. "What's up?" Lee asked, as he dried himself off.

"Gotta drive home tonight," Ray said. "Mom called. Dad's in the hospital, threw his back out, again. She needs me there till he's released. She doesn't drive."

"Sorry about that."

"He'll be okay. He does this once, twice a year, throws his back out, lifting, doing things he shouldn't. Needs a few days' rest, that's all ... and Lee, how about a favor, a big one?"

Lee stopped drying his hair.

"Tammy, could you take her to dinner this evening?"

"Nah, I wouldn't feel right doing that. She's your fiancée, it's your guys' evening."

"Hell, it's only a dinner, Jarrett, not a wedding banquet. She'll love the meal, whether I'm there or not. I even special ordered her a cake. She's been looking forward to it for weeks. You'd be doing us both a big favor."

"Lola too, huh?"

"Hell, Lee, they're going to have dinner at Valley View anyway, the two of them, whether you go along or not. C'mon Mr. K, just for company, it'll help keep the wolves away ... for me?"

"I don't know."

Sensing Lee's resolve flagging, Ray said, "I'm gonna call her right now, set it up. It'll be fine, trust me."

This time, Lee didn't protest.

At the dinner celebration that evening, although Lee engaged in small talk with both girls, he could not take his eyes off Tammy.

"Lee, you're staring," Lola chided him once about it.

"Sorry," he answered, but still continued sneaking looks.

Tammy ordered her favorites, chicken cordon bleu with corn on the cob, oven-roasted potatoes and white wine. Then for dessert, the birthday cake Ray had ordered, pineapple-upside down-cake with whipped cream.

After dinner, Lee dropped Lola at her off-campus apartment. He then drove Tammy to the girls' dorm. "Thanks for dinner, the company too," she said, leaning over and giving him a peck on the cheek. Sliding over to the passenger door, she glanced back.

Her fresh, clean scent washed over him again, so intoxicating it almost made him want to swoon over into her lap. He wanted her to stay and started to speak, but instead, sat there dumbly, frozen under her spell.

"Did you want to say something?" she asked.

Despite their time together, he had never been able to gauge how she felt about him, beyond friendship, that is ... how she truly felt. He hoped it was something deeper. His voice softening, he put his hand over his heart and began with, "Tammy, what about you and me..." In mid-sentence though, he weakened, morphing his question into, "uhh, talking for a few minutes?"

"Some other time, if you don't mind."

Just then, a car pulled up and Sophia Raynes got out. She waved to them and ran up the dorm steps.

"Know her?" Tammy asked.

He nodded. "Art class. Pretty wild rep, I hear."

"I've heard that too," she said, opening the car door.

He gave a nervous chuckle.

"What's funny?"

"Ray ever mention that time she hitched a ride?"

She closed the car door and half-turned toward him.

Chuckling again, Lee tried making light of it, seemingly. "Aw, we were coming out of a movie once last winter, Ray and me. 'The Bells of St. Mary's,' I think. As well as I remember, you had to study. Anyway, Sophia was just coming out too and asked Ray for a lift back to her dorm. Before driving her there, he dropped me off first. Then, he came back late because he had to stop off at the library. Looking a mess when he came back too because he had to fix a flat. He said she tried making out with him, but he was having none of it."

Folding her arms, she frowned.

"Anyway, I needled him some about it later. Told him his story sounded fishy. He knew I was joking. You know how roomies are, nothing's sacred."

Motionless, save for one finger tapping on her knee, she waited for him to continue.

"That's it," he said. "It was nothing. It happened just like he said. I'm sure."

"Then what did you needle him about?"

"Aw, I twisted things around a bit, just to get a rise out of him." He snickered. "You know, kidded him about doing her and making up a story. Just roomie B.S., that's all. Neither of us took it seriously."

"Strange he never mentioned anything about Sophia," she said, fingering her engagement ring ... "We don't have any secrets, Ray and me." She got out and was about to close the car door when he called to her. "About that Sophia business, forget it. Probably just slipped his mind."

When Lee returned to his dorm room afterward, he saw that Tammy's scarf was still on his roommate's bedpost. Perhaps more concerned about his father than he let on, Ray evidently had forgotten it. Before untying it from the bedpost, Lee's fingers caressed it for a long moment.

It was a week later that Ray called him one evening from Pittsburgh. "What did you do?" he demanded. "What the hell did you tell Tammy about Sophia and me?"

Chuckling nervously, Lee tried explaining the events of that evening, characterizing his remarks about Sophia as an innocent attempt at humor that she evidently misunderstood.

Agitated, Ray shouted back in his ear, "Christ, Lee, Tammy said she talked to her later, Sophie, and that screwball claimed I tried to put the make on her. You know what really happened, I told you."

"Aw, shit, why would Sophia say that?" Lee asked.

"Hell, you know why. She's trying to get even 'cause I turned her down."

"Bet you're right."

"But there's something else I don't get," he said, mild suspicion creeping into his voice. "Why'd you tell her about Sophie in the first place?"

"Sorry, buddy. It was a misunderstanding. I was just making conversation, small talk, that's all." He felt his throat tighten. "Told her I was teasing you, that I didn't believe none of the stuff I was saying."

"She's pissed at me now 'cause I didn't tell her about Sophie, claiming I broke my promise. Christ, Lee, you know why I didn't tell her. I was embarrassed." Ray stopped and blew his nose. "She's broken our engagement, thanks to you."

"Let her cool off, Ray. She doesn't mean it. You guys will be back together before you know it." He wiped his mouth with the back of his hand.

"Easy for you to say, she's not your fiancée."

Lee waited, listening. Just when he was certain he had lost the connection, Ray's voice came back again, only pleading. "You know the truth, Mr. K. Tell her what really happened."

"Hell, Ray, I did that already, told her nothing happened. What more can I do?"

His tone grew more demanding. "Dammit, Jarrett, are you gonna straighten this or not?"

"Sorry, roomie, what else can I do?"

"Aw shit, Lee," he said. "Thanks for nothing. Some best friend." He heard the phone click off on Ray's end.

When Lee told his parents he wanted to go to summer school at Hillsboro, they were stunned, pleased but stunned. He registered for two classes the same day and was assigned a new dorm room, again with no roommate because most of the other students had left. The first thing he did though was tie Tammy's scarf onto his bedpost.

A short time later outside the theatre arts building, he ran into Lola. Trying to sound casual, he asked about Tammy. She told him that Ray had driven down from Pittsburgh the night before to talk to Tammy, but that his efforts to reconcile had been futile.

Just as he turned from Lola, he saw Ray coming toward him, a grim look on his face. When the other man caught sight of Lee, he spat on the sidewalk, pivoted sharply and cut across the grass toward the student parking lot.

For the better part of the semester, although he searched every student gathering for her, Lee didn't see Tammy until mid summer. He had gone to the student union to get lunch and there she was, even more gorgeous than he remembered. She was taking notes from an open book. After he bought a sandwich and drink, he walked to her table with his tray. "May I?"

Looking up, she smiled and pointed to a chair.

"Studying?" he asked, sitting down.

Eyes warming, she answered, "Done in a minute."

Shortly, she closed her book and looked up. "Good to see you."

He shook his head. "Sorry about the breakup ... again."

"Don't blame yourself."

"Still feel like it's my fault, partly. Anything I can do? You know, help patch things up?" His feet shifted under the table.

"No, it's over."

"You sure?"

"He wrote me a long letter, telling me his side again. I tore it up, never even read it."

They didn't talk much as he ate his lunch. Finishing, he stood and picked up his tray. "I have to be getting to class. Maybe we can meet later."

She looked up at him like she wanted to say more. Instead, she simply waved and returned to her notes.

As he turned to leave, however, he caught his tray on a chair back, spilling its contents onto the floor.

"Aw, great," he said. Kneeling and crawling under the table, he began retrieving the mess.

She got down on her hands and knees also, using napkins to wipe up the spills. As they crawled around under the table, both on all fours, faces close, their eyes met. On the floor between them was his half-eaten sandwich. Impulsively, he removed the top slice of bread and popped the remaining piece of ham into his mouth.

Tammy put her head down to hide a giggle, then, picking up his napkin from the floor, she did a mock-wipe of his mouth.

Heads down, they both began laughing, shoulders convulsing. Then, for several seconds afterward, every time their eyes met, they did the same. Finally, still on their hands and knees and her face just inches from his, Lee said. "The city baseball team, heard they made the playoffs. Would you like to go to a game?"

At a nearby table, an attractive brunette with a cute, upturned nose was smiling at them behind her hand.

Still kneeling, Lee spoke to the other girl, "Don't you think she should go to the ballgame with me?"

"I never say no to a man on his knees," she answered.

CHAPTER TWENTY-NINE

As Tom Drew ate lunch at work one day, a month or so after his fight with Lee, his eyes drifted aimlessly around the lunchroom. Suddenly he stopped and put his sandwich down. Eating lunch by herself at a nearby table was someone he knew. He limped over to her table. "Cathy, Cathy Pruitt?"

"Tom," she answered, tilting her head up sweetly. "I heard you worked here."

Her face was pure cream with a touch of honey, the final kiss of last summer's sun.

"Uhh, what brings you here, I mean to the mill?" he asked.

"My new Plymouth," she answered. Her eyes scrunched together when she smiled. "Not really new, but my first car."

He smirked.

"I started working here in the front office just last Monday," she explained. "Secretary, same as my last job. This one pays better."

"Mind some company?"

"Heard about the accident," she said as he sat down, "your and Lee's ... your foot too, sorry."

His mouth puckered.

She studied him momentarily. "Someone mentioned you and him were on the outs, but I didn't believe it." She wadded her napkin. "You two were best buddies. What happened?"

He shrugged but under the table, his fingers dug into his bad leg.

"Lee's upset with me, too, for some reason. Ever since you guys came back from the Burnt Tree last spring. Any clue why?"

He rubbed his forehead, fake thinking.

"That's all right," she said, patting his hand. "You'd tell me if you knew."

He looked away.

Head down, she dabbed her eyes. "Pretty sure he still likes me though."

He mindlessly stroked his empty soda bottle. "Would you like to grab a cup of coffee sometime after work, a bite to eat," he asked, "you know, with me?"

She squinted at him, mildly surprised. Using her fork, she played with the crumbs on her plate for a few seconds. "Let me think on it."

She did so that very evening, think on it, and decided to accept. After all, she reasoned, nothing could come of one date. She was still in love with Lee. On the other hand, Pru's mother would approve, her seeing him—Tom's mother was Baptist and Blanche was always hoping.

That one date led to another, however, and that to another and another. In fact, they kept one another company for several weeks afterward. They began exchanging pictures and mementos also. She liked his thoughtfulness, not only on dates, but also at work. She would often find flowers on her desk in the morning, and once at work, after an unexpected shower, he lent her his raincoat. All that time too, he had been a perfect gentleman, giving her a peck on the cheek at the door, and more recently, a kiss on the lips, but only with her permission.

Despite all this, Pru was still at war with herself over the relationship. Marshalled against seeing him were two emotions. One was Pru's resentment over her mother's efforts to control her choice of friends. The other objection was fueled by Pru's feelings of guilt. She knew, all too well, that Lee was still alive in her heart.

At this point, Tom was struggling also. His conflict stemmed from the clash between his original intent to use Cathy to get back at Lee and his growing respect and feelings for her, despite his best efforts to resist these urges. As their relationship grew, he stopped drinking also. Not because of his brother's chiding, but rather so he could focus better on his original purpose, getting back at Lee through her. At least, that's what he told himself in the beginning.

Then there was the issue of his foot, but an issue for him only. She was accepting, matter of fact about it, and sympathetic without pitying. For the first time since losing it, he sensed that another human heart truly felt his loss.

Nor did he have anyone to talk to about this dilemma. Not only were things still distant between David and him over Joyce, but Tom could see his brother was distracted by his own problems with the church.

Both their personal struggles, Pru's and Tom's, came to head one night in early fall.

After saying goodnight to his mother and opening the front door, Tom heard his brother call to him. "Where you headed?"

"Movie."

"Pru?"

He nodded.

"Hope you're minding your manners there, kid. That's a bully fine lady you're dating."

"You've got some nerve," Tom answered. "Seeing as what you and Ma's little helper are doing."

Although the priest answered calmly, his eyes flared. "Joyce," he said, "her name's Joyce. But don't worry; she'll be out of your hair soon."

"So what's up with Miss What's-Her-Name?"

"Father Moore's put me in a box, making me choose, between her and the church."

"Good luck with that," Tom said, slamming the front door behind him.

Later, after Pru got in his truck, she laid his raincoat between them on the bench seat. "Thanks for the loan. Sweet of you."

They went to a movie, and afterward sat in his truck in front of her house, nursing their cokes. She reached over and turned his shirt label under.

"Thanks," he said. "You're kind of quiet tonight. Everything okay?"

She nodded.

Sawyer's Park was just across the street from her house. She looked at the large, full moon looming over its trees. "Halloween in a couple of days."

"Ever see Sawyer's Oak when its dark and its leaves are gone?" he asked. "Spooky, I swear, it looks like some creature in a monster movie." Making a face and hunching his shoulders, he arched his hands over her, claw-like.

She cringed playfully. "I've seen it in daylight, but never at night."

"Them dumb kids say it actually moves once a year, Halloween night. Claim they've seen it." He chuckled. "You know kids, love scaring themselves bug-eyed, as long as they can run home afterward."

"My mother," Pru said abruptly. "We had another argument."

"About?"

"The usual, religion, choosing my friends."

He reached over and rubbed her shoulder. "Did she choose me or did you?"

"A little of both," she answered, pressing her hand over his. "In case you haven't gotten it, she's used to having her way. The reason Lee and I broke up in the first place, trying to please her. All it did though was hurt him, me too. Tom, I need to be honest. I still have feelings for him."

He took his hand away.

"Seems like no matter what I do, that happens, I end up hurting someone." She paused. "That's the other thing on my mind tonight," she said, "not doing that to you. Maybe it's best we stop seeing one another."

An awkward silence followed.

As he turned to say something, he spilled his drink on his lap. He began blotting it with a napkin.

Impulsively, she began helping him until her hand grazed his crotch. She pulled back, blushing.

Tom's eyes rolled over to her. "Would you like to see Sawyer's Oak?" he asked.

She glanced toward her house.

"C'mon," he urged, starting up the truck. "Only take a minute, it's just down the hill. You can see the top from here."

He turned off his engine just down the road from the famous oak and they got out. The massive tree was backlit by the moon.

"Wow," she said, "you were right, it is spooky." She leaned back against the truck's fender, looking up at it wide-eyed.

As they stood side by side, her clean scent washing over him, he drew her close and kissed her long and hard. When they broke, she crossed her arms and hunched her shoulders. "Let's head back, I'm chilly."

"I'll get my coat." Opening his truck door, he found it, but hesitated. Reaching behind the seat, he pulled a blanket out instead. He flipped the visor down and slid a condom from its pocket.

She pointed to the blanket. "What's that for?"

"You said you were cold." With that he wrapped it around both of them. Pinning her body against the fender, he pressed his pelvis up against hers. She tried shifting to one side to avoid him, but he turned her so that his pelvis was up against hers again. He kissed her on the neck near her ear and, breathing heavily, slid his knee up between her thighs.

"No," she cried, shoving him away. "No."

He grabbed her by the hand. "C'mon, Cathy, what's the big deal?"

She shoved him away. "How could you think I was like that?" She flung the blanket off her shoulders and threw it to the ground. Sobbing, she marched back up the road toward her house.

He jingled his keys, calling after her, "C'mon, Cathy. Get back in. I'll drive you home." Limping after her, he fell in the road, and dropped his keys. He crawled around in the darkness, all the while muttering to himself. It took him a minute or two to find them. He caught up with her and drove alongside as she walked. "Don't be like that, Cathy. C'mon, get in." he pleaded.

Putting her head down, she waved him away and continued plodding up the muddy road.

When the main road at the top of the hill came into sight, he implored her one last time, his hand over his heart, "Cathy, I'm sorry. I swear, this'll never happen again. Please, let's talk."

She kept on walking, but never answered.

Finally, at the park entrance, he could only watch as she darted across the road toward her house. Seemingly out of nowhere though, a car's headlights raced out of the night toward her.

He cried out, "Abby, watch out."

The car just missed her, careening on down the road out of sight, its horn blaring.

She ran up the steps to her front door and was gone.

Uncertain why he had shouted the wrong name, he finally convinced himself it was to try and change what had happened that dreadful night when Abby was killed. His hand was shaking. For a few minutes afterward, he sat in the dark across from her house, brooding. True, he had failed in his original intent to use her to get back at Lee, but that didn't explain why he was feeling like he had also lost something bigger, more important.

CHAPTER THIRTY

When Father David walked into the Drew house, his brother was in the kitchen. Tom's face was unshaven and his eyes were hollow.

"Where's Joyce?"

Tom stopped tending the pot on the stove and motioned away.

"Jeez, I told you I'd drive her home." The priest walked over to his brother. "Why are you taking this out on her? It's me you want to take a swing at." Only the bubbling pot on the stove broke the silence. "I'm getting enough crap from the church as it is. I don't need it from you."

"Where you been?" Tom asked, continuing to stir.

"Told you last week, a winter retreat. For the first time, Father David seemed to notice his brother's shabby condition. "Jeez, you look like hell." He paused, studying him. "My God, you've gotta snap out of this. You've been like this ever since you and Cathy ... Wanna talk about—"

Tom cut him short. "It's none of your damn business, like I told you before."

"Go on, I'll fix dinner." He shooed Tom toward the door. "Mind if I doctor this a bit?" he asked, pointing to the pot.

Tom didn't answer. Later, up in his room, when he was skimming the weekly local newspaper, he caught an item on the society page that made him stop. It read: "Mr. Lee Jarrett spent last month's Christmas Holidays with his parents, Mr. and Mrs. Stewart Jarrett, who reside at 354 Fourth Street in Eastbrook. Lee, a journalism major, is currently attending Hillsboro State College in the '50-'51 school year on a baseball scholarship." Tom crumpled the paper into a tight ball and crammed it deep in his trashcan.

Lying down on his bed, he looked at Cathy's lovely portrait on his nightstand and picked it up. With his index finger, he traced her features over and over again, at last acknowledging to himself what his heart already knew: He cared for her ... and deeply.

The next day after work Tom drove by the Pruitt house. Wrapped in a winter jacket, burnt orange fur around her face, Cathy was standing on a ladder in their yard, trimming a trellised rose bush. Impulsively, he stopped. As he walked up behind her, he took his hat off and tried straightening his hair. "Cathy," he said timidly.

Turning, she bristled and began backing down the ladder until he blocked her way.

"Please, Cathy. Just hear me out and I'll leave."

She turned away.

He shook the ladder gently. "Please," he begged. "I'm not leaving till you listen." Despite her stony silence, he began explaining. "It was revenge, just plain revenge. That's why I did it."

She glared down at him.

"I was trying to get even with Lee for something he did. It makes no sense now, but I thought by taking something of his, I could get back at him. No excuses. You can figure out the rest."

She came down one step.

His hand was resting on a rung of the ladder and he put his head down on that arm. "I was wrong, terribly wrong. Please forgive me. I'll never make that mistake again, never." He put his bad foot on the first rung. "What I'd like now is ... for us, you and me to start over, make a fresh start. Could we do that ... please?"

Still turned away, she folded her arms and refused to speak.

The curtain moved in a window of her house.

After he drove away, she came down the ladder and went inside. Mrs. Pruitt met her at the kitchen door. "Wasn't that Tom?" she asked.

"Forget it, Mother."

"Tsk, tsk, pity."

Inside their front door, Pru sifted through their mail, hoping for but not expecting something in Lee's handwriting. But there was nothing. She thought for a moment and her eyes slid toward the kitchen. "Any mail for me, Mother?"

"No, dear, why?"

"Nothing."

Upstairs, Pru opened the drawer to her night table. Two framed pictures were inside, face down, Lee's over Tom's. She walked over to the window. Smoke from the chimney of a nearby house was swirling about in the breeze.

CHAPTER THIRTY-ONE

One early spring day in the lunchroom at Welles Lumber, Tom overheard Pru asking another woman for a ride home. Pru's car, she told her, was in the shop for repairs. Apologizing, the other woman said she could not because she had a doctor's appointment after work.

Since Tom had asked Pru for a second chance, he had seen her eating lunch there frequently, most often with another woman, and although he always wanted to talk to her, he had not mustered up the courage to do so. But that day was different. He had an opening, or at least he hoped he did.

Hat in hand, he approached her table. "Cathy," he called meekly. "Sorry, but I overheard. Can I give you a lift? That is, if you don't mind riding in a truck." When she turned away, he persisted, "We won't even talk, not if you don't want to, please?"

His shirt tag was sticking out. When she turned back and saw it, her eyes softened.

After work, he brushed off the seat and held the door as she climbed in. After driving for a few minutes, he broke the silence. "What's up with your car?"

"The mechanic told me, but I didn't understand. More than I can afford though."

"The work on your car, maybe I can do it."

"Did you know your brother called me?" she asked. "Begged me to give you another chance."

Tom's hands tightened on the steering wheel. "Damn, he had no business..."

"Don't be angry. He was right. I was trying to punish you. You've had enough of that already."

For the rest of the drive, he was quiet until she opened the door to get out. "Can I drive you tomorrow?" he asked. "It'll save you gas money."

Over the next several weeks, they began seeing one another again, watching movies, attending games and even eating lunch together at work.

They became closer than before too, even giving one another nicknames. Tom's for her was Cat. T was hers for him.

Despite this growing bond, Pru was yet again having her share of inner struggles over their relationship. This time, however, she was torn between her old feelings for Lee and her nurturing impulses toward Tom. She worried also about neglecting her mother, although Blanche never brought it up with Tom, like she had with Lee. If anything, Mrs. Pruitt encouraged their relationship, driven by her same motive as before, religion.

As Tom ate lunch a few weeks later at work, a friend asked across the table, "So, are you still on the wagon?"

Tom shushed him with a hand.

"Reason I asked, you've been looking mighty spiffy lately," the friend added. "Better duds, shaved, hair even combed." When he reached over to muss it, Tom slapped his hand away. The friend laughed.

Just then, Pru came into the lunchroom, catching Tom's eye as she took a table. He gathered his lunch, left his friend's table and sat down beside her.

"Thought you were going to eat later, Cat."

"The paper work? I finished it early."

He glanced out the window at the darkening sky. "Looks like snow, but the weatherman said rain. "Bring a raincoat?"

She shook her head no.

"I'll get you one before you leave," he said, pointing to her hair. "We mustn't get that wet." He took a bite of his sandwich.

As he did, she pointed to the back of his hand. "I've been curious. How'd you get those funny, round scars?"

"These?" he asked, glancing at her furtively. "Uhh, a hot engine. I was trying to fix a car, my brother's. He drives to far-out parishes once a month, says mass there."

Her fingers played with the pepper shaker. "Tom ... this Sunday, would you go to church with me, to Easter services?"

"Your mother, did she put you up to this?"

She shook her head.

"I don't think so," he answered, but without real certainty.

She tilted her head sweetly and touched his arm.

The following Sunday, just as Pru opened the church door to go inside, Tom drove up and called to her.

"Why didn't you pick me up?" she asked when he caught up with her at the church door.

"Sorry," he said, tucking his shirt in. "Ma had a bad spell this morning. I didn't have a chance to call. Sorry."

"She all right?"

He nodded.

"Mother didn't come," she said. "Has a sick headache. A nice day though, the reason I walked."

After the services, the minister was shaking hands at the church door. "And who's this handsome fellow?" he asked Pru as she approached with Tom.

"Thomas Drew," she answered for him.

Reverend Paul offered his own name and shook the young man's hand.

"Your mother all right?" the minister asked Pru. "I missed seeing her this morning."

"Headache," she answered.

"Drew, Drew," the minister said to Tom, searching his memory. "Was your mother's name Elizabeth?" Before Tom could answer, the minister went on. "Good lady. She used to come to services. I knew your father too." He smiled. "Catholic, but a good man."

"Tom works at Welles Lumber," she explained. "Good with his hands. He fixed my car in a jiffy."

"Interesting," the minister said, stroking his chin. "We can sure use a good handyman around here."

Tom's foot made a subtle squeak when he shifted from one leg to the other.

"I've heard your mother is not well," the minister said to Tom. Taking the young man's arm, he pulled him aside. "I'll say a prayer."

Back in the truck, Tom wheeled toward her. "What the hell was that?"

She leaned away.

"That thing with the minister back there. Trying to give him an opening so he could ask me to help out."

"Sorry, didn't mean to upset you. Just trying to do something nice ... for both of you."

"Aw, you didn't know. Me and religion, we don't mix."

She arched an eyebrow.

He tapped on the steering wheel for a few seconds, debating whether or not to explain. "Maybe some day."

"Could we stop by Miller's on the way home, pick up a few items?" she said. "Only grocery store open on Sundays."

"Sure, I gotta pick up some stuff too. Just curious, the food shopping: Does your mother ever do it anymore?"

Pru shook her head. "She could though. Same with fixing meals and driving. She could do all that if she wanted. Doctor said she could, even be good for her. But she'd rather I do it. Claims she doesn't like dealing with all the people inside the market and traffic outside. That and she has trouble finding the items on her shopping list. I don't mind, as long as it keeps the peace. I'm all she has, T."

After they finished shopping, he asked, "Mind if we drop my stuff off first? I'd like you to meet my family."

At his house, he introduced Pru around and put the groceries away.

As they drove back to her house afterward, she said, "Your family seems nice, Joyce too."

"She's getting worse though, Ma is."

"Joyce seems good with her, kind, patient."

"You know the deal there, don't you, with her and him, my brother, the priest?"

"I've heard the gossip. I can see there's something between them. Maybe that's all that matters."

He frowned, but then his face softened. "I'll give you this, about Joyce. She is good. Ma takes a lot of watching and she's good with her." He massaged his left calf muscle.

"That numbness again?"

"Yeah, happening more often now."

"Tell the doctor?"

"Did you hear it squeaking at church, my foot? That minister must think I'm some kind of freak."

"You're the only one it bothers, T."

"Always happens at the worst time."

"Next time you do rehab, can I come along?" she asked.

"What for?"

"Maybe I can help."

Tom's eyes left the road ahead and studied her pensively. "You want to help me?"

Mrs. Pruitt came into the kitchen just as they were storing food in the fridge. "Why Thomas," she said, "it's good to see you."

"Feeling better, Mother?" Pru asked.

Mrs. Pruitt smiled.

"Tom's mother's was having a bad day also," Pru explained. "He still came to services though, met the reverend."

Blanche spoke to him. "Poor thing, your mother. I bet she's afraid of being left alone." She squeezed her daughter's hand.

"Reverend Paul asked about you," her daughter said.

"Thanks for helping with the groceries, Thomas," Mrs. Pruitt said.

She turned to her daughter. "The bathroom door's been sticking again. Could hardly open it when I had to go."

Catching Pru's eyes knowingly, Tom smiled. "Got any tools, Mrs. Pruitt?"

CHAPTER THIRTY-TWO

Throughout the following summer and into the early fall, Pru helped Tom at rehab. Although she did feel sorry for him and liked feeling needed, her heart still belonged to Lee, even though she had not spoken to him in over a year. That was why she grew increasingly concerned one day at the rehab center about Tom's growing affections for her.

"This is a new exercise," the therapist said to Pru as she demonstrated on Tom. "You can do this at home using a towel, the wall or just your hands. Main thing is to create resistance, but don't overdo it."

Pru nodded.

A familiar voice called Tom's name. "Thought that was you, young fella. How's it hanging?" Coach Sandy waddled toward him on his new legs and one crutch.

After they shook hands, Tom said, "Cat meet Coach."

The therapist motioned to Pru. "C'mon over here, Miss. I can show you better on this chart."

Tom looked at the coach. "Still haunting this place, huh?"

"These folks are still my team," the coach said, motioning around at the other patients. "Got tired of staying home, staring at my own miseries. Thought I'd hang around here for a spell, see if I can help others look away from theirs. The man upstairs penciled me in this lineup. Better not waste any times at bat he's given me. Don't know how many I got left." There was a light back of his eyes. "I feel like that hooker I told you about once, the one with all the fake body parts. All I got left to toss to others now is me."

Tom shifted to his good foot.

The coach went on. "Too many folks hurting for me to stay home and chase the ol' lady around. Never mind, she's harder to catch nowadays with these," he added, tapping his artificial legs.

Over the coach's shoulder, Tom could see a pretty young woman with artificial arms. She was trying to use some pulleys overhead and her arms were quivering. Stopping suddenly, she began crying. A male aide, his hand on the young woman's back, tried encouraging her. Nearby, a young child, hers Tom assumed, sat filling in a coloring book and humming to herself.

The coach followed Tom's eyes to the young woman. "Seeing as we're both in the same boat as these here folks, you and me, we got a pretty good read on what they're feeling. Not like others with all their body parts." He patted Tom on the shoulder. "Could sure use your help here, son."

"I got my own problems," Tom answered, thumbing at his chest. "Besides, all that work and for what? They'll never be whole again ... me neither."

"Yeah, son, but you gotta work with what you got, take time to lick the other fella's wounds, same as they licked yours when you was hurting." He handed Tom a card. "My number, in case you change your mind." Waving to a man in a wheelchair, the coach hobbled away. Both of the other man's legs were missing also.

Tom's eyes followed after Coach Sandy as he bent over the man in the wheelchair, placed one hand on his arm and said something in his ear. The other man laughed.

The pretty young girl with the prosthetic arms was on the pulleys again, seemingly with new resolve.

Later, as Pru and Tom were leaving, she said, "Sorry, but I overheard the coach talking ... about you lending a hand."

"Ye-ah?"

"That would be a nice thing to do."

He looked away.

"By the way, T., Reverend Paul said thanks again for lugging that fall festival stuff up from the basement. Said he wanted to get a jump on the holidays this year."

He waved his hand dismissively. "Nice of you too, Cat, filling in for Joyce last week with Ma."

She stopped to get a drink at a water fountain in the hall. When she bent down to use it, the stream wet her hair.

They continued down the hall, both laughing as she began flipping her hair dry.

"Just like a cat, your namesake," he said, smiling. "Both hate getting their fur wet." He stopped walking. "Did Lee ever call you Cat?"

"No, always Pru."

Just then a plane passed overhead, and Tom watched until it was out of sight.

"You can still do that if you want," she said, "fly."

"Really think so?" he asked, his tone hopeful.

At her house, just before she got out, he kissed her, not gentle like usual, but harder and longer. She pulled away, frowning, but called back, "Tomorrow, usual time?"

CHAPTER THIRTY-THREE

Tammy and Lee sat by themselves in one corner of the bleachers at Mc-Cloud Field.

She flapped her blouse collar. "Phew, muggy for September."

"Yeah," he agreed. "Glad I wore shorts."

Although it was early in the ballgame, the score read eight to nothing in favor of the opposition. "Not a good sales pitch for next year, the score," he said, pointing to a sign under the scoreboard: '52 season tickets now on sale at the concession stand.

Tammy waved and smiled at another girl several rows down.

The other girl waved back, and then whispered something in the young man's ear beside her. After an appropriate wait time, he glanced back in their direction.

"Sorority sister, Janet Lloyd," Tammy explained. "By bedtime, the whole dorm will know about us."

"Bother you?"

"Not really."

"Game's kind of boring, don't you think?" he asked. "Wanna leave, stay, what?"

She shrugged.

Just then, the home team's second baseman muffed a grounder and another run scored.

"C'mon," Lee yelled, "watch the ball into your glove."

"Second base," she said, "that was Ray's position."

He nodded.

An awkward silence followed until she spoke. "Sort of why I came today," she said, "to explain what happened between Ray and me, you two being such good friends ... or were."

"I was hoping for another reason. You know, so we could get to know one another."

She studied him. "When I first asked Ray about Sophia, what you said, he denied it, said it never happened."

"I hate that, you guys breaking up 'cause of me." He shifted in his seat.

"Don't you dare, Lee Jarrett." She touched his arm. "You've been the one honest person in all of this."

His gut knotted. "He probably just forgot."

She continued explaining. "That's what he said. But then Sophie told me what he did or tried. Of course, he denied it. Claimed he'd forgotten and Sophie was making it up 'cause he turned her down. One way or another though, he broke his word, either by doing what she said or if nothing happened, not telling me. Once you lose trust, you begin questioning everything someone says. You know that."

"Maybe you guys can still work things out."

"You don't understand, Lee. We made promises, you know, the way couples do." Tears welled in her eyes.

He looked down at the gray boards on the seat beside him, their grains heavily etched by sun and rain. "I know what you're feeling," he said, "at least in part." He then explained how his girl and best friend betrayed him, leaving out certain details that might embarrass him.

"Trust, that's the most important thing in a relationship. Don't you think?"

He ran his hand across the weathered seat. "There are other things too, I need to tell you."

Looking at him, she waited.

"They'll keep," he said.

The first batter up in the seventh got a hit and the fans cheered.

Just as Lee turned toward the field, he caught a splinter in his calf. "Dag," he said. It was only superficial, but a small stream of blood trickled down his calf.

She made a pained face. "Better wash that off."

A few minutes later, Lee returned. He handed her a hot dog and Coke. "Didn't know I was a big spender, did you?"

She licked her lips. "Never mind, I'm starving." She pointed to a box under his arm.

"Fudge, peanut butter fudge," he answered. "Chunks of peanuts in it too. They were selling it at the concession. Couldn't resist." He offered her a piece and she waved it off.

"About Ray and me getting back together. That's never going to happen."

"People change."

"He called again last night, still trying to change my mind."

"And...?"

Just then, the crowd booed. The scoreboard told why. A hometown batter had just struck out with bases loaded and two men out.

"How's the hot dog?"

She rubbed her tummy and smiled.

"Sorry," he said with playful eyes. "They didn't have any ham sandwiches."

She frowned.

"C'mon," he said, "you forget already? The student union, my tray, the ham sandwich?"

She nudged him playfully.

Outside her dorm entry, he handed her the last of the fudge. "Give this to your dorm mother. Don't think she likes me. She gave me a sour look when I picked you up. By the way, what's her name?"

"Mrs. Lymon."

Lee gave a wry smile. "Make sure she knows it's from me, the fudge." Taking her hand, he pressed a white, folded napkin into her palm.

Her face puzzled.

He called back to her as he walked down the steps. "Look inside."

She unfolded it. There on the tissue was a handwritten note. It read, "A hillbilly thank you note for your company at the best game I never played in. Love, Lee." She looked up to wave but he was gone.

He had a new desk lamp at the dorm. Unlike the old jittery lamp, his new one cast a soft, surrealistic pallor over the room. Only a white miller pounding on his window screen kept him company as he tried gauging where things stood in their relationship, Tammy and his.

She felt nothing for him, he told himself. Never mind she was looking more and more like that special lady he was searching for, that one true heart he could marry and have a happy life with. Then there was Pru. That might hurt her, marrying Tammy. He hoped so. She hadn't suffered enough yet for her betrayal, not nearly enough. But did Tammy care that she could be that one special lady in his life? Hell no. She was still stuck on Ray, never mind what she was saying.

Just then the phone rang in the hall and someone called, "For you, Jarrett." On the other end, like in a dream, was Tammy. She explained that her mother and father were staying at their lake house just south of Pittsburgh for a few days in early September. She intended to join them for the weekend and invited Lee to be her guest. "And naturally," she added, "I'd like for you to meet my parents."

"Sounds great. Let me check at home first."

"Hope you can make it. Could be your last chance," she said, her tone coy.

Puzzled, he stared at the phone.

She tittered. "To meet my parents, silly. Daddy's not off again till New Year's."

"I'd like to meet him, your mother too."

"Daddy will pick us up around five on Friday at the dorm, tomorrow afternoon. Try to make it. We'll have fun."

After she hung up, he did a victory punch in the air. Although Tammy's father wouldn't pick them up until tomorrow, Lee began throwing things in a bag.

Late the following morning, the phone rang in the hall and someone called his name. This time it was his mother and she was upset. His granddad had cancer, prostate cancer. Doc Gladstone said it had spread to his back, didn't look good.

Lee was stunned. For a few seconds, he couldn't speak. He knew what she had said, yet he still couldn't wrap his mind around it. All he could manage was a weak, "How's he doing?"

"You know him, won't tell you anything. Blood from a turnip."

"What can I do?"

"Come home," she said, "at least for the weekend."

"But I'm tied up, Mom. I promised someone—besides, what can I do?"

"Suit yourself. But it would help, your being here."

After she hung up, he slumped down in a chair. Aw crap. He glanced at his packed bag, then at the hallway where he had just gotten the bad news.

A half-hour later in the shower, he was still weighing what to do, whether to join Tammy at the lake or go home. He let the shower beat down on his head, hoping it might jar an answer loose.

CHAPTER THIRTY-FOUR

His mother looked up from the sink and wiped her eyes when Lee walked through their back door. He touched her shoulder and she put her hand over his. "Glad you made it, dear. We expected you last night for dinner, set a place."

"Couldn't catch a ride till this morning. Been up since five."

"But you made it, that's all that matters."

"I thought about Granddad a lot after you called. God knows I want to help. Not sure what I can do. Got a million questions though."

"Good luck," she said, sniffling. "He never let on he was even sick, other than complaining about his back once and a while. He was at the doctor's when he got the news, there by himself. He just came home afterward and told us, matter of fact like, what the doctor said, that he had male cancer and it had spread. He said too, your grandfather, that he didn't want any fuss made about it either. But that's all we could squeeze out of him. Anything else, we got from the doctor, which wasn't much."

"When was this?"

"A couple days ago. But Lee, don't be mad." She touched his arm. "He made us promise not to tell you, but your father and I thought we should."

"Where's he now?"

"Where do you think?"

"Probably fishing."

"Where else," she answered. "It's either there or the shed. You know that."

The old man didn't own the shed, but it had a pot-bellied stove and held a lot of his stuff, and he often hung out there. That's why they always called it Granddad's shed.

"Dan with him?"

"I swear, that dog's like his shadow."

Opening the fridge, he took a long drink from a milk bottle.

She handed him a glass. "What was it you had planned?"

He looked at her blankly.

"The weekend?"

"Aw nothing. Just a friend at college. Her parents have a place on a lake near Pittsburgh. Promised I'd show up there to meet them."

"By the way, Pru called."

"What did she want?"

She gave him a disapproving look. "Asking about your grandfather, naturally. She cares about him, same as we do. She heard from a neighbor he was sick. Hard to keep secrets in a small town. Said she might drop by later this weekend."

There was a fresh pie on the table. After he pointed to it and his mother nodded, he cut a piece. "This weekend," he asked, his face scrunching up. "Pru's coming here this weekend?"

She studied him. "You seem upset. What is it?"

"I'm fine, Mom. It's nothing."

"Maybe some other weekend you can meet your friend's parents."

"You don't understand," he said, picking at the last crumbs on his plate. "Probably my last chance. Where's Dad?"

"Monkeying with the car. If you're going out there, tell him to come in soon for a bite. Sandwich okay with you, ham and cheese?"

He shrugged.

His father was bent over the fender of their car in the garage with his head buried under the hood.

He glanced back at Lee. "Hand me one of them spark plugs."

"Shame about Granddad," his son offered.

"Won't talk about it, the cancer. Gets upset when I ask." He pointed to the car. "Get in and start her up."

The engine came alive, ran rough for a few seconds, sputtered, and died.

"Hope you're paying attention, bub," his father said as he ducked under the hood again. "All this will be your headache soon."

Lee got out of the car. "I'm watching, Dad, I'm watching."

"Of course, I don't know what's wrong with this ol' gal myself, not yet," his father said, chuckling. "Someday, when you get your own Lizzy, she won't tell you what's ailing her either. You gotta look at how she's acting, then check out each of her systems. When you know what it ain't, you're closer to what it is."

"You like what you do, Dad, being a mechanic?"

His father's eyes smiled. "Working around cars never seemed like

191

work, not to me." He wiped a smudge off the fender with his sleeve. "Your grandfather's hearing angel wings, and he don't like it much."

"What are you saying, Dad, he's afraid?"

"Wouldn't you be, facing what he's facing? Hand me that small crescent," he said, bending over the fender. "It's gotta be the fuel line. I've checked everything else."

Just then, his mother's voice called from the main house through the open side door of the garage. "Lunch, you guys."

His father straightened and looked at him squarely. "Thanks, Lee."

"For what?"

"For coming home, showing up. Mother told me you had plans for the weekend." Putting his hand on his son's shoulders, he walked with him toward the washtub sink and handed him a chip of gritty soap. "Wash up before you go in for lunch. You know your mother and dirt."

"Not hungry, Dad, just had some pie. Ask Mom to put my sandwich in the fridge."

As Mr. Jarrett dried his hands on a grease-stained towel, he eyed his son.

"I'm gonna hang out in the shed for a while," Lee said, "wait for Granddad to come back from fishing, Try and talk to him about ... you know."

"Good luck with that," his father called back as he walked toward their house. "He's been avoiding everyone. Coming in late after everyone's in bed. Looks different too."

Lee's eyes questioned him.

"You'll see."

CHAPTER THIRTY-FIVE

In grandfather's shed, Lee pulled on the cord hanging from the swinging lamp. Its light washed over the high bench and shed floor but left some corners in shadows. He took Ray's baseball glove down and sat in the old man's rocker. The mitt was suede smooth, had a good pocket and molded to Lee's hand like it was tailor-made. He punched the pocket several times with his fist, harder each time.

As he sat in the half-light, rocking gently back and forth, his foot accidentally bumped the wood box under the counter. The old man always kept it well stocked with pine kindling for feeding campfires and the shed's pot-bellied stove. His full name was burned into the boards on one side: Dallas Jarrett.

After a few minutes, Lee's early morning caught up with him and he dozed. A strong wind rattled the shed later and he jumped awake. Seconds later, he heard his grandfather's truck pull up outside.

Dan padded in first, ambling over to Lee, resting one paw on the young man's lap.

His grandfather was next, ducking his head as he came through the door. Lee was surprised at his appearance, even though his father had warned him. Always clean-shaven and with hair neatly trimmed, the old man now had a heavy steel-gray beard, and his hair was long and pulled to the back of his head.

"You look like you're dragging around a dead dog, boy. Why the long face? Your mom making a big deal about what the doc said?"

Lee made a straight-line smile. "How was fishing?"

The old man waffled his hand.

Lee nodded his head. "September can be spotty. Going again tomorrow?"

"Sure as sunup."

"I wanna go with you, okay?"

"Sorry your mother dragged you home for nothing," the old man said. "Hells fire, everyone gets a backlash in his reel now and then."

Lee shrugged.

"Don't go wasting your pity on me. Plenty of good times left in these old bones." Removing his fishing vest, he hung it along with his big knife on a wall peg. On another, he hung his staff by its lanyard, resting his fly rod across both pegs.

As he eased past his grandson, his giant hand squeezed the young man's shoulder. Sitting on the high stool in front of the bench, he faced Lee, tilting the hanging lamp toward the young man. "How's life treating you, boy?"

Lee shrugged.

Dan curled up on the old man's hunting coat. "He likes my stink," his grandfather said, nodding at the dog. "I like his too."

The old man took Lee's fly rod down from the wall over the bench. Pulling it apart, he began flexing the tip, whipping it back and forth in the air. "I fixed your rod, shorter now, stiffer. Not like when it was store-bought, but it'll fish okay." Removing the reel from the rod, he held it under the light and scratched his beard. "Heavier line might smooth it out some. It'll take just a jiffy to change." With that, he began rummaging through a drawer.

"Growing a beard now, huh?" Lee asked.

His grandfather ignored the question.

"Guess everyone wore those in the old days. By the way, you ever know that fella I told you about once, Dan Jagger?"

His head turned slowly toward Lee.

"You remember, don't you? That fellow on the Burnt Tree, the one that restaurant owner told us about. The crazy old guy that killed his wife way back and never been heard from since. Did you know him, ever hear of him?"

The old man's dark eyes hardened.

"Dad said you lived 'round that country once, homesteaded there when you were young, around the same time as that Dan fella, late 1800s."

"What about him?"

"Just wondered if you ever knew him or that other fella. Let's see, what was his name?" He pretended not to remember at first. "Papa, yeah, Papa Joe, that was it."

"Never heard of 'em," he answered sternly. "Neither feller."

The dog squirmed but never opened his eyes.

Pulling a vial from his shirt pocket, the old man removed a pill. At the tub sink, he ran tap water into his blue enamel cup, swallowed some with his pill and threw the rest out.

"The cancer?" Lee asked.

The cup's rim was chipped, its steel heart showing through. The old man gave his grandson a long, thoughtful study, all the while shaking the vial, like he was weighing it. He poured himself a cup of coal-black coffee from a pot on a hotplate. From behind a cabinet, he pulled a half-empty bottle of whiskey and laced his cup with a splash. His eyes rolled over toward his grandson. "Hells fire, boy, fishing and a little nip, that's grabbing life by the balls. Guaranteed to cure what's ailing you."

"But the cancer, what about that?"

The old man stared at nothing. "Tell you what I ain't gonna do, mope around like some people I know." His eyes slid toward the main house.

"They're just worried about you."

"They mean well, but I can't stand all their fussing, that and all them long faces they're wearing. I wanna be treated like before, when I was just an ornery old cuss with nothing wrong.

"And your mother, God bless her, she's the worst," he went on. "All that mothering and trying to steer me into Doc Gladstone's clutches. It's almost more than a body can stand."

He handed Lee the reel and began spooling off the old line. "Got half a notion sometimes to turn the shed light out and leave all this behind. You know, head for the mountains. Just slip my hunting coat on and skedaddle."

His grandfather often talked about doing that, going to the mountains. He would too sometimes, but usually just for a couple of days. But every few years in good weather, he would disappear for weeks, always taking Dan along when he left. They never knew where he went, but he was always flush with money when he came back. Mother would worry when he was gone, but Dad would calm her, reminding her that Granddad had done that for as long as he could remember.

Of course though, when his grandfather came back, she would lecture him. He would always listen politely but never do as she asked.

The old man's eyes ran up the wall to his big hunting knife. "Don't you be worrying old girl," he spoke to it. "You'll be going along too." He turned to Lee and whispered, "She'd never forgive me if I went to the mountains without her."

"But you need more than a knife, don't you, Granddad, in the mountains?"

He thought a moment. "Maybe a dozen things or so, the right things." He cocked one eye at his grandson. "But a body should always have them things at the ready, just in case he gets fed up with all the village nonsense and wants to light out, sudden like." He motioned toward a dark corner of the shed. "My stuff's back there, in my wilding bag."

There, amid the shadows, was a large canvas bag. It looked like a small village was stuffed inside. "She's always packed and ready to go, just in case. Sewed me some straps on her too so I could tote it better. "Don't mention any of this leaving stuff to your parents, especially your mother. She catches me talking this way and she'll have a hissy fit."

"But I don't want you to go away either."

He took a long drink of the spiked coffee, his dark eyes throwing off sparks over the cup's black rim. "In the meantime, boy," he added, smacking his lips and winking, "in the meantime, I'm gonna have me a little of this." He nodded toward the cup. "Hillbilly therapy, I call it."

"Just don't leave, please. We need you, I need you."

The old man touched the vial in his shirt pocket. "I never mentioned it at the time on May's Brook, but that's a fork in the road, a three-pronged one, that I've been stewing about since we went there—whether my two cents is doing you any good or not. My own book of life is the third fork."

His grandson started to say something but Granddad held a hand up. "I'm done wrestling with it though. I've figured how I can do us both a favor, go down two forks at once, so to speak." He gestured to his head. "As long as my rivers topside are running clear, I got a notion or two left that might help you over some rough spots on your own journey, and who knows, might help balance my book too with The Boss, that third fork I mentioned. Then too, as long as you're around, I'll be living on a spell too, in a way. Maybe not in this ol' hide, but my ramblings will, so to speak."

His grandson looked away until his eyes lost their moistness. "Are you gonna do what Doc Gladstone says?"

"That feller's been dying to geld me for years. I ain't about to go along with his program, not just yet. Too many good-looking widows hereabouts to give up saluting.

"I can tell you this much. If a feller has to meet his maker, the mountains is a better place to do it than a damn fool hospital room." The old man walked to the shed's small window and gazed through the Appalachian haze toward the mountains. "Hell, come spring, I could be up there sleeping under an ocean of stars so close I could almost reach up and stir 'em."

"What's pulls you there, Granddad, the mountains, the rivers, critters, what?"

He took the reel from his grandson, and handing him a fresh spool of fly line, began winding it onto the reel. "It's the voices."

His grandson looked at him askance.

"Don't give me that look. We all got 'em." He pointed to the window. "Some of mine are out there. Only I can hear 'em though, mine. You gotta find your own. But they can be tricky, them voices. Some you wanna follow, some you don't."

Lee started to speak, but the old man stopped him with his hand. "I know where you're headed, Lee." Pensively, he studied his grandson for several seconds. "The voices that lead you toward the light, those are the ones you wanna follow."

"The light?"

He started to explain, but stopped and thought for a long moment. "You'll figure it out."

Lee made a face.

He thought for a long moment, finally tapping his chest. "All I can tell you is, it makes me happy in here when I follow them, the right ones. Gets me a little peek at glory's gate."

He winked at his grandson. "Of course, a time or two when I heard 'em, the voices, I might have been sniffing my campfire smoke a mite too long."

Amused, Lee snorted at the line.

When the wind suddenly gusted outside, his grandfather cocked his head and listened. "Voices," he said, thumbing toward the sound.

Lee asked abruptly, "Think there's a God?"

The old man stopped his winding. "Don't rightly know, but even if there ain't, I like the idea of The Boss ... that place where he hangs out, too."

"Think He gave you the cancer?"

He thought a moment. "Who else is running the show down here? Sure ain't Doc Gladstone ... although sometimes he thinks he is."

The young man's shoulders drooped. "But why would God do that?"

"Don't rightly know, again," grandfather answered. "But I still gotta find the right voices to deal with it, what The Boss has handed me."

The old man resumed his winding. "I don't cotton to going under any more than the next feller, but then again, my failings might make certain things a bit sweeter to these old ears. Like the sound of wind hissing through spruce trees alongside a mountain stream, or Dan's raspy trail music when he's hot on some critter's trail. And throw in too a trout stream singing over pebbles it knew when they was boulders." His hand brushed the vial in his shirt pocket. "In the end, the river always wins, boy, be it boulders ... or Granddads." He put the last of the line onto the reel and held it up. "Now, ain't that purty."

His grandson smiled feebly. "Think there's a hereafter?" Lee asked.

"Hope so. But my expiration date's not up yet. The doc said I had a year, 18 months left, maybe more. Besides, what's he know?"

"Not fair, God making you sick."

"Leave that in His lap."

"Don't you ever get lonely up there in the mountains all by yourself?"

"I got Dan and The Boss for company and that's pretty fair starters. I get your drift though. That's the reason I show up 'round here ever so often. Lots of widows need tending hereabouts." He winked, then asked abruptly, "Speaking of that, how's your love life?"

The corners of Lee's mouth curved down.

"You like dancing, boy?"

Lee frowned.

"Always took a shine to it myself," the old man began. "Some fellers don't like it though, the dancing. They'd rather stand off in a corner and dream about hugging them gals later. Of course, like them other fellers, I'd be hoping to do the same. I always figured though, in case later never came, I was for squeezing them pretties tight when the caller was still slapping his leg and keeping time.

"I wouldn't dance with just them hot numbers neither. I'd give them hard lookers a twirl also. A feller never knows what he might find under them feathers, especially if he broke a good sweat looking. Hell, maybe a golden swan or two. Besides, sometimes them good lookers turn out to be turkey buzzards, once you get a good lamplight on 'em."

Lee chuckled.

"Always figured there's nothing wrong with planning on some fun after the fiddles are cased, but I'd best enjoy the jigging while I still got music. You know, in case those pretties go home with some other fellers and them good times I dreamed about having later go up in smoke." He paused. "Same goes for your hereafters ... your Eden Brooks too."

As Lee walked toward the main house, he asked back over his shoulder, "When we go fishing tomorrow, can we talk? I got more questions."

"Just follow your voices, son," the old man said, "the right ones." He smiled wryly at the back of his grandson's head and snapped off the shed light.

CHAPTER THIRTY-SIX

As Lee awoke the next morning, he heard the deep rumble of his grandfather's pickup. He hurried out front, then around back. There was a strange car near the shed, but no sign of the old man or his truck. Lee sat on of the picnic bench, his shoulders drooping. The back door of their house clicked open and shut.

There she was at the top of their back steps, Pru, chestnut hair and big matching eyes over rose lips.

Since the Burnt Tree more than a year before, Lee had plenty of time to think about what she had done. Across that time span, he had felt disappointment, rejection and anger, all those demons cutting him to the bone. The real marrow of the issue though was this: despite those bad feelings, he still loved her. That's why it hurt so much, never mind he had to keep that love a prisoner in his soul.

Lee stood up as she started down the steps. "What are you ... wh-why are you...?" he stammered.

"Good morning to you too," she said. "I brought some cookies over for your grandfather. We talked some too, your mother and me."

"About?"

"Mostly your grandfather, but girl-talk too, a little town dirt," she smiled behind her hand.

"Town dirt?" He folded his arms and sat down again.

"Nothing, really."

He waited.

"Father David's got your mother all worked up. She's worried he might be kicked out of the church. You've heard the rumors, same as me. I told her it might just be gossip, but even if it was true, maybe they don't feel like they did anything wrong, the priest and the girl. I told her those things happen sometimes, people fall in love."

"My God, Pru, he's a priest, a priest. Don't you have any principles?"

"I don't want to fight, Lee." She sat down on the bench beside him.

"Your grandfather's illness too, that has her worked up."

He glanced at the strange car. "Yours?"

She nodded.

He motioned toward the shed. "Have you seen him?"

"Went fishing, according to your mother."

"Damn, told him I wanted to go with him."

"Speaking of that, it's been over a year since we talked, last June in fact. Remember, I called your house just before you and Tom left on your trip, the Burnt Tree. You answered the phone. I told you I called to get your mother's fried chicken recipe, but I just wanted to hear your voice. Everything seemed fine between us, and you said you'd touch base when you got back ... but you never did. Over the last year, I've phoned your house several times." Abruptly, she asked, her tone suddenly sharp, "Why haven't you returned my calls?"

Pausing for several seconds, he ran his fingers repeatedly across the grain on the picnic table. "Sawyers Park ring a bell?"

She seemed puzzled by the remark.

Her reaction bothered him: there were no tells on her face, like she knew what the reference was or had done anything wrong. Despite that, he added, his voice with a tinge of sarcasm, "What about Kenny Harte, your old church buddy?"

She frowned. "What is it you think I did?" she asked, her eyes welling and her lower lip beginning to quiver.

He searched for a lighter subject. "That trip you mentioned, a restaurant owner up there on the Burnt Tree, name was Bud, he told us about a great trout stream way over the mountains called Eden Brook. We spent four whole days looking for it, but never found it."

Lee glanced at the shed. "Damn, Granddad should have waited. Told him I wanted to go with him."

"Knowing him, I'm sure he had his reasons."

"Why are you taking his side?" he asked. "He's no saint."

She frowned.

"A year or so back, Granddad told me a story. It had to do with the death of his first wife, a neighbor man too, from the fever. But not the grandmother I knew." He then recounted for her the tale the old man told him. "Anyway, in the course of his telling," Lee went on, "I learned some things that got me thinking, wondering if I really knew him, my own grandfather."

She tilted her head and leaned forward.

"Well, to begin with, they were just living out there together, him and his first wife, but they weren't even married." He held up three fingers. "Almost three whole years living together and not even married. Told me so himself."

"Perhaps they were, you know, married in a bigger sense."

He cocked an eyebrow.

"Maybe they didn't need a ceremony. They loved one another and that was enough. Maybe that was more important to them than any piece of paper."

"We're back to that, huh," he sneered. "Giving out passes for breaking the rules."

"Aw, corn, honey. I don't want to fight. I'm just saying they loved one another and perhaps they were married ... you know, in God's eyes."

"Okay, okay, have it your way. Let's not get sidetracked. The point is you haven't heard the best part, about Granddad that is. That restaurant owner, Bud, same one that told us about Eden Brook, he also told us another wild tale about how the river got its name, Burnt Tree."

Lee then detailed for her the Dan Jagger story about betrayal and double murder. At its conclusion, he added, "I didn't think much of Bud's tale at the time until Granddad told me his story later. It rang a bell though right off, the similarities. I swear, you could lay one story on top the other, and except for different names and a couple of other changes, they'd be the same story, Granddad's and Dan's."

She leaned away and looked at him askance.

"Hear me out," he said, holding up his hands. "There's other stuff too." He then noted how both tales occurred around the same time and in the same region, the upper reaches of the Burnt Tree, also relating a few lesser coincidences, like the initials of the characters and the wives' favorite flowers. Eyes widening, he finished with, "And what about this? Granddad's dog has the same name as that guy in Bud's story. Don't you see? Granddad even named his dog after his old self."

Momentarily, she considered the two stories. "All right, all right, I'll give you this, there are some likenesses, the characters, what happened. So what?"

"Jeez, don't you get it? They're the same man, Dan Jagger and my grandfather. They have to be."

Frowning, Pru began subtly shaking her head.

"And if they are, you realize what that means, don't you?"

She looked at him blankly.

"What other conclusion is there? My own grandfather could be a murderer ... I didn't want to believe it either, but there you have it."

She crossed her arms over her chest and scowled. "Lee Jarrett, do you hear yourself? That's crazy talk. You know him. He's a good man. He just wouldn't—."

He talked through her. "There is one thing I don't get though, why the wives are buried in two different places, one on the Burnt Tree and the other on Mays Mountain." He bit his lower lip. "The rest fits though."

"Why would your grandfather make up such a story?

"Isn't it obvious? To cover up a murder, escape the law. What else?"

"Look, has he ever lied to you ... to either one of us? If that's what he said happened, then that's what happened." She paused. "My God, I can't believe this. I'm trusting him more than you, his own grandson."

He took a deep breath, exhaled and hung his head.

She thought for a long moment. "Okay, okay," she said, extending her open hands, "let's say you're right, your grandfather was Dan Jagger. That still doesn't make him a murderer."

"How's that?"

"Bear with me. Just for argument's sake, let's say things happened the way your grandfather said, with the fever and all.

"Anyway, over the years, folks changed grandfather's version, trying to spice it up, make it scarier and such. Like, for instance, making Dan a murderer, instead of a victim, which he was. Anyway, you end up with a tale more like what's-his-name told you ... Bud. That's the reason both tales match. They are the same stories, same characters, only Bud's is a juicier telling of your grandfather's 'cause that's what people would rather hear." She paused. "Why couldn't things have happened that way?"

"Oh yeah, there's something else I didn't mention, his leg scar."

"His what?" she asked.

"Grandfather's leg scar. When we were hunting last fall, me and him, and he raised his pants leg, he had a long, wicked white scar running clear 'round back of his right leg."

Still not understanding, her eyebrows lowered.

"Dan Jagger's leg, it was cut in his fight with Papa Joe. I told you that. You forget? The restaurant owner claimed they could tell by the blood trail it was Dan's right leg, same as Granddad's. I asked him about it too, the leg scar, but he didn't give me a straight answer, like he was trying to hide something."

"C'mon, he could have gotten that injury—"

"Sorry, but that leg scar clinches it for me, Bud's murder story."

With that, her shoulders slumped. "Okay, believe what you will." She paused a moment. "But what ever happened to forgiveness? I thought that was your thing, you Catholics."

He gave her a long study. "Yeah, but there's some things a guy can't get past." Holding her eyes knowingly, he added, "Can't forgive either, ever."

"Why that look at me?" she asked.

For several seconds, he tapped on his lips with two fingers. "Aw, skip it," he said finally, his voice trailing off.

"She touched his arm. "Maybe it's an upside-down way to look at things, but like I said before, if his first wife hadn't died, you'd never have been born, wouldn't be here now ... with me."

He liked her touch and wanted more, but instead, pulled away.

She gestured toward her car. "So, what do you think?"

Walking over, he stroked the door chrome.

"Needed it for work," she explained, sliding under the steering wheel. "Maybe you heard. I've been working at Welles Lumber, secretary, for going on a year now. The money's good. Mother got the job for me, went to school with the owner."

He leaned on her car door.

"By the way, I'm sure you know, but your old buddy, Tom, works there too. In fact, he asked me for a date when I first started there."

He looked away and shrugged indifferently.

"Glad you feel that way. We've been seeing one another for several months now. I've been helping him with his foot rehab."

Lee took his hands off the car and straightened. "Forgot to mention, I met a nice girl at college, name's Tammy, Tammy Sturling. We've been dating a lot," he lied. "A real special girl, principled." Capturing her eyes again, he added, "She keeps her word."

Pru eyed him skeptically. "Why that look ... again? You think I haven't done that, kept my word?"

His teeth clenched and he turned to go, but as he did, she held an envelope out toward him.

He was hesitant, but he took it from her, his eyebrows lowering.

Her face softening, she laid her hand over the envelope, now resting in his palm. "Some things that needed saying."

Later, after showering, he sat on his bed and read it. It was penned in her beautiful script.

Dearest Lee,

I hope you read this before you tear it up, but I wouldn't blame you if you did. I love you now and always have. I let my mother do my thinking for me and drove you away. But that's water under the bridge and I'm sorry for that. I prefer, instead, to look to our future. We can still have that beautiful life together we dreamed about. Please find it in your heart to forgive me and call.

   Love you always,
   Pru

  He read it several times. There's those same damn words again, "love" and "always." What a joke. She didn't mean those words before on her picture and she doesn't mean them now, not really. He crumpled her letter.

  He looked out the window and his eyes fell to the picnic bench. Uncrumpling the letter, he tore it into fine pieces and took the Hillsboro fall catalog out of his nightstand.

CHAPTER THIRTY-SEVEN

Lee got back to school late that evening. When he called the girls' dorm, Mrs. Lymon said Tammy had gone to the library. Hurrying across campus, he got there just as she was coming down the front steps.

She was beautiful as always, stunningly so. He always felt that when he first saw her.

"Lee, you're back. Missed you at fall registration."

"Had trouble hitching a ride, again. I'll do it tomorrow, pay a late fee."

She smiled, tight-lipped, and then turned away.

There was an ivy-trellised gazebo across from the library. "Could we talk a minute?" he asked, motioning her toward it.

As he followed her up the steps, her pleated skirt kept time with her swaying hips. Inside the gazebo, it was dark and mysterious. He sat down but after tossing her book on the seat, she remained standing.

"Sorry about missing our weekend at the lake," he said.

She looked down at him, unresponsive. He went on, telling her about his grandfather's diagnosis. "I tried calling your dorm to explain, but they said you were gone. Left you a message."

"I never got it," she said, touching his arm. "Sorry about your grandfather, Lee. I didn't know what to think when you didn't call or show." An awkward silence followed. "Anything new at home?"

He shrugged one shoulder and tried making small talk. "Oh yeah, I did catch some music one night. A Wheeling station, I think. Announcer called it Rock N Roll. Different, but catchy."

"I'll see if I can pick it up sometime, check it out."

He was still seated and she was standing close in front of him. Her breasts, just inches from his face, were full, each like a jumbo snow cone he had once at a carnival. The impulse to wrap his arms around her, pull her close and bury his face in them was almost more than he could resist.

Barely breathing herself, she stared down at him, motionless. It was almost as if she was waiting for him to do that, wanting him to do that.

Unable to read what her eyes were truly saying in the leafy darkness, he rejected the venture, however, electing instead to sit there woodenly, a fearful and indecisive hero, more Barney Fife than Indiana Jones.

His passiveness was her cue and she broke the spell, turning and walking away to the steps.

He picked up her book and padded along after her, like Dan after his grandfather. She took his wrist and looked at his watch in the light from a lamppost. "Curfew." Holding hands, they walked back to her dorm.

"Anything else new in Eastbrook?" she asked.

"Not much. Oh yeah, ran into an old girlfriend, Cathy Pruitt."

She broke hands.

"But that's over," he said. "She dropped by our house for my grandfather. Brought him some goodies."

Just as he started to hand her the book, he accidentally dropped it, sending her index cards, most filled with notes, tumbling down the dorm steps. "Aw jeez, I'm sorry," he said, scrambling after them.

She waved off his apology.

Both began crawling around on their hands and knees, each intent on retrieving the scattered cards. Just as before at the cafeteria, their faces met again, and as before, she stifled a giggle with the back of her hand. "Thanks for telling me about the old girlfriend," she said.

Her warm breath on his cheek made the hair on the back of his neck tingle. He kissed her softly. Her lips were passive, but when she didn't pull away, he kissed her again, only harder. The second time her lips were eager, hungry also, like his.

"Missed you," she whispered.

Another couple passed them on the steps, Lee and Tammy still kneeling. "Looks like someone got their prayers answered," the young man said. The couple laughed, but Lee, his face buried in her hair alongside her neck, never looked up.

Just then, there was a sharp knock on the window panel beside the door. It was her dorm mother, Mrs. Lymon. Tapping on her watch, she glared at them steely-eyed through the glass casement.

Lee held onto Tammy's eyes for as long as he could before the older woman ushered her inside. "Call me," Tammy urged as Mrs. Lymon shut the door.

He stopped at the bottom of the steps and glanced back at the dorm. Guess the fudge didn't work.

Over the next few months, the two began spending almost every evening together, going to movies, attending sporting events or studying at the library. Sometimes also, they lunched with one another at the student union.

All the while, he was becoming more and more certain that Tammy was that one special girl he had been looking for all his young life. Indeed, so certain was he of this that he asked her to spend the Thanksgiving holidays with his family at Eastbrook.

She agreed to come for the dinner, but only if Lee could take her back to the Hillsboro campus afterward. Her father was driving down from Pittsburgh, she explained, to pick her up Thanksgiving evening, so she could spend the remainder of the holiday with her own family.

"Your turkey smells great, Mrs. Jarrett," Tammy said. "And your table setting too, it's perfect."

"We're delighted you could join us for the holiday, dear," Lee's mother answered. Smiling, she motioned to a chair at the table. "You sit there, Tammy, to Lee's right."

As Tammy sat down, Mrs. Jarrett glanced at grandfather's empty chair. "Why he'd rather be out in the cold with wet dogs, I'll never understand," she said.

At the head of the table, his father tried explaining to Tammy the old man's absence coupled with his wife's comment. "You see, him and a half dozen old buddies, most with big fox hounds, they like to head up in the mountains at night. Build themselves a big fire up there, sometimes for the cold, most times for comfort and then listen to their dogs chase foxes. They can tell which animal is in the lead by their baying. You see, each dog's bellowing is different, like people's voices. The one up front is more excited, happier, bawling faster."

His mother cut in, shaking her head. "This young lady must think we're savages."

His father went on explaining. "The ol' guys usually take something along to eat, crackers and cheese mostly, a big round of Longhorn. They talk and joke and lie a lot. You know how stories get blown up over the years. They've been known to pass around a bottle now and then too. Anyway, they stay up there on the mountain till all hours, whooping and hollering, acting like they was teenagers again, but not bothering a soul." Sneaking a look at his wife, he added, "Except for their families."

"I still think you should talk to him again, Stewart," she said to her husband. "You know, about doing what the doctor says."

"You ever try making him do something he didn't wanna do, Evelyn?"

She glared back at him, annoyed but knowing he was right. "Please excuse us, dear," Mrs. Jarrett said to Tammy, "airing family business in front of guests."

"Don't give it a thought. My parents, they do that all the time," Tammy said, catching Lee's eyes and smiling behind her napkin.

"Beans?" his father asked, offering Tammy a serving dish.

After the meal, Lee walked with Tammy out to the shed. Although he feared she might be bored by it all, he gave her the grand tour of his grandfather's world, at least the important corners, including his huge wilding bag. As for the old man's big knife, Stella, it was gone. Lee had to settle for describing it and pointing to the empty wall peg. He pointed to another nearby empty peg also. "He hangs his dut hat there."

"Dut hat?"

He chuckled. "Tell you later."

"That reminds me," she said, turning to leave, "back in a jiffy." When she returned, she handed him a white baseball hat. "I tried finding a better color, sorry. Hope it fits."

He put it on and his eyes said he liked it.

"Call it a Thanksgiving present," she said, beaming.

They embraced and he gave her a quick peck on the lips. "Thanks for making this holiday special, your being here," he whispered.

"Which reminds me," she said. "How about returning the favor?"

He frowned.

"How about spending Christmas with us, my family?"

He hesitated, weighing her request. "I don't know. Mom will have a hissy fit." He suddenly got lost in those blue Crater Lake eyes. "On the other hand, I do owe your parents for missing that weekend at the lake. And you," he added, "I owe you too."

"Great," she said, giving him a hug. "I've told Mother and Daddy so much about you, and they're dying to meet you," She paused. "Your parents, they're nice. I liked them. And what a terrific cook, your mother. By the way, who is Father David?"

"Why?"

"Nothing, really," she said, tittering. "When I was helping your mother with the dishes, she mentioned his name, like I should know him. From what I gathered, he's being transferred from Eastbrook, fooling around with some young woman in the parish," your mother told me.

He took Tammy's hat off and hung it on a wall peg.

"She mentioned something about Cathy too, your old girl, and I think someone named Tom. Who's that?"

"What about them, what did she say about them?"

"Just said they were getting pretty serious, Cathy and Tom, or so she heard."

His teeth ground together. "What else did she say?"

"That was it." Tammy touched his arm. "You okay?"

"Those people mean nothing to me," he answered, his gut tightening, "not anymore."

As Tammy said goodbyes to Mr. Jarrett inside, Lee and his mother walked to the car. Lee motioned his head toward Tammy. "Did I mention she's Catholic, Mom?"

"That's nice."

He slid his arm around his mother's shoulders. "You like her?"

"Seems like a nice young lady."

"Hope so, hope you like her. You may be seeing more of her, a lot more."

She pulled away. "What are you saying?"

"And by the way: I'm spending the holidays, Christmas, with them this year, the Sturlings."

"Aw, Lee, no. You can't, not Christmas."

"It's only fair, Mom. You know, after I cancelled that weekend with them before, and she spent Thanksgiving here."

"But it'll just ruin the family's Christmas," she said, "my Christmas, not having you here. And what about the star on the tree? You always hang it there for the family over the holidays. You've done that forever, it's a family tradition. Why, I remember when your father had to hold you over his head to reach it. If you're not here, it won't be Christmas."

"It'll work out Mom," he said, stroking her back, "you'll see."

CHAPTER THIRTY-EIGHT

It was an early morning at college when a voice called through the door at the dorm, "Phone call, Jarrett, your Mom."

Lee's eyes rolled up. He was suspicious of her timing, calling just a few days before Christmas with the Sturlings.

"What is it now, Mom?" he asked.

"Please come home, Lee," she pleaded between sobs, "come home at once. Something's happened to your grandfather, something terrible." Before he could ask what it was, she hung up.

Lee was certain Tammy would never forgive a second turn down. Surprisingly though, when he called her and explained, she said she understood, insisting Lee go home and call her when he knew more.

Through the misting rain, Lee walked toward his home in Eastbrook. All the lights were on and several cars were parked outside. One red car had "Fire Chief" written on its side. A heavy sadness seemed to be hanging over his little home. His mother was on the front porch, talking to a uniformed man. She waved to him.

The man brushed past Lee and slid under the steering wheel of the red car.

Arms outstretched, his mother met him at the bottom of their front steps. "Lee, oh, Lee," she said. "Something terrible has happened." Sobbing, she pulled him close. "Your grandfather's drowned ... they think."

His mind went numb. He stood there, holding her woodenly, trying to comprehend her words. Over her shoulder, he saw a Christmas wreath hanging on their front door. It had gold bulbs, white frosting and a red ribbon.

The rain pelting on the hood of his rain jacket jolted him back. "What do you mean, drowned?"

"Last night, they found his truck in the Eastbrook River," she said.

For the first time, he seemed to notice she was getting soaked. Motioning for her to follow, he led her onto their front porch and put his rain jacket around her.

The Eastbrook River was normally a lazy, meandering stream, but that night, when Lee crossed the Fourth Street Bridge it was raging. "I've never seen it like that before," he said. "Almost over the arches." Lee sat down on the bannister and motioned for her to sit down beside him. His mother chose to stand, instead.

Sniffling, she explained more. "The fire chief said him and his crew would keep looking all night, but if they didn't find him by daylight, they'd give up the search. He said it was almost certain he drowned, that nobody could have made it out of those raging waters alive. He said they'd have to wait till the river went down before they could drag it." She teared up again.

"I don't believe it," he said.

"I didn't want to either, dear, but the fire chief said—"

"He can't be certain, Mom, no one can." He paused. "Why didn't you call me last night?"

"We didn't want to upset you, dear. We were still hoping, you know, they'd find him, alive."

"Where was this?" he asked.

"West of town." She motioned in that direction. "On the road toward Wilkins. Out near where Stony Run comes in. A bad curve there. You know, where the road swings close to the river."

"What was he doing out that way?"

"Heaven knows." Her voice sounded weary. "He didn't even mention he was going out. Your father had a meeting and I was tired, went to bed early. When I got up once to go to the bathroom, I saw a light in his shed, and then heard him messing around in the kitchen. I thought he was just fixing himself a sandwich, like usual. Next thing I knew, the back door slammed and I heard his truck drive away."

"Strange," Lee said, "when he goes out in the middle of the night, he always lets someone know. Doesn't want you worrying."

"Then later that night," she went on, "the fire chief said the headlights of a passing motorist, fella named Linger, caught some tail reflectors in the river. Most of his truck was under water, only the back end sticking up. Anyway, this Linger fellow got a flashlight, called and searched, then went for help. When they hauled his truck out later, the driver's door was open but the cab was empty. Of course, they searched and searched for hours, the water and the banks as far downstream as Mill Creek Junction, but nothing. 'Like the river just swallowed him up,' the chief said."

"But you're forgetting something, Mom, everyone is. He's a strong swimmer, even won medals for it."

"Maybe you're right, dear," she said.

He started toward the steps. "I'm going out there right now. I'll find him, I know I will. Alive too."

"No, Lee, no," she pleaded. "It's dark. Don't go by yourself. Wait for the others. Some of the searchers are inside having something to eat. Go on in, have a bite and go with them when they go out again." Taking his hand, she led him across the porch toward their front door. "Please, dear, for me."

He hesitated, but then opened the door.

"I'll tell Dad you're here," she said, once inside.

He made his way through the crowded living room toward a table with an almost empty food tray. He picked up one of the remaining sandwiches and sat down on a low stool in one corner.

For the first time, he noticed a red and green banner high on their living room wall: Merry Christmas and Happy New Year '52

All he could see otherwise were people's feet and legs. Suddenly the legs parted, and Dan, looking lost, ambled toward him. Lee scratched the dog's ears and arched one eyebrow. "But why didn't he take you along?" Lee gave Dan the last of his sandwich, and the dog plopped down next to him, facing the food tray, his eyes open a slit. "But we both know he's still alive, don't we, boy?"

Someone waved a bottle of soda in front of Lee's eyes. He looked up into his father's tired face. "Sorry I'm late, Dad. Trouble catching a ride ... again"

"I guess mother filled you in on the bad news," his father said. He put his hand on his son's shoulder and gave a gentle squeeze. "Sorry, pal."

"Yeah, but the car door was open and he's a strong—"

"She told me you said that. Don't you realize that kind of talk is upsetting your mother, getting her hopes up for nothing?" He paused. "Of course, we're going to keep looking. We even got some big spotlights to help, but you gotta face facts, Lee. It doesn't look good."

"I'm going out there with you when you search again," Lee said. "I just know he's out there somewhere, alive too."

"Your mother's motioning for me. I'll be right back," his father said. "We need to talk."

Lee recognized his father's look, his "sermon's coming" look.

Still on the low stool, Lee noticed the people's faces. Most were men with dark beard stubbles and there were a few women. They all looked tired with dark half moons under their eyes. Among the familiar faces, he recognized his grandfather's old fishing and hunting buddies. All of them seemed uncomfortable, lost in this setting, much like he imagined his grandfather would be if he were there.

For the first time, Lee noticed a Christmas tree standing in the corner near him. It was undecorated, but scattered around its base were opened cartons, boxes with strings of lights, silver tinsel and gaily-tinted bulbs.

He picked up a silvered bell and held it up close in his face. He stroked it with his index finger and it tinkled happily.

Off to his right, a woman nodded toward the front door. "It's Father David," she whispered to another woman.

Lee dropped the bulb and it shattered with a pop.

The second woman whispered back, "I heard the bishop wants him transferred. You know, away from that Heinz girl."

"Is he going to accept?" the first woman asked.

The other one shrugged.

His mother called across the room to her son, "Look who it is, Lee, Father David."

The priest walked toward him, extending his hand.

Never looking up, the young man busied himself picking up the larger pieces of the broken bulb.

"Sorry about your grandfather," Father David said.

"Don't worry, we'll find him. He'll be okay."

Father David glanced at his mother. "Hope you're right, kid, hope you're right." He turned to Lee's mother. "What can I do to help?"

Lee dumped the bulb's glass fragments in a trashcan and sat down on the stool again.

"That's nice of you to offer, Father," his mother answered, "that's nice."

"Where's Stewart?"

"The kitchen," his mother answered, starting to walk away. "I'll tell him you're here."

"See you, Lee," Father David said. "By the way, Tom's doing better. Thought you'd like to know."

When Lee didn't respond, but busied himself with the remaining glass shards on the floor, Father David walked away.

Shortly, his mother came back. She stamped her foot. "How could you? How could you be so rude to Father David, refusing to shake his hand?"

"But Mom, you don't know what he did."

"I've heard the gossip, but that's what it is, gossip."

"Please, Mom, don't get upset. It's something personal between him and me." In the overhead light, he could see she was looking tired, very tired. "How long since you got some rest, Mom?"

"Don't change the subject. I can't lie down. Not until I know, know for certain, about your grandfather."

"Really you should, before you collapse."

"I need to keep busy." She scraped some crumbs off the edge of the table into her apron. "If I don't, I'll go crazy."

He made her sit down. "Others can clean up, Mom. You take it easy. Others can do that."

"By the way, I called Pru," she said.

He scowled.

She answered his look. "She cares about him too, your grandfather."

Just then, someone called his mother's name from the other side of the room.

After she left, Dan stood up, and with his head and tail hanging, he ambled toward the kitchen, lost without grandfather, but seduced by the coffee aroma.

Lee followed the dog into the kitchen. His father was making sandwiches. "We're heading back to the river in an hour or so," he said, "once folks get recharged."

"Mom's looking awful tired," Lee said.

"Yeah, I know. Just as well she's busy though. Keeps her mind off, you know." He set up another bread and cold cut assembly line and pointed to it. "Help out, bub."

Lee hesitated.

"Something wrong?"

"There's a grave up on May's Mountain where Granddad's first wife is buried. Ever been there?"

His father stopped stacking cold cuts. "He carted me up there once when I was young. Just cleaned her grave off and said it was his first wife. That's about it. Back then, I was too young and dumb to ask questions."

"He took me up there, too," his son said, "just once, a year or so back. Told me all about the wonderful life him and her had together, then how she up and died."

"Made no sense to me," his father said, "why he'd bury her way up there on May's Mountain." He chuckled to himself. "Funny thing, I met an ol' codger a ways back, told me some things I never knew about him. Claimed, for one thing, Granddad's wife wasn't even buried up there."

Lee's eyes narrowed. "Believe him?"

His father shrugged. "No reason to lie. Anyway, I met this old guy at a family reunion back a ways. Whole bunch of families were gathered down there at Turner's Mill. I'd just gotten me a big drumstick and was sitting in the shade under this pavilion when an old gent sidled up to me. Introduced himself and we got to trading stories and showing wallet pictures.

"Well, in the course of talking, I learned he was raised over 'round Spruce Mountain in the late 1800s, same as your grandfather. Claimed he knew 40 Grit in the old days. I even showed him some old wallet photos to make certain we were talking about the same gent, and he picked him out. Said your grandfather went by another name back then, but he couldn't recollect."

"If not May's Mountain, where'd he say she was buried?"

"Hold your horses. I'm coming to that," his father answered. "Anyway, this old guy went on to say she was laid to rest way up on the Burnt Tree someplace. He mentioned something else I never knew either, her name, grandfather's first wife. He said it was Amanda."

"Amanda? Granddad told me it was Annie. I even remember the initials on her tombstone, A. J."

His father shrugged. "I'm just telling you what this ol' codger told me. Amanda, he said, that was her name. Seemed pretty sure of it too." He paused. "Maybe your granddad put that tombstone on May's Mountain so he'd have some place to visit, think about her, someplace close." He shrugged. "Who knows?"

"Amanda, huh," Lee repeated, weighing the name and thinking. "Now that I think about it, that 'A' on her tombstone could have stood for that too, Amanda." He thought for a long moment. "My God, Dad, if that old guy's right, it changes everything, clinches what I been thinking. Don't you see? They are one and the same man."

His father looked at him blankly.

"Granddad and Crazy Dan. They both lived way up on the Burnt Tree 'round the same time. Their wives had the same first names and both buried up there. Now you've given me something else that confirms it, the name of the place near where they lived. It was called Amanda's Valley, named after Dan's wife. Dad, they're one and the same man, Granddad and Crazy Dan. They have to be. I'm sure of it."

"Crazy who?" his father asked.

"C'mon, don't you remember me telling you about it, that tale he spun, the restaurant owner on the Tree? Had to do with this old guy named Crazy Dan who killed his wife and a neighbor, ran off and was never heard from since. Like I just said, near where he lived was a place called Amanda's Valley, same first name as Crazy Dan's wife, Granddad's too."

His father opened a package of meat, smelled it and made a face. "Where are you going with this, Lee? Hope you're not making your grandfather out to be that murderer. Don't let that imagination of yours set you nuts."

Lee rolled his eyes. "Did he have anything else to say, that guy you met at the family get-together?"

His father shook his head.

Lee began fixing sandwiches, his mind racing. It seemed to him that if he put all the likenesses together, there was only one plausible conclusion: His grandfather and Dan Jagger were one and the same man. They had to be. Goose bumps raised on his arm.

"Maybe it's for the best," his father said, "losing him in the river."

"What do you mean? It's good he drowned?"

He frowned at his son. "I was just saying, it's the way he would have wanted it, going under and quick, with him being sick and all. Maybe it's time you braced yourself for the worst. There are some dreams you gotta toss overboard. Hold onto 'em and they'll lead you down a mine shaft."

"But what about all those ribbons he won for swimming? You've seen them."

"That was more than 60 years ago, Lee," his father said, "when he was in his prime."

"I need some air." Lee stepped onto their back porch. He hated the truth of his father's logic, but knew he was right about how the old man would have wanted it to end, quick and near his voices.

CHAPTER THIRTY-NINE

"Tom's a fine young man," Blanche said. "You're lucky to have him in your life."

Pru lifted the dishtowel off a bowl on the stove and peered under it. There, a mound of dough was rising nicely. Turning to the table, she punched down on another mound, sprinkled it with flour and began kneading it. "Last one, Mother," she said, wiping her forehead with the back of her hand.

Five golden loaves of bread for the church bake sale rested nearby on a dishcloth.

"About him, Tom," Pru began. "I found a hurt baby rabbit once in the road. It was trembling and put on a big show about not wanting help, but I moved it to the side anyway. Tom's like that. He acts like he doesn't need help, but it's just a front. He needs it, at least for now, and that's where I come in. Must say too, I like that feeling, being needed. Lately though, he's been pressuring me for more."

"That's only natural, Cathy. What are you going to do?"

The phone rang and Pru picked it up. She listened, then hung up and buried her head in her arms on the table.

"Who was it, Cathy? What's wrong?"

Head still down on her arms, she answered, "It was Mrs. Jarrett. Lee's grandfather may have drowned."

"Land of Goshen," Mrs. Pruitt said, putting her hand to her throat. "That poor woman." She paused. "We have to send flowers."

"We'll do more than that, Mother. We have to go over there." She tapped her foot, thinking. "I can't tomorrow, Tom's rehab ... but maybe in the evening."

The following day outside the clinic, Pru motioned Tom toward a small children's park across the street. "Mind if we sit a moment? I have something to tell you."

"Me too, mine's good. You seem serious though, like yours is bad."

"You first," she said.

He smiled broadly. "Got my old job in the cutting shop back at the mill. Pays better than before."

"That's wonderful."

He took her by the hand. "All thanks to you."

"Mother said you stopped by when I was out, fixed our sink. Thanks."

"Yes sir, that's me, ol' Mr. Fixer Upper," he said, his tone light. "No big deal. Had my tools in the truck." Pointing to a bench, he took her hand. "What was it you had to say?"

"Bad news," she said. "I waited until after rehab so you wouldn't be distracted. Lee's grandfather drowned ... probably. They haven't found his body yet."

"How'd it happen?"

"Don't know the details, but I'm going over this evening to see what I can do."

His eyes ran over her face, trying to see if there was more.

"Lee's got him a girl at college now," she said. "I think it's serious."

"Good, good for him."

She fingered the heart locket around her neck. "You're right, good for him."

"You really like it, Cat?"

She looked at him blankly.

"My early Christmas gift," he said, pointing to the pin on her sweater. It was a silvered image of a cat. "I love it," she said, touching it.

He dangled his key chain with the letter 'T' in her face. "I like mine too."

She pointed to his leg.

"The numbness? About the same."

Reaching over, she turned his shirt label under.

Anymore, he was leaving it out deliberately. He liked the attention, her touch. He pointed to a children's merry-go-round nearby, "You game?"

"Yes, just my speed."

Giggling, she climbed on and held her legs up. Tom spun it and jumped on the other side.

Her cheeks were glowing from the cold December air, and her smile brightened the somber day.

The carousel was still spinning, but more slowly, and he blurted across its steel bars, "Marry me, Cat?"

Putting her foot down, she stopped the go-around and straightened. She studied him through the bars, head tilted and mouth opened. Deciding he was serious, she answered, shaking her head subtly, "I'm very fond of you, Tom, but I don't...

Ignoring where her answer was likely headed, he went on excitedly. "If it's about where to live, we could move into your house and help your mother. If you don't like that, we got an extra room at our place. You and my family seemed to hit it off. Besides, like I said, I got a raise. Things will be tight for a while, but we'll be okay. As for a ring, I have a little saved."

She folded her arms across her chest. "Sorry, Tom, but I don't feel that way about you."

Still buoyed by the bloom of his ardor, he half-heard her answer. "We'll make it work somehow, Cat, trust me."

She touched her chest. "I need to be getting home."

"What's wrong ... you okay?"

Just then, a young woman wearing a long-sleeved coat approached the playground with a little girl. The woman coaxed the child over to the swings, struggling afterward to lift her up and give her a push. As the little girl swung back and forth, she began giggling. The woman beamed. Tom suddenly realized it was the young woman with artificial arms he had seen before on the rehab pulleys.

They drove to Pru's house in silence. Tom tried making small talk, but it didn't work. On her porch, she turned her face away when he tried kissing her. "I'll drive myself tomorrow," she said.

"Aw no, what's wrong, Cat?"

"Don't call me. I'll let you know," she said, closing the door. She watched through the laced window curtain on the door as he plodded back to his truck, his limp suddenly worse.

CHAPTER FORTY

In the evening mist at the Jarrett house, Lee sat alone on a glider on their front porch. When he first sat down, he felt something gritty under his shoes. It was pine needles.

Before the holidays, his parents always stored their tree on the front porch. Then, with grand ceremony a few days before Christmas, they would put it up inside and trim it. These festivities ended when Lee mounted the star on top, which he had not done as yet. Still half-believing they would find his grandfather alive, he hoped they would not have to skip any of those celebrations this year, but Christmas was nearing.

For the first time, he noticed the foot-high, silver cross in their front window. As far back as he could remember, it was blinking there during the Christmas holidays. His mother always saw to that. Tonight though, it was dark.

The window where it was hanging was open a crack at the bottom. Through the opening, he could hear Father David's voice inside. He felt the gritty pine needles under his shoes.

The smell of fresh coffee drifted out from under the open window. He leaned forward with his face closer to the opening so he could smell it better. He bit down hard, but his eyes moistened anyway.

He heard footfalls on their front steps.

It was Pru. "Lee," she asked, "why are you sitting out here in the dark by yourself?" She collapsed her umbrella and sat on the glider beside him. Putting her head down, she shook her hair playfully in his face. "Look," she said, "it's not wet."

He looked away coldly.

Her eyes saddened. "Sorry about your grandfather. I loved him too, maybe not like you did, but I loved him." She smoothed her hair down. "Remember the time I borrowed his dut hat when we went to the Burnt

Tree? I never told you, but when I gave it back later and told him I liked it, he did the cutest thing. He plopped it on his head, cocked it at an angle and ran two fingers across the front brim in a mini salute. Like I said, cute."

His face started to soften, but he caught himself.

"Has my mother been over?" she asked.

He shook his head.

"Thought I saw her car when I pulled up." She caught his eyes. "Your grandfather, Lee, I'm really going to miss him. He was a great guy."

He swiveled toward her. "Don't say 'was.' We're going to find him, and alive too."

"Sure, Lee, sure." She eyed him sideways. "By the way, how's school?"

He hesitated. "You mean how are things with Tammy and me, don't you? They're fine, just fine, thank you."

"I heard her parents were well off."

"So?"

"Jeez, I didn't mean anything," she said.

"How are things with you and Judas?" he asked.

"Who?"

"Don't play dumb. You know who I mean, your boyfriend."

"Tom, you mean Tom?"

His look said he did.

"You used to be buddies. What happened between you two?"

"He knows, same as you. Come to think of it, you make a great couple: Mr. and Mrs. Judas."

She scowled and stamped her foot. "There you go again. Lee Jarrett. Tell me right this instant what you're talking about."

He didn't respond, but his shoes worried the gritty pine needles under his feet again.

"Then at least, answer me this," she said, her voice starting to break, "Why didn't you answer my note telling you how I felt about us?"

"Still don't get it do you? There is no more us."

Disbelief and hurt written over her face, she recoiled. "Le-e," she pleaded, her voice high, then falling.

"Go on home," he said. "Go on home to your mother, to him. We don't need you here. I got me a real girl now, one who keeps her promises."

She gave a wounded stare and put her hand to her chest. "Lee, you're talking crazy," she said, choking back tears, "What is it you think I did? You answer me."

When he turned toward the dark cross on their front door, she ran off the porch into the night, sobbing.

He yelled after her. "And we're getting married too, Tammy and me."

After she left, he sat alone on the glider in the dark. He felt a sad emptiness that had nothing to do with his grandfather and which he didn't understand.

He thought about why he had not done as she asked, spell her sin out, and have her either confirm or deny it. He finally decided he had held back because he felt trapped between two of his grandfather's voices, one wishing to know if she had broken her promise, and the other voice not wanting to learn if it was true—that when it came to keeping her vows, the girl he loved was weak willed, a leaf in the river.

He walked out to the shed and sat down in the old man's rocker in the dark. When Dan scratched on the door, he let him in and listened as he curled up on grandfather's hunting coat.

In the shadows on the wall, Lee could see the fly rod the old man had repaired for him. Outside, he strung it up and pulled several feet of line off the reel. He cast it again and again. Although it was misting and he could not see his loops in the darkness, the rod's casting rhythm felt better than it ever had.

When he hung it back on the wall inside, the wind suddenly rattled the little shed. Dan whined and Lee did a long thinking stare. Finding one edge of his grandfather's hunting coat in the dark, Lee coaxed Dan off, and then dragged it along the floor so the dog would follow. "C'mon, Boy," he said, "too many ghosts here." Before he left though, he put on Tammy's white hat.

Lee's mother was in the kitchen. "Hungry?" she asked her son.

He waved no and sat down at the table, the dog alongside.

"Pru called. Said she came by to pay respects, saw you and left. Sounded like she was crying. Did you do something to upset her?"

He looked away sheepishly.

She smiled down at Dan. "Did I mention the scrawny little mutt at the river where grandfather's truck went in?"

His eyebrows slid up.

"Fire chief said they found this half-drowned little guy clinging to one end of his tail gate. Said he was scared and shivering his spots off. Some fella upstream claimed him later. He said the dog fell off his back porch and got washed away. It did set the chief to wondering though, wondering if your grandfather lost his life trying to save that little mutt. Be just like him."

Her son's eyes brightened. "Wouldn't surprise me none neither, him doing that. Where's Dad?"

She motioned toward the other room and made a phone gesture.

Lee pointed up stairs. "Tell him to call me when he goes to the river." Up in his room, Lee turned the soft side of the old man's hunting coat out and laid it in one corner for Dan.

When he looked in his mirror, he saw Tammy's hat on his head. If he did marry her, it would serve Pru right for what she did and caused him to do. On the other hand, if she hadn't been untrue, he might never have met Tammy.

He went downstairs, phoned Tammy at the dorm, but got no answer. His mother called from the kitchen, "We're running low on Cokes, Lee."

Their sodas were stored in the washroom, which was just off the back porch. When Lee went for the Cokes, three of his grandfather's old fishing buddies were on the porch, talking.

One was saying to the other, "Yes sir, the chief said Dallas' tire tracks went straight into the river, like he drove in on purpose."

They all looked knowingly at one another.

Lee set the Cokes on the counter beside the sink where his mother was working.

"Your father said we'll need another case too, ginger ale," she said. "Sorry, dear."

When Lee returned to the back porch, only one of his grandfather's fishing buddies was still there. "Don't pay them fellers no mind," he said to Lee. "Your Granddaddy was no quitter, wouldn't have thrown in the towel. Besides, old Frank Conway said he saw some big feller with a huge backpack cutting across his back field same night ol' Dallas disappeared. Frank's spread is just west of where his truck went in. Ten to one, it was your grandfather heading for the mountains. At least, that's the story I'm sticking with, son."

After he took the case of sodas inside, Lee poured himself a cup of coffee.

"Drinking it black now, dear," his mother asked, "like someone else we know?"

On the back porch, he sat on the top step. Dan nosed the door open and sat down beside him. Lee turned his muzzle up toward his own face and stared into the dog's brown eyes. "What I can't figure out though, boy, is why he left you behind."

The door opened and closed behind him. "Here, this might taste good with your coffee," his mother said. She set a plate of food beside him on the opposite side from Dan. On it was a piece of apple pie and a wedge of Longhorn cheese, a thread of rind still clinging to it.

Seemingly pleased, his mother watched as he ate it.

After he finished, there was some Longhorn left and he fed it to Dan.

She put her hand on her son's shoulder. "His favorite cheese, your grandfather's. Never would go to the mountains without it."

She was right. There were certain things the old man took with him when he went wilding. Lee jumped off the steps and hurried toward the shed. "Back in a minute, Mom," he called. Dan bounced along behind him, like he knew what Lee had in mind.

In his excitement, Lee jerked too hard on the light cord and it broke off in his hand. Groping wildly, he found the chain and snapped on the light. He tilted the shade up so its light flooded the wall back of the bench. His grandfather's big knife, Stella, the one he said he would never go to the mountains without, was missing.

He then tilted the light toward the shadows at the back of the shed. It was missing too, the old man's wilding bag.

Walking over to the shed's small window, now painted black by the night, he looked toward the mountains. "He's up there somewhere Dan, I just know it."

His father stuck his head through the shed door. "We're headed to the river now. You coming?"

"Yeah, Dad, be right there," he said, but he knew then they would never find him where they were looking.

CHAPTER FORTY-ONE

One evening a few weeks later, his grandfather's mystery deepened, not about his disappearance, but about his past.

Lee had gone to the washroom, which was just off their back porch, to get the laundry for his mother. After unloading the dryer, the young man lingered briefly, paging through a girly magazine he kept hidden there. He had just snapped the light off, hidden the magazine and picked up the laundry basket when he heard them, the thunderous footsteps coming up their back steps. They seemed to jar the whole house, including the floor of the washroom where he was standing. They were followed, when they stopped, by a giant pounding on their back door.

After the porch light came on, his father stepped out and looked up at the towering stranger. Even though the man's shoulders were slightly stooped, he was big, grandfather-sized big. The other thing that struck Lee was how he wore his hat. His hood was pulled up over his head, a wide-brimmed hat resting over top of that. The stranger took his hat off and threw his hood back. He had a gray, briar-patch beard and matching hair that spilled down in back over the hood of his dark slicker. He put his hat back on and tipped it forward so it shadowed his face.

"Name's Joseph," he said, his deep voice cutting the damp night air, "John Joseph from over 'round Wilkens."

As they shook hands, his father said, "Jarrett, Stewart Jarrett."

"Heard about the drowning last month," the big man said. "Sorry about your pappy, Dallas. He nodded toward the porch light. "Mind turning that off?" he asked, pointing to his face. "I got the eye miseries."

Before his father could do that, the porch-light flickered, and then blinked off on its own, leaving only the light streaming though their kitchen window from inside. Although Mr. Jarrett tapped on the porch-light bulb several times, he could not get it to come back on.

"I know it ain't a good time for you and your kinfolk," the stranger began, "but I'm up against the clock tonight." Pausing, he asked his father abruptly, "Did you ever come across a map, you know, a drawing of some kind in your old man's things?"

Mr. Jarrett searched his mind for a short moment, shook his head no, then asked, "A map of what, where?"

For a long moment, the other man explored Mr. Jarrett's face. "Folks over 'round our way, them that knew Dallas in the old days, claimed he had a map." His eyes narrowed. "Never mentioned it, huh?"

Again, his father shook his head no.

"Sure?"

When Mr. Jarrett suddenly called his son's name, "Lee, you still in there?" the young man jumped, but then pushed the screen door open and walked out.

"Get over here in the light, son," the big stranger said, "so I can get a gander at you." He stuck a big hand in Lee's face.

It was baseball-mitt sized. When Lee shook it, his hand simply disappeared, ending at the other man's. Although vise-like, it didn't squeeze hard, at least not at first.

"When I first walked up," the big man said, "thought I spied you hiding in there, young feller."

His father asked, "Your grandfather, he ever mention a map?"

Only his teeth smiling, the stranger tightened his grip on Lee's hand.

The young man shook his head no, but searched his brain for something to say, some way to save his hand. "He did give me some small rocks once. Found them in the mountains over the years," he said.

With that, the stranger relaxed his hold and Lee flexed his fingers.

Cocking his head to one side, the big man asked, "Rocks, what kind of rocks?"

A minute later, the young man returned with an old, cloth pouch, the kind tobacco used to come in if you rolled your own. Fingers still numb, he dumped the stones into the stranger's large hand.

Lee was sure the first rock the big man looked at was the best. To Lee, it seemed lined with gold leaf that glinted with every turn of his hand. Holding it up in the light from the kitchen window, the stranger turned it over and over, first this way, then that. He finally rejected it though, dropping it back in Lee's small pouch. "Fool's gold," he declared.

Lee held his breath as the stranger checked the next stone. It had sharp, green-hued crystals sticking out all over. As before though, the big man dismissed it too, this time with a simple wave of his hand.

The next small rock, Lee thought the least interesting. For one thing, it did not look like Bud's piece of gold ore at the restaurant. This stone was crystalized rusty-amber.

When the big man assayed it though, his reaction was different. He lingered with it in the kitchen light, and then brought it down closer in his face. He sniffed it once, and then licked it, letting its taste play over his tongue. For an instant, the hint of a smile played through the back of his eyes, but then was gone. Closing his eyes, he squeezed the little stone as if to crush it. He seemed almost in a trance, like the stone was speaking to him. "That's her by-cracky," he said finally, "That's her."

"That's who?" his father asked.

When the stranger opened his hand, Lee expected to see only dust where the stone had been. Instead, it was still intact, except that now, it felt warm in the young man's hand.

"Gotta make tracks now," the big visitor said abruptly, "find her sisters."

"Sisters?" asked Mr. Jarrett.

What Lee saw next though made him freeze. Just as the stranger wheeled, his coat flapped open and there on his right hip was a large, curved knife. At that same instant, the young man thought he saw a large, crescent-shaped scar on the stranger's left cheek. About the scar, he could not be sure, but as for the blade, he was certain.

Before his father or Lee could say anything, the stranger turned, tromped down the steps and strode across their back yard, his broad, dark back melting into the night shadows.

Lee glanced down at the large, wet boot prints on their back porch, and then out into the darkness, but the night had already swallowed the big stranger.

When their porch light flickered on again, they both looked at one another and laughed.

"Kind of fella I wouldn't want to run into on a dark night in the woods."

"I'm with you, Dad."

CHAPTER FORTY-TWO

Over the next several weeks of the New Year, Lee and Tammy saw more of one another. She gave him a portrait and a few other personal items and he gave her his baseball sweater and bought her favorite record for her, Nate King Cole's "Mona Lisa."

Over that same period, he was becoming even more certain she was the one and was looking forward to meeting her parents. And so, when she asked if he could join her and her parents at their lake house, he jumped at the chance. "My Mother's got a bug about spring cleaning this year, wants to get an early start."

After borrowing the family car and following Tammy's directions, Lee arrived at their lake house on a cold February evening. When he pulled into their driveway, he could see her in his headlights. Her face was framed by a white, fur-lined hood and her cheeks had a rosy, cold-weather bloom.

When the car stopped rolling, she ducked her head through the window and gave him a warm kiss. The white hat she gave him was on the seat beside him. Glancing at it, she said, "Guess you liked it." Rubbing her hands together, she added, "I'm cold, let's get inside."

He grabbed his bag from the trunk and sniffed the air. "A wood fire?" he asked.

She pointed to the smoke curling up from a hand-cut stone chimney on the side of their A-frame log home. "We can snuggle in front of it later, if you'd like."

As he followed her up the steps, he could see a boathouse down by the wharf. Over top of that, there appeared to be a small apartment.

"Parents inside?" he asked.

"About that," she answered. "Daddy had a board meeting tonight. Last minute thing. They won't be coming until tomorrow."

He shrugged.

The downstairs was one large room, with huge, oak columns serving both as supports and dividers. All of it was done in a rich, Western motif: Over the center of the room was a large elk horn chandelier; a large piece of cowhide with the letter 'S' branded into it hung on a central wall; around the other walls were pictures of cowboys branding cattle and breaking horses; various branding irons, horseshoes and firearms were mounted in between the pictures; also, most of the chair backs had Indian blankets draped over them.

The walls and high ceilings were finished in blonde knotty pine with soft, indirect lighting. The room seemed bathed in wet honey.

"Got a yummy dinner planned," she called from the kitchen. "Salmon with squash, and a little wild rice, okay? Apple pie after."

"My favorite, the pie." He looked at his hands. "Can I clean up first?" She pointed up the stairs.

His room was perfect too, done in the same western motif as downstairs. The words, "Howdy Partner," were on his door. A large set of bull horns were mounted over his bed, and the bathroom faucet handles were pearl, six-gun handgrips. He felt uncomfortable cleaning up.

When he came downstairs, she called to him from the kitchen, her voice playful. "Men: always on time for food." Across the polished serving bar, she handed him two horseshoe-shaped dinner plates. "Pour us some of that," she said, motioning toward a bottle of white wine.

Holding hands, they ate dinner by candlelight on a glass table mounted over top of a large wagon wheel.

As they finished dessert, he glanced at a picture on a '52 calendar hanging in the kitchen. In the print, two cowboys were hanging over a fence, watching a third man who had just been bucked from a horse. The thrown rider was seated on the ground, spread eagled, trying to regain his bearings. Beside him on the ground was a dark, wide brimmed hat.

"They'll never find him," he said abruptly.

Her look questioned him.

"My grandfather, they haven't found him yet," he explained, "They'll never find him where they're looking, not in the river."

"Sorry, I meant to ask," she said, pointing toward a large, stone fireplace. "Let's move over." In front of the hearth, all hand-cut stone, was a plush, red leather couch.

"We can watch a movie later, if you'd like," she said. "Daddy's got a TV room and theatre downstairs. He likes watching old Westerns. We don't have color TV yet, but I hear they'll be in the stores soon."

Over the log mantle was a large painting of a stampeding herd of wild buffalo. Driving them into a frenzy was a dark, ominous storm approaching from behind over the mountains. With lightning snapping at their heels, the herd had just charged across a raging river, their nostrils flaring, and their eyes wild and rolled back.

The scene was primal, its instincts unbridled.

She handed him a glass of wine and sat beside him on the couch. "To our first time," she said, clinking his glass. "You know, together."

Pulling her close, he kissed her softly.

The phone rang beside her. Answering, she wrote something on a pad and hung up.

"My parents' therapist," she explained, "she called to change appointments."

His eyebrows questioned her.

"They've been arguing more than usual lately, nothing serious. Daddy's under a lot of pressure, his job and all, and mother's a bit high strung. But they'll work it out, I'm certain. They've got it all, the perfect life." She took his hand. "Me too, now."

In the dim light, they sat on the couch holding one another and watching the fire as it licked the oak logs. Lee dozed. When he awoke, the fire had burned down to orange coals. Tammy was lying in front of the fireplace on a shag rug that had the black silhouette of a buffalo head with massive ebony horns. She was on her stomach, her head turned toward the fireplace and resting on her arms.

As he stood over her and looked down, he glanced at the painting over the mantle. Lying there on the shag rug, firelight playing softly over her face, jeans tight over her rear, such that little of her anatomy was left to his fancy, she was irresistible: a thousand 'Our Fathers' worth of irresistible in a confessional.

Haltingly, he laid down on top of her, his hands over hers. His lips brushed her cheek.

She stirred, rolled her eyes sideways up at him, but did not move away. Fully aroused, he began moving his body on top of hers, subtly at first, then harder and harder, and she began pushing back in rhythm with his. Suddenly though, she stopped and whispered up at him, "I care for you very much, Lee, but I can't..."

He frowned.

She tapped her ring finger.

He hesitated. "What are you saying, Tam ... an engagement?"

Her eyes said she was.

He thought a long moment. "Of course, you're right. A girl like you would want that." He started to twist his class ring off but stopped. "I'll get you a proper one."

Filling their wine glasses again, she handed him one and tilted her face up toward his.

He kissed her, long but gentle.

She clinked her glass against his again. "To a happy life."

"Together," he added. He stretched and yawned. "Quite a night." Kissing her on the cheek, she leaned into him.

Holding hands, they set in front of the fire and finished their drinks.

It was then Lee noticed a detail about the buffalo painting that he had missed. The front foot of the lead animal, a huge male with massive jet horns, had just stumbled, leaving it uncertain what was going to happen. The leader might be able to regain his balance, but if he could not and fell, he would surely be trampled under the hooves of his fellows.

The following day, her parents arrived. He liked them, especially her mother, and he spent that Saturday and most of Sunday helping them with the spring-cleaning at their lake house.

Sunday evening, as he was about to leave, Tammy stuck her head through his car window and kissed him. "Feels like snow," she said. "Drive carefully and call me tomorrow."

As he watched her in his rear view mirror, she jogged after his car a few steps, then stopped and blew him a theatrical kiss.

On the drive home, she was all he could think about. Indeed, she was perfect, like the white snow she had mentioned, not cold but pure and true.

A young rain began dotting his windshield. He turned his wipers on but with little for them to resist, they thumped hard back and forth. The night sky began filling with white flakes, warning him that there would soon be more to push against.

Early that spring, Ray Osgood, Lee's former roommate and Tammy's old boyfriend, came back into his life, but not in the way he expected, or as it turned out, wanted.

It began one evening after Tammy and Lee came out of a movie, *Casablanca*. Her engagement ring caught the overhead lights on the theatre front. She held her hand out at arm's length. "I like it, I like my ring."

"Like I told you, it's a cheapie," he said, "stone's not even real, but all I could afford right now. Dad helped me pay for it, said I could work it off. I'll get you a real one later on."

As they walked hand in hand toward the campus, they passed several shops closed for the evening. One had an idyllic picture of a mountain stream in its window. "Still haven't found my grandfather," he said.

She squeezed his hand. "Sorry."

"Like I told you once, they never will ... not where they're looking," he added. "Did I tell you I took Dan to the river where Granddad's pickup went in, hoping he might pick up his trail?"

"And...?"

"On the far bank, he yipped and ran around a minute or so like he scented something, but couldn't straighten it out."

"Good idea though," she said.

"My mother," Lee said, "she wants to put up a gravestone this spring for him." He batted at a low hanging branch. "Wants a service too."

"Nice of her."

Lee shook his head. "No, too final. Means he's really gone."

She stopped and put her arm around his shoulders. "I'm sorry, honey, don't mean to upset you, but I think the river took him."

In a window was a billboard advertising a two night Bogie Movie Festival, part of which they had just seen.

"Did you like it, the movie?" he asked.

"Yeah, but I'd seen it before."

Music was playing softly on a car radio they passed. The singer was Cindy Williams.

"About the movie, he said. I had a guy try to tell me once that they did it, Rick and Elsa. He claimed they made love, all the way, after that scene near the end when she broke down and told him how she felt. He said the viewer was supposed to assume that." He paused. "But it's like you're always saying about promises. If she did what he said, broke her marriage vows, how could either man ever trust her again?"

"It's not that simple, Lee. It depends on her reasons for doing what she did. I know it's just a movie, but don't you see, she was torn between two ideals, two good things—her honor and her heart? She chose love."

In another storefront window, there was an advertisement for a spaghetti dinner one evening that week at St. Peters. When they came to it, Tammy stopped walking and studied the ad for a few seconds. "In fact, it's the same conflict as with your priest friend, Father David, two ideals there also ... the same ones, in fact, his honor and his heart."

"My God, you're sounding just like her now."

Her face puzzled.

"Never mind."

They came to his church, St. Peter's, and she stopped. "Would we have it here, the wedding?"

He nodded. "If that's okay."

She squeezed his arm.

He pointed to a walkway alongside the church. "There's a shrine 'round back. Let's stop a minute? You know, say a good luck prayer."

The shrine was a white marble statue of the Virgin and was inside a gated but low, unlocked enclosure. A frosted glass oil lamp was lit at its base. The light flickered over the Virgin's features, casting her first in light, then in soft shadows.

For a moment, the couple sat in silence on the marble bench in front of the life-sized statue, their heads bowed in prayer.

"I prayed for my parents, you too," she said. "What was yours?"

"That's kind of personal, Tam."

She grew quiet.

"Okay, okay," he said, wiping his mouth. "The same, my parents and you."

She gave him a doubting look. "Honesty, that's the most important thing in a relationship, don't you think?"

He thought a moment and agreed.

"Now that we're engaged," she said, "let's have no secrets, okay? What's the worst thing you've ever done, you know, that you're most ashamed of?"

He leaned back. "Dag, Tam. I'm not sure that's such a good idea. Sure you wanna to do that?"

"O-o-o what dark secrets do you have locked away in there?" she asked, patting his chest playfully. "You kill someone?"

"What's that mean?"

"Just teasing," she said, "lighten up. Let's start with a clean slate, what do you say?"

"I guess," he said, his voice skeptical. "But you first. What's your biggest stumble?" He gave a nervous chuckle.

"Let me think. The worst, the worst," she repeated, searching her past.

"What about with Ray, do anything with him like that?"

She looked at him askance, her eyes annoyed.

"Sounds like you're ready for sainthood."

They both sat silent until a radio began playing faintly from a nearby open window.

"I got it," she said. "Something I did with Forest Smith, half-ashamed to tell you though." She looked at him. "You and him were team mates, the reason I didn't tell you before."

"I played ball with him, but we were never friends."

"Hope you won't think less of me."

He folded his arms across his chest.

"Shortly after Ray and I broke up," she began, "this Forest guy borrowed my math book. Claimed he lost his. Then, one day he called and asked if I could pick it up at his place after school. When I stopped by, he insisted I come up to his room and listen to the new Zenith radio his parents got him. It was beautiful, had a great sound. Claimed he could get stations from all over.

"I don't know about that, but his hands sure came from all over. When I sat down at his desk to listen, he kissed me on the neck, and I swear, that boy grew two extra arms. Anyway, Mr. Octopus was all over me until I slapped him good. Bet his ears are still ringing."

Lee's eyes were amused.

"Of course, then he apologized all over himself, and begged me to stay. But I told him, 'Forget it, mister.' I was about to leave when his mother called from downstairs. Wanted him to pick up her groceries at the market. Always wondered how he explained that to her, my red palm print on his face."

Lee tried hiding a smile.

"I guess it is funny, but then ... I don't know what got into me."

He leaned in.

"Anyway, after he left, I was alone in his room. Naturally, I felt safe, but still burned about the groping. That's when I began searching through his things, not looking for anything in particular, just looking, curious what I might find. Didn't turn up much though until I got a stool and looked on the top shelf of his closet. I guess he thought things were safe up there from his mother. A short lady, you know. Anyway, buried under a bunch of religious books and such were some sex magazines and half a dozen condoms. They did set me wondering though, the condoms, what he had in mind when he invited me up there."

"What'd you do then, Tam?"

She rolled her eyes. "Well, I opened the condom packs, stretched them over the tubes in the back of his new Zenith and left. I knew it was wrong, but served him right." Her eyes were amused now. "Boy, wish I'd been a fly on the wall when he played that radio, those tubes got red hot, and he had to explain the mess and that smell to his mother."

Lee laughed out loud.

"It's not funny, Lee," she said, bumping him playfully. "You asked if I ever did anything bad. Well, there's something for you. It was mean, what I did, seriously mean."

He looked away and straightened his face before turning back.

"Okay, buddy, your turn. What's your darkest secret?"

"All right, all right, don't rush me. Let me think."

She waited, tapping her foot. "Come on, mister, come on," she coaxed playfully. "I told you mine."

"Sorry, Tam, nothing's coming. Can I think about it, tell you later?"

It began misting rain.

She studied him thoughtfully and rubbed her forehead. "Maybe I can help. Ray told me once about you making out with some girl in Eastbrook. I think it was in a park there someplace. He said you told him this one night over some beers. Of course, he was trying to bust us up, so I dismissed it at the time." She looked at him squarely, but her mood was still light. "Any dark secrets there?"

He felt his throat tighten.

When he didn't answer, she went on. "I think he said her name was Abby or something like that." She paused. "Wasn't that the name of the girl you said was killed, the car accident?"

Masked by the darkness, his face grew ashen, "Yeah, that was her name, Abby Wilson. We were just taking her home and there was an accident. But I told you all that before. She was my buddy's friend, Tom. Hardly knew her myself."

Her tone grew more serious. "Is that everything about that night?"

"Jeez, Tam, nothing else happened. Who are you going to believe, Ray or me?"

"Do you know Terry Goodman?"

"Yeah, from over around Eastbrook. Why?"

Her eyes narrowed. "Sorority sister. Anyway, one evening in the dorm we were chattering, just girl talk, and she brought up the name, Abby Wilson. Don't remember what we were talking about, but she said the Wilson girl was kind of slow upstairs and had a shady rep around Eastbrook. Said something like, 'She'd spread her legs for anything in pants.' I thought nothing about it at the time though, until Ray's story later."

"Abby, she wasn't like that. She was a good girl, not like you're saying."

Her mouth puckered. "I thought you didn't know her."

"Jeez, why the third degree?" He considered her for a long moment. "Wait a minute, is that what this come-clean business is about," he asked, his voice higher, "your suspicions about that evening?"

She paused for a long moment, but her look said it was. "Don't change the subject, buster."

"C'mon, Tammy, this is silly."

She pressed harder, catching the scent of deception. "You're stalling."

Chewing on his lower lip, he studied her pensively. "It was Tom's idea in the first place, picking up a girl that night. That's why he went for Abby. From the start though, I could see she wasn't right and I tried stopping him. The guilt over that night has been driving me crazy for two years now, guilt over what I didn't do, stop him. Her death too." He took a deep breath. "About the other though, sex with her. I didn't do it, swear." His eyes wavered in the darkness.

"Ri-ight." Her eyes narrowed. "Then why make up a story like that, the one you told Ray?"

"Aw, it was the beer talking, just guy-bragging after a second pitcher, that's all." His feet shifted.

"Ray, he said you told him some other things too, intimate things about her that no one could know. Like for instance, she had a bad scar near her private area."

He felt his gut tighten more. "That part was true."

Her eyebrows lowered. "But how could you know that, unless..."

"Hold on, let me explain." He swallowed hard. "Tom had sex with her and he was chicken daring me to do the same. You know, 'cause my girl had cheated. I figured though, because it was dark and he couldn't see me, I'd fool him, make out like I did. Kill some time with her, come back to the truck where he was and let him think I did. Never did tell him different."

Her forehead puzzled.

"Aw, just trying to save face, I guess ... the reason I never told him different."

She rolled her eyes. "Tsk, guys."

"Anyway, I had trouble finding her table in the dark. That's when I touched her down there and felt her scar, accidently though. Even told her I was sorry."

"A table, she was naked on a table?"

He hesitated. "Well yes, but—

"And you, your clothes..."

He frowned. "Still had 'em on, of course. But I forgot the table." He glanced at the statue of the Virgin, alabaster in the soft candlelight. "Let me finish. You see, it was a park and there were picnic benches, tables, and she was lying on one of them."

Tammy scowled.

"The damn table-top," he explained further, "was weathered and rough. Must have had a million splinters in it. Tom even got one in his knee when he and Abby..."

She was stoic.

He chuckled nervously and tapped his leg. "Hell, even got one myself when..." Too late, he realized the possible inference of his words, and looked at her side-eyed.

She got it too and scowled.

He laid his head back and blew air out of his puffed cheeks.

Her lower lip quivered and she began crying.

When he stood and put his arm around her, she pulled away and began twisting off his ring.

"Aw no, no, Tammy," he pleaded, "don't do that ... don't do that."

Taking his hand, she slapped the ring onto his palm, turned with her back to him, folded her arms and held rigid, like the statue of the Virgin.

"C'mon Tammy, I'm just doing like you said, no secrets."

She turned to go, but he grabbed her wrist and held fast. "I'm sorry, Tammy. Let me explain."

Jerking free, she closed the shrine gate behind her. The sound of the latch closing in the night had a clang of finality. He called after her, "But Tammy, what about trust?" When he felt his hair and it was wet from the mist, he thumbed his class ring.

In the candlelight shadows, the statue of the Virgin was flickering light, then dark.

Over the next few weeks, he tried reconciling, sending Tammy notes, calling her dorm and trying to talk to her, but all to no avail. And so, by the end of April, he knew it was over between them.

One evening in the dorm later, he sat by himself tossing a baseball in the air. When the phone rang in the hall and he answered, his mother's voice was on the other end. "Sorry to bother you at school, Lee. We set a date for your grandfather's memorial. We knew you'd want to be there."

He studied the phone.

She told him the date, adding, "And Lee, hope you don't mind, but we've invited a few others."

"Like?"

"The Wilsons, his fishing buddies, Father David and Pru ... others also."

"Why them, the priest ... her?"

"It's what your grandfather would have wanted, dear. He was their friend, too."

He thought about telling his mother it was over between Tammy and him, but decided against it because he knew she would ask how come and he didn't want to lie.

CHAPTER FORTY-THREE

Pru bit the thread off of the stuffed doll she was sewing, a smiley-faced fisherman. It was done in cloth, including the hat, suspenders and hip boots, except for the wire rim on the net and the wooden fly rod.

Still hoping she might reconcile with Lee, Pru was making it for him. Although she never mentioned this to her mother, she was certain she suspected whom it was for.

At a nearby table, Mrs. Pruitt was painting two ceramic figurines, a bull and a toreador. "Cathy, would you mind a suggestion for your little fisherman? The fishing pole, it should be dark, not ivory."

Holding the doll up, Pru inspected it momentarily and then dipped her brush in the ivory paint.

"So what are you going to tell him?" Mrs. Pruitt asked.

She gave her mother a blank look.

"Your Tom, of course. He's a good man, Cathy ... taking care of his mother too, I understand. It's been almost three months since he asked you, not fair to keep him hanging."

"Mother, he's not my Tom, and there you go again, trying to shove me toward him."

"Let's face it. We're two helpless women. Lord knows we could use a good man around here."

"Don't worry, Mother, everything will be all right."

"If it's about his foot, I wouldn't give it a second thought." She paused. "Didn't he get you some snow tires last winter too?"

"Mother, I'm not going to marry someone because he got me snow tires."

She glanced at Pru over her glasses. "What's gotten into you? That's not what I meant." She licked her lips repeatedly as she spoke. "It's just that he seems like a kind, giving person, that's all." She leaned back to inspect her daughter's work. "Another suggestion, dear, if you don't mind. A net with a dark, wooden rim would be much prettier than a metal one."

When her mother looked away, Pru continued with the net as before. She glanced at her mother's half-finished ceramic. Her slight, somewhat androgynous toreador seemed overmatched against the fierce, charging bull.

Mrs. Pruitt dipped her brush in red enamel and began working on the animal's eyes. "If you're still holding that Catholic boy in your heart, you'd best give it up. It'll never work."

Pru stuck her finger with a needle. "Aw, corn," she said. The bleeding wouldn't stop and she went to the bathroom. A few minutes later she came back, red-eyed. "Lee's his name, Mother, Lee Jarrett, but you know that."

Hand to her throat, Blanche responded with her best-hurt look.

"I'm very fond of him, Tom, as I've told you. He's like a hurt animal and my heart goes out to him. That's why I'm helping. Sure, I like the feeling I get doing it." She paused. "But I could never feel about him like..."

Blanche gave her daughter a patronizing smile. "That love business, that's not all it's cracked up to be, dear. In the long run, Tom will make you happier. Trust me. I've been there, where you are now." She turned her ceramic around on its pedestal, stopping at the bull's private parts.

"My decision, Mother, not yours."

"My, my, aren't we prickly this evening."

Pru touched her gold locket.

"Don't you see, dear? Your heart can lie to you. Look what it did to me."

"But, Mother, you had some happy times, you and Daddy. I remember. Sounds like you're trying to erase those now, feeling guilty about them."

"Just trust me, dear. In time, you'll learn to love him, Tom that is." She dipped her brush and began stroking the horns.

Pru said abruptly, "It was Lee I was with, Mother, that time on the Burnt Tree."

Mrs. Pruitt frowned, questioning her daughter's statement.

"Remember that baby rabbit story I told you about before? That happened on the Burnt Tree."

"Wha-at?"

"Don't you remember? We were talking about Tom not long ago, and I told you he reminded me of that hurt rabbit I helped once. That happened when I was with Lee, the rabbit incident. He borrowed his father's car and we went there together, not to a ballgame, like I told you."

"You lied, lied to me?"

"Forget that, Mother. Let me say what I have to say. I'm trying to tell you something important."

Blanche folded her arms over her chest.

"Anyway, when we were there, Lee and I, we almost made love, almost but didn't. Not that we didn't want to, but we stopped before we did."

Mrs. Pruitt squirmed.

"We made promises to one another, to God also, promises to be faithful until we were married, to one another that is."

"All young people do that, Cathy: set their sights too high, make promises they can't keep. I did, and look what it got me." She paused. "Don't expect too much of the world, dear. That way, you won't be disappointed." She gave the toreador's sword a final brush stroke. "As for your other young man, he's moved on. Has him a girl at college now I heard ... engaged, too."

Pru's eyes fell to her own empty ring finger.

"Besides, it's not fair to Tom, keeping one young man in your heart while you're seeing another."

Pru laid her doll face down. "Maybe you're right, Mother. I'm going to turn in now. Do you need anything?"

"One last thing, dear. I know Tom's not religious, but he was raised Baptist. "

Pru turned back. "Ever occur to you, Mother, there might have been other reasons why Daddy left? Not like you're always saying, different religions?"

Her mother's head snapped up from her ceramic.

"Because of you ... to get away from you, all your nagging, the bickering, the fighting." Stopping abruptly, she put her head down in one hand and gave a long exhale. "Never mind, Mother."

Mouth open, Blanche leaned back and placed her hand on her chest. She was about to speak, but her daughter disappeared down the hall.

Before going into her room for the night, Pru sat down beside the phone. She chewed on a fingernail, vacillating: Her mother was probably right about Tom. Marrying him would make their futures more secure, and with him, Pru did feel like she was needed. As for love, like her mother said, that would come in time ... hopefully.

Then there was Lee, whom she still loved. But he didn't even care enough to answer her note declaring her love for him. Nor could she forget all those hurtful things he said to her on the porch after his grandfather drowned. That was the same evening he announced his intention to marry that girl he met at college.

She dialed the phone. "Sorry I'm calling so late, Tom," she whispered. "Can you come over tomorrow, after work? I have your answer."

After Pru closed her bedroom door later, her mother made her way up to the attic. There, she dug an old album out of a large trunk, brushed the dust from its cover and began paging through it, stopping at a wedding picture, her own. In the soft glow of her flashlight, she kissed her fingers, and touched the groom's face. Snapping off the light, she sat in the dark, whimpering softly.

CHAPTER FORTY-FOUR

Tom walked over to his chest of drawers, his limp almost unnoticeable, and looked in the mirror. His face was clean-shaven, and his long hair was combed neatly and gathered in back. A photo of Pru was wedged in one side of his mirror. His face warmed when he saw it. Penciled across it at the bottom in black lettering were the words, "She said yes, June 1!"

Stuck in the other side of the mirror was a business card. Pulling it out, he dialed the number, but hung up before it could ring. He flicked the card repeatedly with his forefinger, and redialed the number.

On the other end, a friendly voice answered, "Coach Sandy."

"Coach, Tom Drew," he said. "About the rehab, my helping out. Is that still on the table?"

"Sure is young feller."

"I can't make it till next month, June, and it'll have to be after work, around four or so. That okay?"

"Just mosey on over."

"Thanks Coach, see you."

When Tom came home later that day after work, David was sitting alone on the back porch. He was barefooted, dressed in jeans with suspenders, and no shirt.

"You're giving me goose bumps," Tom called to him. "It's spring, but feels like 40 degrees."

David didn't stir.

Putting his lunch pail down, Tom draped his shirt around David's shoulders and sat on another chair. "How's Ma?"

His brother waffled his hand. "I told her the church is relaxing some of its rules. You know, letting priests wear street clothes now. She bought it. I guess being out of it does have an upside."

"An upside?"

"Yeah, she doesn't have to see what's happening to me, or her little town. All the good people crossing the street when they see me coming. As for my church," he said, hissing, "they're thinking about running me out of town with torches and pitchforks, Joyce along with me. The bishop, he wants an answer about my accepting the transfer. Wants it today."

"Jeez, crapola, you going to accept?"

Father David did a long pause. "I don't know."

"My God, what are you waiting for? You gotta choose."

"I love them both, God and Joyce." He thought a moment. "But you're right."

"You love her that much," Tom asked, "enough to break your vows?"

He nodded. "Like you do about Pru, your girl."

"I call her Cat," Tom said soberly. "A couple of things about her that I need to get off my chest."

"I'm no priest anymore, can't hear confessions."

"Okay, then just listen, listen as my brother." He briefly recalled for the priest how he first told Lee about her cheating, concluding with, "But the worst part is, it wasn't even Cat."

"My-y God, Thomas, not her, not his girl? My God."

"Now hold your horses. I tried telling Lee once it wasn't her, but he wouldn't believe me. Claimed I was lying just to hurt him."

"Can you blame him?"

"But I didn't learn my mistake about her till after the accident. Stopped in Pappy's one night to get a bottle and Kenny Harte was shooting pool. You know what a big mouth he is. Anyway, I overheard him bragging about doing Tracey Smith on a bench in Sawyer's Park that same night. I'm sure now it was her I saw him with, not Cat." He paused. "What can I say? I screwed up. But they do look alike, Tracey and her."

"Jeez, no wonder he's sore at you. Ever tell Pru about any of this?"

Tom shook his head.

"Wow," Father David said. "If she knew, there'd be a special place in her doghouse for you." He paused. "Just curious, why'd you ask her out in the first place?"

"For starters, to get even with Lee."

"For what?"

"Never mind that. Once I saw what a great gal she was, everything changed. I didn't think they made them like her. I was drowning and she reached out and saved me."

When the phone rang, Tom answered. "For you."

David motioned for his brother to cover the mouthpiece. "Who is it?"

"The Bishop's office."

As Joyce did the dishes and hummed to herself in the kitchen, David bit his lower lip and eyed the phone.

Tom waited, hand over the speaker.

"Tell him..." David said, "tell him I choose both: her and God."

Tom did what his brother said and hung up, but his brow was puzzled. "Jeez, does that mean you two are going to...?" He put his two index fingers side by side.

David smiled. "Naturally, we'll tie the knot the first chance we get. That is if we can find someone who'll marry us." He paused. "Maybe we could tell Ma they relaxed that rule too about priests not marrying. You know, in case she asks." He nodded upstairs. "Our spare room, okay if Joyce moves in now?"

Tom shrugged. "It would make more sense, a lot easier to take care of Ma."

"You're still going to be our best man, aren't you," Tom asked, "like you promised once when we were kids? No church rule against that is there, now that you head their leper list?"

"June first, St. Pete's, right ... I'll be there, brother." David glanced at his brother's lunch pail. "Guess I'll have to get a real job now."

CHAPTER FORTY-FIVE

Lee rode to the cemetery through a morning overcast in late May with his mother's sister, Aunt Alice. She lived in Baltimore and worked for a newspaper there. Her husband had to work and could not attend the memorial service for his grandfather. She was his favorite aunt and could always read him well, sometimes too well.

"You're awfully quiet," she said. "Your grandfather?"

"Just wish they were certain he's gone. They can't declare him legally dead yet anyway. Dad told me so, too soon."

"But, Lee, it happened last December. It's going on six months now."

"Yeah, but I've heard stories of people turning up years later, amnesia and such."

"The Fire chief said they might never find him, said his body might have gotten wedged under a log or something."

"They don't know that. Everyone's forgetting he was a strong swimmer."

"Lee, that's a fantasy, thinking he's still alive."

He ignored her remark. "He always took his dog along with him too, Granddad did. But he didn't that night he disappeared, like he was planning something and didn't want Dan to get hurt."

"Drowned, Lee, not disappeared," she corrected him. "Your father said the floodwaters that night were raging and that your grandfather was ill besides." She touched his arm. "I know it's hard to face, but he drowned."

He talked through her. "And another thing, Aunt Alice, his favorite hunting knife. When I checked the shed after he went missing, it wasn't there, where he always kept it."

"What does that have to do with his drowning?"

He didn't feel like getting into the details about his grandfather's love affair with the knife or the mountains. "Aw, nothing, nothing." His fingers worried a loose button on the sleeve of his blazer. "Do you think he might have killed himself, Aunt Alice, you know 'cause he was sick?"

"No, he wasn't a quitter."

"I always heard that if you can swim, that's the wrong way to kill yourself, drowning. Your instincts take over and you fight to live." Lee paused. "But you're right. That wasn't him. He was a fighter. Just seems too soon to declare him dead, that's all I'm saying."

"Your parents, Lee, they need for this to be over," she said, "this uncertainty. Besides, your mother needs some place she can visit, even though he's not really there. They were close. You know that, even though he wasn't her blood."

"Yeah, this has been hard on her especially, losing him," he said. "She's looking awful tired."

"I noticed that in the kitchen overhead light."

"Sorry I didn't wait up till you drove in last night. I was tired and turned in early. Had a long day, college and such."

"Yeah, your mother said you're going to Hillsboro, taking journalism ... incidentally, if you're interested after college, I might be able to get you a job at my newspaper. You may have to be an errand boy to begin, but it's a start."

"Any one there know something about story writing?"

When he looked away, she returned a patronizing smile. "Someone might know a thing or two."

"Thanks, Aunt Alice, I'll keep it in mind."

"As for turning in early last night," she said, "you didn't miss anything. Just a little sisterly talk, your mother and me, you know, family stuff."

Tilting his head, he gestured to himself. "Anything about me?"

She hesitated. "Well sort of ... Evelyn told me a little about you and two girls, one named Cathy, the other Tammy, and your history with them. Even showed me one's picture: Cathy, I think, pretty gal."

"Aw jeez, why did she do that?" He blew air out his puffed cheeks. "Pru, that's what I call Cathy," he said. "She did something real bad, Aunt Alice, something I can't get over, even talk about." He shook his head. "Besides, those bridges are all burned."

"Bridges can always be rebuilt, you know."

"Maybe it's best not to, sometimes."

"That may be true for some bridges," she said, "but this morning at the house, before the mourners left for the cemetery, I saw you both, you and Cathy, sneaking looks at one another when the other wasn't looking."

His head dropped to his chest. "It's complicated, Aunt Alice."

She pulled the car over along the cemetery driveway. "Glad we got to talk. I have to drive back to Baltimore today, right after the service," she explained, "work." One last piece of aunty advice though about judging. It can get mighty lonesome up there on Mt. Olympus, all by yourself." As they got out of the car, he frowned at her comment. Waving goodbye to him, his aunt walked over to an older couple and embraced them.

As Lee walked up the cemetery hill toward where the other people were gathered, he passed her grave. The mid-morning sun broke through the clouds, illuminating its tin marker. It read Wilson. He stopped and lingered for a second, glancing at the date of her death. "My God," he whispered to himself, "has it been that long, almost two years?"

A large granite stone marked his grandfather's gravesite, too formal and pretentious for the old man, thought Lee. The name Dallas Jarrett was chiseled into its face. Two dates were there also, March 1870 and December 1951.

It all seemed strange to Lee: his grandfather's name on a headstone marking his burial site, except he wasn't there. Both were empty, the grave and the coffin. But it was how his parents wanted it. Before lowering it in, each family member and friend threw something personal, something treasured in the coffin. Lee threw in his favorite baseball, the one signed by the Pirates. They buried something of his grandfather's too: his swimming ribbons.

All through the service, Lee found himself sneaking looks at Pru. It gave him goosebumps just looking at her. Even with the somber occasion and in black, she had a wondrous aura: her glowing skin, the rich, chestnut hair haloed from behind by the early sun and those big, brown eyes, always those eyes. Once, when he glanced across the grave and his eyes caught hers, he started to smile, but caught himself and looked away. He heard only the last line of the priest's eulogy: "And so dear friends, in the midst of our mourning, always remember His promise..." Pausing and repeating his last words for dramatic effect, he ended with, "His promise of eternal life."

After the ceremony, Pru walked among the mourners, embracing and talking to each for a few seconds. She spoke briefly to a stranger in work clothes standing on the fringes. His shoes were muddy and he had a heavy set of keys dangling from his belt. Not until he took his hat off though, did Lee recognize who he was. It was Abby's father, the cemetery caretaker.

Just as Lee started down the hill toward the cars waiting for the funeral procession, someone called his name. Recognizing Pru's voice, he kept on walking.

When she caught up, she caressed his arm. "Sorry about your grandfather, Lee. I know what he meant to you."

He looked into those eyes again and his resolve melted. Putting his hand over top of hers, he squeezed it tenderly. As he did though, he felt a ring. Looking down, he saw what it was: her engagement ring. He stiffened and pulled away. "Thanks for the pity, but no thanks," he said.

Her eyes were hurt.

Hurrying down the hill past Abby's grave, he got into the back of a car in the procession.

"Sorry about your grandfather," the driver said. "Ray Osgood," he added, thrusting his hand back over the front seat for Lee to shake. "You and my son were roomies, played ball together at Hillsboro. Read about the memorial in the paper."

"Yeah, sure," Lee answered, "I remember Ray. Good guy. How's he doing?"

"Don't know," Ray's father answered. "He's in Korea, joined the marines. Doesn't write much."

"I didn't know."

"Sorry to bring it up at a time like this, but something I never understood," Mr. Osgood said. "Maybe you can help. Ray's sophomore year he was doing fine. All he talked about was you and Tammy. Then that summer after they broke up, he didn't mention you anymore and dropped out of school. Just moped around the house till he joined up. Could never get him to talk about it either." He turned again toward Lee. "What happened between you guys?"

"Why you asking me, like it was my fault?"

"No, no, it's just that you were best friend. I thought you might have some clue."

As they drove away slowly, he saw Pru walking arm-in-arm with Tom. She smiled when he whispered something in her ear. Lee swallowed hard trying to bank his feelings.

Ray Sr. looked in the rearview mirror, "Let it out, son. I heard he was quite a guy, your grandfather."

On the backyard patio at their house, his parents were greeting mourners and serving food. Lee tried to avoid them, entering the house through the side door.

Dan was in one corner of his room, snuggled up on the old man's hunting coat. He wagged his tail once when Lee entered.

Seconds later, his mother came in and set a piece of cake and glass of milk on his night- stand.

"Tammy and I called it quits, Mom," he announced abruptly.

"Oh," she answered with seeming indifference. She glanced at the dog. "Looks like you got a new buddy." She walked over and began scratching Dan's ears.

As she did, Lee sifted through the mail on his nightstand, stopping and frowning at an envelope addressed to him, the name Pruitt embossed on the return address.

About to leave, she noted her son's scowl and the envelope in his hand. "Wedding invitation," she explained. "We got one too. Your old girlfriend, Pru, she's getting married next weekend, first of June."

His gut knotted.

Mr. Jarrett came up to his room later. "You should come down and say something to the guests. They've been asking about you."

His father's hand was behind his back. Pointing to it, Lee asked, "What do you have there?"

Mr. Jarrett tossed a hat on the bed. "Thought you might like this."

It was familiar, yet strangely different.

"Your grandfather's," he said, "his dut hat."

Lee frowned. The hat's edges were crisp and the stains on the band and crown, although still there, were faint.

"After he got sick, Ol' 40 chucked it in the trash," his father said. "Asked him about it once and all he said was, 'When the hunting's over, you call in the dogs and piss on the fire.' I tried pressing him more, but that's all I could get. Not like him, giving up though. He was old but still feisty.

"Could be he saw the handwriting on the wall," Mr. Jarrett went on. "Then too, he might have been scared of dying, like the rest of us, but still talking big."

Lee shot his father a dark look.

"C'mon Lee, I loved that ol' man too, but he could be preachy at times, a bit windy, you know that."

"He just liked telling stories, Dad. No harm in that. Maybe he would dress them up some, but that was just to make 'em sound better, more interesting."

"You know your grandfather, Lee. He liked picturing the world as it should be, not like it is. Most times, he'd go along if it was hanging crooked on the wall, his picture of life, but every once in a while, he'd get an itch to straighten it."

His father continued, "I don't know where he got those notions. Maybe from his mother. She used to read to him in the evening after chores, poetry and such. His father didn't approve much. Thought it was a waste of time, that she was spoiling the boy for real man's work, like he done, cleaning out stalls and such."

"Why does it look so different, his hat?"

"Had it cleaned and blocked. Thought I'd give it to him if he ever, you know, got well. Guess he won't need it now. It's yours."

Lee turned the hat around admiringly.

Walking to the door, his father turned back. "Oh yeah, almost forgot. Came across something else too. Remember that big, scary fella who showed up on our back porch one night, the one asking about Granddad's map?"

"Yeah?"

"Well, I found one in the old man's bank box, a map. Might have been just what that big feller was looking for. I'll get it."

"Hold it, Dad. Remember his name, that big stranger's?"

His father stroked his chin. "Joseph, John Joseph, I think. Why?"

"And remember that tale about how the Burnt Tree got its name, the one I learned from that fellow, Bud? Remember me telling you that?"

"Yeah," he answered, his patience waning.

"Well, I've been thinking about it and this John Joseph fellow."

"Where you headed with this?"

"Let me finish, Dad. You could make Joe out of the big feller's last name real easy, like that Papa Joe character in Bud's story."

He eyed his son.

"Something I never mentioned. The big stranger on our porch that night had a scar on his cheek and a wicked looking knife on his right hip, just like Papa Joe, or so Bud claimed. I saw them both in our porch light that night."

Mr. Jarrett's face said he wasn't following Lee's program.

"Don't you see? It changes Bud's tale. That big stranger on our back porch could have been him, Papa Joe, the guy Crazy Dan supposedly killed. And if it was Joe, who did they bury on the Burnt Tree way back?" He paused. "It could change Granddad's story too. There was a character in his version a lot like that Papa Joe, only with a different name."

His father cocked an eyebrow. "Do you hear yourself? That's a bunch of nonsense. You're letting your fancies take the reins." He paused. "You want the map or not?"

Lee nodded.

A few minutes later, his father threw a folded, yellow parchment on the bed beside his son. It was wrapped in old, wrinkled wax paper. "Looked at it myself, but couldn't make heads or tails. See if you can figure out anything. Be back shortly, I have to get more chairs for the guests."

Lee rolled off the bed and stood up. Hands trembling, he removed the map from its waxed paper. He unfolded it carefully and laid it open on the bed. Bending over, hands behind his back, he examined it closely.

On the upper right hand corner was a directional cross. There were two lines on the map snaking back and forth. One line went north, the other branched off from it and headed west. These, he assumed, were rivers, although not marked as such. Labeled at the confluence of the two rivers were the words, "Gates of Stone."

"My God," he whispered. "Could that one weaving line be the Burnt Tree and the other Eden Brook? The directions were right, north for one and west for the other. And Gates of Stone: Could those be Bud's giant, stone slabs guarding the entrance to Eden Valley, the same ones the Indians called 'Spirit Gates?'"

Far up the Eden Brook squiggle were two large, upside down Vs with stick trees drawn inside. Although not labeled as such, Lee took them to be two mountains, big ones, again like in Bud's tale.

Back down the valley from the mountains, the weaving line made a big northerly bend. Near it was something that made him stop and bend closer. At the bend's northern apex were the words, "Indians Drawings."

Most puzzling of all though were the words at the bottom of the map—"Where stone runs blood and dies the flood, there be your prize but the demon lies."

From the doorway, his father asked, "So what do you think?"

Momentarily fingering the map, Lee shrugged. "The line heading north could be the Burnt Tree and the other Eden Brook, but I'm not sure. Can I keep it a while?"

"Later. I wanna show it to a couple of your granddad's old buddies first. See what they make of it."

Lee handed it to his father. "I'd sure like to study it more."

"There's something else too," his father said, "a box of your grandfather's. He said to give it to you if something ever happened to him. Don't know what's in it. It's out in the shed."

"A box of his?"

"Mother and I decided to wait till after the service to give it to you." Mr. Jarrett pointed to his bedside table. "Key's in there." He then motioned away. "Gotta go now, see to our guests."

After his father left, Lee yanked the table drawer open and there it was resting alongside his tarnished holy medal, the key to what was left of his grandfather's world. And perhaps too, the key to unlocking some other dark mysteries about him, at least his grandson hoped so. Cradling the key in his fingers, he plopped grandfather's hat on his head and hurried out to the shed, Dan padding along after him.

On a peg over the workbench, he hung the dut hat. Sitting on the stool, he slid the small wooden chest over in front of him.

It was about the size of a large wooden pistol case, only deeper. He ran his hand over the darkly varnished lid. Its edges were worn round by a thousand hands. Carved into its top, between two ornate brass hinges, was an animal's head. In the half-light, he could not see what it was, so he slid the box under the lamp and bent closer.

It was the head of a big cat with barred teeth, ears flat to its head like it was angry. Inscribed under it were the initials, D.J. But what did those letters stand for, he wondered. Dallas Jarrett or Dan Jagger?

Hands trembling, he opened it slowly.

CHAPTER FORTY-SIX

The smell of musty cedar greeted him from inside the box. On top was a small packet of yellowed letters bound with a bow. A note on top of the letters read, "Destroy, don't read."

He put the letters aside to burn later.

The only other things inside were an envelope with Lee's name and a badly scorched piece of brassy metal.

The charred metal was half an animal's head, a cat's head, a big angry cat with barred teeth. For several long moments, Lee studied it. "My God," he cried aloud finally, "could that be a jaguar?" His excitement growing, he considered further. And if it was, could it once have been a doorknocker, a knocker on a certain cabin, Crazy Dan's cabin? And if it was ... that clinched it. He answered himself, "Granddad and Dan were the same man. They had to be."

A sudden blast of wind made the little shed quiver. Lee cocked an ear toward it and smiled. Voices, he thought.

He removed a note from the envelope with his name. As he did, a photograph fell out. It was the partially burned picture of Pru. Evidently, his grandfather had rescued it from Lee's letter-burning episode two years before. It was the snapshot that once had, "Love You Always," at the bottom, but now read only, "Love you," the last word having been burned away.

He turned to the note. It was from his grandfather, but penned in two different handwritings.

"Lee,

The Widow Taylor helped me with this next part, saying what I had to say. She's school-taught and dying to repay me for some pleasures I done her. Her writing's next, but like that little girl's skirt, it's short and sweet. Don't let her flowery scribbling throw you off the scent though. It's still me in here.

Someday you may find it, your Eden Brook. Be certain though, that is your true quest. But should your efforts fall short, do not lose heart. Perhaps your journey was the end.

Till then, though your river be dark and troubled or sunny and calm, say yes to what it brings. But should your waters be unkind and you meet another struggling too, offer your canteen and staff to ease his way, your own as well.

And when you stop amid tide to quench your thirst, drink upstream of the herd, but do not then fault that gathering if your cup has dregs. Look instead, to your own stirrings.

Left some money for you at the bank."

It was signed by his Granddad. Also in his script was a P.S. that read: Wish I were going with you."

Although the second part, like his grandfather said, was not his writing, he was clearly in there. It was like the old man, his wont to say things around a corner, rather than straight out. Some of it Lee got, but he needed to think more about what the note was saying, underneath the words.

He picked up Pru's singed photo. It was taken three years before in the spring, and on the occasion of her first time fly-fishing. It was also the day they had sworn their oath of fidelity to one another.

In the picture, she was holding his fly rod and sporting his grandfather's dut hat. The old man had loaned it to her in case it rained. When she first put it on, it fell down to her eyebrows. She liked it anyway though, because it was Granddad's. The Burnt Tree, which they fished later, was in the background.

Earlier that same morning three years before, he had pulled up in front of Pru's house in his father's car. Her green duffle was on the front porch and she was seated on the swing.

That was the first time he saw the pretty, young girl next door, Miss Denim Shorts, as he later tagged her. He only saw her a few more times after that, but he always looked forward to it.

That morning, her back to him, she had just bent over to pick up the newspaper on her front steps. Straightening, she turned and waved to him, her mussed ponytail dancing back and forth. It disarmed him such that he had not waved back.

Later, on their way to the Tree, Pru insisted they stop so she could help a young, injured rabbit. She took it from the road, but its thrashing feet scratched her arm.

Lee shook his head at her as she got back in.

"Can't help it," she said. "I hate seeing anything suffer."

"How's the scratch?"

"It'll be okay. He couldn't help it, he was just scared."

He shook his head again, but liked that she was that way.

Later that morning when they got to the Tree, he parked near where Tom and he always camped. He waded out into the stream first. Although its spring-fed waters made him shiver, once he was there for a few minutes, it felt warmer than the air. He motioned for Pru to follow. She began wading toward him over the slippery rocks. By the time she was up to her thighs, her will faltered, and she began wading back toward shore.

Lee chicken-squawked behind her.

"Sorry, honey," she called, her teeth chattering.

It warmed up as the day moved on, and Pru caught one small brook trout. Lee dipped it using Tom's net he had borrowed.

They were always Lee's favorite, brookies. He liked the jeweled ruby spots along their emerald sides. They reminded him of Pru's lips, those spots. Once you hit their heads on a rock though, the red spots never looked the same again.

It was then that he snapped the picture of her holding the fish. Later, he had a duplicate made so she would have a copy also.

Afterward, she asked if she could release it. She knelt in the quiet shallows, wet jeans tight over her thighs, cradling the trout in the current. The little brookie, ever pulsing, wriggled free. When it did, it flipped water in her face. She looked up at him, her lips rounding in surprise.

They found a quiet pool to swim and cool off in that was shaded by a tall fir.

Afterward, they sat on a blanket as she dried her chestnut brown hair. Her body was tanned and firm with those wondrous "S" curves that girls have at their hips and around behind. Pulling her down on the blanket beside him, he kissed her, long and open-mouthed and fondled her breasts under her swim-bra. Her nipples firmed and she began breathing heavier. Embarrassed by his own hardening, he embraced her sideways.

Thunder rolled overhead and it suddenly began sprinkling.

"Every time," he said, smirking.

Jumping up, they gathered their things and ran for the car. Once they were settled inside, he looked over and saw her eyes were moistening.

"What's wrong, honey?"

"You know how much I love you, Lee Jarrett, and want to, but let's save that for when, you know."

"You're right, honey. I'm sorry ... again."

His mother's rosary was dangling from the car mirror. With rain pounding on their windshield, she put her hand around its cross and he put his hand over top hers.

It was Pru who then suggested they swear the oath of fidelity to one another. That pleased him also.

255

CHAPTER FORTY-SEVEN

The late afternoon sun crowded the cool shadows where Lee was seated at the bench in the shed. He held the picture with Pru and the Burnt Tree up. "Okay, what now?" For several minutes, he struggled with that question, finally resting his head on his arms and catnapping.

Dan dug behind one ear, his paw drumming on the wooden floor.

At the sound, Lee straightened. "Hey boy, can you spare a couple minutes?"

The dog's eyes opened a slit and rolled up at him.

"Got this problem I've been wrestling with. Hope you can help. Still don't know about college, but that's not the big one, problem that is. It's about a girl. Matter of fact, you know her. She always brings you biscuits. Name's Pru."

The dog's tail flopped once.

"Anyway, it's about getting past something she did, or might have done that is, with some other guy. I tried getting even with her for it, but that went sideways."

Dan stretched stiff-legged.

"But that's not my big headache, boy."

The dog's eyes grew heavy, and he began to nod.

"Pay attention, buddy, this is important." He patted the dog's head. "You know me. I always believed things were either right or wrong, no in-betweens. It's what I was taught, Mom, the nuns.

"Anymore though, I see they're not always in stone, right and wrong. If you have an eye on fairness, you see they can change shades ... depending on lots of things.

"Then too, I always wanted my world to be perfect, like a beautiful painting, bright colors and all, especially when it came to Pru and others I cared about. But the subjects in my beautiful picture began fading, falling down that is. I blamed them for making it fade and tried hurting them, but all it did was hurt me.

"But now I see it wasn't their fault, my beautiful painting going bad. I doomed it from the get-go. They were imperfect before the first brush strokes, my people... me too, but I refused to see that."

The dog snapped halfheartedly at a vexing fly.

"Stay with me, Dan... but maybe that wasn't such a bad thing after all, my getting hurt." Heavy-eyed, the dog looked up at him with what Lee imagined was a frown. Lee touched his shirt pocket with the note. "It helped me see what Granddad was saying."

Overhead, the old shed's rafters suddenly creaked; Dan's sleepy eyes chased feebly after the sound.

Lee was silent for a long moment. "I wasn't saying yes to the river."

The dog rolled over, stretched and yawned.

"Sorry, boy, I got side-tracked. Back to my point, about Pru that is." He took a deep breath. "I'm not sure what to do about her. If I stick to my old black and white way of judging, like in the Bible, things can get 'iffy,' like I said. But if I go against what I was taught and give her a pass for what she did ... might have done that is, reasoning that it's because she's flawed like the rest of us, and that right and wrong are not in stone anyway, and the Guy upstairs doesn't like my thinking, we both could burn in Hell. As for Pru, one way I'm bound to lose her for sure, the other..."

The dog stretched and grunted.

"Yeah, you're right about that too, boy, the Bible's no help there. It can lead you both ways sometimes. Good point, though. Shows you're paying attention."

Dan began licking his genital.

Lee's gaze slid up to the white baseball hat on the wall over the bench. "That girl at college? I never loved her, not really, not like Pru. Something farther south was holding my reins there." He smirked at Dan. "But you're playing with me now, aren't you? You knew that already, that I loved Pru."

"Her name was Tammy, that other girl. Gorgeous, perfect, too perfect." He paused. "We were both chasing smoke."

He glanced at the smudged baseball on the shelf, the one Tom had given him after Abby. Taking Ray's baseball glove down, he blew the dust off and hung it carefully back on its peg.

Dan got up and stretched like he was about to leave.

Lee patted the dog's bed. "C'mon buddy, settle back down. I'm all done."

Then, he thought to himself, Tom did claim he made a mistake about Pru. Said it was some other girl he saw that night with Kenny Harte, not her.

Finding a pair of scissors, he trimmed the burnt edges from Pru's photo, careful to leave the words, "Love you."

Lee reached down and scratched the sleeping dog's head, but Dan didn't stir. "Sorry to cut into your beauty rest, but thanks for listening. You're the only ear I got left, now that he's gone." Suddenly, he snapped his fingers. "Double dag. Sorry, buddy, but one last thing if you're still with me. Any advice you have, better come soon. She's getting married this Saturday, or did you forget that?"

Dan whimpered in his sleep and his legs began spinning in place like he was running from something in a bad dream.

Lee started to awaken him, but stopped and spoke to him quietly. "All this time, I've been telling you what I need, never asking what's best for Pru." He considered his own words for a moment, and then shrugged. "Probably too late now anyway, but I still gotta do it, tell her how I feel."

Dropping the old man's note and Pru's photo in his shirt pocket, he slipped into the house, Dan tagging after. He called Pru's house and work place but she wasn't at either. The wedding, he thought to himself, she was probably off somewhere busy with the wedding.

When he checked with a teller he knew at the bank to find out how much his grandfather had left, he was stunned. It was over $5,000.

Just as he put the phone down, someone called his name. A man approached him from down the hallway. "Had to use the terlet," he said. Capturing Lee's hand, he held onto it as he talked. "Joe Murray. Sorry about your grandfather."

"Thanks."

"I hope you know how proud your folks are, you going to college and all."

Lee didn't answer.

Up in his room, he lay on the bed, searching the ceiling for answers, mostly about Pru but college and writing also. He paged through his journal, reading the entries he had made about the Burnt Tree, most from the day he had spent with his grandfather on May's Mountain.

He pulled the old man's note from his shirt pocket and reread it — stopping at the words, "... drink upstream of the herd..." Abruptly, he clapped the journal shut.

Downstairs, he dialed the phone, hoping his aunt was there, that she had enough time to drive back to Baltimore. A woman's voice answered on the other end. "Aunt Alice," he said, "it's Lee."

PART THREE

CHAPTER FORTY-EIGHT

" And so," Lee finished explaining to his parents, "Granddad, he helped get my head straight about both Pru and Tammy. Other stuff too. Helped me see how much she still means to me, Pru that is. I'm going to tell her so too, while there's still time."

His father, who was seated at the kitchen table, looked up from the newspaper. "And that's all there was in Ol' 40's box, the note, a check and a hunk of metal?"

Lee nodded.

Mr. Jarrett flicked the ashes from his cigarette, missing the tray. "I'm surprised, thought for sure there'd be other stuff. Still $5,000 is a nice sum."

His mother swept the cigarette ashes off the table with a dishcloth onto the floor. "Naturally, we're happy for you," she said. "Cathy's like a daughter to us, a decent young lady, unspoiled."

Lee's eyes fell to the ashes on the linoleum.

"We always knew things would work out for you guys, somehow," she added.

Lee shook his head. "But it's not a done deal, Mom, us getting back together. Lots of stuff to be ironed out yet."

His father lowered the newspaper. "And just when are you going to tell her all this?"

"Soon as I can. Jeez, she's getting married this Saturday."

"Naturally we're happy for you, son," Mr. Jarrett said. "Fine girl, Pru, and we want things to work out. But what if she doesn't feel the same anymore? Might only upset her, telling her all that." He ground his cigarette out in the ashtray. "How long's it been since you and her broke up, two years?"

Lee's head dropped. "Maybe you're right, Dad, maybe she's changed, forgotten all about me by this time." Momentarily, he worried the lino-leum pattern with the toe of his shoe. "But I still have to tell how I feel, Dad, just have to."

At the sink, his mother rinsed a cup she was washing. "Cathy hasn't changed how she feels."

Lee frowned at her back. "But Dad could be right. By now, I could be just another page in that girl's diary."

She patted her chest. "Trust me, a woman just knows." Pausing, she dried the same dish for a second time. "Like with that other girl, Tammy. She wasn't right for you. A nice young lady, but you never felt about her the way you do Cathy. You know that."

Lee sensed she was talking more about her own feelings than his.

Mr. Jarrett gave his wife a doubting look, but then weakened. "Okay, okay, let's go with that. Let's say she still feels the same. But he'll still have to work things out with Tom."

Lee's teeth clenched together.

"Won't be easy, convincing him. The word around town is he'd be a goner if it wasn't for her. Hard for a fella to do, give up someone he cares about and who's saved his hide."

"Maybe you're right, maybe Tom and I should talk."

"Yeah, you guys should try and iron things out," Mr. Jarrett said. "Go easy though. Remember all he's lost, and could lose yet."

"What he's lost? What he's lost? In case you haven't noticed, every-thing's turned out pretty good for him. He's getting married this Saturday ... and to my girl."

"You and him used to be pals." He looked over his glasses at his son. "What happened between you guys?"

"He's to blame, mostly. My shoulder, that girl getting killed, his leg too."

"Hope this is not about payback, son. Remember what happens when you point fingers."

His son looked away and rolled his eyes.

"Back to when you get together, you and Tom," Mr. Jarrett said. "He's never going to like it, losing her, so don't try making him feel better about it. That could upset him even more. All you can do is try and help him accept it, what she's doing. It's a woman's right to change her mind." He glanced knowingly at his wife. "As to the rest, you have no say, that's between them two, Cathy and Tom."

"That's true," Mrs. Jarrett added, "she did give her word to Tom. That's true."

"But surely he wouldn't stand in her way if she doesn't love him." Lee shrugged. "If he does, she'll just have to break it, her word."

Mrs. Jarrett touched her son's arm, her face pained. "You know we want you two to be together, but I'm sorry. I know that girl ... so do you. She just won't do that."

Mr. Jarrett looked up from his newspaper. "She'll just have to reason with Tom and ask him to let her out of it, her promise."

Mrs. Jarrett's cross pendant caught the overhead light. "But haven't you ever done that, Mom, gone back on your word?

"Certainly not," she said, worrying an old chip in a serving dish. "Why would you ask such a thing?"

"What about your word to Him?" Lee asked, motioning up.

Eyes wavering, she looked at her husband for help.

"Sure," his father broke in. "We've all done that sometime, gone back on our word. We're no saints, but—"

Lee cut him off. "But that's what you and Mom taught me to do, always keep my word. Sounds like you're preaching one thing and doing another."

His father stiffened. "What does that mean?"

Lee opened the icebox and cold air greeted him. "Aw, nothing."

Afterward, both parents eyed him skeptically as he made himself a peanut butter and jelly sandwich and poured a glass of cold milk.

The first bite stuck on the roof of his mouth. "I've decided something else too, about college."

His mother's eyes darted over to him.

"I'm leaving school."

"Aw Lee no, please no," she said.

"Too tough for you, bub?" Mr. Jarrett smirked.

He faced his father squarely. "You're not going to talk me out of it this time, Dad. It's not that it's too hard. Staying would be easy." He took another bite of his sandwich. "College is just not for me, at least right now. Maybe someday."

"What are you saying?" asked his father. "There's not a thing, not one thing at Hillsboro you liked, no courses, nothing?"

"It's stuff I don't care about, Dad, mostly freshmen stuff and program requirements. I want to write stories, stories that make people feel, think."

"Hell, Lee, you can switch what you're studying."

"I checked that out, Dad, their catalogue. You know, other programs, courses; they don't have much there either, not what I want."

His mother pleaded from the sink. "But your degree, get that first, dear."

"Mom, I don't want to look back some day and wish I'd done something different with my life. Of all people, I thought you'd understand that."

Not following his point, she frowned at her husband. "But Lee, you're ruining your life, Cathy's too."

"Look, college is something you guys want. Sure, baseball made it okay for a while, but that's gone now, that's over."

"No it isn't, not if you still want it," his father said. "That doctor, he can fix it, your shoulder. Said he could."

"But we both heard him, Dad. He said I might be okay, my shoulder might be okay. No thanks, Dad, no maybe-surgeries for me."

"I didn't like him, anyway, Evelyn, that doctor," he spoke to his wife. "Maybe we should get a second opinion. You know, see another specialist."

Lee put his head down in his hands. "I just want to hold on to what's left, writing and maybe Pru, if it's not too late. Is that asking too much?"

His father pointed to the headline of his newspaper. "That's another thing. There may be a war coming. You ready for that? Quit school now, and you could end up in Korea."

His son shrugged indifferently.

"What are your plans in the meantime, mister? Just gonna bum around here?"

"Peanut butter," he said, pointing to his mouth and swallowing hard. "Aunt Alice, she said she could get me a job on her newspaper in Baltimore."

Mr. Jarrett shot him a sarcastic look. "When did she say that?"

"On the way to the funeral. Dad, will you let me finish?" he asked, a hint of irritation in his voice. "Anyway, I called her today, and she okayed it. Wasn't crazy about it, seeing as I hadn't finished college, but said she'd go along if you guys would."

"What are they paying?" his father asked.

Lee returned only a blank stare.

"Answer me this then. What will you be doing there, to begin with? And Aunt Alice, will you be working with her?" He gave a pleased with himself chuckle. "And what do you know about newspapering? Hell, Lee you might be just filling inkwells."

"Sure, Dad, maybe for starters, I'll have to empty trash cans and be a go-for, but I'll be around writers, story-writers. Aunt Alice said so. Who knows where that could lead?"

"I can tell you: straight to a bread line," his father answered.

"But there's Granddad's check. I'll use that till I get on my feet."

"Money down a rat hole," his father said.

"But that's what Granddad said I should do, follow my voices."

"Your voices?" his father questioned.

"Yeah, my own dreams. What's wrong with that?"

"I don't know how to say this, son, but your grandfather wasn't the best role model for ... for how to live your life. The perfect world he longed for can never be, like chasing smoke. That won't get the bills paid either, son, smoke."

His mother broke in defensively, "But we loved him just the same, dear, your grandfather."

His father went on. "Why not do like your mother said, finish college and do the writing thing later?" He jabbed a finger at his son. "No one likes a quitter, boy. That other dream, the Baltimore one, too many if's and maybe's ... smoke."

"But, Dad, haven't you been listening? I want to learn how to write, write good stories. I can't do that studying courses like state history or principles of economics." He leaned on the table and put his head in one hand.

Taking Lee's silence as a weakening, Mr. Jarrett pressed again. "That way, you can get back together with Cathy. Finish your dreams with her too."

Lee swallowed hard on the last of his sandwich and hacked on the table with the side of his hand, like he was chopping though his father's reasoning. "No, Dad, No. I'm going to do like I said, take that newspaper job."

"But, Lee," implored his mother, "you're not ready for such a big change, not yet. Wait a year or so."

"I'm going on 21 now."

Her eyes teared. "But just barely." She stooped and filled the dog dish with water.

"I'm only going to Baltimore, Mom, not Timbuktu."

She wiped her eyes on her apron. "Besides, all your friends are here. You'll be alone there, a total stranger."

He took a deep breath. "I'm going to ask Pru to go with me. If she says yes, we'll have one another. Might get me a deferment too, Korea."

Mr. Jarrett scowled. "My God, a wife on a clean-up boy's salary?"

"You keep forgetting, there's Granddad's money."

"And Cathy's mother?" Mrs. Jarrett asked.

"May be the best thing for Pru," Lee said, "getting away from her. It's one reason I'm hoping she'll go, not the big one though."

"What a rotten thing to say," Mrs. Jarrett said. "If Cathy goes with you, that lady's all by her lonesome and no money besides."

"Yeah, but what about us, don't we deserve some happiness?"

"You mean don't you," his father offered. He turned toward his wife. "We've spoiled our son, Evelyn."

He heard it coming, one of his father's sermons. His son had titled them all in his head. This one he called, "Tennis Anyone?"

Mercifully though, his father gave him the abridged version. "Get this through your head, bub. Life's not about what Lee Jarrett wants. It's about serving, serving others."

His mother interrupted. "Why can't you just be happy here in Eastbrook? Find a job, a writing job if you want, and stay here? We can help. Not easy for a young couple starting out."

"It might be the best thing for us," Lee said, "Being on our own to start."

She ignored his answer. "That way too, Cathy can help care for her mother."

"Don't worry, we'll send her money every month."

"I don't just mean money, Lee. There's other things a daughter can do, unspoken things."

Lee made a face. "That's all Pru has done her whole life, try to keep her mother happy. Doesn't that girl owe something to herself, some chance at happiness? Besides, that Mrs. Pruitt, she's not as helpless as she makes out."

She frowned. "And all this too, I suppose, without a Catholic priest, a ceremony?"

"I promise, Mom. Once we get to Baltimore, we'll do it."

At the sink, his mother began turning a coffee grinder. "When are you going to ask her?"

"Soon as I can. Got to, I'm leaving Friday late."

Her shoulders slumped.

"But if her answer's no," his father asked, "what then?"

Lee did a short thinking stare. "If that's her answer, there's no reason to stick around."

His mother's eyes teared, and Lee put his hand over hers and helped turn the coffee grinder. "I didn't mean that the way it sounded, Mom." He looked at his father and his voice softened. "I love you guys. Nothing will ever change that. Besides," he added, "we'll be back so often you'll get tired of us."

As he turned to go, she hugged him, pleading in his ear, "Please give it more thought, dear." She tossed a coffee bean onto the floor for the dog.

Paws spinning, Dan scrambled after it, pinning his prize to the linoleum. Afterward, as he sat crunching it down, he seemed pleased with himself.

They all smiled.

Mr. Jarrett put his arm around his wife and walked her to the bottom of the stairs. "Let's sleep on it. Things look different in daylight."

As Lee started up the stairs, he called back, "Hey Dad, I'm going to stop off at the Burnt Tree and fish a few days. Don't have to be in Baltimore for a couple of weeks or so."

"Isn't that out of your way, son?"

"Not much, I checked the map. And Dad, can I borrow the camping gear?" He scrambled on up the stairs, calling back to his father at the top. "And oh yeah, almost forgot. Help me get a car, a good used one tomorrow? We gotta do it early though."

"Sure you're ready for that headache?"

"Gotta have one."

His father gave his mother a helpless look. "Let's talk about it in the morning, son."

CHAPTER FORTY-NINE

When Lee first saw the Drew house through a thin, early morning fog, his knuckles whitened on the steering wheel.

As he approached, a policeman flagged him down. Over the officer's shoulder, Lee could see two cars in the middle of the road. The one facing him had a dented front end and the other's radiator was steaming.

The policeman pointed to the stalled cars with his flashlight. "Some folks had an accident. You gotta go around."

Lee motioned toward the Drew house. "I'm just going right there," he said, pointing, "the gray house just past the cemetery. Can I drive around on the berm, instead?"

Shaking his head no, the officer pointed toward the open cemetery gates. "Go through there, and then hang a left at the first crossover. That'll bring you in from the other side."

Lee frowned. "That the only way?"

"You can go back to the interstate and around if you want, but that's longer."

Lee eyed the cemetery gate.

The officer's mood lightened. "What's wrong, son, afraid of a little graveyard?"

"O-o-o," Lee played along. "Anyone hurt?" he asked, nodding toward the accident.

"A few bumps and scratches, that's all." Another car pulled up behind Lee's. "Have to move it now, son," the officer said, waving him toward the cemetery gate.

As Lee drove along the rows of granite tombstones, he searched for his grandfather's, stopping just down the hill when he spotted it.

Waving atop some graves were small American flags. The VFW always put them on the veteran's graves for Decoration Day. There was none on his grandfather's. No one knew whether he had gone off to war or not.

He knelt on one knee beside the old man's grave, bowed his head and blessed himself. "About Pru, Granddad, am I doing the right thing?" He took the old man's note out and reread it.

Way off, a groundskeeper was cutting grass. The mower's metallic whirling spoiled his thoughts.

He looked up at the mountains. Above them, low clouds were sliding across the tops, just out of their reach. He asked the same question toward the mountains. Only the wind answered though, fluttering the small banners on the veterans' graves.

As he walked back down the hill toward his car, something drew him toward Abby's burial site.

No stone honored her resting place, only a small tin marker shoved in the ground with a paper insert. Maybe he could do something about that someday. Across the top of the tin marker, someone had printed the name Wilson in large, black letters. Lee bent over to get a closer look at the paper inside the glass. Although the ink had run and was faded, the name and dates were still legible—Abagail Grace Wilson, born June 1932. Close to his own, he noted.

There were some wilted flowers on her grave and he tossed them aside.

Wild flowers lined the cemetery fence. Some had yellow petals and cores stained like old blood and others had white petals with untainted yellow centers. He didn't know his flowers, but he thought both were daisies.

He picked a small bunch, careful to choose only those with yellow hearts and white petals. Their green stems were tough. Afterward, he laid the flowers on her grave.

An unsteady wind began blowing from the west, whining across the gravestones. It rose and fell like notes in a sad ballad. Her sweet, honest voice haunted him still.

He picked another bunch of flowers for Pru, the same kind as for Abby. Just as he stood up, he heard a mower stop nearby and saw the groundskeeper walking toward him. His shoes were muddy and a set of keys were jingling at his belt. It was Abby's father.

Lee hurried to his car. As he drove away, he could see the man in his cracked mirror. One hand was holding his hat and resting on one hip, the other scratching his head.

CHAPTER FIFTY

As Lee sat in his car in front of the Drew house, he looked at his hands. Although they were stained from the daisy stems, he could still see the white scars from his fight with Tom.

He rapped on their front door and waited, but there was no answer. Just as he was about to pound again, it eased open a slit.

From the darkness inside came a woman's timid voice. "Yes, who is it?"

"Mrs. Drew?" he questioned the voice, but got no answer. "It's Lee, Mrs. Drew."

"Who?"

"Lee Jarrett, Mrs. Drew. Is Tom in?"

"No," she answered.

He glanced at Tom's truck out front, patted his leg for a few seconds and shrugged. Just as he turned to leave, the door opened wider and there he was, his sworn enemy, Tom Drew.

He had long hair that was pulled back in a ponytail and he was leaning on a cane. His face, Lee noted, looked more like the old Tom, only softer.

"Lee, Lee Jarrett," Tom said, his voice strong and warm. "I was getting myself a glass of water when I heard your voice." He leaned forward and stuck out an open hand.

Lee shook it half-heartedly. "I tried calling. Phone not working?"

"Disconnected," he said, motioning Lee inside. As Tom stepped back, his artificial foot made a noise and he looked down. "My squeaky wheel," he said. "Doc claimed he fixed it, the squeak, but still acts up when it's gonna rain." He peered over the other man's shoulder at the car parked out front. "Yours?"

Lee nodded. "White walls and all. Got it just this morning. Dad helped me. Granddad's money."

"Sorry about your grandfather. Looks good though, your car. I still got the old truck."

"Yeah, I saw it."

Tom motioned again for Lee to follow him. "I'm doing some work out back. C'mon, we'll walk through. Watch your step."

Lee followed him through the darkened living room. As he stumbled along behind him, the other man's foot squeaked in the shadows.

Tom pointed to the closed drapes. "Sorry it's so dark. Ma's idea, claims it's cooler." He stopped and shook his head. "Not the real reason, though. She thinks the neighbors are spying on us."

In the kitchen, his mother was hunched over a sewing machine, her face down close to the pumping needle. She looked smaller and more stoop-shouldered than Lee remembered.

"Ma, look who it is: Lee Jarrett."

She recognized him this time, or appeared to. "Lee Jarrett. Where've you been hiding, boy? Come over here, and let me get a look at you."

When Lee bent over to hug her, she slid her fingers through his blonde hair, and then, holding him close, ran her eyes over each pore in his face. Finally, she gave him a wide, toothy grin and gestured for him to do the same.

Lee grinned back.

"Good," said Mrs. Drew. "Hang onto them teeth, your hair too." Looking at her son, she motioned toward Lee. "Your friend here's handsome as ever." She turned back to her sewing. "Don't be such a stranger, Lee Jarrett," she said over her shoulder. "And stay Baptist, boy."

He gave Tom a puzzled look.

Tom rested his hand on her shoulder. "We'll be out back, Ma, if there's anything."

She put her hand over his and smiled. "You're such a good son." She looked at Lee. "He's helping other folks who lost their parts too."

"I heard."

"He even got a prize for it." She touched a referee's whistle hanging around her neck.

Tom spoke to her gently. "Ma, that's not a prize. Just a gift from a friend. I told you that."

"See, they even wrote something on it." She handed it to Lee.

Lee read the inscription, "If you need a friend, just whistle, Coach Sandy." His eyes questioned Tom.

"Just a friend I'm helping out ... he helped me out too."

His mother added sweetly, "She comes over just to see me sometimes, Miss Cathy."

Tom explained, "Ma needs someone with her at night when I'm out. Sometimes Cathy fills in. Won't take any money."

"Don't let the door slam, dear," she said, "when you go out."

Tom pointed toward her whistle. "Remember, Ma, blow if you need help."

On the porch, Tom glanced back at the kitchen door. "Never sells anything nowadays. Sewing seems to keep her calm, happy. Doc Gladstone said it was good for her. Keeps calling people though, perfect strangers. We get complaints, the reason we had the phone disconnected. She's been worse lately, especially at night." He shoved a chair toward Lee.

"No thanks. Can't stay long."

"David's dropping by later. He'd like to see you, I'm sure. Why don't you stick around and say hello." He leaned his cane against the bannister, but it fell over.

Lee glanced around the porch, but saw no crutch.

"Guess you were right about David. You know, what you said once about him fooling around. He seems happier now though. They both do, him and Joyce."

"I heard," Lee answered. "But there's other things we have to talk over, you and me."

Tom pointed to a saw on the floor beside his cane.

Lee handed him the tool, and then leaned the cane back up.

Tom patted his left leg. "Been getting numb lately. Nerve damage, the Doc says. But I only need the cane once in a while. Don't feel sorry for me, though, losing my foot. I've been helping out at the rehab center. Met a lot of fine people. Many a lot worse off than me ... you haven't seen guts till you see the special hell those folks are in."

"Yeah, heard you were helping out down there," Lee said matter-of-factly.

Lee pointed to a padded board resting across two sawhorses. "What's that?"

"Kneeler, church," the other man explained. "Minister said the pad was coming loose. Told him I'd fix it. No big deal."

Lee eyed him skeptically.

"About what?" Tom asked.

Lee frowned.

"Said you wanted to talk."

"Uhhh, I quit school. Got me a newspaper job in Baltimore, or my aunt said she could. Leaving today, in fact."

"Baltimore, jeez ... your parents, what did they say?" He chuckled. "Don't tell me, I know."

"It doesn't matter, I'm going anyway."

Tom studied the other man. "Damn nice of you, Lee, stopping off to say good-bye."

"Oh yeah, yeah ... sure."

"So you're gonna chase that dream, huh, writing?" He touched Lee's arm. "Happy for you, Jarrett."

Lee's eyes slid down to the other man's bad foot. "Are you, really?"

"Sure, why wouldn't I be?"

Lee arched an eyebrow.

Tom hesitated. "You mean our fight?" He waved it away dismissively. "I was screwed up back then, Lee. Did some things, crazy things I'm still ashamed of. Hope there's no hard feelings."

"Not just that," Lee continued, "there was other stuff ... you lied about Pru cheating. Truth is, you started the whole downward spiral between me and her." He thought a moment. "But things worked out pretty good for you, didn't they?"

"You're right, I did some crappy things."

Lee hissed back. "It was a lie though, wasn't it, her cheating?"

He nodded once. "But I didn't know it at the time, swear."

Lee glanced at the other man's fishing hat hanging on a wall peg. "Forgot to mention: I got a couple of weeks before I start my new job. Thought I'd camp for a few days on the way, fish the Tree."

Tom's eyes brightened. "Good for you." He thought a moment. "Gonna search for it, that brook we looked for?"

"Eden? Don't know, maybe."

"Wanna borrow my net?" He glanced down at his bad foot. "Hell, just keep it. My wading days are over."

Lee shrugged.

"You ain't getting my knife though." Tom grinned. "The only way you get that is when they throw the dirt in."

"Never asked for it," Lee said, unsmiling.

Tom sat down. "Ah-h, that feels better. Enough about me though, what about this fishing trip?" He chuckled. "Hey, Jarrett, gonna stop at St. Pete's, like usual?"

"Hadn't thought about it."

"Those were great times, weren't they, on the Tree. If we ever do it again," Tom said, pointing to his prosthetic foot and smiling, "I'll bring the firewood."

Lee started to smile, but caught himself and wiped it away. "We're getting side-tracked T.D. We need to talk. Set some things straight."

"I think I know where you're headed, Lee. But me first."

Lee's face puzzled.

Tom bent over and began working on the church railing. "Been haunting me ever since that night. You know, that Abby mess. The other stuff too." He paused, his head down. "Shame we don't have confession in our

religion, like you guys. Maybe I could have unloaded some of this guilt."
He pointed to the rail for Lee to hold.

Lee steadied it as Tom began planing one side.

"Why did I do some of those things, act that way?" he asked himself.
His eyes thought a moment. "Jealousy, pure jealousy. That's what was
underneath it."

Lee took his hands off the rail. "Jealousy? Jealous of...?"

Tom looked up and held the other man's eyes.

"For God's sake," Lee cried. "Of me?" He hesitated. "Then why all
that buddy, buddy stuff back then?"

"No Lee, that was real. I liked you, always did." Running his hand
over the board, Tom found a rough spot and began planing it. "I'm embarrassed to say it even now, but I was jealous of everyone, especially you,
what you had that I didn't, a perfect life."

"Hell, T.D., if it was money, all you had to do was—"

"It wasn't that, what I wanted was..." He stopped, searching for the
right words. "I'm not sure, but money couldn't buy it."

"Go on," Lee urged.

"Jeez, does it really matter? Let's just say I was royally screwed up
back then and leave it at that." He pointed to the rail again. "Keep the pad
stretched tight while I tack it."

Lee did as he said, all the while eyeing the other man.

Tom began tapping in the small nails. "Then, after the accident," he
went on, "I blamed you for that whole mess, especially my foot. That's
what that fight was about. Stupid, huh? Anyway Lee, I'm sorry. Okay?"

Far off, Lee could hear the metallic whirl of a grass mower. "And
Abby?"

"I feel so bad about what happened to that girl ... her folks too." Tom
motioned toward the cemetery. "She's buried over there, you know, right
next door. Her dad's the caretaker."

Lee nodded.

"Family's saving for a headstone someday. He doesn't make much
though, so I've been putting away a little. You know, help out some."

Lee was stoic.

Tom continued tacking the pad. "Been around two years since the
accident," he said, "but Mr. Wilson still hasn't gotten over it. Keeps her
grave looking pretty nice, but last Christmas Eve, I asked him if I could
tend it that evening. Anyway, while I was talking to him, I noticed a red
paper-cross in his buttonhole, one corner bent over. I got a late start but
set up some lights and worked on her grave till late. You know, pulling
weeds, planting grass and flowers, watering and such. When I gave it a
final check early next morning, there on her grave was a small red cross,

one corner bent over. Evidently, he'd visited her grave sometime in the dead of night." He stopped hammering and shook his head.

Lee brushed the sawdust off his hands. "Never know what to say when I see him. I know it's not right, but I try avoiding him, mostly."

"Once and a while too, when there's nothing on her grave," Tom added, "I jump the fence and put fresh flowers on it."

"I was just over there. Those flowers, yours? I tossed 'em away, wilted."

Tom glanced at the cemetery. "Crapola. Thanks, I need to pay better attention. Back to what I was saying, how screwed up I was. I even started dating Cat to get back at you, at least at first."

"Who?" Lee asked.

"Cathy, Cat, you know, like the animal, c-a-t."

Lee smirked.

"Anyway, cats hate getting their fur wet," he explained. "Same with her. She hates getting her fur wet too, her hair." He paused. "But you know that. Anyway, that's why I call her Cat." He chuckled. "She calls me T."

"That's dumb. Pru's, her name, everyone knows that."

Tom let the remark slide. "Anyway, that's how it all started, my dating her was to get even with you, but she changed all that. She's a great gal, but hell, you know that too." He drove the final tack in the kneeler. "I gotta pinch myself sometimes—we're getting married tomorrow."

"Yeah, I heard." Lee half-sneered.

"Hope there's no hard feelings."

"Nah, no hard feeling," He gave a cynical laugh. "But you've got a damn good act going there."

Tom frowned.

"All this goody-goody stuff with rehab, church work and the grave, this sudden concern for others. That's not you. Why the big change?"

He thought a moment. "A lot of people to thank, but Cat mostly. She helped when there was no one else, like with Ma, my rehab. Shoved me toward others too, giving them a hand ... the clinic." He looked squarely at Lee. "Cat gave me a reason to live, Jarrett. Can you understand that?"

"You think that balances the scales?"

Tom blew air out his puffed cheeks. "It's crazy, Lee. I know I've done some rotten things, hurt others, but maybe some good came of it too."

He looked at Tom askance.

"Didn't we both find someone?"

Lee's eyes narrowed.

"I found Cat.

"Yeah, good for you maybe, but—"

"Hold on, I heard you found a girl at college too, even got engaged. That's good isn't it?"

Lee answered matter-of-factly. "Turns out, she wasn't Miss Right after all, least ways, not for me. My own damn fault, though."

"Buck up. Maybe you'll find her. You know, in Baltimore."

Lee felt his throat tighten. "Which is why I'm here."

The screen door slammed shut and they both looked over.

It was Mrs. Drew, a senseless smile on her face. She was carrying a pitcher and three glasses on a tray. "Thought you boys might like some lemonade."

Tom pointed to the extra glass. "Joining us, Ma?"

"No silly, it's for your father."

Tom's eyes rolled to the other man.

Lee took a sip and gave his glass a sour look.

Tom did the same. "Sorry," he said as he walked toward their back door, "I'll get us some sugar."

"Have you met my son's fiancé?" she asked.

Lee nodded he had.

Mrs. Drew began speaking low. "She's his whole life, Miss Cathy is. He didn't want to live before she came along." She looked around cryptically. "God only knows what might happen if he lost her. You'll like her, Miss Cathy," she said, turning to leave. She let the door slam behind her when she went back inside.

Tom looked away from Lee. "Good lady," he said, wiping the side of his eye with an index finger. "Sawdust."

Lee studied the other man for a long moment, and then looked at his watch. "I gotta be going."

"Hold on, what was it you wanted to talk about?"

Lee waved his hand away.

"Sure?"

"I'll leave around the side. Tell your mom goodbye."

Tom pointed toward the back door. "Hold on, I'll walk you through."

Inside the front door, Tom grabbed his hand and shook it again. "David will hate missing you."

"Say goodbye for me."

"Hey, almost forgot, my fishing net. Back in a second."

"Say, could I use your bathroom?" Lee asked.

"One down here's broken," he said, pointing upstairs.

After Lee used the facilities and came out, he stepped inside Tom's open bedroom door. The room was bright and cheery. Several model planes rested on the shelf over the bed, and on the far wall was a large poster of a U. S. Air Force Mustang. An oak chair with one cracked rocker sat in the middle of the room.

There were two pegs on the inside of the open closet door. On one was a neatly pressed blue suit. The wedding, Lee thought, his mouth twisting to one side. On the other peg was Tom's green hooded raincoat. It was just like Lee's only larger. They bought them together years before.

On the dresser in front of his mirror were a signed baseball and a picture of the two friends in better times. Their faces had wide smiles and their arms were around one another's shoulders. An inscription at the bottom read, "Brothers, through thick and thin." Knowing the bad blood between them of late, Lee was puzzled why the other man kept the picture there.

Tom's room was much the same as Lee remembered, except for one difference. On his nightstand was a color portrait of Pru's beautiful, smiling face, her chin resting on the back of her hands.

He picked it up. Her lips were full and ripe, but as always, it was those large, walnut brown eyes that stirred something deep within him. There was a reserved dignity in them also with just a hint of devilry. He stroked her cheek in the frame, the glass cool under his fingertips.

Tom's voice at the doorway startled him. "What a bunch of crapola. You didn't stop off to say goodbye, did you? You came here to take her away. What's wrong, didn't have the guts to tell me?"

Setting her picture down, Lee fumbled for the right words. "I tried to, but your mother, your foot..." and finally blurting out, "You're right, I'm going to ask her to go with me."

Tom's bad leg buckled slightly, but he caught himself and straightened. "And what about your word?"

Lee frowned.

"You told Cat once it was over between you and her."

He studied Tom's twisted face. "I was wrong." He wiped the back of his hand across his mouth. "Look, I know it's a rotten thing to do, especially with the wedding and all tomorrow, but I wanted you to know, first."

"Just like that, huh?" Tom snapped his fingers. "Same ol' Lee. Me first, and the hell with others."

"Hold on, T.D. Was that all about me, that night with Abby?"

"Okay, maybe I do understand. You paid a price too." Tom glanced at Pru's photo. "But, for God's sake, don't be thinking of yourself, not now."

"That's why I'm going to ask her to go, for both your sakes."

"Ri-ight," Tom sneered. "Thanks but no thanks. Sure, you'll feel good, but all it's gonna do is upset her, send her world in a spin. If you really cared about her, you'd just go on to Baltimore, to your big newspaper job." The last words were heavy with sarcasm.

"Now wait a damn minute. Let's say she loves me and marries you, you both could end up miserable. Don't you want her to do it because she loves you, not because her mother wants it or because of a promise she made, or..." He glanced down at the other man's foot.

Tom's eyes flared.

"Why not let her decide?" Lee went on. "She knows how you feel. Let her hear what I have to say and decide for herself. Besides, if you're so sure of her, what are you afraid of?"

Tom stared blankly at her picture for a full minute, struggling with Lee's words. When he finally spoke, his voice was almost pleading. "I do love her, very much, never cared for anyone that way before, and I'm afraid of losing her." He paused. "But maybe you're right. Maybe we should do that, let her decide. After all, that's what we both want, isn't it? Her happiness?"

Lee glanced at his watch. "I'm running late."

The other man followed Lee to the front door, limping worse now. "She know you're coming?"

Lee shook his head no. "But don't call, let me talk to her first."

"Oh yeah, my fishing net. Couldn't find it. Must be at Cat's."

"I'll get it when I see her."

"And Jarrett, it was Tracey Smith I saw that night in the park with Kenny Harte, not Cat." He nodded toward the cemetery. "Swear it on her grave."

Lee stared back, trying to gauge how much truth was in the other man's voice and eyes.

When Lee got in his car, the seat springs squeaked like Tom's foot. That nice guy act didn't fool me, he thought. Two peas in a pod, Tom and that lip-licking Kenny Harte. Can't trust either one.

Back inside the Drew house, Tom sat bumping back and forth in his rocker with the cracked runner. Pru's portrait was on his lap. He glanced at the picture of Lee and him on his dresser. He took his hunting knife out of its top drawer and ran his fingers along the side of its finely honed edge. Sheathing it, he stuffed the knife down into his pants under his belt, slipped a jacket on over it and grabbed an extra raincoat and baseball cap. Limping to the front door, he called back toward the kitchen, "Be back in a while, Mom. Gotta set some things straight."

CHAPTER FIFTY-ONE

As Lee started the car, there was a tap on his window. It was Father David. His neck was thin and he was wearing wrinkled pants and a red stained T-shirt. He wasn't as tall as Lee remembered.

"Father," he said, then changed it to, "David."

"Good to see you, Lee. Sorry I missed your grandfather's memorial." He patted him on the shoulder. "Saw you coming out of our house. What's up?"

Lee looked away.

David motioned toward the house. "Tom's losing feeling in his bad leg. Needs surgery but can't afford it. Doc says it's nerve damage. Could be permanent if he puts it off."

"He never mentioned the operation."

"Hubris," said David.

"One of your fancy, college words?"

A frown rolled down David's brow. "Pride, too much pride. Why don't you stay for a while so we can catch up?"

Lee shook his head no. "I quit school. Got me a newspaper job in Baltimore. I'm leaving today."

"A writing job, huh? Good for you, glad someone's dreams are coming true."

Lee's eyebrows lowered.

"In case you haven't heard," David explained, "I've got the plague. Least ways, that's how the church and town folks are making me feel."

"I heard you left the orders."

"Got a couple minutes?"

Lee hesitated.

"For old times' sake?"

It began to rain and David looked up. "Mind if I get in?"

Lee shifted Pru's flowers to the back seat.

Once David was seated, he wiped his wet face with his sleeve. "Got any blueprints for an ark?" he asked.

Lee didn't smile. "You asked before why I stopped by. I'm going to ask Pru to go with me." He thumbed toward the house. "I just told him."

"Afraid of that," David said.

"You and him cheated me out of a life once, lying, stealing my girl. It's not going to happen again."

David pointed toward his back. "Climb on. Always room for one more."

"Don't be cute, you know what I mean."

David studied the other man. "Just hope you're doing it for the right reason. I've tried it, payback, doesn't work."

"You know how I feel about Pru, always have. Sure, I did some stupid things that got us off track, but that's all behind us now."

"But Lee, my brother, he's not well. It may seem like it, but he's not. This could push him over the edge again, losing her." His eyes shifted to the house. "Not many know it, but he tried killing himself once, ramming a tree in Sawyers Park. But then she came along, Cathy, and he had a reason to live."

"In case you've forgotten, he brought most of this on himself."

David talked through the remark. "Now, you waltz in here and take that away. Are you really that insensitive? Don't you realize they're getting married tomorrow?"

"Hey, he's the reason we broke up in the first place, Pru and me. We'd be the ones getting married tomorrow if it wasn't for him."

David's upper lip curled, like his brother's when he was angry. "Same old Lee, never happy unless life's pitching you a perfect game."

Lee sneered. "Don't put this on me, mister. What about you? You broke your word, let a lot of folks around here down, good people who trusted you."

He studied Lee for a moment. "I know I disappointed you and a lot of others. I'm sorry for that."

"Me? Not me, you didn't disappoint me. Others."

"Have it your way. What else is on your get-even list?"

"Doubt if you have enough time. For starters, your brother cost me a baseball career and got that girl killed." He paused. "Top it off, he ends up marrying my girl. Is that enough for you?"

David was silent.

Lee glanced at his journal on the dash. "And oh yeah, he put some snakes in my head too, about my own grandfather."

David held his hands out, palms up, questioning the remark.

"Never mind. The point is, you guys took a chain saw to my life, the two of you."

David scowled.

"When I asked for your help after the accident, you deceived me, my own priest, my friend. You played along with Tom's lie about Pru's cheating. On top of that, you knew he wanted her and never told me."

He held his right hand up. "Lee, I swear to God, if he was lying at the time, I never knew it, and if he had his eye on her, I never knew that either."

"Ri-ight," Lee said, doing a mock laugh. "That's rich, coming from you, swearing an oath to God. It was you that greased the skids for your brother with her in the first place, telling me to drop her, the girl I loved. Remember?"

"That was the church talking, Lee. For the most part, they don't work, mixed marriages. My position back then too as a priest."

"Sure, hide behind that."

"I'd give you a different answer today."

"Yeah?"

He thought a moment. "Listening to the church is not always the same as listening to your heart."

"How does that help me?"

"Guess it doesn't."

David studied him for a moment. "Let me tell you a little story about pain."

Lee's eyes rolled up.

David ignored the reaction. "The next day after his suicide try, I noticed some funny round, red marks on the back of Tom's hand. I asked him about them and he said he fell asleep in the car with the cigarette lighter in his hand. Can't prove it, but I think I know what happened. The night of the accident, he was sitting in the truck mulling over how to end it. He got to hurting so bad that he began pressing the hot cigarette lighter to the back of his hand, hoping the pain would help him forget. Of course, it didn't work because he went through with it anyway, ramming the tree."

"He's a big boy now. He'll get over it," Lee said, patting his left shoulder, "same as I have."

"Sure, he screwed up, and may have cost you some dreams. But the last time I checked, you don't walk on water either."

"You mean Abby, don't you?" Lee smiled sarcastically. "That's rich. You giving moral advice, after what you've done, breaking your priest vows. And for what?" He hesitated. "A few minutes rolling around on a church pew with Miss What's-Her-Name."

David grabbed Lee's shirt and stuck his face close, almost nose to nose. "Are you crazy, sex in God's house? I haven't lost it completely, mister, my soul, not yet anyway." He let go of Lee's shirt. "And for your information, her name's Joyce, Joyce Heinz."

Lee's eyes widened and he leaned away.

Hands trembling, David stared out the passenger window for a long moment. "Look at me, a fine role model. I've done a lot of thinking about that, what you just said, me giving others counsel after what I've done. Maybe I am going to Hell, but you tell me. Is it a sin in His eyes, having sex, if the couple loves one another and are willing to live with the consequences? Not sure of the answer anymore, not like I was once."

"If you're not sure, then why'd you choose her over Him?"

He thought a moment. "At one point I felt that whichever I chose, God or Joyce, I was going to burn in Hell. It was just a question of when that would happen. Burn now if I chose Him and lost her, and suffer in Hell later if I chose her."

"Didn't know you felt that way about her, loved her that much."

"She's a bully girl."

"How'd you decide?"

David got out of the car, walked around and shook Lee's hand through the car window. "About your question, how I chose. I figured out a way to keep them both happy, God and her. Then again, you're never sure about Him."

A question started to form on the other man's lips, but David held up his hand. "Let me finish."

CHAPTER FIFTY-TWO

As Lee closed his car door in front of Pru's house, his eyes dragged across the road toward Sawyer's Park. They found the tops of the park's tall trees and the opening where the picnic benches were.

On her front porch, he tried making a sharper cuff in the legs of his turned-up dungarees. After checking his reflection in the door's glass panel, he knocked. Shortly, a window curtain moved and he caught a glimpse of Blanche. He took his hat off and put Pru's flowers behind his back.

Blanche, her eyes dark and flinty, opened the door. "Ye-es?"

"Good morning, Mrs. Pruitt. It's Lee, Lee Jarrett. Is Cathy home?"

"What do you want?"

He tapped his hat against his leg. "I'd like to see her."

She frowned. "About?"

"I'm leaving town today, Mrs. Pruitt, and I'd like to see her before I go. For just a few minutes, that's all."

"I'll tell her you stopped by," she answered, starting to close the door.

"Wait please, would you just tell her I'm here?"

"She's busy." She opened the door wider. "In case you don't know it, young man, she's getting married tomorrow." Her eyes grew stonier. "And to a good man, one who loves her. She could never be happy with you."

"Just five minutes? Five lousy minutes, Mrs. Pruitt?"

"It'll just upset her."

He held up two fingers. "Just two minutes, please, then I'll leave."

She folded her arms across her chest.

He took a deep breath, his throat tightening. "Mrs. Pruitt, I'm not leaving, not till you tell her I'm here."

"Tsk, tsk, such childishness." She turned and disappeared, leaving the door slightly ajar.

Shortly, Pru's lovely face appeared in the doorway. "Lee," she said, surprise in her voice. "What's up?" Her hair was in curlers.

From inside, beyond the front door, her mother's cold voice cut through the darkness. "Cathy, don't be long."

"Okay, Mother."

He tried sounding casual. "I'm heading out of town ... today. Don't know when I'll be back."

She frowned. "Leaving Eastbrook?"

"Yeah, thought I'd stop off and say goodbye. Saw your car out front when I pulled up."

"That's a shame. I sent you an invitation. You know, for the wedding. It's tomorrow. I was hoping you'd come."

"I forgot," he lied.

"Why are you leaving?"

He made a nervous laugh. "Sorry, I'm getting ahead of myself. I quit college, got me a newspaper job in Baltimore, full time."

"Oh?"

"Yeah, like I said, I'm leaving today, later on this afternoon."

"Your aunt, the one in Baltimore, she get the job for you?"

He nodded yes. "Granddad left me some money too, a nice sum. It'll carry me till I get on my feet. He motioned toward his car. "Got me some wheels too. Dad helped me pick it out, said it was a good starter."

She nodded toward Lee's arm behind his back. "What do you have there?"

"Almost forgot." he said, thrusting the flowers in her face. "I picked them myself on the way over. They're for you."

She opened the door wider and motioned him toward the living room. "I'll get a vase."

He sat on one end of their couch from her. On a table next to him was a flattering portrait of Tom. Beside it was Blanche's favorite porcelain figurine. She called it her joker clown. One side was a smiling clown done in bright, happy colors with one hand up, the other side was a sad-faced clown done in drab hues with its hand down, lesser details supporting each side.

He was always surprised it was Blanche's favorite. To him, the figurine seemed the very embodiment of her deserter-husband's philosophy about life's duality.

When he picked up the porcelain, it felt cold. He turned it upside down. Its unfinished bottom felt rough, like a cat's tongue. There was a hole in the underside and Lee could see it was hollow.

Pru returned and set a vase with his flowers on an end table. She sat down on the other end of the couch from him. Her skin was fair and unblemished, like the daisy petals on the end table next to her.

She tittered and held up her green stained hands. "Daisy stems."

"Me too," he said, holding his up also.

Her lips pursed. "So you're leaving little ol' Eastbrook?"

He nodded.

"Your mom and dad, how are they taking this?"

His eyes rolled up. "You know."

"How far is to Baltimore?"

"Three hundred miles or so."

"Long drive by yourself."

"Don't have to be there for two weeks. I'm gonna stop on the way and fish the Burnt Tree. Probably camp near where we swam and lunched." He glanced out the front window. "Weather report says rain, then clearing. Hope I don't get caught," he said. "You know, like we did?"

She smiled. "Are you going to look for your brook again? What was it called? Don't tell me. A girl's name, started with A?" Her eyes tried remembering.

"Amanda, it was called Amanda's Brook," he prompted. "Bud's father renamed it Eden. That's what I call it anymore, Eden Brook."

"Yes, I remember now." An uneasy silence followed and she repeated, "So, are you going to look for it?"

He shrugged.

"Ever?"

"Maybe, maybe," he said, nodding, "it haunts my dreams."

Pru casually glanced out the side window. "She has a crush on you, you know."

He questioned her remark with an open hand.

"That pretty young thing next door, Mary Lou Harris."

"Nah, she acts that way with all the guys. She's just trying out her flirting wings."

"Don't know whether I mentioned it or not, but after we broke up a couple years ago, she grilled me about you. Wanted to know why you weren't coming around. Told her it was just a temporary thing. She asked a lot of other questions too. Seemed curious about you ... and the Burnt Tree also. Definitely interested."

"That's natural," he said, "they used to live there. Lots of boys still hanging around?"

"A few," Pru answered.

"I hope she hasn't given it up yet."

She gave him a disapproving, yet slightly amused look. "I still think she has a crush on you."

"When are you leaving? What time?"

He looked at his watch. "By four or five, if I can."

"Same time as rehearsal. You know, for the wedding."

"Congratulations," he said, his tone dead.

"You too," she said more sincerely, "congratulations."

He frowned.

"Your girl at college, what's her name, Tammy? Someone said you two were engaged. I guess she'll be joining you in Baltimore."

Lee stared at her and chewed on his lower lip like he was wanted to say something, but didn't.

"I guess in a way, I have you to thank for everything that's happened, Tom and me, the wedding."

His brow unfurled.

"You never answered my note. You know, when I wrote how I felt and tried getting back together. You never answered it, my note."

For a few seconds, neither said anything.

"Speaking of notes, Granddad left me one. Read it, but I haven't figured it out, everything he's saying."

The hint of a smile played across her lips. "Your grandfather, I've been lighting a candle for him every afternoon at the Virgin's altar. Saying a prayer."

"At St. Pete's?"

"Yes, your mom's idea to start. But I can see why you do it. Stop by when your church is empty, quiet. You can feel, see things more clearly." She smiled. "Your mother even showed me how to bless myself. It isn't that different from ours, your church, not really. God's God."

"Nice of you, the candle, the prayer."

"Didn't do it for you. I loved him too, you know that."

"I didn't mean anything. Still nice of you."

Just then, Blanche yelled from down the hallway. "Something's wrong with this thermostat again, Cathy. Says 70, feels like a hundred. Thought Tom fixed it."

"I'll check it, Mother," she said, turning back to Lee. "Thermostat's fine, probably hungry."

"I stopped off at Tom's house this morning before I came here. He said you had his fishing net, that I could have it."

"I'd better fix her a sandwich, Lee. Take me just a minute. Can you wait?"

He nodded.

"Tom's net is on the back porch. Can you get it?"

As Lee walked through the house, he could see several white flower arrangements. On the dining room table was a large centerpiece, several stacks of dishes and a large punch bowl with cups around it.

Blanche's room was drab and stark.

He retrieved the net and started back. When he came to Pru's bedroom door, he stopped and pushed it open.

A fresh breeze was pouring through the half raised, ground level windows. It was playing with the curtains. A white dress and bridal veil were draped neatly over the back of a rocking chair near the window. A brown suitcase rested on the floor, all packed for their honeymoon, he assumed. Sun filtered through the shrubbery outside and fell across her bed.

His gaze shifted to her night table, hoping but not expecting to find his picture. It wasn't there, but Tom's was. Blanche probably trashed his.

When he returned to the living room, Pru was sitting on the couch next to his daisies. Lee sat on the other end from her again.

"Mother's napping."

He laid the net on the floor beside the couch. "Remember the first time we fished the Tree?"

Her eyes softened.

"Anyway, when I went through Granddad's stuff, I found an old picture of you. It was taken that time we fished together." He stared, remembering. "Those were good times."

"Boy, that water was cold."

"Hey, remember when we used to go swimming at Wildcat?"

"And that farmer's heavy wooden gate," she added, "the one you always had to help me open."

"And what about all those basketball tournaments?" he asked. "Remember the time we got soaked running to the car after the championship game?" His eyes brightened. "Practically had to wring us out afterward."

She smiled behind her hand. "And that little restaurant we'd eat at after the games. The Rainbow, I think it was called. I can still taste their hot meatloaf sandwiches."

"And those picnics at Holly River." He chuckled to himself. "Remember that time we were playing basketball in our bare feet and I stepped on a hot cigarette butt? Boy, did I dance."

Smiling, she nodded. "You're right, we had some great times, didn't we?"

When the wall clock chimed two, she motioned toward it. "Been running fast. I'll have T. check it." She paused. "I hope you and Tom can bury the hatchet."

"Did he ever tell you what's between us?"

"Whatever it was, I know he regrets it."

Walking over to a wall display, she spoke with her back to him. "Tom lost more than his foot. He lost his dreams, his self-worth. But he's trying to put his life back together now, and I'm part of that." She placed her hand on the display. "He made the case for me, my doll collection."

In 10 of the 12 compartments were stuffed dolls, all peering out with big eyes and stitched smiles.

"You've been busy," he said. "You only had four two years ago. The clown still your favorite?"

She nodded. "Tom's also. Still have the baseball player I made you?"

"Sure, it's on the car dash right now."

When she turned to face him, she was tearing. "Don't mind me." She wiped her eyes with a sleeve. "It's your leaving, the memories, the good times, the end of things."

Their eyes locked. Walking over, he was about to take her in his arms, but she turned toward the casement. She pulled the clown out, set it in her palm so it faced him and held it up. Its legs danced crazily. "T needs surgery," she said, "but he can't afford it."

"David told me. He said if it wasn't for you, Tom would be dead now. In fact, he said you're his whole world."

"He's exaggerating."

He asked abruptly, "Does he love you?"

She hesitated. "Certainly, why would you ask such a question?"

"It's just that I don't trust him. He put on a good guy act with me at the house, but you don't know him like I do." He glanced at Tom's picture. "Do you love him?"

She touched her chest up high. "Mother says that will come in time. Let's just say for now, I'm very fond of him and he needs me. And like I said, he's hurting. Besides, there's more than that to a marriage."

"Yeah, like?"

"He's a big help to us, Mother and me. She likes him too."

"Hmm, wonder why that could be?"

"Don't be funny," she said. "Besides, there are promises I've made ... to both of them."

"Pru, please don't let her run your life, like she did with us. Do what's in your heart."

"In other words, forget my promises, do like you're doing?"

"My promises? My promises?"

"Never mind, I don't want to fight."

"My God, Pru, don't you get it? My leaving Eastbrook, the job, Baltimore, this whole damn thing is for you ... at least in part."

"For me?"

Capturing her eyes, he took her hands gently in his own. "Pru," he said, his voice half whispering and plaintive, "please, go with—"

Her mother's flinty voice killed both his plea, and the moment. "Has he gone yet, Cathy? It's getting late, the rehearsal..."

Eyes still on Lee, she said, "Don't worry, Mother."

Mrs. Pruitt banged on the wall. "Cathy, I need you, now."

Pru stood up. "Tsk. I have to go Lee, sorry." Their eyes locked again, she took a step toward him, but then stopped. "Good luck, Lee. Drop me a line once in a while. Let me know how you're doing."

"I'll let myself out." He watched as she disappeared down the dark hall and probably out of his life forever. All the while, her dolls were smiling their stitched smiles, like all was still right with the world.

When Pru's footsteps faded, he picked up Blanche's joker clown statuette. "Damn, damn you," he cursed at her. From far down the hall, Mrs. Pruitt's sharp voice counterpointed her daughter's gentle tones. Lee glanced at Pru's portrait beside the vase with the white and yellow daisies. Meanwhile, the wall clock was hurrying the afternoon forward.

He eased the front door shut and stood on the porch. The sky overhead looked like fresh cement. Thickening clouds were rolling across it and a wind was rocking the porch swing. Pulling his collar up, he tucked her mother's figurine under his jacket. He glanced next door, hoping to see her, Miss Denim Shorts, but she wasn't there.

Just then, a delivery truck pulled up out front. The driver took out several flower arrangements, glanced at his notebook, and then looked up at the Pruitt house.

When they passed on the steps, Lee didn't acknowledge him.

After Pru heard the front door close, she walked to the living room window. Standing back so Lee would not see her, she watched as he drove out of sight.

When she turned to leave, she saw his fishing net on the floor next to the couch.

She called the Jarrett house and Lee's mother answered. "Mrs. Jarrett?"

"Cathy, dear," she answered warmly. "I was hoping you'd call."

"Lee forgot his net, the fishing net Tom gave him."

"Were you surprised?"

"Beg pardon?"

"Baltimore, Lee asking you to go, the rest."

Cathy frowned at the receiver, and then listened again.

"You know how we've always felt about you, Cathy, like a daughter. You know that, don't you?" Mrs. Jarrett paused. "You there?"

"Yes, I'm here."

"It's a shame about Tom though," his mother pattered on. "In time though, it'll all work out for the best, you'll see."

"But isn't Lee engaged to that girl at Hillsboro? What's her name, Tammy?"

"That's history, they broke up. I'm surprised he didn't mention it. But your plans, dear. Tell me all about them."

"Can I call you back, Mrs. Jarrett?"

"Certainly, dear. Call us before you leave. And don't worry about your mother, she'll be all right. We'll see to it."

After Pru hung up, she gave the phone a long stare and worried her engagement ring.

Suddenly, from the other room, her mother's needy voice cut her thoughts short.

CHAPTER FIFTY-THREE

Lee had never had that mystical feeling in church before, not till that time two years before. A few times out in the mountains or on a river he had felt it, but never in church.

They had been on their way fishing, his grandfather and he, and the old man had made a brief stop at St. Peter's to make an electrical repair for Father Moore. When his grandfather and the priest went downstairs to check the wiring, they left Lee in the church by himself.

The young man had attended hundreds of church services before, but this was the first time he had been there when it was empty with sun shafting through the colored windows the only light.

It was then he felt it: a mystical sense that everything would be all right if he trusted in the right voices, that the rest was out of his hands.

It was a feeling he had never gotten during services but he wanted again. Other times later when he felt it in an empty church, he almost had to will himself to leave. All too soon on that first occasion, however, when the lights flickered back on and he heard grandfather's voice, the feeling left him.

When he thought about it later, he decided it was mostly the quiet and solitude that did it.

And so after that, it became a tradition with Lee. Anytime he was going fishing, he would stop off first at St. Peter's. Not for a blessing from the fish gods, as Tom had needled, but hoping for that special feeling again.

After leaving Pru's house, he entered the empty church and blessed himself. The holy water felt cool on his fingertips and forehead. It was shadowy and still inside. He folded the kneeling bench down and it echoed clear back to the choir loft. When the sounds faded, a hushed holiness replaced it.

He knelt in the cool, quiet twilight, hoping he would get it again, the feeling. The late morning sun was shafting through the colored windows, just as he liked it.

Although the feeling only came when the church was empty and quiet, he didn't always get it. If he thought about it too much or got distracted, it didn't happen. Things had to be just right, an empty church, unlit except for colored sunlight, quiet, cool and the world shut out.

Not like during services when the people were there, getting up and down, uttering words out loud, even repeating the same prayer over and over again. The priest too, he was always busy doing something, interrupting Lee's thoughts, so that he could not hold onto those feelings, if he even got them.

Although everything was right for it that day and he waited and waited, it never came. His mind wandered too much: the trip, his new job, Pru.

There were two life-sized statues on both sides of the main altar, each with rows of lit candles at their feet. The one to his far right was St. Joseph. The other statue, just in front of him, was the blessed Virgin, looking young and beautiful. The Virgin's face, with the candlelight playing over her white marble features, reminded him of Pru. Mary was holding a small bouquet of real flowers close to her bosom. They were yellow and white.

He slid a quarter in the box at her feet, lit a votive candle and made a request to the Madonna.

To his immediate left on the side was a large stained glass window. Its caption read, "St. Thomas in the Temple." In it, the saint, his face looking fatherly and wise, was holding the Christ child in his arms. Standing close by, her hands folded in prayer, was the blessed Virgin. Unlike the youthful statue, however, this Madonna looked more matronly. St. Joseph was in the background holding two caged doves. All the figures had haloes around their heads.

Lee's eyes fell to the bottom of the encasement. There, the Virgin's right foot was crushing a serpent's head.

"Snakes again," he whispered. "Damn."

Just then, he heard the church door open and shut. The candles fluttered; his quiet time was over.

When he heard footsteps coming down the aisle behind him, he looked over his shoulder. Like in a perfect dream, there she was, Pru.

Eyes straight ahead, she walked to the statue of the Virgin and knelt down.

His mind was spinning.

Lighting a candle, she bowed her head.

Why was she there? He didn't have any answers, but he did know one thing for certain. Watching her kneeling there in prayer with the holy light washing over her features, he never wanted her more.

CHAPTER FIFTY-FOUR

As Pru started back up the aisle, she suddenly stopped at his pew and held Tom's fishing net out toward him. "Called your house and talked to your mother." She looked at him knowingly.

"Sorry, Pru. I tried, but..." He shook his head.

As he turned to lay the net on the seat, she slid in beside him, half kneeling. She rested her forehead on one arm and took his hand. "I love you, Lee Jarrett. Don't you know that?" she whispered. "Always have, always will."

His eyes caressed her face. "God, how I've wanted to hear that," he said, folding her into his arms.

She nestled closer to his chest. "I was so afraid it was over. That night on your porch when they were searching for your grandfather, those angry words."

He stroked her cheek. "It's okay, Pru. I'm not mad, not anymore."

"And Kenny Harte, what was that about?"

"Just me being stupid. Trying to get even."

She tilted her head in a question.

"Aw, your promise," he said, "I thought you broke it."

She stared at him, trying to make sense of his words. "My God," she said, giving a low cry, "with Kenny Harte?" Holding his eyes with her own, she took his hands. "Lee, I've always been faithful to you."

He stole a look at his green stained hands. "I have too," he whispered.

She stroked his cheek with the back of her hand.

He pulled her close. "David, he said something today that stuck with me. Had to do with why he left the orders, chose his girl over God. He said he could best serve Him by being a whole person, which meant having her by his side. I can't be whole either ... unless you're there with me."

She kissed his open hand and her eyes welled. "Lee, when you leave today for Baltimore, will you take me with you? I can't lose you again, not now, not ever."

"But what about tomorrow, the wedding?"

"Aw corn, I don't care. I'll break my word and call it off, do what I have to so we can be together." She pressed her face against his chest. "Here's where I belong."

Falling into one another's arms, his open mouth found hers. They lay down on the church pew, Lee on top. Just as they did, however, his foot kicked the net off the seat. Its clattering echoes made them both sit up, still clinging to one another and breathing heavily.

His gaze found the lamp with the red flame over the altar, the one that, if lit, meant Christ was present. At least, Father Moore always said that's what it meant. "Sorry," he said, blessing himself, "our promises on the Tree." He brushed a wisp of hair off her forehead. "Hey, almost forgot. Granddad, he left me some money, around $5,000."

"Wow, nice."

"Hopefully, it'll carry us till we get on our feet."

Fingering the mesh on Tom's fishing net, she started to speak, but hesitated.

"What is it?"

"Aw nothing."

"C'mon,

She held back another moment. "It's just that we have everything, one another, a bright future and Tom has nothing." Laying her hand softly on his chest, she asked, "Would you mind terribly if we gave him just a little of it, your money? You know, to help with his operation, leave him with some glimmer of hope?"

"Give Tom our money?" Pulling away, he stiffened. "Is that what this 'be nice to Lee' is all about?"

"No, silly. I meant every word," she answered, squeezing his hand. "I just thought if we did that, helped with his surgery, it might help ease things for him. You know, make up for me breaking my word."

"We can't do that," he said, folding his arms across his chest. "I won't be making that much to start and we may need every cent. He'll just have to find it elsewhere, the money."

She gave a long sigh and her chin slid down to her chest.

He studied her momentarily, and began gently rubbing her shoulders. "But I guess in a way, it is yours too now, the money ... or it will be soon, so you should have a say in how it's spent. What do you think we should do? What I said before though still goes, about our needing it to get started."

As she struggled with the question, she stared hard into his face, but not seeing it. Finally, removing a prayer book from its holder, she mindlessly paged through it, hoping for some answer there, but not expecting one.

He glanced at the stained glass window with the serpent and matronly Madonna. "And your mother, what about her?"

Pru leaned away and put her hand to her chest.

"Are you okay going to Baltimore, just you and me?"

Her face twisted, like she was in pain.

"I know you want to care for her and feel like you're breaking your word by leaving with me, but for God's sake, Pru, don't let her run your life again, not like she did before with us."

Her eyes were drawn to a stained glass window on the far side of the church. Swaying tree branches outside were making its colored light brighten, then fall. The window depicted Christ in the Garden of Gethsemane. She began tapping on her lips with one finger. "Aw corn."

"So why can't you make up your mind?" Lee asked. "Is it about hurting others, again?"

Hesitating, she nodded and shrugged one shoulder.

"But Pru, it's like you're always telling me, someone's bound to get hurt." He paused a long moment. "Is it that ... or are you just trying to dodge decisions, trouble?"

Her shoulders sagged.

He tried lightening her mood. "Money, maybe we can send your mother a little from time to time. My parents, they said they'd help too ... and who knows, maybe later on she can come live with us." The last words stuck in his throat, but her brightening face told him she liked hearing them.

He studied her for a long moment. "You're probably fed up with Granddad stories, but bear with me please one last time. He even had this one titled, called it 'Road Apples.'"

"Road Apples?"

"Yeah, horse droppings. If there were some in the road, that's what he'd call them, road apples." He chuckled to himself. "Their shape, I guess. Anyway, he said one day a team of horses left a big pile of them in the trail. No traveler was willing to clean them up for fear of getting crap on themselves, so eventually everyone did just that, stepped in it and got some on them." He paused.

"You get it, don't you, Granddad's point about making decisions? Dealing with a problem can bring trouble, but so can not dealing with it. If you choose to walk around a pile of crap that others are stepping in, sooner or later you'll be cleaning it off your own shoes. So, be a cleaner-upper, make the path better for the next traveler, yourself too."

At first, her eyes were amused, but afterward, they became more serious and pensive. Pocketing her engagement ring, she pointed to his class ring. "Can I have that back?"

He slipped the class ring onto her third finger.

Just then, there was a faint sound behind them, maybe as far back as the vestibule. He shushed her with a hand, turned an ear toward the sound and held his breath for a few seconds.

"What is it?" she asked.

"Not sure. I might be crazy, but it sounded like Tom's squeaky foot."

She looked at him skeptically.

He shrugged. "The old church's bones settling, maybe, that or a mouse." He dismissed it with a snort.

He looked at his watch. "I gotta swing by the house and pack before we leave." His voice turned lighter, "Pack warm," he said to her, "it can get mighty cold in those mountains at night."

"Pick me up in a couple hours or so?" she asked, smiling. "I've got a lot to do also. My duffle will be on the porch."

"They're calling for rain. I'll bring a raincoat."

She toyed with a lock of her hair and shrugged indifferently.

He frowned, but then his face softened. "You were right, you know, what you said once about Granddad and his first wife, them not needing a piece of paper." He hesitated. "But we'll get one anyway, Baltimore."

As she turned to leave, she put her hand over her heart. "Always have, always will."

After she left, he knelt at the foot of the Virgin. There were no matches, so he used someone else's candle to light his. The wax felt warm and soft like Pru's face.

He thanked the Virgin for her blessings, but he was surprised he felt no guilt about touching Pru the way he had in church. Maybe that was the way real love was, sex without the guilt. He hoped so. Nonetheless, he would probably tell it in his next confession, just to be on the safe side.

His step lighter now, he hurried back up the aisle, glancing once at the stained glass casement with the Virgin and serpent.

CHAPTER FIFTY-FIVE

His father was slicing a cucumber when Lee came in the back door. On the kitchen sink was a colander of ripe, red strawberries."

Lee sniffed the air. "Something smells good."

His father pointed to the stove. "Bacon and onions. Your mother's helping out at church. Said she might be late. I'm fixing dinner. Want me to set a place?"

"No thanks, Dad. I have to pack if we want to make the Tree before dark. If you get a chance though, throw some canned food in a box for me. And, oh yeah, par boil a few potatoes."

"She agreed to go, huh?"

"Yeah, we got things straight, finally."

"Hope your mother gets home soon. She'll blame me if she doesn't get to say goodbye."

"Camping gear in the shed?" his son asked.

Mr. Jarrett nodded.

After Lee packed the car, he went to his room for one last check.

Following him, his father asked from the doorway, "How's the new jalopy?"

"Okay, Dad. Thanks again for helping."

"It's a holiday weekend," he said, "watch out for all the road-crazies. How you fixed for cash?"

"Granddad's, remember?"

His father's mouth twisted to one side and his gaze wandered to Lee's fly rod. "Still saving for a bamboo?"

Picking up the tip section of the glass rod, his son whipped it back and forth in the air. "Nah, Granddad fixed it. It'll do fine."

"Them mountain streams can be awful cold. Wanna take along my waders? I ain't using them."

"They don't fit, Dad, too big."

"Back in a jiffy," his father said. Returning momentarily, he threw a pair of hip boots at his son's feet. "Take 'em along just in case. Yes sir, them boots will feel mighty good when that cold mountain water starts nipping at your toes. Of course, you can't hike in them. They'd rub your feet raw. Blisters ain't much fun."

Lee pointed to his father's arm that was behind his back.

When Mr. Jarrett brought his hand around, the young man recognized the yellowing waxed paper. It was grandfather's map.

"You may as well have this. Who knows, might come in handy someday."

Lee smiled broadly. "Thanks, Dad. About that big guy that showed up on our porch one night asking about a map, remember? Well, I've been thinking. If he really was Papa Joe, like I was saying, who was it they buried up on the Burnt Tree alongside Crazy Dan's wife?"

"Let it go, son," he said, his tone indulgent.

The young man laid the map on his bed. "I'll take good care of it."

His father waved it away, "It's yours. I got no use for it. Might have once, but not anymore. Are you gonna look for it, Eden Brook?"

"Maybe Tom was right, maybe that restaurant guy made it all up just to get our money. Tom claimed he was full of wind."

"But I wouldn't toss it away, son, that dream. Sometimes a little wind can clear the air, help you see things clearer."

He hesitated. "Maybe," he answered, "maybe I'll look for it."

"Gotta check on dinner. Give me a shout before you leave."

After he left, Lee glanced at the map. Who knows, he thought, it might answer some questions about his grandfather too. After all, if he was reading the map correctly, it was near there where the different tales occurred, Bud's and the old man's."

Lee picked up the dut hat. He turned it 'round and 'round by its brim, stopping occasionally at a faded stain, musing about what marvelous adventure might lie behind it.

The dog was curled up on Granddad's coat. "Were you there for any of these, Dan?"

At his name, the dog got up.

"Now hold your horses. Don't go away. No more talk, promise." Lee chuckled. "But remember what I said, you're the only ear I got left."

When he was packing, he threw the tarnished Miraculous Medal into his things, although he wasn't certain why. Both his mother and his priest had let him down.

Lee ran the last of his things out to the car and stopped by the kitchen where his father was shucking corn.

"Before you head out, you might wanna swing by the cemetery," he said to his son, "pay respects to your kinfolk. Decoration Day."

"Did that."

"All of 'em?"

Lee shook his head no. "Just Granddad's."

His father gave him a weighty stare. "Why just him?"

"I needed to talk. Could always talk to him."

Mr. Jarrett frowned, wanting more.

Lee didn't offer.

His father opened the oven door and forked three potatoes baking there. "How'd things go with Tom?" Steam rose from the tine holes he had made.

Lee shrugged.

His father cocked an eyebrow. "And Mrs. Pruitt?"

"I can't save the whole world, Dad," he replied, an edge in his voice.

"Don't get smart, young man," his father snapped. "You know perfectly well what I meant. I ain't asking you to save the world, just one little corner of it."

"Sorry," he said, "Didn't mean anything."

Mr. Jarrett nodded at the hip boots. "If they're too big, try stuffing newspapers in the toes. But remember what I said about not hiking. Try that and you'll wear your feet bloody. He looked down at the dog. "Going to miss Lee, boy?"

Dan scratched his ear once with a half-hearted swipe of one hind leg, almost losing his balance.

They both smiled.

"Can I take him along, Dad, you know, for company? Just till Christmas?"

"Um-m, I don't know. Your mother won't like it, losing you both. You know how she feels about Dan, only piece of your grandfather she has left."

"I'll take good care of him. Just till Christmas, please?"

"He would be good company, good watchdog too. Guess it won't hurt. Just till Christmas, though."

"Thanks, Dad." He washed out the dog's dish and gathered the rest of Dan's things.

"Better eat before you leave though," his father said. "Liver and onions."

His son looked at his watch. "I'll grab a bite on the way. Thought I'd stop at Wilkens and get a couple hot dogs."

"Been a while since I've had a good dog with chili," his father said. "Have one for me. Call your mother first thing when you get to Baltimore.

You know how she is." He looked down at the dog. "She'll have a hissy fit, not getting to say goodbye to either one."

Near the back door, his father held him long and close for a few seconds. It was the first time Lee remembered him doing that since he was small.

Stepping back, Lee gestured to grandfather's dut hat on his head. "Pru likes it. Thought I'd give it to her."

"Find a place to stay?"

"Yeah Dad, small motel just west of Baltimore. Brown's, I think, is the name."

Mr. Jarrett took a small white box out of the pantry and handed it to his son.

Lee sniffed it. "Fudge, peanut butter?"

His father smiled. "You guys need anything, call, you hear?" He held his son out at arm's length, one hand outside each shoulder. It reminded Lee of a scene from Pinocchio, one he remembered or just imagined. In it, the puppet's maker, Geppetto, was giving his creation one last check before cutting his strings and sending him out into the world.

Bending over, Mr. Jarrett tilted Dan's muzzle up and looked into his eyes. "Mind your P's and Q's, boy, what you been taught."

Lee was certain his father was talking to him through the dog. He checked his shirt pocket one last time for Pru's photo and his grandfather's note, and then patted his leg. "All set, boy?"

Wagging his tail once, Dan padded after him.

CHAPTER FIFTY-SIX

Humming to himself, Lee bounded up the Pruitt's front steps, two at a time. Her packed duffle, the one Lee had given her, was not there as expected. When he surveyed the porch more carefully, he suddenly froze. Hooked over the armrest of the porch swing was Tom's cane. He started to knock, but instead, walked around the side of the house. Halfway there, he froze again. There, behind the Pruitt house, was Tom's truck. He felt his teeth clench and his jaw slide sideways. "Son of a bitch," he whispered.

Starting back toward the front of the house, he stopped outside her mother's closed bedroom window, hunkered down to one side and peered in. Mrs. Pruitt and Tom were standing in the doorway to her room. He still had his coat and hat on. Her hand on his arm, she was telling him something. Although Lee could not hear the words, she seemed distraught. Finally, when Tom spoke, she shrugged and held her hands up. Afterward, she sat down in a straight-backed, cushion less rocker. Both her hands were resting on a Bible in her lap and her shoulders began shaking as she cried.

Putting a hand on her shoulder, Tom whispered something in her ear. She looked up at him, smiled, said something back and patted his hand. Before leaving, Tom bent down and kissed the top of her head.

How sweet, thought Lee. How phony.

After Tom left her room, she closed her eyes and her lips began moving, like she was praying.

Lee moved over to Pru's window, stooped down and hid behind the dense shrubbery. Her window was partially open and she was humming along with a song on the radio. At the bottom of the bed was her packed duffel for the trip with Lee. There was a soft knock at her door, she opened it and Tom stepped inside. "T.," she said, sounding surprised, "I didn't hear you knock. Mother let you in?"

"Knocked on the front door, didn't get an answer but I could hear music playing. I let myself in. Hope you don't mind."

She pointed to the radio. "Didn't hear you."

Lee crept closer and cocked an ear toward her open window.

She followed Tom's eyes to her packed duffle. "I'm so sorry, T. I was going to write you a long letter." She hesitated, searching for the right words. "To try and explain why, I mean apologize for breaking my ... no, I mean for everything. It's better this way though, you hear it from me."

"No need," he said. "Your mother told me everything. Said she was hoping you'd change your mind."

"Yeah, she's pretty upset."

"Don't suppose you'd consider putting off leaving, at least till she gets used to things?"

"Lee's got a job waiting," she said.

"And just when do you plan to tie the knot, you and Lee?"

"Not till Baltimore."

"But that may not be for a week or so. Lee said he was going to stop off at the Burnt Tree for a few days. Isn't that the cart before the horse?" His upper lip started to curl, but when she reached up and turned his shirt label under, it straightened.

"Just a piece of paper, the marriage license."

He frowned and looked at her side-eyed.

She put her hand on his arm. "Never mind, T. It'll be all right, trust me."

"Maybe your mother can join you later. You know, once you get settled."

"Lee said that too," Pru answered, "once we get on our feet."

"In the meantime, don't worry. I'll keep an eye on her."

"What about your mother?"

"Joyce, David's girl, she's helping out. Ma's in good hands there."

Pru held her engagement ring out toward him. "I'm sorry. I feel like such a dog, going back on my word."

He took the ring from her. "No need. I release you from it, your promise." He held the extra raincoat and baseball cap across the bed toward her.

She frowned.

"Fair trade, Cat," he said, trying to manage a smile. "My raincoat and cap for the ring. You don't wanna get that fur wet."

She managed a pursed smile. "But how'd you know I'd go with him, say yes?"

"No secret. You two have been sweet on one another since you met." His hand brushed the knife handle under his jacket. "Truth is, I've been afraid of this all along, that he'd come back into your life and that would be the end of us."

When he sat down beside her, she pressed her forehead against his. "This is so unfair. What will you do now?"

He gave her a thoughtful stare. "I'm not going to hurt myself if that's what you're wondering. Too many people depending on me."

"One good thing," she said. "There'll be plenty to keep you busy. You know, church, your mother, rehab. And those flying lessons we talked about too. Promise me you'll follow up with those."

He looked away. "None of that means much without you."

"I'm so sorry I'm causing you more pain. You've had enough of that already."

"It was worth it, Cat. Getting to know you, almost having you for my wife."

Her lower jaw trembled as she fought back tears. When the clock in the hall struck four, she glanced toward her mother's room.

He handed her a tissue from a nearby box. "C'mon, Cat, you can't be looking teary-eyed when Lee gets here. When's he picking you up?"

"Any time now."

After he limped to the door, she hugged him. His face was close to hers and he studied her eyes, trying to read if there was anything left unspoken behind them. There wasn't.

"Lee Jarrett's never been out of here," she said, patting her chest. "But you'll always be in here now too, not like Lee, but in here."

He stepped out the door, but then stuck his head back inside. "If you ever change your mind, I'll be right here."

When Lee heard the front door close, he hunkered down and hid behind the shrubbery. After a long pause, he heard a car door open and shut out front of her house and Dan bark once. It sounded like his car door and he was puzzled.

A few seconds later, Tom came limping past without his cane, his foot squeaking. Just after he passed Lee, his leg collapsed and he fell to the ground awkwardly with a grunt, face down. He lay there for a few seconds, before rolling over onto his back. Tom was so close to him then that Lee was almost afraid to breathe.

He was startled when Tom began speaking up toward the heavens. "Thanks for bringing her into my life, if only for a short while. She's a wonderful gal and I love her, but she's his now. Lee's okay and will take good care of her, probably better than I could. Hope he can forgive me for everything, you too."

Lee frowned and squirmed.

Tom removed something from his shirt pocket. Holding it up, he studied it momentarily. Even in the fading light, it sparkled. Suddenly, he flung it over his shoulder and it landed in the bushes near Lee. Wiping his eyes with his fists, the fallen man got to his feet, still wobbly, and limped away.

Seconds later, when Lee heard Tom's motor fading down the street, he crawled out from behind the bushes, and found the object the other man had thrown. It was Pru's engagement ring. Not sure why, he dropped it in his shirt pocket.

CHAPTER FIFTY-SEVEN

Now the road for Pru and him was clear. Nothing stood in their way, not anymore. He even had Tom's blessing. And yet, as he walked back to the car, he felt no real sense of victory. Why was that?

When he opened the car door to get in, Dan was on the driver's seat. Beside him was Tom's knife. Eyebrows puzzling, he picked it up, stared at it, and then looked in the direction the other man had left.

Dan jumped in the back seat, laid his head down and closed his eyes, one ear drooping over Mrs. Pruitt's statuette.

Lee sat in the car, still suspicious that Tom had shown up at Pru's house hoping to win her back, never mind the Mr. Nice Guy routine. Tom knew his presence would make her feel guilty about going back on her word, rethink her decision.

In fairness, Lee countered in his head, it did seem like the other man was sincere, truly loved her. As for that good guy act before at Tom's house, and what Lee had just witnessed outside, both appeared genuine. Of course, that made it harder for Lee to dislike him, but it still didn't change how Pru and he felt about one another.

Tom knew also that Pru had trouble with decisions. He was probably banking on that, however, hoping it would confuse her so she'd have second thoughts about choosing Lee over him.

Then again, he considered, maybe Tom saw him hiding there in the bushes and that entire prayer business on the ground was all a charade to throw Lee off. No sir, he didn't trust that guy.

Leaving the car door open, he walked back to Pru's window. Her radio was still playing softly. She was on the bed with her back up against the headboard. Lee's framed picture was leaning against her drawn-up knees. Her eyes caressed his portrait. But then, with the same caring gaze, she looked over at her wedding dress hanging on a closet door.

Abruptly she stopped and lifted her brown suitcase onto the bed alongside her canvas duffel. She stood there for several seconds, one hand on each, looking mournfully first at one, then the other. At one point, she also glanced down at Lee's class ring. Her breathing suddenly became labored and she placed her hand high on her chest.

Moving the bags over, she crawled onto her bed. Like a small child, she gathered herself into a ball, hugging her drawn up knees and rocking back and forth.

Blanche's sharp voice suddenly cut through the wall, although what she said was inaudible.

Pru jumped at the sound but didn't answer. Instead, she began a low whimper that turned into a tortured moan. Throwing herself face down, she began weeping full out then, her shoulder's convulsing with each sob.

Lee crouched outside her window for a minute afterward, confused by what he was seeing. *As Time Goes By* was playing softly on her radio, its words registering vaguely on Lee's consciousness.

Once again, he returned to the car and sat for a long while, trying to sort things out.He suddenly felt like he was in the climax of his own *Casablanca* movie. There was the beautiful Ilsa, torn between love and honor and naturally performed by Pru, the dual-sided villain Tom, and facing the biggest decision of his life was the story's hero, Rick Blane, obviously played by Lee himself. Sadly though, there was no Louie, no surrogate character to share his pain, to emote for him.

As Lee mulled over what course to follow, two things became crystal clear. Pru's old demon was back, indecision, and over the same emotions as with Ilsa in *Casablanca*. Lee realized too, he could never make the love sacrifice that Rick had in the movie: give Pru up to Tom. Not certain why, his eyes were drawn to the back seat and Blanche's dual sided statuette.

The pewter skies opened up then and it began to rain. His thoughts chased the raindrops on his windshield, both headed down.

Not certain why, he took his grandfather's map out of his backpack and carefully opened it. He was almost certain now it showed the way to Eden Brook, but the riddle at the bottom still haunted him.

The torrent began drumming harder on his car roof and he cracked a window open to clear his head.

He turned to the dog. "What do you say, boy? Wanna try for it tomorrow, Eden Brook?"

Dan's tail was happy.

Lee slid the map into its pocket, resting his hand there afterward.

CHAPTER FIFTY-EIGHT

Shoulders aching from his full pack and leg muscles cramping, Lee stopped wading. He was exhausted, bone weary from trudging endless days up the Burnt Tree. Following his grandfather's map and traveling dawn to dark, he had journeyed way past where Tom and he had stopped two years before. What started as an adventure had become an ordeal.

To keep from losing his way, he had kept to the river mostly. Even so, he had gotten lost twice. Once he took a wrong fork that came in from the west. The other time, the canyon became so choked with huge boulders that it was impassable and he had to skirt the river to find a way around. Over the course of those same days, he had to wade swamps, slog through endless, tangled forests, detour around log jams, crawl over and under deadfalls and at times, in narrow canyons, he had to throw his pack on top of boulders, clamber up and tumble down the other side. His knees and elbows were skinned and bleeding. All the while, the grade was up, the steepness varying, but always up.

Save for a broken beer bottle on the riverbank days back, he had seen no human sign. He was seeing more wildlife tracks though: turkey, bear, even the paw prints of a cat in the river sand yesterday, a big one. He knew it was a mountain lion. His grandfather told him how to tell. There were no claw marks, unlike with bears or wolves.

All of that day, he had followed the river's course through its tree-lined canyons, beautiful yet mysterious, surrealistic in the shadowy light of their misty-green loneliness.

Taking off his hat and leaning unsteadily on the staff, he studied the river to the north. Ahead of him the valley opened up. He mopped the sweat from his eyes with his sleeve and cupped his hands over the brim of his hat to block the sun. Far upriver, he thought he recognized a familiar landmark; a stony outcropping that had been described to him two long years before. "My God," he asked aloud, "could that be them, the Gates of Stone that Bud pictured and the map mentioned?"

Throwing off his pack, he climbed a small rocky prominence. Only then did he taste it on the breeze, a familiar scent, yet one never so rich, so pure. It was the fresh green taste of damp pine and laurel. It beckoned to him, calling him to a land he had dreamed about for the last two years ... perhaps all of his life. It was a place where there would be good fishing, and much more. But at least now he knew it was real and within his grasp.

"That's it, Dan," he said, "our Shangri-La, it's gotta be." He patted the dog's head. "Thanks for pointing the way. Couldn't have done it without you."

Dan had seemed happy, almost exuberant since they left base camp. At times he would run ahead, stop and with his nose high, sniff the air, yip, and run on ahead again. It was as if the dog knew where they were headed, had been there before and remembered the way. Those times when he did take the lead, the young man followed along and the dog's instincts were unerring.

Before climbing down from the crag, Lee shaded his eyes and studied the valley far upstream, making sure one last time he hadn't imagined it.

It all fit, what he was seeing, Lee's kingdom in the clouds. Even after two years, some of the restaurant owner's memories, if not his precise words, rang fresh in Lee's soul. "... you'll see a giant, ash-blue, limestone wedge with a big crack down the middle, like it was struck by Thor's hammer. That's the gates to it, Eden Valley."

So high were those stone gates that billowing white clouds seemed to be rising out of them. Against their whiteness, he could see a faint dot wheeling on high thermals over the entrance. The dot was there, then not there, depending on where it was in its curling glide. He was certain it was an eagle, a regal bird posted there to guard that sacred portal.

And carpeting the banks of Eden Brook, from the valley entrance down to where it spilled into the Burnt Tree, were bright yellow wildflowers. "Bud's path of gold," he whispered to himself.

He tucked the compass on the chain inside his shirt. The eagle would be his guide now, beckoning him on toward his prize.

It beguiled him to think that his grandfather had homesteaded near there long ago, carving out of the wilderness an ideal little kingdom that the gods destroyed because he dared steal perfection from them.

Only now, that world was not just a fantasy, like Tom had insisted, but a real land, one more mystical than Lee ever imagined.

He realized too that Eden Valley was yet far upriver, but if he leaned into the fading light, he might be able to camp beside its waters that very evening. The first thing he would do before entering the valley though was to kneel and give thanks. Then he would bathe in that sacred brook. He could even envision how its crystal waters might feel: As clear and cool as the holy water in the marble fount at St. Peter's. And, trusting he wasn't pushing his blasphemy too far, he might even dip his fingers into its sweet currents and bless himself before entering.

Perhaps tomorrow, he might search for the spring that Bud had dipped the fingerling from long ago during his own pure moment in time. And if I find it, Lee told himself, I'll drink from it out of my hat.

Resting momentarily on the bank, Lee could picture the valley, not exactly as Bud had described, but close enough to the waiter's words to sharpen his memory. Its floor was inlaid with white and yellow wild flowers with Eden Brook, like a golden thread, weaving through it ... peaks scraping the clouds, once higher than the Himalayas ... and the waiter's father, a changed man, after all the glory he had witnessed that day.

A thin, early mist began ghosting over the Burnt Tree then, casting everything in shades of black and white. He could no longer see the opening to his valley. He couldn't miss it though. All he had to do was follow the river. He could do that even in the dark. Encouraged that his goal was finally close, he hurried on, wading and resting over and over again, but now oblivious to his heavy pack and any pain.

Several miles back, Dan had decided to run along the rocky shore rather than wade with Lee. Once, the dog stopped though and did a long stare back downriver.

"What is it, boy?"

The dog lifted his nose to the air, yipped once, but then loped on.

Later, when Lee stopped and glanced back, he thought he saw something. A deer perhaps. He waded on but when he stopped again, he saw it a second time, a movement, only this time more clearly. He froze. It was the faint silhouette of a human figure, probably a man from the way he moved, a big man, wading far behind him, two hundred yards or so back. The man was knee deep in the water near the bank, but so indistinct in the mist, he almost seemed an apparition.

Lee waved to the figure, but he returned no sign. He called to him also, but if the other man called back, he could not hear it over the rushing waters. And when Lee motioned for him to catch up, the figure merely stared back at him. Through the mist, Lee could not make out any of the man's features, but something about him seemed familiar. Although he could not be certain, the figure appeared to be wearing a wide brimmed hat like his own. He appeared also to have either long hair or a hood under his hat.

Pointing, Lee asked the dog, "Who is that, boy?"

After briefly surveying the direction Lee gestured, Dan headed upstream again. Every few steps though, the dog's eyes pulled his head back downriver.

Lee thought a long moment. "It had to be Pru," he told himself. "The low light and mist were probably distorting her size and movements." After all, she had promised to join him. It happened right after he had gotten in the car to leave. She had tapped on his window, telling him that she needed more time to call the wedding guests and cancel the reservations. She insisted that he go on ahead, and tearfully gave her word that she would follow along. They agreed to meet and camp at their favorite spot alongside the Burnt Tree. Although at the time, Lee was disappointed she wasn't going with him, he understood and agreed.

Once he decided to try for Eden Brook, he left her a note at the campsite, explaining where he had gone. Sure, it had to be her, he reassured himself. She had found his note and decided to follow along. Who else? Certainly not his grandfather, he drowned. Nor Tom with his bad foot. Neither of them made any sense.

He continued wading toward Eden Valley, the figure always trailing, but keeping the same distance between them.

Eventually, Lee began having serious doubts about it being Pru. If it was her, he reasoned, she would have caught up by this time and joined him.

As to who else the stranger might be, he had no idea. He refused to unbridle his imagination though. That way might gallop him off a cliff.

At this point, the mysterious figure was becoming more than a curiosity. Its presence, let alone the mystery of its identity, was beginning to annoy him.

Looking upriver, Lee could see a sharp fishhook bend in the Burnt Tree where, if he rounded it, and then cut back across its arm, he could confront the trailing stranger.

Alongside the river, just before it hooked, was a section of marshy shoreline. Over time, hundreds of deer hooves had churned the brown river sand into a strip of thick, deep slurry. The river there was swift and angry. It did not seem like a good place to ford, but evidently it was. The animals always seemed to know.

After making certain the stranger was still following, Lee rounded the bend in the river, and climbing the bank, quickly found an old game trail. Not bothering to take off his pack or throw his staff down, he stumble-jogged along the green, shadowy tunnel, tennis shoes sloshing, limbs slapping his face and briars scratching his bare legs. Dan loped along easily in front of him, certain it was all a game. Finally, Lee could see daylight flickering dimly ahead through the leafy curtain. His throat tightened.

Breathing heavily, he broke through the last brush wall onto the riverbank. Just as he did, his foot caught a vine, throwing him off balance. Turning as he fell, he slammed down hard onto his back on the rocky shore. At the same instant, he heard a sharp crack and knew what it was. Rocking to one side, he could see the butt section of his fly rod splintered on the ground. "Aw, shit," he muttered.

When he rolled back to face the stranger dogging him though, there looming over him was a dark, foreboding presence. Fear clutched his chest and crawled up the back of his throat.

CHAPTER FIFTY-NINE

He could now see that the figure's head was hooded with a wide-brimmed hat over top that. The sun's fireball was hanging low in the sky and rested just over the stranger's shoulder, blinding Lee, so that when he tried looking into the other man's face, all he could see was a black emptiness. "Why are you following me?" Lee demanded.

The faceless man didn't answer.

When Lee fell onto his back, his staff landed alongside. If he could just retrieve it now, he would not be completely defenseless.

Dan cowered nearby under a bush. Lee was surprised. He had never seen the dog so frightened, not even the time he treed a bobcat and got his muzzle clawed. Trying to buck up the dog's spirits and perhaps his own, Lee shouted, "Sic him, boy, get him." It didn't work. Dan only backed up further under the bush, his rear end beginning to quiver.

"What do you want?" Lee shouted at the man.

Tilting his head to the side like he was trying to understand the young man's question, the figure hesitated. That's when Lee made his bid for the staff. The hooded man, however, anticipated his intent. Just as Lee reached out to retrieve it, the stranger slammed his foot down on the young man's bad shoulder, grinding his heel back and forth afterward. The twisting reawakened the old pain in Lee's shoulder injury and he almost passed out.

Finally the grinding stopped, but his shoulder felt weak and the big man was still standing over him. "Aw dag," Lee uttered under his breath. The figure was now holding the young man's only weapon, his wading staff.

"Who are you?" Lee demanded. "Why are you doing this?"

The dark stranger returned no answer. Instead, he gave a cruel, chilling laugh, as if there was some private joke on Lee over his questions.

Bud's story about the Demon from Hell flashed into Lee's head, but lost some of its frightening grip when Dan suddenly rediscovered his old fire. Darting out from under the bush, he grabbed the man's pants leg and began tugging on it, growling all the while. Wheeling toward the nuisance at his feet, the hooded figure began stabbing at the dog, using Lee's staff like a spear. Dan held fast to the pants leg though, his rear dancing away from each jab.

Lee saw another chance then, perhaps his last. He suddenly remembered the sharp, splintered section of his glass fly rod. Reaching back over his head, he blindly searched the ground for it.

Meanwhile, Dan was bouncing back and forth, still dodging each of the vicious jabs, all except the last, but that's all it took. When that final thrust stabbed him in the ribs, he yelped, let go of the pants leg and limped off to one side, whimpering.

Still groping back of him for his broken fly rod, Lee at last found it. As before though, the mysterious stranger anticipated the young man's intent, and using Lee's own staff, pinned the back of his hand to the sharp river-cobble. A blinding pain shot up Lee's arm. Then, leaning on the staff, the faceless man began twisting the tip back and forth into his palm. As the sharp stones and sand cut into the back of his hand, Lee writhed in agony.

After a few seconds though, the man eased his pressure. The intense pain lessened, but it left the back of his hand throbbing and bleeding.

Now, with both his shoulder and hand injured, the young man felt truly helpless. The dark figure could finish him off whenever he wished and Lee could do nothing about it. That prospect made him sick with fear.

It also dawned on Lee that, for whatever reason, the stranger wasn't ready to do that, end his life, not just yet. But why? He seemed to be toying with Lee, the way a cat does a mouse ... before killing it. Could the hooded figure be enjoying his pain?

From somewhere close by, a raven gave a raspy warning. Great, another bad omen, Lee thought cynically, like what happened before the bad storm on the Tree. At the bird's squawking, the figure glanced in its direction, but then whirled back toward the young man.

The late sun still in his eyes, Lee could still not see his enemy's face. The young man's hat, having tumbled off when he fell, was lying nearby. Perhaps he could use it to shield his eyes, so he could know the identity, or at least see the face of the mad stranger who seemed determined to end his life. With that in mind, Lee pointed to the hat. Then, open handed, to show it he meant no harm, he began inching his hand over toward it.

The figure watched, watched, seemingly curious about his intent. Then, something possibly clicked in his primitive, reptile brain, and he slammed the staff into the side of the young man's head, rendering him near senseless. Possibly tiring of the cat-mouse game, the faceless man then leaned back and with both hands, raised the staff over his head, as if to deliver one final life-ending blow.

Through a foggy haze, Lee suddenly became aware of a dog barking somewhere far off. Momentarily, the haze parted, and there was Dan, again, now bravely limping back and forth at the stranger's feet. The dog's eyes were terrified, whites showing big, but he was barking gamely at the dark presence looming over Lee with the club.

But matters were different with the dog this time. He was slower, easier to strike after his injury. With one glancing blow to his head, the figure stunned him also, just as he had the young man. Now, the dog lay helpless on his side, his eyes beginning to glaze over. And as before with Lee, the stranger raised the staff over his head with both hands, only now intent on crushing the life from Dan.

Something snapped in Lee though, and he snarled up at the dark presence, "Get away from him, you big S.O.B. That's my dog."

At the sound of Lee's voice, the faceless man swung back toward him, and with the staff still raised in both hands, brought it down in one murderous, hissing stroke toward his head.

At the last second though, Lee rolled out of the way, and when the club slammed into the ground beside him, he grabbed for it. Still on his back, but holding on as best he could with a bad shoulder and hand, he struggled with the other man for control of the weapon. Meanwhile, the stranger was swinging his end of the staff back and forth in a mad frenzy to regain possession. Lee felt his strength beginning to wane, however, and the staff, slick from his own blood, began sliding inch by inch from his grasp.

When at last the young man lost his grip on the shaft, it happened so suddenly that it caught the other man by surprise. Losing his balance, he staggered backward down the riverbank, finally ending up thigh deep in the deer crossing slurry at the water's edge. There, muttering angrily, he struggled to free his legs from the muck, but could not. Finally, he tried steadying himself with the staff, but when he did, the sticky goo held it fast also, causing the man, once again, to lose his balance, fall backward into the water's raging torrents and go under. Only his hat marked the spot where he disappeared.

Lee jumped to his feet and ran down the bank to where the figure had gone under. Dan limped along after him.

Before being swept away by the rushing waters, a hand came up once, its fingers clutching, like they were searching for something. But for what? Lee asked himself. Was it for his help or his throat?

For several seconds after the stranger disappeared beneath the waters, Lee chewed on his lower lip. Throwing off his backpack and twisting his staff from the muck, he bolted downriver through the dense undergrowth. Meanwhile, the dog trailed along behind, barking a hot warning and questioning the young man's intent.

As Lee hurried along the bank, he kept close watch on the rushing waters, checking for any sign. The sun was about to duck below the mountains. When Lee came to the first pool 50 yards or so down from where the man went under, he waded out into an eddy up to where the water was under his armpits. Too late, he remembered that Pru's picture and his grandfather's note were in his shirt pocket. Both were soaked. "Damn," he said, slipping them under his hat and backing out into shallower water.

The stranger's hat suddenly came floating around the river bend above him. Plucking it from the water, he shook it off and frisbeed it toward shore. Growling, Dan grabbed it by the brim and began shaking it.

River shadows were growing longer now. Seeing no sign after several minutes, he began wading back toward shore.

It was then the hand seemingly ghosted up from the depths behind him. From shore, Dan sounded a frantic warning. Lee looked back, startled. As before, the hand's fingers were clutching, seemingly frozen in that pose, their intent still unclear. The hand was coming closer too, so close now that he could see white scars on its palm.

Lee raised the club over his head, determined to end the life of the faceless man that so recently was bent on ending his.

Just then, the western sun flashed its last rays through a gap in the peaks, lighting the river's surface around him. There under the water was a twisted face. But was it his own reflection or the face of the stranger, and if the latter, were its features benign or malevolent? Lee stared hard into the water for several seconds, but so distorted was the image in the failing light and his own stirrings, he could not be sure of either.

Brow yet troubled, Lee gave the face one last study and slowly lowered his staff. Uncertain what to do next, he gripped and regripped the handle for several seconds. Then, ever so tentatively, he held the staff out toward the stranger's hand, as yet frozen in a claw-like pose.

All the while, Dan was limping back and forth on the river bank, barking a frenzied, "No, no, are you crazy?"

CHAPTER-SIXTY

Lee jumped awake to the sound of his own moaning and Dan barking in his ear. "It's okay, boy, everything's okay."

His head was strung with cobwebs. Once he swept them aside, he realized he was still in his car in front of Pru's house, and the Eden Brook ordeal had all been a dream. Most disappointing of all though, the part about Pru agreeing to join him on the Burnt Tree was not real either. He had dreamed that too.

Dirven by the fresh, vivid dream and somewhat chagrin, he glanced at his fly rod. It was intact. He then took Pru's photo and his grandfather's note from his shirt pocket. Her picture was dry but not the note.

It was damp, like it had been in water. The words were streaked, faded and illegible. He felt inside his shirt for sweat, but there was none. Puzzled, he studied the note for a long moment, finally shrugging and returning it to his pocket.

He looked at the dog. "Sorry I upset you, Dan. Had a bad dream. In it, this big, scary guy was trying to kill us. Never did learn who he was though, not for sure, but I have suspicions. Anyway, you and me were looking for Eden Brook and..." Lee stopped. "Say, is that why Granddad left you behind? Did he show you the way there once so that someday you could show someone else? Me, for instance?

"As I was saying, in this dream that scary guy, he fell in the Burnt Tree and drowned ... I think. Before that though, you were sort of a hero. That big fella was about to smash me to a pulp when you grabbed his pants leg and stopped him." He chuckled. "That was sure brave of you, boy. I know you were scared. I sure was."

Dan yawned.

The young man's gaze fell to the dut hat on the seat. For Lee, the best stain was still there, faint, but still alive. "Hey boy, remember that time we drank from our hats on May's Brook, Granddad and me, and he talked about the river. I think I have some of it figured out now, what he was trying to tell me. The same as with his note. There's still a lot I haven't figured out yet, but I will, I will."

One of the dog's eyelids slid open.

"One last thing, Dan. Its palm was scarred just like mine, that scary guy's." He held his hand up for the dog to see. "Wonder why I dreamed that?" He glanced up at Pru's house and Tom's net on the car floor. He thought for a long moment. Raindrops streaked down his windshield but a strong wind sent them scurrying back up the glass.

As thunder rolled across his car roof, he spoke up toward the rumble, "It's my own stirrings I'm tasting, isn't it, Granddad?"

He slipped his raincoat on, pulled the hood up and put the dut hat over top that.

Searching for his face in the rear view, Lee found instead, the dark stranger in his dream. Like the cracked mirror said, his heart was split, but he knew then what he must do.

He took the chain with the compass from around his neck and picked Tom's fishing net off the floor. Holding the net's steel rim against the magnet's side, the needle quivered toward it. He then moved the compass away until its needle pointed true north. The fishing net, its bag still torn, he lay on the seat next to him.

Lee sat for a long time, staring out his windshield, seeing nothing. Finally, letting his head fall to his chest, he blew air out his puffed cheeks. Penning a quick note and gathering a few things, he trudged over to the Pruitt mailbox.

Just in front of it, another car had dripped a few drops of motor oil onto the road. There, oil on water was rain-bowing the blacktop.

He stuffed the items he had gathered inside the mailbox and draped his raincoat over it. Behind him, the wind slammed his car door shut with a sickening thud. Rain trickled down his face and he licked it off his lips. It was salty.

Once back in the car, he hammered the steering wheel with the butt of his fist. Dan stirred. Fiddling with the rear view, he found the dog's eyes. Dan was still watching him, as if waiting for something more, or so Lee imagined.

He touched the faint scar on his forehead. "Yeah, you're right," he said to the dog. "I should have told Pru about Abby, the whole story, but you can't tell that kind of thing in a note, Dan. Besides, I didn't..." He took his wallet out and removed a condom from inside. It was wrapped in gold foil and one edge was torn. He stared at it momentarily, and stuffed it in the trash.

The dog didn't move.

"Okay, okay, I'll help with that too, her gravestone ... happy now, Dan?"

Lee suddenly felt sick to his stomach. Opening the car door, he gagged, but did not throw up. Leaning forward, he rested his forehead against the steering wheel.

His eyes fell to Tom's net, then the cigarette lighter. He punched it in. After it popped out, he spit on its glowing coils and they sizzled. Holding his breath and gritting his teeth, he clamped the red-hot coils against the back of his hand. A searing jolt shot up his arm, but he pressed the lighter there until it made him whimper. When he pulled it away, there was an angry, scarlet welt.

As he drove away from Pru's, he glanced at the house next door. On the porch was a young woman in a yellow and white print dress and she waved. He suddenly realized whom it was, the same girl who always waved to him, Miss Denim Shorts, Louie. She was more a woman now, in fact, a beautiful woman, and with that fine Rolls Royce motor still purring somewhere inside. For the first time, Lee waved back, slowed the car, thought about stopping, but didn't.

He took the Miraculous Medal from his glove box and hung it on the rear view mirror as he drove into the early evening dusk. It dangled there, still tarnished. Lee's eyes softened and he squeezed it gently for a few seconds.

Later, the burn on his hand began to throb. For a short while, the pain helped him forget her, but only for a while.

CHAPTER SIXTY-ONE

When Pru heard a car door shut, she hurried to the window. Puzzled, she watched as Lee stuffed some items in their mailbox. She hurried onto the porch and called his name, but it was too late. The taillights of his car were disappearing around a corner down the street. Oblivious to the rain soaking her hair, she ran to the mailbox. After draping his raincoat over her shoulders, she puzzled at the first thing she found inside, her mother's favorite statuette. Shrugging, she put it under her arm and peered inside again. More curious yet, a ring, her own engagement ring no less, lay inside on a piece of paper. Frowning, she picked up both. The paper was a check for two thousand dollars. It was made out to Tom. She turned the check over. On the back, Lee had scribbled a note. "The ring's for tomorrow, the check's for a rainy day. Tom will understand. Love you, always have, always will. Lee."

"T's foot," she said, teary-eyed. About to close the box, she saw something else stuffed deep inside. Reaching far back, she pulled it out. It was a hat, his grandfather's dut hat. She put it on, and clutching the other items to her breast, stood in the rain, staring in the direction his car had disappeared. Hand over her mouth and her breath catching, she began weeping.

Back in her bedroom, rain was pelting softly against her window. Both Lee and Tom's raincoats and hats hung on a chair back near the door.

Just then, her mother banged on the wall. "Cathy."

"There in a minute, Mother." Taking a photo album from a drawer, she leafed through it until she came to two photos opposite one another. One was from the time she and Lee had fished the Burnt Tree for the first time and almost did it.

On the page across from it was a color photo of Tom from the waist up. He was standing in front of a small airplane at a local airfield, his hand resting on its propeller. She had encouraged him to go there, but he had resisted until she agreed to go with him. In the picture, he was beaming.

She looked again at the Burnt Tree photo. On her head was grandfather's dut hat. Behind her, ever frozen in its passing slide, was the Burnt Tree. For several long moments, she studied the Burnt Tree photo, finally running her fingers gently over the dut hat. After her eyes slid toward her mother's room, she whispered knowingly at the Burnt Tree picture, "Road Apples."

Pru brushed the last tears from her eyes, and her face brightened. When she peered out her bedroom window, she could see the skies to the west were clearing.

Pru took a bag from the bed and slipped on a raincoat and hat at the door. Car keys in hand, she looked in the hall mirror. Around her neck was the heart locket her father had given her. When her eyes rolled up and glimpsed her hat, she half-smiled and ran two fingers sharply across its brim in a mini-salute.

She strode to her mother's room and knocked. Voice firm, she spoke through the closed door, "Mother, we have to talk."

CHAPTER SIXTY-TWO

A night-wind awakened Lee alongside the Burnt Tree and he sat up. The night before, he had unrolled his sleeping bag alongside a fallen willow. The fallen tree had left an opening in the tree canopy. Overhead, a luminous river of stars ghosted across the night sky.

The wind suddenly blew harder, tumbling his hat off the log. He had bought the hat when he stopped at Wilkens for hot dogs and provisions the evening before. Felt and wide-brimmed, it was like grandfather's dut hat, or as close to it as he could find.

As for his grandfather and Crazy Dan being the same man, Lee was certain now they were. But the question still remained, which story was true: Bud's in which Dan was a murderer or the old man's in which he was an innocent victim of circumstances?

He wanted the old man's to be true, but wondered if the question really mattered. His grandfather was gone and never coming back. He was a fine, decent man and Lee loved him, would always love him, regardless of what he had done or not done, and that was that.

He pulled the fallen hat over next to him and pinned it down with his staff. Tom had mocked him about it once, his staff, saying that Lee should always hold onto it as a reminder that some dreams were impossible.

"I think the opposite is true for me, boy. I need them, those dreams. They help me get through the darkness on the river."

His jaw line hardened and he stared at the dog. "Still want to try for Eden Brook tomorrow, buddy?" he asked, his voice upbeat.

Either at the mention of Eden Book or Lee's tone, the dog wagged his tail.

Lee pulled a small jar of coffee beans from his pack and fed a few to Dan. For several moments afterward, the dog's eyes were fixed on him, his head tilted right, like he did for his grandfather. Lee recalled *Casa-*

blanca, the movie that somewhat paralleled his own predicament, or at least, he thought so. "Is this the beginning of a beautiful friendship, Dan?"

The dog licked once at the pinesap on the young man's burn.

Lee smiled. "I'll take that as a yes."

The sweet smell of wood smoke from his campfire drifted toward Lee. He inhaled it deeply and let it wash over his face. His eyes smarted, but he did not mind. It was his grandfather's kindling, the last he would ever chop. Lee buried his eyes in his shirtsleeve.

His gaze slid to his jeans on the willow log. In the dim light with the legs folded under, they looked like denim shorts. Shaking his head, he half-smiled.

The wind whined across the bark of the fallen willow at his back, and just beyond the firelight, some leaves rustled. Barely breathing, he listened hard and searched the dim shadows, but only empty darkness greeted him.

A whippoorwill called from somewhere deep in the forest. It was a lonesome cry and went unanswered.

He batted at the insects dancing in his face. At Wilkens he had bought a Rum-Soaked-Crook Stogie. Although Lee didn't think they worked, Tom claimed they kept the little nasties at bay, and he always insisted they take them along camping. Lighting his, Lee blew its smoke up at the spinning bugs. It made them dance wildly but not go away. He fingered the scars on his palm, then ground the stogie out and hurled it into the fire.

He dug in his pack for a book he had brought along, hoping to read in the dim firelight until sleep came again. It was a story Bud had recommended. His hand found instead, the handle of Tom's knife. Drawing it out, he tilted it back and forth, its blade flashing in the dim campfire light. He started to slide it back in its holster but stopped. Burned into the sheath was the letter T. "Damn him," he said, as he flung the knife out into the darkness.

Just beyond the bank, the Burnt Tree sang over the rocks as it rolled back home. It had many secrets to tell if one listened. His grandfather had listened and told Lee which voices to follow.

Taking the note out of his shirt pocket, he looked at the blue ink stains that had run down the page. His grandfather's words were gone, but they were still in Lee's heart, would always be there, along with the memories.

The young man looked at his black and rust stained wading staff, its truths tested in fire and blood. I'll take it along tomorrow. Granddad told me why—it'll lead me toward the light. Taking the staff in his right hand and resting the other on his journal, he closed his eyes for a few seconds.

For a long moment afterward, he studied the night toward Eden Brook and chuckled. "Hell, Dan," he whispered, "Tom could be Rick Blane, the hero in this movie."

Lee stared into the darkness where he had thrown the knife, all the while tapping its sheath on his palm. Using a torch from the campfire, he found the knife and returned it to his backpack.

Searching his pack again, he found his grandfather's map and unfolded it. There was not enough light to make out the details, but his young eyes traced the two weaving lines on the drawing, marks that he was still certain were the Burnt Tree and Eden Brook.

He refolded the map and slid it down deep in the wood bag, rocking it afterward so it fell to the bottom, the way Tom showed him when they left anything behind for safekeeping.

From his plastic fly box, he removed some gray flies. These, he hooked onto his hatband. The red and white Eden Brook flies he left in the box. Holding his hat at arm's length and turning it slowly, he gave it an approving nod.

The Eden Brook fly box he pushed deep into the wood bag, rocking it afterward, like with the map, so it too fell to the bottom.

His voice lowered. "Sorry, Dan, we're not going to look for Eden Brook this trip."

The dog whined low.

He patted Dan's head. "Maybe we'll make it there someday, boy. Till then, the Tree will do just fine ... it's perfect."

His father's hip boots were draped over the log beside him. Crumpling a few sheets of newspaper, he stuffed the wads into their toes and threw the boots over the log for tomorrow. Perhaps they'll fit someday.

Lee snuggled down in his sleeping bag and up against the dog. Out on the main road, he heard a car far off, its engine at first sounding like a mosquito's whine, then closer and closer until the mountains swallowed it up. He could not tell whether the car had stopped or gone on.

A breeze gusted and the dog raised his head like he heard something beyond the young man's senses. He wagged his tail once.

"Who is it, Dan ... is it her?"

The night before, he had parked downriver from his campsite, near where Pru and he had lunched and swam. For a long while, he studied the darkness in that direction, but nothing. Afterward, he lay there listening, hoping, but again nothing.

The last smoke from his campfire curled up into the night sky. Reaching back, he patted the dog's head. "It's okay, boy. Go to sleep. It's just the voices."

Although Lee fought it, his eyelids grew heavy. He slid one hand under the pillow beside his notebook, the other he rested on his shirt pocket. Just before drifting off, he said a prayer that he would want what the river brings.

Somewhere far off in the night, a whippoorwill called. This time another answered.

Jerry Bonnell was born and raised in Weston, West Virginia. His first loves were basketball, fishing and creative writing. After attending St. Patrick's School in his home town, he enrolled in Glenville State Teacher's College in 1950, graduating from nearby WV Wesleyan shortly later. After serving in the Navy, he taught English Literature in the Baltimore County school system, married, and had one son, both of whom passed. He has one grandson, Christopher, from that marriage. Bonnell remarried in 1966, secured a master's degree from the University of Maryland and continued teaching in Baltimore County until he retired. Recently widowed, he now divides his time between Montana and the Florida Keys, pursuing fly fishing and story writing.

Printed in the U.S.A.

www.riverfeetpress.com